Friday Night Fighters

FRIDAY NIGHT FIGHTERS

A FORENSIC VETERINARIAN MYSTERY

—⁖⁖⁖—

GAIL BUCHALTER

Photographer: David Harp

Dedication

———✸———

To my son, Jordan, and all the animals
that have shared our home.

Acknowledgements

THANK YOU MICHAEL VICK, THE NFL quarterback whose arrest for hosting pit bull fights at his Bad Newz Kennels shined a light on a "sport" that had previously lived deep in the shadows.

I also wish to thank:

Editor Charlotte Herscher, for her talent, kindness and ability to always ask the right questions;

Editor Salvatore Manna, for helping to shape the book and keeping me on track;

Forensic veterinarian Dr. Melinda Merck, who assisted in the prosecution of Michael Vick and whose support and expertise helped turn this project into a fact-based novel;

Kathryn Destreza, Director, Investigations Division, ASPCA, who was always accessible and supplied the information concerning the investigative aspect of this book;

Commander Jeff Thibert, Bloomington (Minnesota) Police Department, a K-9 officer earlier in his career, who provided insights into tracking and arresting criminals;

Dorchester County Sheriff James Phillips, and the Maryland State Police, Easton Barracks, for answering my never-ending questions about police procedures;

And finally, my appreciation to Robert Borden, Renee Jones-Lewis, Patty Crankshaw-Quimby, Amanda Showell, Candes Kehn, Betsy Skye, Cindy Orbany Smith, and Woodlief Oliver for their encouragement and help.

ONE

— ⊶⊷ —

I WAS SLEEPING THE SLEEP of the dead, which is kind of ironic since death is my business. I am Dr. Allison Reeves, a forensic veterinarian. It wasn't a job I grew up dreaming about. In fact, I didn't even know it existed. I only discovered it a half-dozen years ago, when I was a bored vet at a small animal hospital in Southampton, New York.

Now, one ring of my phone brought me to full consciousness.

Such is the nature of my work.

I looked at my cell phone and smiled with relief. I was staring at the picture of my boyfriend, John Thibert. I was surprised to see it was already 10 o'clock in the morning.

"Dr. Reeves," he said, formally.

My heart sank. This was business. Otherwise he would have called me Allison or maybe even Babe. John was a Senior Trooper with the Maryland State Police's K-9 unit, based in Easton, which oversaw three predominately rural counties: Caroline, Dorchester and Talbot where we lived.

"What's going on?" I asked, throwing off the covers and jumping out of bed.

"I'm going to send a photo. Take a look. Then we'll talk." He paused, and I headed towards the bathroom. John was a man of few words, sometimes irritatingly so. He came from a large, boisterous farming family and learned to keep his own counsel. I, on the other hand, was an only child raised in a home where my parents divorced when I was 10 years old.

I had taken only a couple of steps before my phone pinged and the picture came across my screen. I was staring at a dead pit bull, a big black boy with a white stripe under his chin, wearing fighting scars all over his visible body. The dog was lying on a tarp, so I knew he had been moved. My stomach cramped. Always my visceral reaction to sights like this.

"What killed him?" I asked.

"A bullet."

"Well, I guess that's good. At least it was quick," I muttered. "Where are you now?"

"I'm at the Cambridge animal shelter with the dog and the bitch," he whispered, referring to Michelle Manning, the president of the shelter's board of directors. "I was just going to drop him off," he continued in his hushed voice. "I wasn't fast enough. She got to me and began – what's the word? – venting. Yeah, fucking venting. That's why I'd like you here."

"As a shield?"

"Exactly, I want to hide behind your skirt. Oops, I forgot you never wear one." John was nothing if not wry. Then he added, "I want you to pick up the dog and necropsy him at your lab. Nothing less is going to make her happy, which I realize is a good reason for you not to show up. But I don't want this left to the board's vet."

It was like he was throwing me a bone, but I didn't bite. Instead I tried to figure out an escape plan. Nothing came to mind, so I was forced to ask about the crime scene.

"It washed away with last night's rain."

"Damn it," I groused, knowing there was no evidence left.

I had driven through that exact storm, hydroplaning half the way home. I was returning from a raid on a cat hoarder in Chestertown that lasted into the early hours of the morning. Several cats survived the triage process. We were too late to save a couple that had already died. I brought their bodies back to my lab in Trappe. It should have been a 45-minute drive. Instead it took me 90 minutes. I planned on performing the necropsies after a few hours of sleep. They would have to wait.

"How come you're doing cleanup?" I asked. "This is certainly below your pay grade."

"Saturday. No Animal Control," he answered.

"Yeah, but why you?"

"A bunch of bikers, no, let me rephrase that – a group of sparkly, iridescent cyclists," John said disdainfully. "You know, the ones you always want to run over for taking up the entire road."

"Yes, dear," I said. "Dog?"

"Getting there," he grumbled. "Anyway, they were riding down the back road and pedaled right up on the dog. Someone had tossed him in the town's illegal dump. You know the one off Hawkeye Road. Well, there he was. Everyone freaked out and started calling 911. They demanded action. Some of those Baltimore boys waved their political connections at the idiot dispatcher. She called me because of the K-9 thing. And I took the call so I could get out of the barracks. Duke had told me he was bored hours earlier."

Duke was John's K-9 companion. He was attractive for a Belgian Malinois, if you had a thing for pointy-faced German Shepherds that had been sheared of their long, luxurious fur, which is how I viewed all Malinois. But looks didn't count. He was John's protector and would die for him. I loved him dearly. Besides, who wouldn't be impressed with a talking dog?

"Hang on a sec," John said. "I'll send you a photo from the scene."

My phone pinged again and this time I was ready. Or so I thought. "What the hell?" flew past my lips, right before I said, "Tell me he's not laying on a Barcalounger."

"Honey, I wish I could," John said. He was all talked out.

The photo said it all, anyway. The pit bull's body was stretched across the seat of the discarded recliner while his neck was draped over the armrest and his massive head hung down, jaw twisted open and tongue nearly touching a puddle of rainwater mixed with his blood.

"I'm on my way," I said.

T W O

---꘎꘎꘎---

THE COLD SPLASH OF WATER swept any remnants of sleep from my eyes and left me staring in the mirror. My exhaustion stared back at me. My icy blue eyes seemed to turn more glacial with every year. I saw weariness competing with wariness in them. The laugh lines that once creased the corner of my eyes were barely perceptible, and my lips were pressed together with a new, unwelcomed tightness.

Yet I loved my job. I loved bringing to justice people who abused animals. John and I shared that same passion, but it came at a personal cost. I did lots of yoga. He occasionally shot people.

I ran a brush through my long, dirty blonde hair, quickly twisted it up and out of the way and grabbed my work clothes from the closet: white T-shirt, black jeans and thick black lace-up boots. My underwear was lacy and pricey, a gift to my feminine self and John.

I poured a cup of cold coffee from the pot he had left for me and, without taking the time to reheat it, drank it down in a few gulps. I grabbed my jacket off the nearby kitchen chair, where I had left it to dry just hours before, and slipped it on. It pretty much told my story: On the front pocket was the inscription ANIMAL CSI. Emblazoned across its back was HSPAC (Humane Society for Prevention of Animal Cruelty) FORENSIC INVESTIGATIONS. The only fact it omitted was my title, Director of the mid-Atlantic Region.

My lab was in the woods just a quarter-mile from our house on the banks of the Windy Hill River near the tiny town of Trappe. Outside was parked the HSPAC Mobile Unit, where it stood when we weren't chasing down crime scenes. I thought about jogging to it, but even with my long legs and crushing desire to get some fresh air, I knew my car was the practical answer. I peeled out of our garage and parked it at the lab where I swapped vehicles.

I entered the 26-foot, state-of-the-art Mobile Unit that was essentially a traveling veterinary clinic. There was a large sink with drainage space set between two examining tables against one wall. Next to it was a portable generator and high-intensity lights. On the opposite wall was a long desktop with a digital microscope affixed to it; underneath were stacks of drawers that held slides and vials for evidence collection, and packs of wrapped instruments. The no-frills workspace also included portable anesthesia/oxygen machines and an X-ray machine. On a less optimistic note, the Mobile Unit contained grave detection and exhumation equipment and a large refrigerator.

I cranked the engine and it roared to life. I made it to the Cambridge shelter in 16 minutes without getting pulled over. I drove past the bare-bones cinderblock building that housed the abandoned and the abused. I figured John would be in the back, since his original plan was to drop off the pit bull in the shelter's refrigerator and flee.

I was correct and found him talking to Michelle Manning and Helen Taylor, the shelter's director, on the other side of his squad car. Duke was seated in the back, taking it all in. John's grey eyes locked on mine. At 6-foot-4 he could easily see me, just shy of 6 foot, over the others. As soon as we made eye contact I noticed his shoulders relax a bit.

He ran his fingers through his long dark hair, always a source of dissension at the barracks, and resettled his regulation felt Stetson hat on his head. John had recently traded in his summer uniform – straw Stetson and short sleeves – for his tan long-sleeve one. The black tie and olive pants with a black strip down the side never changed with the season.

"Dr. Reeves," he said, acknowledging my arrival.

My eyes fixed on the tarp on the ground as I gave them a nod. In my line of work, the dead come before the living. John knew that and immediately squatted down with the agility of a field hand, pressed his boot heels into the earth and pulled back the tarp. The dog, an American Pit Bull Terrier, as pumped as baseball's Barry Bonds, hadn't diminished much in death. His overdeveloped muscles screamed steroid use, his earflaps had been sliced off for fighting and healed bite marks covered his body. The fatal wound, according to John, was the bullet that landed between his eyes.

I had my Nikon D5000 in hand and snapped photos. John held a clipboard with his report detailing his involvement with the dead dog. He signed off on it and gave it to me. I signed on. Thus we continued the chain of custody with words and pictures.

I read his report and noted with surprise that the dog had been microchipped. That was very unusual. People in the fighting world didn't want a dog, especially a dead one, traced back to them.

"You want me to put him in your refrigerator?" John asked.

"Not yet," I said quickly. "I want to bag him first. But I do want your tarp for now. Okay? Will you wrap him up while I get the bag?"

"Sure," he said in his gentlest voice.

I finally turned my attention to Helen, and gave her a smile. I had known her for years, since she was a vet tech at my friend's clinic in the nearby town of Easton. She uncrossed her arms and put her hands on her full hips and smiled back.

Helen was in her late 30s, heavyset, with a long, brunette ponytail, calm brown eyes and a sugary drawl that was steeped in the Deep South. All that softness belied her true nature: autocratic and demanding. But the kennel attendants, who survived her arduous training period, adored her.

"Have you had time to call Avid?" I asked, noting the name of the microchip company on John's report. It not only provided the chips, but kept a registry of pets and their owners.

"Yeah, Doc," she said quickly. "According to Avid's records, he belonged to Patricia and Marcus Everett who live in Altamont Heights."

"A rather upscale neighborhood for pit bull fighting," I noted.

"It's really weird," Helen said, re-crossing her arms across her chest again as if she were hugging herself through more bad news. "The Everetts reported the dog stolen three years ago. They were devastated. That's why I already have their address and phone number in my files. The dog's name was Benji."

"How old was he when he was stolen?" I asked.

"Around two. Maybe a little older."

I was rendered speechless. I couldn't imagine a dog that age being turned into a fighter. I knew their training began when they were just a couple of months old. I was having an even harder time dealing with the fact that a pet was stolen from a loving home to be turned into a fighter. It really pissed me off, which is what made me so good at my job. I never told John, but I really wanted to do horrible things to these awful people. I knew if I admitted that to him, it would be like unleashing the crazy in him. He found life to be pretty film noir. No grey areas of justice – and nothing can be more black and white to him than law enforcement."

I gave myself a moment and turned to Helen.

"I'll necropsy the dog this afternoon. Once I've finished and know what I'm looking at, I'll call my partner and we'll take it from there," I said, referring to Jackie Vincente, my counterpart with the HSPAC. She was the Lead Investigator for the mid-Atlantic Region, so we worked together most of the time. Also, she was my best friend.

I excused myself and walked to the Mobile Unit, my laboratory on wheels. I was back in seconds with a large, heavy duty, white plastic bag. John lifted the covered dog and I slid the bag around it, tied it closed and attached a tag with the date, time, location and contents written on it.

"Want a hand?" John asked.

I nodded and he hoisted up the dog and walked behind me, carrying it into the Mobile Unit. I opened the refrigerator, glad I had transferred the dead cats to my lab last night. John carefully placed the pit bull inside. After I closed the lid, he put his arms around me and gave me a deep kiss.

"Good morning," he said, this time his smile reaching his eyes.

"Not really," I said a little gaspy from his kiss. "You should make a break for it while you can."

"I can't go yet," John said, shrugging with annoyance. His shoulders were speaking volumes today. "I promised Helen I'd look at some horror story pit bull. She's going to ask you, too. Besides, I'm not sure it's safe to leave you with Manning. You look pissed already."

"Maybe I should let you hold my Glock; but I'm supposed to carry it for protection and right now I think I am in danger." I tried a smile, but even I could hear my whiny tone. I really disliked her and just wanted to go home with the dead dog.

It says a lot about your day when removing a bullet from a dead animal is preferable to talking to the living.

THREE

JOHN LED THE WAY BACK to Helen and Michelle, then stopped so I could walk around him and move in closer. He had already done his stint; now it was my turn. I planted myself in front of him and breathed. One look at Michelle's enraged face actually calmed me down.

I was raised in an angry house, too often the recipient of my mother's rage, especially after my father's abrupt and total departure. I would retreat into my bedroom and bury myself in my schoolbooks. Even she couldn't object to that. After a couple of years I developed a mantra: "It's her, not me." I said it until I believed it.

My other escape was to walk my neighbors' dogs. There was a Cocker Spaniel in one apartment and a German Shepherd puppy in another. I never thought to ask for money; I was so thrilled to be playing with their dogs I couldn't believe they didn't ask me to pay them. I bonded with animals long before I learned to trust people. I was meant to be a veterinarian and an avenging one at that.

I looked at Michelle and saw my mother. Fortunately, they shared no physical attributes – my mother was tall, blonde and willowy, traits I inherited except I was bigger-boned. Michelle, on the other hand, was a thick woman who insisted on packing herself into tight black leggings and a matching zip-up sweatshirt. Both items should have been at least two sizes larger, if not for her comfort then for those who had to look at her. She had lots of lifeless, dyed black hair that rolled past her shoulders in big waves and did little to soften the harshness of her black eyes and heavy jowls.

While Michelle continued her rant, my old mantra popped into my head. I repeated it just as I did as a child, and found it easy to tune her out. I just stared at her.

Michelle was a realtor whose life unraveled as the real estate market crashed. And, depressingly, she took the shelter down with her. One way was overpaying her out-of-work husband, a contractor, to do unnecessary projects there. She had stacked the board and bullied them into never questioning any of her decisions.

But her worst failure occurred three years ago, right after she and her board members decided that the facility would become a No Kill shelter for both dogs and cats – a place where no animal would be euthanized. More cachet and more grant money.

The only problem was there was already a No Kill Cat Sanctuary that housed approximately 60 cats on the property. Most of them would never be adopted, so Michelle viewed them as a financial liability, not lucky rescues. It also took a lot of effort to spay/neuter and vaccinate all of them. With Michelle's blessing, the board veterinarian Kathleen Dreyfus, a.k.a. "Dr. Death," declared an epidemic of Feline Infectious Peritonitis in the Cat Sanctuary. It wasn't true. A few cats were infected, which occasionally happens in shelters. They die. The others live.

But Dr. Death ordered every cat euthanized. She called it humane; I called it genocide. The fact that scores of animals died so they could replace that No Kill cat shelter with one that housed only a few adoptable felines was beyond ironic, it was immoral. Yes, the shelter now had a No Kill facility for dogs, but it had such a limited admission policy that most surrendered canines were turned away. And, what really made me crazy was they barred all pit bulls. I had volunteered my services on a regular basis at the shelter since I moved to Maryland. But that ended with Death Day, as I would always call it, and the enforcement of its new "closed door" strategy. This was the first time I set foot on the premises since then. Michelle's grinding yammering brought me back to the present.

"I'm sick of trying to deal with the pit bull problem," she said, pounding her fist into her open palm, I guess, for emphasis.

"What problem?" I pointed out, though I really wanted to tell her she was the problem. "You refuse to admit them in your shelter."

She ignored me and continued at top screech, "A few weeks ago, Helen got a phone call from someone saying there were pit bull fights going on in a backyard in downtown Cambridge in the middle of the day. He was too scared to call the police, but Helen did. We never heard back from them. I'll bet anything pit bull fighting is going on all over the area.

"And now this," she snorted, waving her hand towards the HSPAC Mobile Unit. "This isn't about one dead pit bull. It's about dozens of dogs. And I'm talking only about the ones we see here."

"Oh, I didn't realize you were accepting pit bulls again?" I reiterated, in my most scathing voice. I once darkly joked that all it took for a dog, not just a pit bull, to be refused admission to the Cambridge shelter was a crooked canine tooth.

"I don't know what you're talking about," she said. "We have a pit bull here that Helen found tied to the fence with a dying litter. In fact, the newspaper is coming over to do a story on her."

"And then what?" I asked, clenching my fist because I just knew what she was going to say next.

"Oh, we'll send her to Animal Control. They're better equipped to deal with pit bulls."

Bingo! I wondered if I suddenly dropped to the ground I could count on John to draw his gun and shoot her to put me out of my misery. I stood there and half-listened as she continued her self-satisfied rant about how she was saving the animal world.

The other half of my brain began flipping through the menu in my mind. I always found food comforting in a way that went beyond mere sustenance. It was emotional comfort. Hopefully, John would take me to a restaurant tonight. As Michelle rampaged, I made it all the way to dessert – warm bread pudding steaming under the coolness of vanilla ice cream – and she was still complaining. I started to back away and would have stepped on John's feet if he hadn't backed up. I was done. Michelle wasn't.

"I'm not finished. You need to hear this," she ordered. I felt John stick his finger in my back like it was a pistol. I was trapped.

Until she crossed the line.

"And what are the police doing? And you? You're the HSPAC. What is your group doing? Nothing. You have all the money and the resources, but neither of you has provided any help."

"Enough," I snapped. "You've been sitting on this dog fighting info for how long? You didn't think about calling the police and following up yourself? You refuse to take in pit bulls and now I'm the problem and you're the solution?

"I was notified less than an hour ago that Trooper Thibert brought in a dead pit bull," I continued, my ire intensifying. "I was here within 20 minutes. I have taken possession of the dog. I will necropsy it this afternoon, making it my number one priority. So get out of my face."

I turned towards Helen. "You wanted to show us another dog?" I said. Michelle stepped back quickly to avoid my pivoting shoulder. I was so mad I knew better than to say anything more to her. I was trying to be more politic, or at least more than usual. "This would be a really good time."

I started walking towards the shelter with Helen. John could fend for himself. I needed to save a life – my own.

We went to the back enclosure and Helen stopped in front of a large kennel. I looked inside and suddenly none of the politics mattered. Helen put a comforting hand on my arm.

"This is Ella. And how's my beautiful girl?" she cooed, sliding into the kennel. I followed. We both knelt down.

The "beautiful girl," was a tan pit bull with white markings, covered in scores of cigarette and cigar burns. Some prick had used this emaciated dog as an ashtray. But Ella, with her true pit bull nature, didn't hold a grudge against humanity. She wiggled her back half as she mannerly sat and let her tongue loll about until it could connect with Helen's face.

"How did she end up here?" I asked.

"I showed up for work a few days ago and this little girl was tied to the fence," Helen said, looking drained as she recounted her introduction to the tortured dog. "It was raining and she was drenched but trying to protect her four puppies. She had tucked them under that skinny little body of hers. Whoever dumped her threw a blanket over her, but it was soaking wet."

"What happened to her puppies?" I asked, expecting to hear the worst. It was only half as bad as I anticipated.

"We were able to save two. Don't ask," she warned.

If Helen didn't want to discuss it, I knew I didn't want to hear it. I had turned my attention to Ella. Some of her newer burns were infected. I ran my hands over her body. Her ears, like the big dead pit bull, had been sliced off with a razor blade and scarred from old infections.

"I guess she wasn't up to their standards of a fighting dog," John said in a low growl. I hadn't noticed him standing outside the kennel until he spoke. "Doesn't look like she was used as a breeder, either. Her nipples aren't dragging the ground. God help the hump that did this to her if I find him."

I shifted into a cross-legged position and Ella immediately flopped into my lap. She dragged her tongue across my right hand and I cradled her snout so she could deeply inhale my scent. John bent down on her other side and began kneading what was left of her ears and I think I heard macho man murmuring sweet nothings into them. Ella rolled over, which elicited a shudder from me. Every inch of her belly had been burned.

"Where are the puppies?" I asked Helen.

"They're being bottle-fed right now, but we're slowly introducing them to wet food. They'll be back in a few minutes."

"Did Dr. Death look her over? Rabies shot?" I asked.

"Yeah, she came in and gave her the once-over. I had already started putting antibiotics on her infected sores. Got rid of the fleas and we took turns taking the ticks off her. God, there were so many."

"She eating well?"

"Ravenously. Thank God her organs hadn't started shutting down."

"I'll be right back," I said. "I'm going to get my bag. I'll examine her completely before I go."

"Thanks, Doc," Helen said, looking relieved.

John walked me back to the Mobile Unit where I grabbed my vet bag. Michelle had disappeared so I wouldn't have to see her for a long, long time. Or so I thought. Then I walked John to his car. He opened the door to let Duke out, and I gave him a big pet before he walked over to a tree to lift his leg.

"I'll call you if I'm going to be home late," John said wrapping his arm around my shoulders. "Let me know if your exam of Ella reveals anything more than the obvious, okay?"

"Sure," I said, wondering why he wanted to know.

FOUR

———⚬⚬⚬———

I LOOKED AT THE CLOCK on the dashboard and was relieved to see I had most of the afternoon left. I was itching to necropsy the pit bull (the equivalent to an autopsy in humans), but was glad I had taken the time to examine Ella. I had drawn a blood sample from her, which I'd run later to discover any hidden problems. Helen was taking care of the dog's obvious ones.

I turned onto our property and drove past our caretakers' house, which wasn't nearly as grand as it sounds. It was the old farmhouse John's grandparents had left him, where he lived until we built our own place. He offered it to a family friend, Gina, and her husband, Vernon Williams. She took care of our house and he took care of the property, including farming a couple of acres for all of us. We built our own home closer to the water, and I put my lab nearby. Since John had inherited 20 acres, we all had plenty of privacy.

I pulled in the driveway of my lab and marveled, as always, that this small, compact building was my creation. I built it two years ago with some of the money I inherited from my father. His money also built the house that John and I lived in, but I considered the lab my most fulfilling project.

Now I parked as close to its front door as possible, shortening the distance I would have to carry the pit bull. I jumped out of the van, opened the door, and walked into my lab, a 1,000-square-foot space illuminated by several rows of hanging fluorescent lights. A large, box-like X-ray machine was rolled against one wall and at the center were a couple of long metal tables, each large enough to display the skeletons of several animals at a time or even a small horse.

The exam table was on the opposite side of the lab. I prepared it for the dog, pulling a long piece of white butcher paper off the large roll attached to the wall next to the table. The paper would catch any traces of evidence that might come off the dog and anything it left on the tarp.

I walked over to the floor scale and flipped the switch, and the platform rose to waist level so I could easily put the dog on it. I went back to the Mobile Unit, opened the refrigerator and retrieved the pit bull. It was a bit of a struggle, but I moved him into the lab.

I placed the dog on the table, removed the bag and then opened the tarp. I lifted the dog and put him on the scale. I then carefully shook out the tarp on the paper and collected the droppings that had fallen off the dog and put them in a bag. I folded up the tarp to return to John and then weighed the black pit bull. He was a solid 58 pounds and I had felt every ounce of him as I carried him to the examining table.

My voice-activated recorder was sitting on a tray near the edge of the table. I would talk my findings into it, which would later be transcribed as part of the necropsy record. I placed my surgical pack on another nearby tray, opening its outer wrap, and began talking into the recorder, giving my name, job description, the date and time, and a description of the animal, including its length and width, which I had measured.

I manipulated the intense directional light attached to the ceiling, using a foot pedal to shine the beam on the pit bull's head. Next to the light was a long tubular fume extractor that probably wouldn't be needed since the dog hadn't started to decompose. Throughout the necropsy, the table could be tilted downward into the large stainless steel sink beside it so any refuse could be hosed away.

I was finally ready to begin the necropsy. I stuffed my hair into a surgical cap, slipped into a gown, opened a package of gloves and pulled on a pair. Next, I unwrapped the sterilized instrument pack, gauze pads and consecutively numbered envelopes for collecting evidence.

I paused before I began the necropsy. I had long ago stopped wondering how people could be so cruel. There was no satisfactory answer. How they were abused as kids made no difference to me; I only cared how abusive they had become. As always, I promised the victim – this time the black pit bull with the white stripe - that I would do everything in my power to find his killer. I was successful often enough to keep myself positive and, if not hopeful, at least involved. I petted the dog, apologized for his harsh life and prepared to slice him open.

But first I scraped under the nails and clipped them, hoping I'd find some human DNA, and put the scrapings in the first numbered envelope, narrating my actions as I went along.

I then took a fine-toothed comb and ran it in a grid over the entire dog. This process didn't reveal any other contusions, wounds or lesions, but it did reveal some foreign hairs – with roots. They could be tested for DNA. I separated them by color – white, beige and brindle – and placed them in separate envelopes. Next, I took samples from every orifice, put them on slides and placed them in slide holders and more evidence envelopes. I took radiographs and didn't find any internal injuries or projectiles. The dog had no fleas, no ticks, no visible health problems at all, other than a bullet in its brain.

Now it was time to shave the dog and soon all its fur laid on the floor. I switched to a number 40 blade in the clipper, the kind they use to prepare surgical sites for humans as well, to remove any stubble. I found the unexpected.

The dog had two sets of scarring. One had to have been inflicted before the Everetts took possession of him. The other was from after he was stolen. I had never seen anything like this and my heart ached for this dog. He had been ripped from what seemed like a caring home to be returned to the world of dog fighting. A few photographs with my Nikon detailed this part of the procedure.

Putting on another pair of sterile gloves, I turned off my emotions and slipped a new blade on the scalpel holder, which glinted in the reflection of the overhead light. It required little effort to open the dog from its neck to its pelvis and pulled back the sides, exposing the rib cage and several organs. The next part of the process was to slide the scalpel under the skin and separate it from the body. A quick check revealed nothing but the previously noted scarring. The abdominal and thoracic cavities followed. I examined one organ and collected tissue samples and discarded its remains.

It was time to look at the heart, which I had already removed and placed on a tray waiting to be dissected. Just as I suspected, the left ventricle was enlarged and the walls had thickened. This was the result of prolonged anabolic steroid use. Still not satisfied, I collected a urine sample from the bladder which would offer definitive proof of steroid use.

Almost at the end of the necropsy, I dropped my gloves in the trash, gave my temples a quick rub and leaned back and then forward, putting my palms on the ground to stretch out my spine. Now I was ready for the brain, the final piece of the puzzle.

I took the Stryker saw and cut a cap around the top of the skull. I put on a new pair of gloves before pulling it off, exposing the brain and the bullet hole. The tissue around it was torn and shredded. I moved the light so it shined on the pulpy mess and I saw the glint of the bullet. Using the long, straight forceps, I fished around until it grasped the end of the bullet. It came out easily. It was a flattened 22-caliber bullet, used because it's small and bounces around in the brain, tearing it up. I rinsed off the blood and tissue revealing a portion of the bullet's land and groove, which could be used to determine the gun that fired it, if it ever was found. I dropped it into another evidence envelope.

Once the cranial nerves and spinal cord were severed, I lifted the brain and looked it over. Other than a third of it that had turned to mush, the brain didn't show any abnormalities. I now knew what I suspected 3 hours and 52 minutes ago: The dog had been killed by a bullet.

Only now I could testify to it. If the pit bull's killer was ever caught and tried, I hoped I'd be called to the stand.

The first time I was asked to testify for the prosecution, I wasn't even a forensic vet. I was working at a veterinary clinic where I'd had a run-in with an abuser. It was the first chance I had to make a difference in an abused animal's life and it made a huge change in mine.

F I V E

———⊶⊷———

I MOVED TO SOUTHAMPTON ON Long Island in New York a few years after I graduated from veterinary school. I had first returned to Manhattan to take care of my mother who had been diagnosed with terminal cancer. There I began my veterinary career at the Animal Medical Center.

My mother's death two years later freed me in many ways. I was glad I was there for her at the end. I pretty much made my peace; she died a lot less angry. I still wish our relationship could have been different but, over the years, I learned to accept it – through lots of continuing therapy.

I was now officially an orphan. My father had died from a massive heart attack when I was 16. I never saw him during the years since he divorced my mother and me. But at least he left me a boatload of money that was put in a trust. I was allowed to use it to pay for a therapist, which helped me to work out my painful past and prepare me for a healthier future.

Some of the money went towards my college tuition; hence, I went to the University of California at Davis for my undergraduate degree and then its well-respected School of Veterinary Medicine. I had also been accepted at the University of Colorado, but California was even farther from New York.

I had just graduated and planned on settling on the West Coast when I received my mother's phone call asking me to return to New York to care for her. I was outraged. I ran to my therapist. There was so much to work through. I was forced to deal with my feelings of dread and anger that I had been tapped to take care of her. I vacillated between "Are you crazy?" and "I love you." Once I realized they weren't mutually exclusive concepts, I packed up my life and returned to Manhattan.

I hired a caregiver to help with my mother so I could go to work. We maintained a reasonable relationship until she died. I settled her estate, which included her mother's charming beach house in Southampton, which had become a rental property in the summer.

I took it off the market, sold my mother's apartment and moved into the house. It was small on a good-sized piece of property. Perfect for a couple of dogs. I spent weeks looking for two that had been raised together. Finally, I found my adoptees, despite their given names, which were Julia and Angelina. They were pit bull sisters – one brindle, the other tan – that were seven years old and had spent the last four years in a shelter. Each was a sweetheart and so grateful for any kindness I bestowed on her. Not only did I find my dogs, I also landed a job at a busy animal hospital in town.

I honed my surgical skills mostly by removing testicles and ovaries. Over and over and over. This was the land of minimal reproduction, be it dogs, cats or people.

Every so often, I went searching for ingested objects, removed cancerous tumors and repaired the damage of car on dog. The worst part of the job, by far, was the owners. Too often they demanded I pay more attention to them than their animals.

I did, however, love my two-story, shingled house on Peconic Bay. I'd take my girls for long walks on the beach and, on clear nights, I could see the lights of Long Island's North Fork across the bay. Life was good, yet I still felt like I was marking time. Until I met Daisy.

One day, a woman rushed in with an unconscious cat and a surly younger man. A vet tech quickly ushered them into an examining room. I was right behind them. I introduced myself and began checking out the black and white long-haired cat.

"Oh, Dr. Reeves, something's wrong with Daisy," the woman, Jeanine Reilly, said, stating the obvious. The scent of whiskey rode on her breath and collided with my face. It wasn't near noon. I looked up from the cat to glance at the woman and was surprised to see her staring at the boyfriend who, in turn, was looking me over.

I ignored them both and felt a contusion on the side of Daisy's head. I checked her eyes and found them rolled back. Then I used my stethoscope to listen to her heart and lungs. Her heartbeat was steady but faint, her breathing shallow.

"Mrs. Reilly," I said sharply, "how long has Daisy been unconscious?"

"I don't know. I found her like this in the kitchen," she wailed. "I met a friend in town for brunch and when I got home, Daisy was unconscious. I yelled for Steve, this is Steve Hudson." She almost batted her eyelashes at him. That's about all that moved on her face, an immobile mask of Botox. He was pushing 30. She'd never see 50 again.

"Does she go outside?" I asked, trying to get her to concentrate on the cat. "Could she have been hit by a car?"

"Oh no, I would never let her out," she said indignantly. "She could get hurt."

I worked hard to keep my own eyeballs from rolling back in their sockets. "Mrs. Reilly, she has a large lump on her head. I'd like to X-ray her."

"Of course," she answered, finally sounding concerned.

The vet tech picked up the limp cat and followed me to the X-ray room. I decided to check out her entire body. I was glad no skull fracture appeared, but there were newly healed fractures of three ribs and the humerus of the front right leg. This was an abused cat. The only question was by whom. My money was on the boyfriend.

I had no intention of returning Daisy to her owner. But I wasn't ready for a confrontation, either. Instead, I simply told Mrs. Reilly her cat needed to remain overnight. She and the boyfriend walked out, talking about getting a drink to calm her nerves.

I found my boss and told her about Daisy's situation. I explained that I wanted to contact Animal Control and have it begin legal proceedings to confiscate the cat. She agreed. I called the head of Animal Control, a real badass when it came to animal abuse, and she asked me to forward my findings. I faxed them over to her. She called back a few hours later to tell me she contacted Mrs. Reilly. She told her Daisy wasn't coming home pending an investigation, and she quite likely would be facing animal abuse charges.

Daisy rallied and returned to consciousness. I stayed with her until I was sure she was okay. I gave her one last look before I left. Julia and Angelina were waiting at home.

I was heading towards my car when I saw Steve the boyfriend, obviously waiting for me. "Hey, bitch!" he shouted, fury contorting his slick, good looks. "Who the fuck do you think you are? Telling the police we messed up that goddamn cat!"

"Get away from me!" I snapped. I wasn't scared. I was pissed. I looked up at the roof of the building and pointed.

"Those are cameras," I said, lowering my voice. "You come near me and I swear I will fall to the ground, screaming. Then I will make sure you go to jail." I picked up my phone. "I already dialed 911. All I have to do is push Send. I am not a defenseless cat!"

He looked startled. I brushed past him, jumped in my car and cranked the engine. Then I drove so close to him that he was forced to jump back – my moment of childish revenge for Daisy. I stopped halfway down the street, pulled over and cut the engine. Within moments, Steve's car raced past me. He never looked sideways. I waited for his taillights to disappear. Then I restarted the car, did a U-turn and went back to the clinic. Just in case, I put Daisy in a carrier and took her home with me.

But I never saw Steve again. He didn't come to court when the case against Jeanine Reilly was finally heard. He simply disappeared, leaving Reilly to defend herself. She blamed him. But mostly she blamed me for ruining their relationship. I had been granted temporary custody of Daisy. And I was the main witness for the prosecution.

On the stand, I testified Daisy had been continually abused. I made the case that even if the abuser were the boyfriend, Daisy's owner had permitted it to happen, one broken bone after another. Reilly received a hefty fine and was told Daisy would not be returned. I petitioned the court for custody and Daisy is still with me. It took one simple court case for me to discover my calling. I found my voice on the witness stand and became the protector of the speechless. The thrill of seeing animal abusers in handcuffs was only topped by rescuing the abused animal.

Once I realized my mission, I began researching the field of forensic veterinary medicine and discovered Melinda Merck. She had pioneered the field of forensics, becoming the director of Veterinary Medicine for the ASPCA. She had investigated famed, and now infamous, NFL quarterback Michael Vick, and testified against him for holding dog fights at his Bad Newz Kennels. The case became a headline screamer that swept across television, the Internet, newspapers and dinner conversations.

Vick had denied his involvement in pit bull fighting until Melinda's findings proved him to be a liar. He claimed ignorance. He was never there, didn't know dogs were being fought and had no idea betting, drugs and weapons flowed on his property like blood.

Melinda oversaw the exhumation of eight dogs buried in two mass graves, all belonging to Vick. They had died from hanging, drowning or being brutally slammed into the ground. Melinda's findings validated the co-defendants' version of how Vick had killed his own losing pit bulls, not his fabrication. The bite marks on the dogs' bones added irrefutable proof that they were fighting dogs. Eventually, Vick was prosecuted and sent to prison. What the case did for forensic veterinarians is what the television show "CSI" did for police work.

Duke's woof brought me back to the present. I yelled "Come in," before John could knock. The door opened and he ambled in. Duke sat guarding the doorway. I guess he was still on the job. John noted I was wrapping up the surgical instruments.

"You done?" he asked.

"Almost," I said, and slipped out of my gown, throwing it in the washing machine, pulling off the cap and tossing it in the trash. John turned me around and rubbed my shoulders. Not nearly long enough. Then he gently pulled me towards him and gave me another one of those knee-bending kisses. Granted I was weak from hunger, but I was wobbly for other reasons.

"I have a bullet for you," I said, pulling away so I could finish my job.

"You could have just said 'no'," he replied, dropping his hands for emphasis and sliding into my desk chair. "I did take sensitivity training."

"No, you didn't. In fact, I distinctly remember your reaction when your sergeant threatened you with the possibility. It was 'Fuck him.' And you threatened to call in sick for several days. I was so glad I was testifying out of town while you were sulking."

John chose to ignore me. "Duke, come boy," he ordered softly. His dog instantly stood up and went over to John and laid down, tail wagging. John petted his head, looked at me, held out his other hand and said, "Give."

I handed him the bullet. He felt the envelope while he looked at the paperwork I also gave him. He scribbled his name, signing off on accepting the bullet.

"Twenty-two?" he asked. I nodded yes. "What else you got?"

"How'd you know I found anything else?" I asked, surprised.

"You mean besides your 'God, I love my job look,' which isn't that different from your shit-eating grin?"

"Nice," I said, but laughed anyway. That's how good I was feeling. "But you're right. I found three different colored hairs on the dog's coat. It could be a potential goldmine since they all had roots. I'll FedEx them to Barbara first thing Monday morning."

Barbara Montrose was the director of the Veterinary Genetics Laboratory at UC-Davis, the largest domestic animal testing site in the world. She also maintained the first criminal dog fighting DNA database, known as Canine CODIS (Combined DNA Index System), established after a multi-state federal dog fighting investigation.

I pointed to the three glassine envelopes that contained the different color hairs I had discovered on the pit bull, which were labeled with the case info on the outside of each. Glassine was the preferred packaging material because it kept the nuclear (chromosomal) DNA intact during transit, allowing the hair sample to "breathe." If it were placed in a closed environment, such as a tube, it could create enough moisture to promote bacterial growth that would digest the DNA. I put each hair in its own FedEx envelope and labeled them with Barbara's name and address.

John watched the whole process. He was waiting for something. I knew what it was: word about Ella.

SIX

———— ∽∾∾ ————

THAT WAS THE BEAUTY OF having a home lab. I already started testing Ella's blood. I wanted to know if she were malnourished because of starvation or if she was also eaten up with other diseases.

I performed a Knott's test to determine if she had heartworm, spinning down a sample of blood mixed with formalin. I looked at the results through the microscope and didn't detect any microfilaria (baby worms) circulating in the bloodstream. I gave John a thumb up.

"Now, for part two," I said. I did a serology test to make sure there were no adult heartworms living in the pulmonary arteries. This is easily determined by checking for a specific protein in the bloodstream only produced by adult heartworms. It wasn't there and my other thumb went up.

Ella proved negative for the tick-borne disease Ehrlichia, but she did test positive for Lyme – not that unusual for animals on the Eastern Shore. I'd do a quantitative test later, which would provide a base point for further testing. I gave John the results and called Helen immediately. I told her the good news and the not-so-bad news, and recommended she just continue the regimen of Doxycycline that Ella was already on.

"Hey, Doc?" Helen started. "I know tomorrow's Sunday, but I'm concerned about some of Ella's burns. They're not healing like they should and our vet hasn't bothered to come by. I haven't even heard from her and she's had the blood work for more than 72 hours."

"I can come right now if you want."

"Oh, God, no, I'm sure you've had a day of it. Tomorrow would be fine," she said, her voice filled with relief, and added, "Have a great night. I know I'll sleep better. I really worry about that one."

"Helen, I want to interview the Everetts first. I hate having to tell them Lassie isn't coming home. I'll call you when I finish there and know what time I'll be by," I said before I disconnected.

I walked over to John and sat down in his lap and leaned my head against his shoulder. I kissed him on the neck.

"Helen wants me to stop by and see Ella tomorrow. Want to meet me there?"

"Yep."

"Thought so," I said, and smiled so wide I think some happiness might have worked its way back into my being. "Why don't you go home, make dinner reservations, draw me a bath, fix me a drink and whip up some hors d'oeuvre?"

"How 'bout knocking off the food order? Everything else is doable."

"Well, good," I said, suddenly looking forward to getting home. "What's a bath without you?" I said and smiled again. I had insisted we build a tub large enough for the two of us.

Once John and Duke left, I called my partner, Jackie. I had met her at the same time I met John, but I only had eyes for dead bodies, bugs and him. And not always in that order.

We had attended one of the first workshops offered to both law enforcement and veterinarians at the University of Florida in Gainesville, headed up by Drs. Melinda Merck and Jason Byrd, a forensic entomologist. Byrd was known worldwide for his expertise in assessing a body's decomposition by the manifestation, type, and age of bugs.

That's when and where I met John Thibert. Together, we studied the life cycle of bugs and plant growth, an important part of the exhumation process. And Lord, did we exhume animals. The dead had been buried at various times, so each body we dug up was feeding a different cycle in the life of a bug. We worked in the field and then the lab. I was dirty, smelly and sweaty, and John couldn't get close enough. He was as funky as I was, and that was just fine with me.

We had dinner together and, yes, we both looked really good scrubbed and wearing clean clothes. Kind of like a sardonic wedding cake couple. We talked about death for most of the meal. I had the feeling the waitress tried to avoid our table. We switched the conversation to ourselves while she cleared the plates.

I told John I had been born and raised in Manhattan. He chortled. I didn't know why. He really laughed when I explained I lived in my grandmother's house in Southampton. I also explained that I was an orphan who had adopted two dogs. But I was more interested in the details of his life, so I shortened the version of my life to include: always wanted to be a vet; became one; testified in court and found my calling – forensics.

John Thibert, I learned over dessert, was from the Eastern Shore of Maryland, an area some visiting Washington, DC, politico recently compared to Mississippi.

His family owned and farmed hundreds of acres. He hated farming. He hated hunting even more. He told me about sitting in a deer stand at dawn, snow all around, waiting to kill something. Passing the bottle around with his father and two of his four brothers made it bearable, but he silently prayed he'd fall out of the stand and be rushed to a warm hospital bed.

Yet John had no problem driving his chopper in any kind of weather. He loved everything motorcycle and worked summer jobs and after school to buy one. His mother cried about his riding; his father threatened to destroy his chopper if John didn't at least graduate from high school. He was in constant trouble. He had so many tickets, he lost his license. He still tore up and down the road. He finally ended up in jail. His family refused to bail him out. They figured he and everyone else would be safer if he stayed there for a while. I thought that was a weird choice, but maybe that's why I chose not to be a parent.

Anyway, he was found guilty on numerous charges. He appeared for sentencing before a judge who knew the family well – this was small-town America. He made John an offer: A suspended sentence if he graduated from high school and became a motorcycle cop or he could remain in jail. John asked if he could think about it. The judge stared at him in disbelief. John finished high school, became a motorcycle cop and eventually graduated from the University of Maryland with a degree in criminology.

Just before we met, he had traded in his beloved motorcycle for a cadaver dog. Though in the land of marijuana and meth, Duke was also a drug dog. John's Commander and mentor, Lieutenant Bill Andrews, had tried to talk him into taking the detective exam and think about transferring to the homicide division, but so far, John said, he wasn't interested. I, the overachiever that I am, had somehow learned to keep my mouth shut.

But back then, we were both looking for something new, and were very surprised when it turned out to be each other. We walked back to the motel and barely made it to my room before we were having sex. Standing up, clothes on, eyes wide-open, wall-banging sex. The next day, John moved his things into my room.

He had driven down from Maryland, and I had flown. By the time the seminar was over, we'd arranged for me to drive back with him so we could grab some extra days together. We stayed in the brick farmhouse where his grandparents had lived in Trappe, just over the Choptank River from Cambridge. John never wanted any of the huge tracts of farmland in Dorchester Country that his parents and brothers had inherited. He just wanted this plot of land. And his grandparents willed it to him.

Maryland's Eastern Shore reminded me of the East End of Long Island, long before the potato field famine. It took me back to when there were acres of farmland instead of miles of subdivisions. I was happy there. John wanted me to stay.

I wasn't ready. It took me six months before I was. During that time, John would visit me or I'd go to Trappe. Finally, he moved me and Daisy. Angelina and Julia had died the previous year, within weeks of each other. I rescued a few old dogs when I first moved down here, knowing their time was limited. John was fine with it, understanding I wanted to give each one a good life, however short. A year later, we moved into the house we built on John's property on the Windy River.

I was surprised how easily I gave up my solitary lifestyle. I had had several short-term relationships, and always kept my own house. But John gave me closet space willingly and let me choose my side of the bed. We were like gifts to each other that we just couldn't stop unwrapping.

He introduced me to the Talbot County Coroner, Dr. Max Greene, who enjoyed most of the time we spent dissecting bodies. Just as he appreciated my curiosity, right up until it became tedious. A lesser man might have told me to shut up; he would only growl "Look it up." But Dr. Greene, shaggy-haired, pale and a tad paunchy from too much snacking at work, liked teaching. I followed him around like a dog.

I exchanged emails with Melinda to let her know what I was doing and studying. After 18 months, she called to invite me to join her team to investigate a hoarder in Florida. A few months later I worked a puppy mill case with her in Pennsylvania.

I returned to Trappe with new confidence and growing professional credentials. I continued offering my services to law enforcement agencies and local animal rescues to help prove cases of animal abuse. I became a fixture in the courtroom, the area's first forensic veterinarian, and a welcome witness for the prosecution.

Melinda also threw some cases my way. After three years, HSPAC offered me a full-time position overseeing the mid-Atlantic district. I accepted on the proviso that I could build my own lab, using money I would raise, near our house. I spent so much time traveling to crime scenes and courthouses that I wanted to stay close to home when I could.

I used Melinda's lab as a template in designing my own. And every time I worked in it, I followed her procedures for processing and preserving evidence. Equally important, she taught me how to translate that information into a successful presentation that would lead to a conviction in a criminal court case.

I felt the need to call Jackie and update her on today's events. I told her about the dead pit bull I had just necropsied, the purported rise of dog fighting in the area and our getting involved. She was all for it. We would try to interview the Everetts tomorrow morning, if they were amenable.

I found their number in my notes and called them. I introduced myself to Mrs. Everett and gave her the sad news. It made her cry. I set up a meeting with the couple for 11 o'clock, after they returned from church. She wanted to know what happened. I decided to hold off on the details until I had a better sense of who they were. Lots of bad people went to church.

SEVEN

⸺◦◦◦⸺

I WAS SITTING AT THE breakfast table, looking out on the Windy River. John went off to the Church of Crime; he was working Sundays this month. It was finally too cool to sit outside on the deck with Daisy, who was old and creaky and lived for sunlight. She was resting on the sun-drenched window ledge. Tom was sitting next to his empty food bowl glaring at me.

He was our gargantuan grey cat. The first time I saw him, I thought he was an amorphous fog, a grey shape-shifter. That's because it was dusk and the air was thick with humidity after days of no sun and not a drop of rain. It was like living in a translucent saturated sponge.

The cat appeared and disappeared as the heavy mist thickened and thinned. I called to him. He heard me and ignored me, but he didn't run. I was sitting on the screened-in porch, letting Eric Dolphy lull me further into the day's melancholia with his alto sax rendition of "Tenderly." Next was his bass clarinet version of Billie Holiday's "God Bless the Child." After a particularly sweet solo, the grey cat walked towards the porch. I opened the door, he walked in and he never left. To this day, I can't tell if it was the lure of jazz or blues that spoke to him.

I called John and told him about our visitor. He was fine with the cat as long as Duke didn't eat him. John soon pulled into the garage, but left Duke in the car while he came in to suss out the situation.

"Jesus Christ," he marveled at Tom, as I had unimaginatively but accurately named the cat (I planned to neuter him the next day). He was sitting next to me on the living room couch. Daisy was on my other side sound asleep. I don't think she spent more than 45 minutes awake in any 24-hour period. "I was worried about the cat. Now I'm more concerned about Duke's eyes."

"He is huge," I said. "And you thought I was spinning another fish story. I think he's probably pushing a muscular 30ish pounds. I'm going to guess he can bench press 250."

I gingerly carried Tom, waiting for the first sign of my blood, and John retrieved Duke. We placed the two within eyeshot and neither one cared. Tom yawned and Duke lay down, blinked a few times and closed his eyes. That's about as much as Duke and Tom have interacted in the four years since he entered our lives.

Tom was now resting on the couch and turned his head in answer to the quick knock that preceded Jackie's entrance. The never-ending summer had finally come to a windy end, and a gust of cold air followed her down the hallway on her way to the kitchen. I met her there.

Jackie Vincente was compact in size, motion and speech. She was 5'-4", a size 6, yet could lift Tom with one finger. Her looks, like her last name, kept her tied closely to the Mediterranean shores her family had left two generations ago. Her olive skin had darkened in the summer sun. Her long bangs reached to her eyebrows and her thick brunette hair was loose with loopy curls resting on her shoulders. Jackie's eyes, the deepest, darkest shade of brown, carefully shielded her feelings, lest they bubble over and out at an inappropriate time.

"Coffee?" I offered. "Fresh pot. Food?"

"Just coffee." She walked over to Tom and petted him. She picked up the mug I poured for her and sat on the bench under Daisy and the window ledge. Daisy actually woke up to enjoy having her head scratched.

"Did you pick up a rental or do we need to get one in Cambridge?" I asked. We had established this investigative procedure that neither of us ever drove our own car unless it was the HSPAC Mobile Unit. It was a precaution in this day of instant information, a way of protecting ourselves from someone jotting down our license plate numbers and traveling the Internet highway to our doorsteps.

"I picked up a convertible," Jackie said having the good grace to look sheepish. "It's such a beautiful day. I kicked up the heater to boil, zipped up my jacket and put on a wool cap. Very efficient."

"Your cheeks are somewhere between scarlet and whipped," I noted. "I thought maybe you were suffering from adult onset Rosacea."

"Fine, I'll put the top up. You know you used to be fun?"

"Really?"

"No."

We laughed. Drank our coffee and went outside.

We latched the top in place and took off with Jackie at the wheel.

I kept the heat on, but lowered it to simmer.

"I can't believe last week I was making jokes – well, what I thought was a joke, if I were funny – about grilling the Thanksgiving turkey outdoors." I shot Jackie a look but she blithely kept her eyes fixed on the road. "But now I'm seeing that turkey covered in goose bumps, chattering its way off the grill, waddling into the kitchen and hoisting itself into the nice, warm oven."

"Okay, that's funny," she laughed.

I was about to tell her to screw off when she took a right turn and a quick left placing us in a welcoming neighborhood of tree-lined streets with views of the Choptank River.

"That's the house on the right, the one with the opened garage door," I said, and Jackie slowed down.

We could see the rear end of an Audi Quattro resting comfortably in the darkened interior of the garage and what looked like a Volvo wagon in the bay beside it. The house was a beautiful, turreted, three-story Victorian with three types of shingle. It was painted a soft, pale green with dark green shutters, arched windows and maroon and cream trim.

It was perched on a lovely chunk of property adjacent to the water with a large fenced area perfect for a dog. "I hope they got another dog," Jackie said, giving voice to what I was thinking.

As we pulled into the driveway, we could see an African-American couple in their mid-to-late 50s through the tall vertical windows in the foyer. They were trim and athletic-looking, both greying at the temples.

"I don't get it. They look more like Golden Retriever people," Jackie whispered. "A large pit bull like that is a rather unusual choice for a middle-aged, middle-class couple. Not that there's anything wrong with it."

I hid my smile because the front door opened while we were still walking up the porch steps. We introduced ourselves, and Patricia and Marcus Everett invited us into their house.

EIGHT

———— ❀ ————

I NOTICED TWO SETS OF golf clubs leaning against the wall next to the hall closet, probably heading for winter retirement or Florida. The house was warm and inviting. They slid open a set of mahogany pocket doors and led us into a living room awash in deep blue wallpaper dotted with creamy stars, a throwback to the Victorian age. It was a large house, especially for the two of them. But once I noticed the family photos on the tables, hearth, piano, end tables – in other words, every available flat surface – I realized this home had raised a brood of children. Gaggles of kids, grandkids and their pets were memorialized in pictures during Christmas and summer vacations.

Mr. Everett had disappeared while his wife seated us and returned with a pot of coffee, cream and sugar on a tray. Cups and saucers had already been placed on the sidebar. He poured and handed them out. Jackie and I sipped our coffee and murmured our collective thanks. She had pulled out her notepad and pen and placed them next to her.

"We just wanted to ask you a few questions about Benji," I said with an easy smile.

"You reported him stolen three years ago," Jackie interjected, taming her bouncing curls by tucking them behind her ears, before she took over the gentle interrogation. "Please tell us the circumstances."

"Of course," Mrs. Everett said. "We go to church every Sunday, and would always put Benji in the yard if the weather was good. It was a beautiful day. Until we got home. That's when we found the lock on the gate was broken off, and Benji was gone."

"Was there any sign of a struggle, like he had been subdued?" Jackie continued, picking up the pad and jotting notes into it. "Most people are a bit nervous around pit bulls."

"There was a beef jerky wrapper outside the fence. Fools, they could have had him with a Saltine," Mrs. Everett said sadly. "He was such a big baby. At least with people. He was very dog aggressive though, so we were extremely careful with him."

She turned towards me suddenly. "He was shot? It doesn't make sense. Why steal him and then shoot him?"

I didn't say anything. I was finding the couple less suspect, and therefore more likable. But I was still bothered by one unanswered question.

Jackie paused and took a mouthful of coffee and then tapped her mouth with the linen napkin she had been provided, giving me time to jump in if I wanted to. I didn't. So she continued, "That's what we're trying to find out. Tell me, Mrs. Everett, how'd you get Benji?"

"Some crack addict was selling him and had him tied up with a piece of rope," Mr. Everett said, sitting next to his wife on the loveseat. He put his hand over hers. "That poor dog was so skinny and had scratched himself raw. He also had fighting scars all over his body.

"I couldn't help myself. I offered the guy $100 for him, all the cash I had in my wallet. He took it. The jerk didn't realize it, but I would have gone to the ATM window if he had asked for more money."

I smiled at Mr. Everett. I liked them.

"We took him straight to the vet," said Mrs. Everett picking up the conversation. "He couldn't find any ID, no microchip or tattoo. We decided to keep him and had him chipped. We had him for a little more than two years." Her voice cracked.

"Who named him Benji?" I asked, betting the answer would make her smile. I peeked at Jackie, whose dimple was showing. She knew what I was doing.

"Our grandson Daniel," she said and, indeed, she smiled. "His parents had bought the movie for him and he watched it umpteen times. As soon as his mom told him we got a dog, he called us and asked if we'd name him Benji. How could we say no?"

"Any idea who could have taken him?" Jackie said.

"We talked about it," Mr. Everett said with a thoughtful frown. "The crack addict who sold Benji never left the area. I swear I saw him on the other side of our street a few days before Benji disappeared. Afterwards, I drove around looking for him.

"I finally found the creep standing in front of a liquor store a few blocks away," he continued, standing up to retrieve the coffee pot. "It was a couple of weeks later. I pulled over and told him Benji was missing. I didn't say he was stolen. I asked him if he had seen him around. He told me he didn't know what dog I was talking about. I couldn't tell if he was lying, or he was so messed up he really couldn't remember. I called the police and they pretty much told me 'tough.'"

"Would you give us his description?" Jackie pressed on. "And the location of this liquor store?"

"It's four blocks south of Maryland Avenue on the corner of Pine Street," Mr. Everett said quickly. "He wears a Dodger baseball cap, which is pretty standout in Maryland. And he has no teeth. Well, that's not exactly correct. He has one upper tooth. I couldn't stop looking at it, it's kind of mesmerizing.

"He's skinny, too," he added, leaning forward in his seat. "I've only seen him wearing filthy jeans and an orange T-shirt, but never a jacket or coat. I drive by a lot, hoping to catch him with Benji. At least now I can stop looking."

By now, Mrs. Everett had tears in her eyes. "The other thing that's so sad," she said, "is Daniel found a female red pit bull puppy in the street. He brought her home and named her Scarlet. No one claimed her so they kept her. Daniel wanted to breed her so he could have a Benji puppy. Then the other grandchildren started clamoring for one. We were going to have the one litter and then neuter him. First we had to wait for Scarlet to mature enough to have puppies. Then she had 'female troubles.' It would have been so nice to have Benji puppies, especially now that he's gone for good."

She looked at her husband, who reached into his pants pocket. He took out a white handkerchief, such a reassuring, caring gesture from another era, and put it in his wife's hand. She dabbed her eyes and leaned back in the loveseat, clutching the handkerchief in one hand and rolling the pearls of her choker between the fingertips of the other.

I leaned forward a hair. Jackie, the best partner ever, noticed and paused. Mrs. Everett had just unknowingly answered the one question I had about the couple's potential culpability. Why hadn't the dog been neutered? The grandkids wanted puppies.

I was ready to get going. My foot started rotating at the ankle, which I thought was quite an improvement over its loud nervous tapping that drove Jackie crazy.

"I have one more question," Jackie said, "and then we'll be on our way. How old do you think the guy in the Dodgers cap is?"

"Who knows?" Mr. Everett said. "He looks about 50. But he could be 25. Life has definitely been hard on him."

Suddenly I had an idea. I wasn't sure if it was a good one or not, but I pushed onward. "I know you are just getting used to Benji's death," I said. I always had trouble saying "passed." For me, dead is "dead." Nothing mystical, never soft and fuzzy; always ugly and unnecessary in my world. "But there are some adorable pit puppies at the shelter. They are being transitioned to puppy food and should be ready for adoption soon. Maybe you'd like to think about it."

The room warmed up a couple of notches immediately. Mrs. Everett's lips curved upward in a hesitant smile.

"Oh, my God." Mrs. Everett appeared startled. "A puppy? Lord, that's a thought. Honey?" She turned to her husband with a look of anticipation. "What do you think?"

"I think we need to slow down," he said, and saw the disappointed look on his wife's face. "Well, I guess it's time to take the candle out of the window for Benji, now that we know he's not coming home. Maybe we could go look at them."

She grabbed his hand. "Maybe Daniel would like one of them. Oops, I'm getting ahead of myself." She smiled.

I handed her a piece of paper with Helen's name and the shelter's phone number. "I'll tell her you might be calling. I'm going over this afternoon to check out the mother."

"Was she abused?" Mrs. Everett asked hesitantly. I nodded yes, knowing where she was going. I was ready. "Was Benji abused?"

"He died instantly," I fudged. Neither of them pressed my answer. Sometimes you just know you don't want to know.

NINE

———— ⌾⌾⌾ ————

JACKIE AND I DROVE STRAIGHT to the liquor store where Mr. Everett had last talked to the dog thief. We cruised down Water Street, occasionally breaking for ambling geese heading to and from the river. We hung a right on Talbot Avenue, heading away from the water and the historic district with its huge, rambling Victorians and gingerbread Princess Annes. After a couple of blocks, we made a left on Washington Street, driving deep into the heart of Cambridge, passing small two-story houses stuck on small strips of land that gave way to apartment buildings a few blocks later.

Soon we were in the land of no return, skirting the edges of the sprawling public housing project that operated under the misnomer Rosewood Gardens.

"Such a lovely name for an awful ghetto. Oh, excuse me. How politically incorrect. I meant to say 'inner city,'" I grumbled. "How'd they do that? Find the ugliest, drug-dealing, murder-driven, dog fighting, women-beating area of this charming town and call it Rosewood Gardens? No roses, no woods, no gardens, go figure. Just so many victims, people who are stuck here and will never get out. Dealing drugs, fighting dogs, smuggling guns, herding whores, committing any heinous act in order to rise to the top of the heap. Those are the heroes of the neighborhood." We were less than a half-mile from the Everett home, yet this was a different world.

"You really are depressing today," Jackie griped.

"I'm just being realistic," I corrected her. Then I pointed to the corner. "There's the liquor store."

43

We drove by it slowly and looked around for a drugged out guy wearing an orange shirt and a Dodgers baseball hat. He wasn't there. So Jackie and I went for lunch and gave it another try after we finished. Still no sign of him. Neither one of us wanted to give up so we cruised around the neighborhood for a couple of hours hoping for a sighting. I was ready to pack it in, thinking about the cats I needed to necropsy. We had finished all our bottled water, so we went back to the store to buy some and give it one more look-see.

We pulled into the store's parking lot. A desultory group of druggies leaned against any structure that would keep them upright: walls, Dumpsters, step rails.

They all stared at us. I got out of the car. As prearranged, Jackie stayed seated and scanned the wastelands, looking for a guy in Orioles country wearing a Dodgers cap. I strode into the store, more bodega than 7-Eleven, and bought a couple of bottles of water. The young guy behind the counter looked at me with surprise. I wanted to ask him about the orange-shirted crackhead oh-so-badly, but Jackie had sworn me to secrecy. I just smiled and thanked him when he handed me my change.

As soon as I walked out the door and slipped into the passenger seat, Jackie put the car in drive and peeled out of the lot so quickly I was thrown back in the seat. We flew down the street.

"Check it out," she marveled and said, "Look!"

I followed her gaze and saw a flash of orange turning right and out of sight onto Cedar Street. Jackie barely braked as she took the corner, and then had to surreptitiously slow down since we had overshot our shambling quarry. She deftly pulled into a parking space several car lengths ahead of our suspect.

We left the car and walked nonchalantly towards him, looking around, not wanting to scare him. Well, Jackie didn't. I wanted to tackle him from behind and lie on top of him until he literally and figuratively spilled his guts. But I, not Jackie, had just necropsied Benji and seen the terrible beatings he had taken.

This scarecrow of a man was exactly as described – wearing an orange T-shirt, filthy jeans cinched at the waist with a piece of rope to keep them from falling down and a ravaged Dodgers cap. His stench arrived several feet before he did. Once he caught up to it, he looked at the two of us.

Jackie mildly gestured for him to stop. She smiled; he wavered. His foot was tapping out one rhythm while a facial tic kept his jawline shifting to a totally different tune.

"Hey," Jackie said, all sweet and nice. She could do that. I've seen her smile at violent, abusive offenders, politely and regretfully handcuff the perps, and watch them hit their heads against the roof of the squad car while placing them in the back seat. Then she would take out a wet wipe, wash her hands and shake them like a healer flicking off bad energy.

The crackhead almost registered puzzlement at our interest in him, but he couldn't quite muster the energy. I was happy to leave him to Jackie. I wished I were back in my lab with the cats that were still waiting to be necropsied. Jackie and I had discussed the best way to get information from him. I was a believer in checkbook interrogation – especially if it would get me away from this creep more quickly.

"I was hoping to get some information," Jackie said softly, pulling herself inward, looking really small and non-threatening. I lingered behind her, out of the way.

He didn't say anything. He looked downward and ran his tongue over his tooth, circling it, caressing it. Now I knew what Everett meant when he used the word "mesmerizing."

"I'm Jackie Vincente. This is Allison Reeves. We're looking for information about the black pit bull with the white stripe you found and gave to a nice couple a few years back. I'm sure you remember that."

Jackie avoided "stolen" and "sold." She was trying to make it easy for this guy to come clean. He just mumbled to himself. I was getting impatient. Jackie remained quiet and looked at me, a go- ahead signal if I ever saw one.

"Okay, let me try this," I said, moving forward. There was no way on Earth I could look tiny, so I drew myself up and looked down at this miscreant. "I don't ever want to talk to you again. But I am willing to buy the information we want. My partner? She looks nice and sweet, but trust me, she's not. Really. I, on the other hand, can be turned into a cash cow. Now I want you to think about how much it's going to take. Think about your drug of choice and washing it down with some booze. How about a coat? Going to be a real cold winter, I hear."

I knew Jackie was throwing me a withering glance, so I didn't look at her. Why open yourself up to criticism? I stared at the tooth. The man mumbled something unintelligible.

"What?" I said, now the voice of patience.

He repeated it, "Five hundred dollars."

"That's a lot of coat," I said. "I hope your info is worth it."

"I want my money first!" he said suddenly belligerent. I looked at Jackie who tilted her chin up and down. We both knew we could take the money back if we didn't like his story.

"You got the money?" he asked.

"Yeah," I said. "Now pretend you're giving us directions. People are starting to notice us. Then go around the corner and we'll meet you at the end of the street and pick you up. We'll give you the money, drive around while you tell us what we want to know, and then we'll drop you off. Okay?"

He answered by pointing straight down the road, held up three fingers, and then jerked his thumb to the right. We thanked him, slipped into the car and pretended to follow his directions, went three blocks and took a right and backtracked.

"You had to get a convertible," I griped. "Do you know how close he's going to be? Put him in the back seat? What back seat? He might as well be sitting in my lap. Roll down your window."

"Sssh," she said. "Here he comes."

"I know. I can smell him."

TEN

I OPENED THE PASSENGER DOOR and grudgingly pulled myself out of the car so the dog thief could get in the back. He took off his baseball cap and revealed a blend of wild, wiry, grey and black hair that reminded me of a used Brillo pad. He recaptured his hair under his cap and squirmed past me. I wondered why I could smell death and not be affected, but his stench made me want to throw up.

"We want to know what happened to that black pit bull with the white stripe," Jackie said. "It went missing from that couple about three years ago. You were seen hanging around the neighborhood. Wondered if you might have noticed anything going on."

"What you need to know for?" he asked, and began pulling on a thread that hung from what had long ago been the hem of his T-shirt. He gave it his full attention.

"Look," I jumped in. "You want the money? Talk. You don't, then get out of here. This car is way too small for the three of us, so make it quick."

"Just tell us what you saw hanging around. Did you see who might have taken the dog?" Jackie questioned, giving him a plausible out from a dognapping charge and still land us at the buyer's feet or, better yet, house.

He looked nervous for a nanosecond and the rhythm of his jaw sliding back and forth increased. He looked up so I could see the conflicting emotions of fear and greed wage a tug of war across his face.

"Look," Jackie said encouragingly. "There's no reason you ever have to be involved in this. We need a name or two and we're gone. An address would be an extra hundred."

I pulled the cash out of my pocket, which I always kept for just such occasions, and flashed it to hurry along his decision-making process. I didn't know if he were thinking about what he'd smoke, drink down or shoot up, but he now seemed as anxious to get this over with as I was. Words tumbled out of his mouth without teeth to hold them back. Jackie and I listened, but it was as if he were speaking a foreign language. He had to repeat himself several times until we finally figured out what he was saying. He had heard about some guys who were always looking to help pit bulls. He was walking down the street one day and saw this black pit bull in the road. He had no collar, so he figured the dog had no owner. He took him and sold him to the guys who wanted him so the dog could have a good home. That's all he could remember.

"Did the dog have a white stripe under his neck?" I asked.

"Don't know," he mumbled and asked belligerently. "What difference does it make?"

Jackie put her hand on my knee, stopping me from doing him bodily harm.

"Do you want the money or not?" she asked pleasantly. Then she added, with a jarring change of tone, "Because that was a bunch of bullshit. Now, who wanted pit bulls?"

"I don't know," he said, his eyes shifting back and forth trying to conjure up an escape route. Now I was kind of happy we had a two-door car. I watched him squirm in the rearview mirror.

"Who did you give the pit bull to?" pressed Jackie. "Did you bring it to him? Or did he get it from you? If you don't answer right now, we're done. So speak up or get out."

I saw her cross her fingers. Big bluffer. But it worked.

"Guy hangs out at the liquor store put out the word. I told him too bad I didn't know it a while back. I found this dog and gave it away."

"And?" I said my anger growing, sure he was talking about when he sold Benji to the Everetts. We maintained our silence, and won the waiting war.

"But I found another black pit bull on the streets. I went by the liquor store with it, but the guy wasn't there. Hung around with the dog, figuring he might show. Had to keep it all night. Guy came around next day. Looked over the dog and made a phone call. Took a picture of the dog and sent it, too. Told us to stay there. An hour later, a black tricked-out ride pulls up."

"Do you know what make?"

"Sure do," he said with a sly smile. "Even heard the name of the guy he called. But that'll cost you that extra hundred."

"Name first," I insisted.

"Two guys get out," he said, ignoring me. "Man, they were real scary. They look at the dog. One pulled out a hundred and gave it to the other guy. Then they took the dog from me! Not a fuckin' word to me! The guy pocketed the hundred. Fuck 'em. Hope he OD'd on it! Fuck 'em all!"

"You heard a name," Jackie said, ignoring his tirade. She began picking at her fingernails, a sign she was getting fed up, her patience all but gone.

"Never forget it," he paused again. This one turned out to be worth waiting for. "Got their license number, too. I wrote it down and memorized it. Now you give me my money."

I looked at him hard. Jackie pulled out her notepad and I was about to hand him the cash.

"Hang on a sec," Jackie ordered, looking at me. "Now, give me the license number first."

He winced at the delay, but acquiesced. She wrote the mumbled number down and handed it to me. I called John. He ran the tag number for us. The car belonged to an Antonio Rivera. A minute later his rap sheet and photo arrived. John took it upon himself to send the police records of his known associates. I stared at my iPad, registering each face.

I passed the tablet to Jackie. She looked through each photo and returned to Antonio Rivera. She showed it to our captive.

"Is this him?"

The body tics reappeared with staggering intensity. Sweat beaded up above his lip, across his forehead and ran down his neck, causing the dirt there to slide downward. His tooth didn't seem to offer him any comfort, though we could hear a constant sucking sound.

"That's him. That's the guy. Now let me out of here."

"Hang on," Jackie said, once again scrolling through what I figured was Rivera's rap sheet. "That was only one. Let's see if we can find the other man. Then you can go."

She showed him another photograph. He shook his head. Then she showed him another. This time his head bobbed up and down and his anxiety level increased to near panic. He emitted a sound that was almost like a moan.

"That's him. Now let me the fuck out of here." he screamed.

"You said you heard a name. What was it?"

"Shit!"

"Give us the name and we're gone," Jackie said.

"Guy I brought the dog to said some other guy might want it, name Crown or Brown or, maybe, Town. That's all I know. Now give me my money."

I slapped six $100 bills in his outstretched hand and started to reach for my door. Before I could open it, Jackie jumped out of her side and held the door for him. He grabbed the back of the driver's seat, to pull himself up but his foot twisted and he fell out the door onto the street. I will go to my grave believing that Jackie could have broken his fall, that she had time to reach out and grab him by the arm, the shoulder or the belt. It happened so quickly, but I know how fast her reflexes are. I'd seen her snatch dogs and cats out of mid-air flight when they were attempting an escape. He would have been an easy catch for her, but she didn't move to help.

"Oh, my God," she said, dripping concern. Again we chose not to make eye contact lest we laughed. "Here, let me help you up. I'm so sorry."

"Get away from me!" He scrambled away on his hands and knees before slowly getting to his feet. "Ain't got nothing more to say."

That's how I felt when I thought about what horrors he had inflicted on the luckless Benji. I, too, was beyond words.

ELEVEN

I STARED INTO THE MACABRE faces of identical twins, Antonio and Jorge Rivera, captured in the moment by a police camera. Antonio had a wide, slashing scar that ran up and over the left side of his jawbone and stopped at his temple. The scar permanently lifted the outer edge of his lip and nearly closed the lid of his left eye. In case the scar, the snarl and the squint didn't provide enough identity independence, he also had a spider web tattooed on his shoulder that crept around his neck and ended with a black widow devouring her mate under his right ear.

Antonio's brother, Jorge, shunned such understated minimalist artwork and instead turned to the Maoris, a la Mike Tyson, for inspiration and total facial tats. His brown skin was barely visible under an intricate pattern of black ink.

As 6-foot-2-inch twin towers, I guessed they figured they were never going to fly under the radar, so they decided to travel at the speed of sight. Their faces were unforgettable. Their bodies, too. They were as juiced as poor Benji.

Jackie's fingers were drumming on the roof of the car, the noise dislodging my eyes from the iPad. But not before I had read that the Riveras had been charged with aggravated assault, drug dealing, gun trading and, there it was, dog fighting. They had beaten all the charges, either having them dismissed or pleading them down to misdemeanors, payable with a cash fine and probation.

"Hey," she said, once she had my attention. "You want to drive so I can find out more about these creepy guys? I want to work up a profile of them and their known associates."

We performed a modified Chinese fire drill and switched seats. The wind had been picking up all day, and now warned that winter was barreling down on us. We didn't care and simultaneously lowered our windows, releasing the last remnants of unwanted smells. I did, however, turn up the heater.

"The Riveras live on the same street, or rather, lane, in Cambridge," Jackie noticed. "Why don't we drive by and see what's going on?"

"Sure. Then I need to go by the Cambridge shelter," I explained. "I promised Helen I'd take a look at a dog there. Another pit bull. But at least she's alive."

"So why are you going to see her?"

"Jeez, Jackie, I am a vet," I said, verging on huffy. I wasn't enjoying this day. "Sorry. The dog was burned all over and some of the wounds are infected. Helen asked me to stop by. I ran the dog's blood work yesterday, since Dr. Death hadn't bothered. Anyway, John saw her yesterday too – her name is Ella – when he brought in the dead pit bull. He wants to meet me there."

"Oh no, is this puppy love?"

"Gee, I'm blushing," I pretend giggled.

Jackie was busy breezing in and out of law enforcement websites while I drove down the empty road heading towards the outskirts of Cambridge. I watched the wind whip the high clouds across the sun. Its rays flickered across the native plants that had reclaimed several empty lots. The plants, "weeds" to the uninformed, were an ecological miracle sustaining bugs and birds and even humans. I recognized the Narrow Leaf Mountain Mint with its cluster of white flowers that were greying with the approach of winter. It leaned against Orange Coneflowers that stubbornly held onto their tiny, vibrant blossoms, and contrasted with the pale, straw-like Switchgrass. Our own property was a safe haven for these generally unwanted plants. We had a few acres of wildflowers that pulsated with the arrival of spring every year, breaking out in orange poppies, wild irises and marsh marigolds.

"Can you talk?" I asked.

"Sure, what?" Jackie said, glancing in my direction.

"I want to collect Benji's remains, as best I can, and have them cremated. My gift to the Everetts."

"Have I told you I love you?" she said, patting her heart for emphasis.

"Never enough."

I drove us to one of the many Cambridge subdivisions that was built during the boom-that-went-bust. We passed the sign for The Chesapeake Estates and turned onto Larkspur Lane.

"Say what you want about those Rivera boys, but they do know how to invest in real estate. They bought four houses when the market tanked. Each twin took a place and they moved in Mom and Auntie who-the-hell-knows. These goddamn thugs are making enough money to buy up a bunch of property. Piss me off," Jackie spit out.

"Yeah, but the houses are ugly."

"Great. I feel so much better," she turned her head and glowered at me.

I ignored her as we drove by Antonio's house. There were no cars in the driveway. We went a few houses down to Jorge's, where a white Esplanade was parked. Jackie surreptitiously photographed the car and the property. Sparse grass. No trees. No flowers. All the blinds were drawn. The houses were as inviting as the Riveras' faces.

I drove around the block so we could gauge the depth of the back yards. I continued onwards and back to the street, leaving the barren lawns of Larkspur Lane behind us and headed towards the shelter. "They can't train dogs there. The yards aren't very large and there are too many people around. I can't believe these tattooed assholes are part of the landed gentry. You find any known associates? Anything interest...."

"Hey, I have a name," Jackie cut me off. "Actually two names. The one I find more interesting is Jefferson Brown, as in Crown or Town, who lives at 412 East Main Street in Hurlock. And here's a photo. It's about 20 years old."

We were stopped at a light. I turned to look and found myself staring at a dark-skinned African-American with a shaved head, fierce eyes, a gold grill, and a stack of thick gold chains sitting on his shoulders. The necklaces only emphasized the fact that he had no neck. Jackie scrolled and enlarged and flicked her way through a series of screens and landed on his rap sheet.

"Brown hasn't been charged with anything in more than 20 years. That was when he beat a murder rap when the witnesses were all killed off and the charges Had to be dropped. Then he fell off the Earth as far as the police were concerned." Jackie paused and added triumphantly, "In any case, I think we found out who's the top dog."

"Ha ha," I felt obliged to say.

Jefferson Brown, she continued, never did any jail time, but his criminal history was decades long and he was only 47. Brown dropped out of school at age nine, obviously anxious to make his mark on the streets if not the classroom.

"This is interesting. When he first began getting picked up, he would spout legalese at the arresting officers. Stuff that was well beyond a nine-year-old's skill set, especially an elementary school dropout. Someone investigated and found that when he wasn't taking care of business, he was at the library."

"An autodidact?" I wondered out loud.

"Self-taught?" Jackie questioned.

"Exactly. So what was the boy crime wave doing back then?"

"Looks like he was already an aspiring drug kingpin. He was picked up in a sweep when he was nine and, according to the officer who released him, he was polite, innocent and quite surprised to be at a police precinct. His "charming" act wore thin by his fourth visit. But he still wasn't charged. That didn't happen until he was 12.

"Jefferson Brown entered the system, not as a drug runner, but as a full-fledged drug dealer, in charge of his own area," Jackie continued reading. "He was rumored to have won over his crew with loyalty and profit-sharing, not violence, though that always seemed to be an option."

"Profit-sharing?" I asked incredulously. "Are you kidding me?"

"No. Check this out. He was only 15 when he took over his neighborhood. That was when he began to beat murder charges."

Jackie's monologue continued: "Once he consolidated his authority over Fort Howard Park, his hometown, his tentacles crept through Baltimore County, systematically and literally squeezing the life out of his competitors. He was a true vulture capitalist, picking clean the bones of his enemies and taking over their businesses. Today, he owns construction companies, bars and restaurants, and gambling interests, both legal and more often not, and distributes drugs and arms. But he also opened several small libraries in poor neighborhoods around the city. So I guess that evens out his karma."

"When did he become involved in dog fighting?" I asked, the question leaving a sour taste in my mouth.

"When Arnie Diaz got out of jail," Jackie answered, still perusing his multi-paged file. "He was Brown's best friend growing up. Diaz served 12 years for voluntary manslaughter. When he was released he began buying dogs with his good buddy's money; they became partners. That was eight years ago. At least that's what a couple of busted dog fighters said when trying to cut a deal. Someone entered that info in Brown's file."

Jackie paused, reached for her water bottle and took a swig, "Here's a picture of Diaz."

He was a slender nearly-white guy with green eyes, freckles and tightly curled red hair. He was puny in comparison to Brown and the twins, but there was a lot of madness in his eyes. According to his rap sheet, he had a penchant for guns – the great size equalizer – and a hair-trigger temper.

"Is that it?" I asked Jackie hopefully.

"We should be so lucky," she replied instantly and handed me her iPad again. "Meet Duncan Stanton, the king of behemoths. He became the face and voice of Jefferson Brown once he entered the world of dog fighting."

"Jesus," I muttered. "That's one scary-looking guy."

Stanton had thick features, a head full of flopping dreads that looked like spun cotton candy stuck to his scalp, reminiscent of Bart Simpson's nemesis, Sideshow Bob, and a waxy, thin Cab Calloway mustache.

"Wow, and even creepier than I expected, and that's saying a lot," I said, bringing my eyes back to the road. "And not one of these guys can fit through a doorway without turning sideways first. Except for Diaz, who they can use as a battering ram."

TWELVE

———— ⊶⊷ ————

HELEN WAVED FROM HER OFFICE window once she realized it was me behind the wheel. Jackie popped out; I gingerly unfolded. Then I wrestled my vet bag out of the trunk.

Helen opened the front door and smiled as we walked through. It was a nice change, since most people aren't happy to see us.

We hugged hello and she turned to Jackie. They had met several times over the years and they shook hands, smiling at each other.

The inside of the shelter was barebones, poor town practical. The board liked to think of the furniture as donations; I found "castoffs" to be more accurate. Plastic and aluminum chairs backed against two of the walls, facing Helen's desk. There were large double doors on the wall opposite the front door that helped soundproof the kennel quarters. We passed through them and entered the land of howls and yowls. We followed Helen to the isolation room where Ella was sequestered with her two surviving pups.

"I put her here because it's the quietest spot. She seems to do well in this environment." Helen gently pushed Ella back so we could all crowd into the room. There were a couple of recovering cats in kennels high up on one wall who pretty much ignored the goings-on below. Ella was beside herself with all the attention, twisted up like a pretzel. She herded her puppies in front of her, and sprawled around them.

I petted her scarred head and began my examination of her oozing wounds. Nothing that local antibiotics wouldn't heal, I thought, along with the meds she was continuing to take for Lyme disease. I cleaned up the leaking sores and applied salve to them. I told Helen not to worry – the wounds were healing albeit slowly. Suddenly I saw John's boots at eye level and looked up. He was smiling down.

Ella looked at him, too, and began to whine. John dropped down beside me and put out his hand toward her. She sniffed, licked and returned her head to my hand.

"Helen, you have time to do any temperament testing on her?" I asked. "I think John and I are interested in adopting her." John nodded his assent. Often he didn't have to talk for me to understand and interpret for him.

"We've walked her past cats and she had no reaction. I don't know about dogs."

"Is she well enough to meet Duke now?" John asked.

"Sure," Helen answered. "I can't imagine her flipping out. Lord, she's such a good-natured girl. But we'll all be close by in case we're needed."

I finally had a chance to look at Ella's pups. They were tumbling over each other. There was a black male with a white stripe similar to Benji's and a brindle female. On a whim, I pulled out my phone and took photos of them. I then called the Everetts.

"Hi, Mrs. Everett, this is Allison Reeves. I have a couple of things I wanted to talk over with you and your husband. Is he there?"

"Yes, he's sitting next to me. Hang on and I'll put you on speaker phone."

I got to the point quickly. "I've been thinking about you and Benji and, if it's okay with you, I want to send his remains to be cremated and returned to you. Also, I'm at the shelter and I have some photos I'd like you to see. When we were at your house I mentioned some pit puppies. This is the first time I've seen them. I was hoping you might be interested in looking at them. Please don't feel pressured. I don't mean it that way. But they are adorable."

"I wish the same could be said for their mother," I sighed. I wasn't above tugging at their heartstrings in any way possible. "She's been burned all over. My boyfriend and I are going to adopt her."

"Oh, the poor thing," Mrs. Everett said. "But the puppies are okay?"

"Yes, they just need a loving home and I thought of you." It was John's turn to roll his eyes.

"This is so sudden," Mrs. Everett said and paused. I heard a mumbling in the background and then she was back on the line adding excitedly, "But we'd love to see them."

I sent the photographs. Sounds of gushing came across the phone lines. I guess the pictures had arrived. "You don't have to make any decision now. I know it's a lot to consider."

"Dr. Reeves," Mr. Everett said, taking over the conversation as the voice of reason. "They are adorable. We're going to talk it over. It's a big responsibility, as you well know. Is the black one a male?"

"Yes."

"He reminds me of Benji," he said before he hung up.

"They're thinking it over," I reported.

"Well, why don't we introduce Ella to Duke in the large run out back?" Helen suggested.

John and I went outside and walked to his cruiser. He opened the back door, tapped his left thigh and Duke instantly appeared next to him. John reached in his pocket, pulled out a treat, offered it to him and rubbed his head, whispering, "Such a good boy." Duke's eyes dripped adoration.

John reached into his car, took out a leash and tucked it on his hip, a just-in-case precaution. Then he turned with Duke glued to his side and jogged him into the large fenced grassy area. John held up the heel of his hand and Duke sat. He flattened his hand and Duke's belly hit the ground.

Soon Helen came walking in with Ella tugging at the leash, eager to go anywhere. She spotted me, her new best friend, and tried to drag Helen my way. No chance. Helen gave a very slight tug on the leash and a hopeful "Heel" command. Ella ignored her, but stopped pulling, especially once she was handed off to John, who had walked 10 feet from Duke.

He turned to Ella, who was staring at Duke. John recaptured her attention with a treat and held it over her head, telling her to sit, while he patiently backed her up until her butt had no where to go but down. He flipped her another treat from his pocket. He tossed one to Duke, who hadn't taken his eyes off the two of them. When Ella bounced up, he held the treat overhead again and backed her into a sit again. A smile played across John's face as he watched the dog try so hard to please. It made all of us laugh. We were a pathetically easy crowd.

He slowly walked her over to Duke, whose eyes remained fixed on them. Ella excitedly moved towards him, tail whipping furiously back and forth, trying to pick up speed. John kept her under control. She finally arrived at Duke's nose and sniffed. He, the ultimate dog of discipline, did nothing but watch John's eyes and hands for clues.

When Ella seemed satisfied with Duke's scent, John flipped his palm up and raised it a few inches, willing his dog to rise. They continued sniffing, Ella under tight control though she couldn't stop her squiggling enthusiasm. She rolled on her back in a defenseless position. Some dogs, I thought, are alpha, others are beta. There was no doubt where Ella fell on the Greek authority alphabet: omega.

John gave Duke a one-word German command that seemed to mean "Play," because right before everyone's eyes, Duke turned into every dog. He sniffed back at Ella and gave a big waggie-tail motion. She was ecstatic and dropped her belly, extended her front legs and then bounded up. The minute-long chase was on, each dog taking a turn running after the other. Ella stopped after one pass and turned towards us. She was exhausted.

"You ready for a new dog?" John asked, picking up the tired pooch. "A young one?"

"Yeah, I don't know why, but we just clicked," I said thoughtfully. "I think we have the exact home she needs. We'll take the puppies and pray real hard the Everetts want them. Truth be told, I actually wouldn't mind if they stayed."

"Sounds good to me," John said readily. "It's been a long time since I've been around puppies. I'm sure I'll remember why as soon as we get them home."

He handed Ella to Helen standing outside the fence. We walked to John's car where I opened the door for Duke. We stood there taking a private moment to talk.

"Are you ready for this onslaught or do you want to take a day or two?" I asked John. "Ella's in good hands here. This is pretty sudden."

"It's up to you," he answered. "Whatever you want to do."

"You really mean that?" I stared into his eyes. He let me in, showing warmth and enjoyment. I suddenly realized he was mirroring my feelings. "Okay, let's take them all home."

Jackie had sidled up to us in time to hear the last sentence of our conversation and said, "Wow, good for you guys. As much as I hate to leave this 'Norman Rockwell moment,' I'm going to get going now that your ride is here. Okay?" Jackie said.

"It's not going to get any cuter, so go home," I answered with a grin. She would meet me tomorrow to do the necropsies.

We were gathering up a kennel for the puppies when my phone went off. It was the Everetts.

"Are you still at the shelter?" Mrs. Everett asked. "We were wondering if we could come and see the puppies."

I relayed the Everetts' desire to come to the shelter. Helen was overjoyed at just the possibilities of adopting out two pit bull puppies. We hadn't had time to tell her that we would be back up if the Everetts bailed.

It took Patricia and Marcus Everett less than 10 seconds to lose all their dignity once they saw the puppies. They were crawling on the ground, playing with them, while I cuddled Ella. Just as I hoped, they didn't want to break up the bond between the siblings and decided to take both.

Jackie had waited to watch this moment and then said her goodbyes. She left and John moved Duke to the front seat. Helen and I put the crated puppies on the back seat.

The Everetts stood outside the car looking stricken. "I'd just like to keep them for a few days to make sure they're okay," I said.

They nodded with relief as Helen offered them adoption applications. We went back to the office to fill out our paperwork for Ella. Helen was my reference for her, and I was the Everetts' for the puppies. We insisted on paying the fees, though Helen wanted to waive them.

"I'll call you when they're ready to be picked up," I said.

"That's so nice of you," Mrs. Everett said but I could tell they wanted the puppies yesterday.

THIRTEEN

———∞∞∞———

THE EVERETTS LEFT AND I looked at Helen. She was a tad teary. I was unprofessionally close to tears myself. Every so often, the inner-child in me erupted, usually set off by an imminent adoption.

Those feelings originated in a childhood incident. I was 13 and had spent most of my life begging both my parents first, and then my mother, for a dog or a cat. They said no. One day, I found a starving grey tabby kitten in the street. I quickly raced to the grocery store and bought a bag of cat food. I returned to the kitten that was still hiding under a car and put out a handful of food next to it. Soon I was holding the cat.

My mother was out at a luncheon, and the housekeeper was in the kitchen. I snuck the kitten into my night table drawer. Then I went to the store and bought a litter box and litter and put that in my closet. I have no idea why I thought I could pull this off. I guess I still had hope back then.

Of course, my mother quickly discovered the kitten. She told me to take it back to the street where I found it. I refused. She yelled. I still refused. She screamed for the housekeeper and ordered her to take the kitten outside. I wouldn't let go. My mother squeezed my wrists so hard the kitten fell from my hands. It was removed from the apartment and returned to the street where I knew it would die. That was the moment I vowed to become a veterinarian, so I could save animals.

Now here I was with the very savable Ella, who was anxious and watchful and much relieved when I placed her next to her puppies. I squished in on her other side. John seat-belted Duke into the front passenger seat. We were the happy car.

"Ah, he's just like the son we never had," I said, and saw John's grimace reflected in the rearview mirror. I could have smacked myself for my thoughtlessness. Also for stupidly picking the scab off a wound that just wouldn't heal. John wanted children; motherhood terrified me. The thought of it made me queasy, as in "mourning sickness." My unfortunate comment gave way to an uncomfortable silence.

Finally we were winding through the woods to our house. We pulled in the driveway and my heart fluttered, as always. Our compact two-story home was perfectly backlit by the descending sun. Its rays ricocheted off the still waters of the Windy Hill River. I was amazed that we had built my dream house – an A-frame that sat high on four poles. We were both believers in the rising tides of climate change.

Plus we both had a thing for sloped ceilings, so we tucked the master bedroom and bath on the top floor. The main level flowed from kitchen to dining area to living room. A huge fireplace was the center point of that floor. Glass walls – actually huge sliding pocket doors – were on each side of it and faced flowerbeds withering in the death throes of winter's imminent arrival. Behind them, the lawn rolled down to the river.

I had the architect carve out space for two small offices, each tucked against a side wall. Both rooms had long, vertical windows that looked into the woods. The garage was on the bottom floor with guest rooms and baths, all with high horizontal windows to let in some natural light. We liked having company, but just not too close.

We settled the puppies and Ella in the sunroom and fed them. John and I returned to the gleaming white kitchen with its long blackish-navy, marble countertop. He fed Duke while I pulled leftovers and salad makings out of the fridge and, together, we reheated, chopped and tossed our dinner in less than 15 minutes. The sun had gone down and I flipped on the outside lights and lit the inside candles. Then I blew them out.

"Let's take Duke and Ella for a walk," I said. "That way we can eat without guilt. Or cleaning up. I have no idea if Ella's housebroken."

"Yeah, I'm sure between burnings, her they took her outside and walked her 'til she went," John said, wearing his sardonic look.

"Well then, I guess that's a 'no,' and I'd better hurry up since she just ate," I said.

We freed Ella from the sunroom and I made a quick stop at the hallway closet between the kitchen and the garage and took out a leash.

"You really think you need that?" John asked, leaning against the kitchen counter and watching Ella press her full weight against my body. "I doubt you could ply her from your side with a crowbar."

"I know," I acknowledged, "it was love at first sight. And I can't lie. For me, it was all physical at the beginning. But now that she's turned into a big slurpy, we will go off into the sunset."

"How 'bout the woods instead?" John asked, cutting me off. He bent down to pet Ella and kissed me on the top of the head when he straightened up. He tapped his thigh and Duke jumped up. We all went outside.

Ella was enraptured with Duke and would follow him until she realized she had left me a few feet behind. Then she would scamper back to my side. She was becoming a tad frantic, which John noticed. He slowed Duke's pace so we formed a tight-knit family unit. A nearly full moon lit the pathway and we walked deeper into the woods.

"How'd your day go?" John asked, surreptitiously taking Duke's ball out of his pocket. "What do you think?" He tipped his head towards Ella.

"I'll hold her so Duke can have his playtime," I said, and lifted her up. John let the ball sail down the path. Duke flattened out, skimming inches above the ground, reaching his top speed. Ella barely noticed, pressing against me. I returned to John's initial question.

"We found the guy who allegedly stole and then allegedly re-stole the hapless Benji," I said.

"How?" he asked somewhat surprised. "That was fast."

"Jackie and I met with the Everetts and they gave us a great description of the crackhead who sold them Benji. He was hanging out exactly where they said he'd be. We waited awhile and, sure enough, he showed up. Life rarely works out so well."

"Checkbook investigation?"

"Okay, just a tad," I sheepishly admitted, and went on defense as I followed up with, "Well, I couldn't beat the information out of him; I'm not a cop."

"Nice," he said, and without missing a beat punched me lightly in the arm.

We looked at each other and laughed. I wrapped my scarf tighter around my neck and pulled up my hood. John put his arm around my shoulders and drew me into him.

"To continue," I said, "as much as I would have preferred to subject that crackhead-douchebag to extraordinary rendition, I handed over cash instead. As soon as I mentioned my willingness to pay him, he was miraculously able to describe the two guys who picked up Benji – Antonio and Jorge Rivera."

I explained how Jackie had located their homes and our subsequent driveby. John's expression was somewhere between consternation and impressed.

"But they don't check out," I said, disappointment pulling my lips down. "I think they're low-end, very large enforcers, you know, like secretaries on steroids. We looked at their known acquaintances and Jefferson Brown, now of the hamlet of Hurlock, interests us."

We turned around and started home. Once there, I put Ella in the sunroom with her puppies and gave them all food. Then we fed ourselves. I lit the fire and John picked a wine. We carried plates to the living room, put our feet up on the coffee table and the plates on our bellies. It had been a long, long day.

After dinner I turned on the alarms and shut down the house for the night and followed Duke up the stairs to the bedroom. I heard the water running in the bathroom. I walked in and found John's back facing the glass shower door, fogged with mist and cascading water. I could make out the outline of his long dark hair, dripping water onto his square shoulders and his back that tapered down to his butt and thoroughbred-length legs.

He turned towards me and moved closer to the misted glass shower door. Though we'd been together for five years, he still had the power to make my breath catch. I was out of my clothes and next to him in mere seconds.

Eventually we made it to bed and fell asleep immediately. I awoke to an orange fireball dispelling the night's darkness. John was gone. The smell of coffee moved me out of bed and eventually down the stairs. Ella was waiting in the sunroom, looking up at me as if she'd seen a miracle. For her it was. I let her and the puppies out.

John walked out of the kitchen, looked at us and couldn't help smiling. The puppies landed at his feet and Duke was staring at them with horror mixed with a smattering of disdain. John already had the coffee pot on the table. I heated some milk and brought it over while he pushed down the French press, capturing the coffee grains at the bottom of the glass container.

"Did Tom or Daisy see Ella yet?" I inquired nervously, noting neither cat was hanging from the ceiling fan. They were on the counter. But both had their hackles up and their tails bushed out as they stared at the little rodents, or as we called them, puppies.

"Yes, to both. I don't want to be mean, but I'm not sure Daisy could see, hear or smell Ella, which," he paused, "might not be a bad way to go through life at her age."

"She's not the Helen Keller of cats," I grumped, hating how old Daisy had grown. "At least Ella's not wearing Tom like a coonskin cap and she still has both her eyes."

We ate and watched for the red-tailed hawks that nested high in a tree across the river. This was their time of day to scream across the sky in search of breakfast, sometimes flying with their offspring, other times celebrating empty nest syndrome. This morning, they were flying up and down with military precision, searching their territory for edible intruders.

"Oh God, you think they smell the puppies?" I asked.

John didn't even crack a smile. He was miles away, but not soaring with the eagles or hawks. He stared at me. I knew what was coming as soon as he asked what Jackie and I had planned for the day. His face was impassive when I discussed the cats' necropsies. Then I told him I wanted to do some followup on Jefferson Brown.

"You're not going after him, are you?" he asked with a distinct note of disapproval that only emphasized his frown. "I looked him over and he's a real prick. Allison?"

I refused to have this conversation. He hated thinking I was in jeopardy. I did, too, but sometimes my job took me to scary places, not just depressing ones. I knew exactly how John felt: I worried about him all the time.

FOURTEEN

——∞——

THE BOYS WERE LEAVING FOR work just as my phone rang. John paused in the doorway and started to turn around, stopped himself, shook his head and exited. It was as if he knew it was Jackie.

"What?" I said to her warily, always suspicious when she called right before I expected her to show up. It usually meant a change in plans, and I wasn't good at that. I didn't like to think of myself as a control freak, but I'm pretty sure everyone else did.

"Now, now," Jackie, who knew me so well, chided. "This isn't a big deal. You can handle it. In fact, you'll probably like it."

"What?" I said my voice tight, still not convinced.

"Do you think we could find time to tour Hurlock today?"

"Oh, that would be great!" I laughed with relief. "I'm glad John has left already, so he won't know. I think he'd put up a roadblock to stop us."

"Well, I wouldn't blame him," she said, her voice becoming serious and thoughtful. "These are dangerous guys."

"I know, but we'll just drive by. If we are onto something, I certainly don't want to be noticed. Speaking of which, do you want to rent a car on your side or wait until you're here?"

"I'll get one here. My car needs to go to the shop, anyway. I'm on my way to drop it off now. See you in about an hour."

"Jackie," I warned, "if you find yourself drawn to anything small and cute, I will drag you behind it – think 'National Lampoon's Summer

Vacation.' I wouldn't do it to a dog, but I would do it to you. I still have indentations under my chin from my kneecaps."

Jackie gave a full-throated laugh. I hadn't intended my warning to be that amusing.

"You know, the cats can wait a few more hours," I said, changing my mind out loud. "I'm really curious to see what we'll find in Hurlock, so let's go there first. It shouldn't take too long. Then we'll come back here and do the necropsies."

"Perfect. See you soon."

I slipped on my jeans and T-shirt, grabbed a heavy jacket and Ella, and headed outside. She was oblivious to the fact that she was leashed and couldn't roam freely. She couldn't have cared less. She was exactly where she wanted to be: next to me.

The wind kicked up and dropped the last of the flame-colored leaves from the trees. The recent breeze that had offered relief from the unusual heat of late fall now carried the chill of winter. I shortened our walking time, worried about Ella's lack of insulating body fat. She needed a coat pronto.

Once back at the house, I waited impatiently for Jackie's arrival. I Google-mapped Jefferson Brown's house and found the most direct route. I noted it was on a large parcel of land on the edge of the town. Large enough to keep dogs. I was even more impatient by the time I finally heard the crunch of gravel under Jackie's tires.

I peered out the window to see what she was driving and was surprised to see Michelle Manning and her husband, Dwight, piling out of their car. They stormed up the driveway and would have pounded on the front door if I hadn't opened it. I surprised the two of them, which I could tell irritated good ol' boy Dwight.

He refocused his mean, little brown eyes on me and glared. Forget a beer belly; the man was a walking keg. Dwight pulled his faded and frayed baseball cap over his thick forehead. Then he unzipped his navy, quilted, bomber jacket revealing his button-popping, flannel shirt, so he could dig his thumbs in the waistband of his jeans and saunter up the front steps.

I slipped outside and closed the door behind me. I knew this wasn't a friendly visit; they weren't friends.

"I want my dogs back," Michelle screamed, her voice strangled in fury; her face flushed and twisted, before Dwight could utter a word. They were both so tightly wound they seemed to be pulsating.

"They're not your dogs, Michelle," I said calmly, knowing that's why they were here as soon as I saw them. "The Everetts and I filled out the adoption forms and were approved. We paid the fees and I, as a veterinarian, brought the puppies home with Ella. When they are healthy enough to leave, they will go to the Everetts."

"Helen had no right to give them to you," Dwight said, his voice harsh, probably afraid he'd been outmanned by his wife. "Michelle set up a bunch of interviews to talk about the burned-up dog and she needs her there. So give 'em all back."

He moved his bulk towards me aggressively. I stood my ground and stared him down.

"I thought you don't accept pit bulls at the shelter," I said, switching my gaze to Michelle without even trying to conceal my distaste for her.

"We already arranged for them all to go to a rescue," Michelle said with a dismissive wave of her hand. She lifted her large, black-framed sunglasses and stuck them on top of her head in her usual gesture. I always wondered if they kept her brain from crawling out of her skull in embarrassment.

"Are you kidding?" I exploded, letting them get to me. "Why in the world would you send three dogs to a rescue when they already have homes? They are not a publicity magnet for you to stick on the front door of your shelter."

"No, you're right," Michelle snapped. "They're pit bulls. Between you and me, who cares? You know the stats. You know everything."

I couldn't resist answering since I was passionate about this topic.

"Do you even know 'pit bull' isn't a breed?" I asked, sure they wouldn't care, but I was unstoppable. "Nearly 100 years ago, pit bull bloodlines diverge into two breed: the American Pit Bull Terrier and the American Staffordshire Terrier. But now they have been interbred as well as bred with other bully breeds, such as Bullmastiffs, Olde English Bulldogges, Perro de Presa Mallorquins, so that now no one has the same definition of what is a pit bull.

"In fact," I continued, unable to stop myself, "the Animal Farm Foundation, which is devoted to pit bulls, states they are an ever-expanding group of dogs that includes whatever animal control officers, police, shelter workers, owners, trainers or politicians deem them to be.

"Top dog fighters, the big money guys, prefer American Pit Bull Terriers because of their agility and strength. That kind of negates any reason you'd have for not accepting American Staffordshire Terriers. They're sweet dogs that, granted, can look scary when they're bred to weigh 125 pounds with gargantuan heads stuck on short, thick bodies, but they're not really fighters."

"That's all bullshit! I can pick out a pit bull without any trouble," Dwight said, ignoring everything I had just said. So, undaunted, I tried a different tack.

"According to the American Veterinary Medical Association, dog ownership was 70 million in 2012. Today, it's estimated that more than 5 percent of those pets are pit bulls. That's over 3.5 million. So for every horrible pit bull maiming/murdering headline, there are hundreds of thousands of pits living a peaceful, loving existence.

"And," I added, "go to any shelter but yours, of course, and you'll find it overflowing with pit bulls. They are the ones that aren't aggressive enough to be fighters – which is most of them – and end up in shelters where they are euthanized. Pit bulls are the throw-away dogs of our universe."

"Bullshit," Michelle interjected this time, wearing a self-satisfied smile that also showed off a smear of lipstick across her front teeth. "They train pit bulls because they're killers to start with."

"God, you are such an ass." It popped out of my mouth before I could stop it. But I was so angry I didn't care. "I've owned pit bulls for years. They are the most generous and loyal dogs I know of. With your attitude, it's no wonder you're known as the director of the board of the Inhumane Society."

Both Mannings looked as if they wanted to kill me. I decided not to give them the opportunity and I put my hand on the doorknob. "I am not giving you back the dogs. Just get out of here."

Dwight squared his shoulders, puffed out his chest and started to step into me.

"Oh, go away," I said, tired of the two of them.

I walked into the house and closed the door on Michelle's tired threat, "You haven't heard the last about this."

I was sure that was true.

FIFTEEN

ANOTHER CAR PULLED INTO THE driveway after the Mannings sped away and I saw with relief that it was Jackie, driving a nondescript, large-assed sedan. She popped the trunk and I threw my HSPAC jacket into it in case I needed to look official. It landed next to hers. I noticed she'd also brought her metal case filled with cameras, binoculars and a fingerprint kit. I slipped into the passenger seat. Jackie was dressed in civvies, but like me, I knew she was wearing her gun and bulletproof vest.

We left Trappe, heading east towards Hurlock while I related my conversation with the Mannings for Jackie. We passed through several small towns that dotted the countryside and drove across large tracts of farmland. Thirty minutes later, we were entering Hurlock.

Jackie stopped at the blinking red light, the town's one and only major intersection, and turned onto Main Street. The houses were packed close together in this underwhelming blue-collar neighborhood. Yards and garages were at a minimum, though some basketball hoops grew out of cement slabs in lieu of trees. This no-frills area had its share of foreclosure and rental signs staked in front yards. As we headed away from the town's center, the houses gained ground and even more realtor signs.

"I'll bet that's Brown's place over there," I said after a while, pointing to a large, old brick house. The giveaway was the brand-new, high wooden fence that shut out any view of the grounds.

According to the street numbers on the mailbox, it was indeed Brown's. A new cherry red Mustang convertible was parked on the street in front. Three other cars were in the driveway. One was a BMW, less pricey than the Benz, but more tricked-out, with lots of chrome and deeply tinted windows. The S-class Mercedes sat in front of the open garage where I could see a Hummer parked against the wall. A white Esplanade nosed up to the back of the Beemer. I checked the license number and it was the same one that was parked in front of Jorge's Cambridge house. Pretty ritzy cars for this neighborhood. I quickly snapped photos of the license plates and we drove slowly down the street.

Jackie called her contact at the police department. He was out on sick leave.

I picked up my cell phone, put it down, picked it up again, and put it down.

"Debating?" Jackie asked, her full lips forming a grin. "Who's winning?"

"Not John," I said, returning her look with a grimace, feeling my neck muscles tighten like they were attached to a winch. "But I want to know who owns these cars. He can run the tags immediately, and he's the only cop I'm sleeping with who'd probably help. I'm betting he'd rather do that than have us wait around to see who gets into these cars."

I hit speed dial. "Where are you?" he asked.

"Hurlock," I said as innocuously as possible, and glared at Jackie, daring her to say something. "Sweetheart, I need some info on four tag numbers."

"Oh, I thought you were calling to twist the knife in my gut," John said. "Just give them to me. I'll send you the info if you leave there right now. Okay?"

"Sure," I said without hesitation.

He waited a split second for me to say anything else and when I didn't, he disconnected without another word. The only thing wrong with cell phones, I thought, is that you can't slam them down like an old-fashioned receiver. I had a feeling he would have preferred ending our conversation that way.

But he did email me the requested names and addresses in seconds. I rattled them off to Jackie, who kept the car moving along side streets. "The Mercedes and the Hummer are Brown's. The Beemer belongs to Duncan Stanton, the Caddy is still Jorge Rivera's and the Mustang is owned by a Sandre Washington. Her address is in Cambridge. Wow, it seems as if she's cohabiting with Antonio Rivera on Larkspur Lane at the lovely Chesapeake Estates."

"I have an idea," I said suddenly. "Turn around."

"We're not going visiting, are we?" she said and shot me a quizzical look.

"I didn't say I had a stupid idea. Jeez, Jackie," I said and returned her look with a big smile, "this could actually be brilliant."

I pulled out a notepad and pen, and wrote down the name and number of the realtor on the For Sale sign next to Brown's house. As Jackie continued driving, I jotted down the addresses of a couple of other available places in the neighborhood.

"Are we going house hunting, honey?" Jackie questioned. I nodded.

"Why?" Jackie asked, while she tapped her fingers on the steering wheel.

I elucidated. My idea was to get a warrant to set up cameras looking into Brown's backyard. I listed the causes – the crackhead heard his name as Benji's buyer making him the recipient of stolen goods, and the Rivera brothers worked for Brown and picked up the dog. Plus we knew Brown had been involved in dog fighting. Oh, and he had a suspiciously high fence. I'd give us a warrant.

"Why don't you call around and see if there's a judge that will sign off on a surveillance warrant this afternoon," I asked Jackie. "Can you get it done that fast?"

"You drive and I'll type," she said, pulling over so we could switch seats.

Jackie called the office of the Circuit Court and put us on speaker with Judge Ethan Bainbridge's secretary, Bob Hampton. He put Jackie on hold for a moment after she explained the situation and then came back on the line. The judge, he said, would make time for us when we arrived. Bainbridge was pro-animal and anti-abuser. When Jackie asked Bob if we could bring our request for a warrant on a flash drive, he chuckled (probably realizing we were writing it on the fly) and assured us he'd be happy to print it out. Jackie's fingers were now tapping out a different rhythm; this time on her keyboard. As we pulled into the court's parking lot, she saved the document on a flash drive and handed me her laptop. I scanned the request, nodded my approval and closed her computer.

"Now let's come up with a reasonable story for the realtor about why we would want to live in this godforsaken area," I suggested. "How about your parents live nearby and your father just had a stroke and you want to be close, but not too close, to help out?"

"Why me?" Jackie asked suspiciously.

"Because my New York accent would probably make anyone wonder why my parents would move from Manhattan to Hurlock."

"God, you are such a snob, but we can go into that later," Jackie said, relenting though her lips were compressed, holding back a snarky reply – almost.

"For now, I'll just thank God for my cracker roots. They keep me from becoming a judgmental jerk," she said and made us both laugh. Jackie had more than come to terms with her past.

Her mother had three daughters by the time she was 17, sired by three different men. Jackie was the oldest and became the acting parent at way too early an age. Her mother was around just enough to snatch the government checks.

A couple of years out of high school, when her sisters were old enough to take care of each other, Jackie saw a sign in a U.S. Navy recruitment office offering a college education in return for military service. She just walked in and signed up. Over the next six years, she made her deployment work for her. She became a paralegal and learned enough about law to know she never wanted to be an attorney. But by the time she was discharged, she had an undergraduate degree. Jackie had become everything she could be in the Navy.

She returned to New Orleans to be near her family. She found a studio apartment, a homeless dog and a scruffy three-legged cat, she told me years ago. Then Jackie landed a job with the Louisiana SPCA as an Animal Control officer, working for then-Chief Humane Officer Kathryn Destreza. With Jackie's legal background and Destreza's guidance, she soon became an investigator. Five years later, she landed the job of Lead Investigator for the Southern district when Destreza accepted an offer from the ASPCA.

Jackie had spent her years in Louisiana breaking up dog fighting rings, shutting down puppy mills and liberating animals from hoarders. In addition, she was often in charge of rescuing and relocating animals in the aftermath of disasters.

Then she met Thomas Livingston at a No Kill conference in DC. He was a litigator for the SPCA of Anne Arundel County, a venerable nonprofit organization. She fell for the rumpled, grey-haired attorney with the soft brown eyes and unyielding sense of justice. He had, in fact, helped write some of Maryland's harshest animal abuse laws.

After a year of interstate dating, Jackie became pregnant. She and Thomas got married right away; she had learned from her mother's mistakes. Jackie moved to Annapolis where they bought a house, and she transferred to the HSPAC's mid-Atlantic district. I was delighted. We had kept in touch and followed each other's careers since our first meeting at Melinda's workshop years before and had teamed up occasionally. Now we were partners.

I picked up Jackie's phone and dialed Carol Hayden, the realtor who had the listing on the house next door to Brown's. I put her on speaker and poked Jackie to talk. She introduced herself and brought up the property at 410 Main Street. Jackie asked Carol to describe it. I gave her an encouraging smile; she gave me the finger.

Carol launched her pitch: the house was expensive for the neighborhood, but well worth it. It was $229,000 ("but make an offer"), a large rancher with a deep backyard and all new everything. Better yet, she said, she'd be happy to show it to us. Jackie arranged to meet Carol at 10 tomorrow.

To add credibility to our story, Jackie asked her to pull some other less expensive listings. I felt bad lying to Carol and using her, but I felt much worse for the dogs.

SIXTEEN

THE CIRCUIT COURT WAS HOUSED in a modest two-story structure set on a prime piece of real estate on the Choptank River. It had to be rebuilt two times since the 1700s, burning to the ground the first time and outgrowing itself the second. Crime never sleeps, though justice is often caught napping.

Jackie and I breezed through the metal detectors since we had locked our guns in the car and put the car in the police lot. We said our hellos to the two security guards on duty. Lord, I thought, looking at the pleasant, doughy, balding men nearing retirement age, what could they possibly secure except our handbags? They gave them a cursory look and us an agreeable smile.

We turned left and went down the long hallway, stopping at the last door. We walked into Judge Bainbridge's outer office and exchanged pleasantries with Bob Hampton. He took the flash drive from Jackie and was soon printing out the request for the warrant.

Then Bob ushered us into Bainbridge's chamber and the judge stood up from behind his desk and walked halfway across his spacious office to meet us in the middle. He was middle-aged with a sparse spray of greying hair circling his scalp like a fallen halo.

"Allison. Jackie," he said in a welcoming voice and gave us each a warm handshake. "Have a seat while I look over your request. Coffee?"

"That would be wonderful," I said, noting the etched sterling silver coffee pot with a trace of steam rising from its tip. It was set on a matching tray on his mahogany sideboard. The courthouse may have made a boring architectural statement, but the judge's office was a testament to bygone eras of taste and tradition.

"Okay if I pour?" I asked.

"Help yourself. I take mine black. Bob just put out the cream."

I fixed three cups, served them and sank into the striped maroon and beige silk upholstered chair next to Jackie. I recognized a Chippendale-style tilt table separating us and wondered if it could be authentic, but decided not to ask. I put the saucer on the coaster and brought the cup to my lips. The coffee was delicious. I wasn't surprised.

The judge adjusted his glasses and scanned the pages he held in his thick fingers. When he came to the end, he slapped them against his thigh in disgust and popped up and off the settee. He walked to the door on small feet with a surprising amount of grace, opened it and told his secretary to prepare the actual warrant for his signature. He turned over Jackie's paperwork to him.

"I heard about the dead pit bull on Sunday," he scowled. "One of the Baltimore bigwig cyclists had the need to call me. Once I heard Thibert was responding to the call, I knew I could rest easy and return to my golf game. He didn't shoot anybody, did he?"

I laughed as I shook my head no. We chatted about pit bull fighting in the area until Bob knocked lightly on the open door, walked in and put the paperwork in the judge's hand. He quickly read the warrant and signed off on it. Jackie and I were legal. We continued sitting and half-heartedly drank our coffee.

"Oh, get out of here," the judge ordered. "I know you're just being polite. Go get those bastards, but be careful. I only hope I get to sentence them."

I refrained from hugging him and instead collected our cups and saucers and returned them to the sideboard. The judge walked us to the door, said goodbye and told us to be careful again. We both thanked him.

"Let's call Carol Hayden and see if she can meet us later this afternoon at 4:30," I said barely out of the judge's chamber. "Sunset should be around five."

"I'll tell her I can make it after work today if she's available," Jackie said and added with a grin, "I haven't picked out a career for myself yet."

"Oh, you still don't know what you want to be when you grow up?"

"Well, now I'm thinking judge," she said. "That was some nice office."

Jackie picked up her cell phone and spoke to Carol, who was more than happy to move the appointment up a day.

"What now?" she asked me.

I looked at my watch and saw we had enough time to necropsy the two cats I'd brought back from the raid on the hoarder. "Let's close out the Chestertown case."

"Sounds good."

Once on the road, I called Gina at the house. I had spoken with her before Jackie picked me up and asked her to check on Ella and the pups. She answered her phone on the first ring.

"Oh, my God," she gushed. "I'm in love. I just finished bottle-feeding the babies. I gave them a bowl of wet food and they're standing in it. They seem to like it. I fed Ella, too. Jesus. Need I say more?" Gina had the wonderful capacity of self-censorship, refusing to overstate the obvious.

She mentioned she had left some vegetable curry (I knew the veggies would be home-grown from her husband Vernon's garden) and brown basmati rice on the stove for our lunch. I asked her to join us, but she said she had already eaten. My phone call caught her, she said, just as she had finished cleaning our house. I told her we'd probably see her, but we barely did. She was backing out of the driveway as we pulled in. She slowed down, waved and gave us her radiant smile.

Gina was a petite, attractive, auburn-haired woman with sinewy muscles and bristling energy. She was the perfect counterpart to Vernon, a handsome black man who turned women's heads, but he had eyes only for Gina. Even after 25 years of marriage. I hoped John and I would have that kind of future.

"Jackie," I said as she turned off the car's engine, "if it's okay with you, I want to check on the pups and pick up Ella so we can take her to the lab with us."

"No, it's not," she grumbled. "I thought we were going to eat first."

"Can you get through one necropsy? I'm beginning to feel guilty."

"What, about starving me?" she was now going into full pout mode.

I looked at my watch and realized she'd been on the road since eight o'clock. It was lunchtime. I opened my door and extricated myself from the rental.

"You're right, we should eat first. I'm hungry, too," I lied out of kindness.

SEVENTEEN

AFTER A QUICK LUNCH, JACKIE and I loaded Ella and Frick and Frack, as I called the puppies, until the Everetts gave them their grown-up names, in the car. We drove the quarter-mile to the lab that had been carved and curved out of the woods to create a meandering pathway that ensured the most spectacular trees remained standing.

Ella continued to stick to my side as we entered the building. For all she had been through, she was still luckier than the two cats in the lab's refrigerator.

We had been too late to save them by at least a day. They were both out of rigor mortis by the time we arrived on the scene. They were just lying dead on the kitchen floor, near the empty food bowls. Somehow I could never get the hate on for hoarders that I had for puppy mill breeders or pit bull fighters. Usually there was something pathetic and insane about hoarders. I never met one who didn't think he or she was "saving" the animals they were, in fact, slowly killing. That included the crazy bitch whose house we had recently raided.

But this case put me over the edge. The fact that she didn't even notice the two dead cats in her kitchen killed any empathy I might have felt. She had abused these cats for years. No one noticed. She was just a middle-aged, middle-class woman passing for neighborhood normal until the stench of cat urine, excrement and death seeped out of her closed doors and windows and spread across her neighbors' yards. The police were called first, then Animal Control. Jackie and I were next on speed dial.

I barely glanced at the hoarder whom the police were restraining while a variety of people crated and cared for her cats. Jackie and I recovered the dead ones. Only then did I give the hoarder my attention. I wondered if her waist-length hair marked her descent into cat hell. Her brownish/grey roots took up two-thirds of her hair length, leaving the bottom part a washed-out pale blonde. If hair grows approximately six inches a year, she was well into her third year of bat shit. Her clothes were as filthy as her stringy, unkempt hair. Sobbing, she was taken away.

The two dead cats in the lab were reminders of her insanity. Jackie and I went to work. She spread the white paper over the examining table while I took one of the dead cats from the refrigerator. Jackie turned on the computer and the tape recorder. The procedure was always the same. I stated the date, time and crime, and put on my surgical gear. Then I literally let the first cat out of the bag and emptied its contents on the paper to catch any remnants that might have been dislodged from the cat's fur. I noted piles of flea feces had fallen off the tabby. I would analyze the droppings later. For now, I put the cat on the scale and found it weighed a pathetic four pounds, six ounces. It was emaciated. I said it; Jackie typed it.

I don't think I've ever performed a necropsy without thinking back to the first few I completed at the beginning of my career. They were tough even when the animal died of natural causes. I never threw up in those early days, but there were a few times I interrupted the process, gagging my way outside, where I had to gulp fresh, soothing air. That reaction ended with experience.

But I had to readjust my response once I began examining abused animals. I would look at those tortured beings and simply become furious. The anger had a purpose. It would tamp down the tears that otherwise would have bubbled up and out of my eyes, rendering me useless. I learned to compartmentalize my feeling of grief so I could perform my job. I relegated that sadness to a place deep inside me. What rose to the surface was what I saw as a more positive use of my emotions: I was hell-bent on finding the pricks that hurt these animals and hoped to cause them the pain they deserved.

I shaved the cat until I had removed all its fur. I noted the animal was covered in scabs and pustules that were the results of flea bites. There were no bruises or lesions to be found. I was ready for Jackie to photograph my findings, and turned the cat over so she could get a complete series of pictures.

"Look how pale and yellow-tinged the cat's gums are," I said, opening its mouth so Jackie could see. "If the organs are that color, the cat probably died from anemia caused by all those flea bites. It definitely suffered from severe chronic malnutrition."

I picked up the scalpel and drew a line that opened the cat from its neck to its pelvis. I pulled the skin back on both sides, and noted out loud that the visible organs were, indeed, unusually pale with a slight yellow tinge.

"What does that mean?"

"Hang on. I'll know for sure in a few minutes."

I slid the scalpel under the skin and completely separated it from the body. I held it up to the light and saw scarring caused by the cat constantly scratching its flea bites. Then I opened the rib cage and, one by one, removed the organs. I took tissue samples from each and placed them in formalin, which would preserve them for a later pathology examination.

"So what does it mean?" Jackie asked in true-friend fashion. She knew how much I loved to pontificate, especially if my findings confirmed my expectations.

"Okay, this is what happened," I explained, knowing that she thrived on this type of information. "Initially, the cat was suffering from starvation. See, there's no fat under the skin or around the organs. It caused hepatic lipidosis, a severe liver disease, which created generalized jaundice, hence the yellowing and the enlarged liver.

"In addition, the flea bites caused chronic severe anemia so the bone marrow could no longer produce enough red blood cells. Other organs were forced to take over its production. That's why the spleen is also enlarged. In other, non-medical terms, this cat didn't stand a chance."

I quickly processed the remaining organs and went to work severing the head at the top of the spine, removing the crown of the skull and taking out the brain. It showed no abnormalities.

I began the final stage of the necropsy. I picked up the femur, the large leg bone, and scooped out some marrow. I continued explaining what I was doing and Jackie kept on typing. I smeared a tad of the marrow on a slide and took it over to the microscope.

"Ah," I said with satisfaction.

"You're not going to say 'Eureka,' are you?" Jackie warned. "I might have to kick you in your tibia."

I had to laugh. If we didn't, the job would be just too depressing. "No, I'm satisfied just saying I was right – as always," I said, sure I was wearing my smug look.

I stripped off my gloves and went to the refrigerator and pulled out the second cat. We went through the same process and came up with the same results: malnutrition and severe chronic anemia. Or as I thought about each flea bite: death by a thousand pricks.

EIGHTEEN

I THREW MY SURGICAL GOWN into the washing machine and emptied the hamper next to it of all the towels, surgical wraps and additional gowns that had accrued over the last couple of weeks. I started to reach for the laundry detergent and pulled my hand back like it got snakebit.

"I can't do it now," I said dramatically, dragging the back of my hand across my brow. "I'll worry about it tomorrow. I want to go home and have a drink. I'll never be thirsty again."

"Well Scarlett, I'm afraid you'll have to wait because right now we have to meet Carol," she said looking at the clock on the wall over the sink. "We barely have time to clean ourselves up and get back to Hurlock. God, I hope this goes fast. I need to call home and tell them I'll be late."

She was right. It was nearly four. Then I looked at Ella, who was starting to squat. I gently but firmly picked her up and took her outside. The puppies scampered after us. Jackie grabbed my glasses, threw them in my handbag and grabbed her own stuff.

While she locked the lab door, I maneuvered Ella onto the grass. As soon as we stopped, she and the puppies peed. Jackie and I filled their heads with "Good dogs!" We were from the school of positive reinforcement.

Jackie gathered up the puppies and I put Ella in the back seat next to them. We sped back to the house, dumped the dogs, and headed towards Hurlock and Carol. We somehow managed to arrive at the appointed time, probably because I was driving.

Carol Hayden was slipping the key in the lock of the front door when we pulled into the driveway of the house for sale. She turned around instantly and secured a welcoming smile on her face. It did little to soften her sharp, hardened features; neither did her helmet-headed, dyed-blonde hair. Her nose was broad and bumped like a log, and her lips were pressed together and painted so dark they reminded me of a thin chocolate mint. She didn't even try to disguise the hungry look of a realtor whose business had bottomed out with the market.

Carol left the door ajar and walked to the edge of the porch as we were coming up the steps. What we could see of the grounds was quite lovely. It was thick with rhododendrons that had shed their blooms, but still retained their shiny, dark green leaves. Red-berried hollies followed the side of the house to the backyard, where we could see the tops of old sycamores and red oaks. I noticed some fruit trees peeking around the back corner, but I was mostly interested in the line of large white pines that dripped their limbs over the fence.

We introduced ourselves with handshakes. Jackie took the lead and explained her supposed situation.

"I'm looking for a place in this area," she said, nailing the accent perfectly – somewhere north of Mississippi and east of Tennessee. "I've been living in Baltimore, but my parents have a house in town. My father is recovering from a stroke and doing real good. But I need to be closer to them, just not too close. I think I'd rather buy than rent, but I'm not sure."

She gave a rueful smile and Carol, implying understanding, nodded with such intensity her hair almost moved.

"Well, this is a nice area, safe and getting better all the time," she responded, her eyes darting to the large fence as if she couldn't control them and back to Jackie. "I'm not sure exactly what you're looking for, but we'll narrow it down as we go. I've picked out three other houses. Two need fixing up; they're foreclosures and very inexpensive. The other is key ready."

"I don't want to fix up a place," Jackie said, glancing my way for agreement. We already knew this house was in good shape. Also, we just wanted to see enough properties to make our story believable. "I might end up just renting, but it's such a buyer's market I could be persuaded."

"Well, as I said on the phone, this house is in perfect condition," Carol said, swinging the door open, "but see for yourself."

I slapped an interested look on my face as we wandered through the living room. When they headed for a bedroom, I broke loose and went roaming. I quietly went out the back door. The yard was huge and ended at a chainlink fence. Yet as deep as the property was, the seven-foot high stockade fencing went back even farther.

I walked around the yard like any good looky-loo, but was only interested in the fence. I noticed there were scores of knotholes, but they had been filled in, probably with wood putty. Then I saw sunlight glinting through a hole and peeked through. Brown's yard was empty except for a large red oak tree. No grass, no flowers, no nature. Just a lot of dirt.

I quickly returned to the house. God bless Jackie. She was in the guest bedroom asking about closet space. No one could play a role better. It's what made her such a good investigator. I went into the large master bedroom and texted her: "I'm thinking the pine trees."

She replied: "I'll get the cameras."

I walked into the bedroom and rejoined the two of them. Jackie was putting her phone back in her handbag and telling Carol that she had to check her car and see if her husband had left his glasses in it.

"I'll be right back," she said, and winked one dark eye in my direction as she slipped past me.

We stood silently, since I wasn't very good at chitchat. Carol seemed fine with that, maybe because I wasn't the perspective client. Jackie was back in a couple of minutes, her large handbag slung over her shoulder, her hands thrust deep in her jacket pockets.

"Brrr," she said, pulling up the collar on her jacket. "I couldn't find the glasses. It's getting pretty dark out there. I'm going to look around the backyard while I still can. Carol, Allison is more of a cook than I am, so would you show her the kitchen? I'll be right back."

Jackie was on her way out before Carol could say a word. I did my job and asked if the appliances were new, and feigned interest in every aspect of them.

Jackie returned to the house and let out a "Wow, it's gorgeous back there. Are those apple trees?" Carol nodded. "Well, I guess I don't have to worry about the neighbors in the brick house stealing any of them. Lord, that's a big fence," she elongated each syllable so it seemed like it took her an hour to say the shortest sentence. She had definitely redis-covered her Southern roots.

Carol's eyes dulled and she looked down as if she were afraid she'd give away something. I wasn't sure what she knew, but I sensed her dis-comfort. Jackie looked at me. I could tell from the deepening lines across her forehead she was feeling the same thing, and weighing the worth of pushing it. She didn't have to.

"The couple who lived here before had a little dog," Carol said with a sigh, patting her unmoving hair unconsciously in a gesture that bespoke her frustration. She did not want to say anything, but we were in a state that required full disclosure of any problems that came with the house. "The people next door have a few large dogs. They started digging un-der the fence and the little dog went through the hole and got into their yard. They killed the little dog. The next day this fence started going up. The gentleman who owns the house and the dogs sent someone to apologize and pay for the dog and their distress."

"Was Animal Control contacted?" I wondered out loud.

"Not that I know of," said Carol. "I think everyone just wanted to let the incident go. I believe the owners were paid enough to forget. Also,

Mr. Brown has done everything to prevent any more problems from occurring."

"When did it happen?" Jackie asked, her brow now knitted like a cabled sweater.

"About six months ago."

"Is that why the house is on the market?" Jackie questioned.

"Gosh, no," Carol responded quickly. "Mr. Brown has proven to be a good neighbor. They were fixing it up to sell before the dog incident."

"How long has Mr. Brown and his dogs lived there?" I asked.

"Years," Carol said, her voice clearly wanting to put a period on this conversation. "Not that anyone else has complained about him. Or his dogs."

"What breed of dogs does he own?" Jackie asked curiously.

And so ended Carol's brief moment of easy breathing. She nearly gagged on the words: "pit bulls."

NINETEEN

———⊶⊷———

IT WAS DARK WHEN JACKIE and I left Carol in the driveway. We had looked at one more property to lend an air of reality to Jackie's story, and then begged off any more house hunting due to the late hour. Carol perked up, her eyes brightened and her spine straightened imperceptibly, when Jackie said she'd like to look at the first house again in a day or two.

Once again I felt a pang of sorrow for the realtor who was unwittingly working so hard without any possible reward. C'est la guerre. Jackie and I pulled out of the driveway and drove around the block, returning to Main Street in time to see Carol's taillights. We parked a couple of houses down from Brown's place.

I figured what we were about to do was, at worst, semi-legal. We had the warrant that permitted us to survey Jefferson Brown's property, but we didn't want to warn him that we were aware of his existence. So I planned to spy on him from his neighbor's yard which we had just legally entered. The fact that we were sneaking back into it in the darkness of night could be perceived as a grey area. I could live with that. We would re-enter it legally to meet with the realtor and collect what would hopefully be evidence against Brown. and tiptoed our way into the backyard we had just left.

Jackie pulled the tiny camouflage cameras from her handbag and dropped them into my outstretched hands. That was because the tomboy in me was elected to shimmy up the pine trees closest to Brown's fence and stash them in the sweeping branches. We anticipated that the trees would offer views of both the side and back yard.

"I slipped the two receivers under the bottom step," Jackie said. "They can pick up a signal from the cameras up to 250 feet away."

"How do they work?" I questioned, while I tucked my pants cuffs into the tops of my boots so they wouldn't snag during my climb. I stuffed the dark green duct tape into one pocket and the two teeny cameras in the other while I listened to Jackie's explanation.

"They're heat and motion activated, so as soon as someone or something steps into the yard, they begin recording. Another cool feature is that we can remove and replace the receivers' memory disks so we can view them instantly on our laptops."

"Here's hoping I can strategically place them to get a good view of the yard," I said as we tiptoed down the driveway. Well, here I go!"

I stopped at the first tree I suspected would provide a broad view of the side yard. I wrapped my arms and legs around it and shimmied up it, so I could tape the camera on top of the first limb that did, indeed, look into Brown's property. I quickly and silently dropped to the ground and then climbed the pine tree nearest to the back of the chainlink fence. I placed the second camera so it looked into the back yard. Again, I noiselessly landed and joined Jackie so we could make our getaway.

Suddenly, we heard a muffled dog bark next door. Then the sound of a door opening. Soon we could hear a dog running up and down the length of the fence, growling and barking. The porch lights went on.

"What's going on?" a deep voice boomed. "Someone out there?"

"Jazz, shut the fuck up and get in the house," a different, more threatening, male voice ordered. The dog immediately stopped barking. The person continued, "Stanton, stop asking stupid questions to the night air and get the fuck out there. See what's going on."

Jackie and I hurried away as fast as we could and still be silent in our departure. We made it to the street and our car in several convulsing heartbeats. We jumped into the front, I flipped off the overhead lights, and we slid down in our seats. We would have been noticed if we pulled away from the curb at that point. So we held tight. Soon we saw the bright beam of a flashlight coming from Brown's driveway. It zigzagged up and down the street, flickering through our car windows.

I peered over the wheel and saw the unmistakable shape of Duncan Stanton turn towards Brown's house and walk back up the driveway. The behemoth, with his huge mop of dreadlocks, blocked out the porch-lights like a lunar eclipse. We waited in case he came back. He didn't.

But a woman, cradling what appeared to be a blue nose pit bull puppy, left the house and walked down the well lit driveway. I couldn't make out her features, but noted that she was tall and thin. She was wearing a baseball hat with its brim nearly covering her face and a large shawl wrapped around her body. She walked over to the Mustang and placed the puppy on the passenger seat. Then she entered the driver's side. The car lights had remained on long enough so that we could see her talking to the puppy. This was a pet; not a fighter. Serious dog fighters shunned blue nose pits, considering them to be mutations. She stopped petting the dog, started her engine and drove away.

Jackie and I waited a few more minutes before we took off without turning on the headlights. I kept the speed down so I could take the corner without using the brakes so its lights didn't reveal our movement. You never know if someone is smarter than you give him credit for being. I gave anyone who was not only twice my size, but also violent and drugged-out, the intelligence of a Mensa member. In this particular case, I put Duncan's IQ in the neighborhood of Steve Jobs.

Once I flipped on the headlights and pulled onto Route 392, heading away from Hurlock, I allowed myself a smile – it crinkled its way across my face. We had escaped our prey, targeted them and we had a plan in place. The gathering clouds that were rolling in from the west and the increasing winds that bowed the trees lining the road did nothing to negate my rare, sunny feelings. Until I felt my concern, which was hiding below the surface, bubble up. I worried about the fate of the dogs we had left in Jefferson Brown's clutches.

"How soon do you think we can go back and pick up the spy stuff? Do you think tomorrow is too soon," I asked Jackie. My mood clouded at the mere thought of waiting.

"How about the day after, in the afternoon? We'll get the disks out of the receiver and put in new ones. Hopefully it will be enough time for those pricks to do something illegal. And not too awful."

"Yeah, I'm sure they're the masters of moderation," I griped. "Let's at least make it early afternoon. Lunchtime? I know how you hate to ask your boss for time off."

Jackie managed a grin to make me feel better, I'm sure, and nodded. Leaving animals in jeopardy was one of the more difficult aspects of the job.

"I wish I could just kick in their door, break their faces and take their dogs home. It sucks that the law limits our options. Damn it."

"You can think about it tomorrow," Jackie said, cutting me off. "Right now, I want a drink."

I managed to shave a few minutes off our travel time in search of that elusive cocktail. I felt my stomach begin to relax as soon as we entered the house.

But before I could belly up to the bar, I sighed and dragged myself to the sunroom. I cleaned up the mess the dogs had made and fed the puppies. I took Ella with me and fed her in the kitchen where she could eat in peace.

"God, I'm beat," I moaned. I sat down on the couch, unlaced my boots, kicked them off and left them where they fell. I took a couple of minutes before I pushed myself up and went to the kitchen, fed the cats and moved over to the bar. Ella found Jackie on the couch and curled up next to her.

"Wine?" I called to Jackie.

"Oh, yes!" she said without hesitation.

"Red or white?"

"I don't care as long as I get a whole bottle," she said.

My phone rang as I pulled a bottle of Barbaresco off the wine rack. John's name came across the screen.

"I'm home and safe and I love you," poured out of me. "And your information was really helpful. Thank you. Are you coming home soon?"

"Wow, I should get pissed off more often!" he joked. "I was calling to say I'm almost home and I didn't want to feel like it's a 'wait 'til your father gets home' moment. Be there in a few. Bye."

Jackie took in my side of the conversation. "All is forgiven?"

I smiled my answer and opened the bottle. Jackie had roused herself and pulled two glasses off the bar, and took them with the wine to the coffee table.

"Does 60 seconds count as enough breathing time?" Jackie asked.

"I'm thinking that may be overdoing it today," I answered glumly.

TWENTY

———✣———

JACKIE'S EYES WERE WIDE AND fixed on the platter of cheeses, crackers and an assortment of olives I had placed on the coffee table. I walked out of the kitchen and her head rotated on her neck like an owl to see what I was now carrying. She actually ran her tongue over her lower lip when she saw the hummus and a sourdough baguette.

"That's the beauty of not having children," Jackie said with a sigh. "You have food, instead. Every time I go to get something to eat, someone's already eaten it. I've tried hiding stuff, only to learn I was just making a game out of it. And I always lost."

I smiled as I flipped on the outside lights. The living room was a sweeping, simply furnished space that made the outside world the focal point. Two long, plush, deep grey sofas faced each other with a glass and chrome coffee table in between. A large Italian designed, marble-based lamp with an extended thin metal arch that held a circular lighting fixture, moved gracefully when the glass pocket doors were slid open and a breeze swept through the living room.

Tonight warranted a fire, so I lit one and finally threw myself on the couch opposite Jackie. Groaning with delight, I sank into the deep pillows. I sipped some wine and thought about sitting upright to get some food. Too much trouble. Drinking was much easier. Jackie, either hungrier or more industrious or both, sat up, filled two plates and passed one to me. I put it on my stomach and managed to move hand to mouth.

Jackie was looking at me. "What?" I asked.

"You really have a nice life," she said, looking both anxious and pensive. "I always thought marriage and kids were a necessity. I'm sure that's because of the way I wasn't raised. But sometimes I feel trapped. Not very often, but...."

I looked at her sharply. She startled me with her comment. I took a deep breath, not sure what to say. I aspired to be Jackie. We had both come from loveless homes, yet she had been able to commit to a marriage and motherhood. I felt there had to be something lacking in me that made me so terrified of marriage, even to John. I loved being with him but feared one day, as my father did to my mother, he would walk out the door. I didn't want to be left resentful and raising a child by myself. I knew I had worked out a lot of my childhood fears of abandonment, but I had believed Jackie had surpassed me in the emotional stability department.

"Oh, no!" I groaned, staring at her. "I wanted to be you when I reached maturity. You and Thomas are such a perfect fit. And Michael's the coolest kid in the whole world. I'm thinking how nice it would be to settle down and know you're with the person you want to be with forever. I see you as having found it. Don't tell me you're having a seven-year itch thing?"

"No. No. I love Thomas," Jackie said leaning forward and looking directly at me. I could see the uncertainty and pain in her eyes. "I don't want to be with anyone else. If anything, I want to be alone. I'm scared I'm turning into my mother. But not really. It's just every so often I feel trapped," Jackie said. She leaned back with a sigh.

"In a way you are," I said, surprised by her confession yet felt compelled to offer her advice, though this was certainly not my area of expertise. "You have a kid, and you are tied down. But he'll be off to school or his own life in a dozen years. And you just said you love Thomas.

"Hey, Jackie, we both know too well it's never perfect," I added. "But you know my feelings about life: any day that's better than bad is really good. You have it good."

"I guess you're right," she said though her voice was uncertain. Then she nodded. "Yeah. Maybe I'll just take a long weekend."

"Perfect," I said and smiled with relief. "Now that's an easy fix."

Then I heard the only sound that could easily lift me from my languor other than someone shouting "Fire!" It was the garage door sliding open. I jumped up and arrived in the kitchen just as John and Duke came through the door.

John walked over to me and I hugged him. His hand cupped the back of my head, his fingers threading their way through my hair. I hated any acrimony crossing the threshold of our home. I'd had enough of that as a kid. And he knew it.

"Hey, Jackie," John called out, throwing his arm over my shoulder and propelling us towards the living room. He gave Jackie's shoulder a squeeze. Then he petted Ella.

"Pull up a bottle and join us," Jackie said, swinging herself into a seated position. "Wow, I thought we had a long day. You look like crap."

He did. His uniform was smeared with dirt and sweat marks. He had obviously taken his boots off in the garage and was standing in his socks, which were the cleanest part of him. His eyes were exhausted.

"Jesus, Duke and I tracked some autistic kid this afternoon through the woods for miles. And miles. It felt like we chased him all the way to Florida. His parents said he got away from them once before, but that time he ran down the road so they were able to follow him in their car."

"God, how awful – for everyone" I said. "How old was he?"

"Fourteen and long-legged," John said, with a weary shake of his head. "He was unconscious by the time Duke found him. Scared the shit out of me. I just didn't want him to be dead. Seems he just ran until his body gave out. Once I had a location on him, they sent some ATVs into the woods to get him back and then transferred him to an ambulance. I called the hospital on my way home and he was conscious, at least."

"You want a drink?" I asked.

"Yeah, but first I want to take a shower. Do me a favor, Babe, and feed Duke."

"Sure. Prepare yourself. I'm going to let the puppies out of the sunroom while you're gone."

"Thanks for the heads up."

He returned barefoot and clean, wearing a white T-shirt and jeans, but his tired look remained. He stopped off at the bar and took a rocks glass and the bottle of Pappy Van Winkle Family Reserve Rye, a gift from me.

"Have I told you how much I love you?" he asked, his slow smile reaching me on the couch.

"Every time you pour a drink from that bottle, sweetheart."

He collapsed next to me and threw his leg over mine. He raised his glass to Jackie and me and took a long drink.

"From the look of you two, I'd venture you had a long day yourselves. Why'd you call in those particular license plates? Do I need a few more drinks before you answer?" He reached for the knife and sliced several pieces of bread. He popped an olive in his mouth and passed a hummus-laden slice of bread to Jackie and then me before taking some for himself.

I told him about our day in Hurlock. As soon as I got to climbing the tree and placing the camera in it, his body tensed. He finished his drink in one gulp.

"Honey, I appreciate your concern. I truly do," I said gently, not wanting another confrontation. "But this is what we have to do sometimes. I have to leave the safety of the lab. Every day that you and Duke walk out the door, I have to talk myself down. The anxiety would be overwhelming if I didn't. Compared to you, I'm hardly ever in danger. Besides, I have Jackie to protect me."

John's moan was audible: he did an Eddie Cantor eye roll. We all tried a laugh that didn't quite make it.

"Look," I lifted my right hand and swore, "If we find out anything, I'll let you know. And we won't put ourselves in any unnecessary jeopardy. I'll call a cop."

"You're so funny," John said, his grey eyes still flinty, but I could tell he was somewhat assuaged. He continued absent-mindedly running his hand over Ella's head, who had left my side as soon as she realized John was a human food dispenser. She licked his hand, which he immediately wiped on my leg. I, in turn, punched him in the arm. We had gotten beyond the moment of his discontent.

"You know, I can go home and watch the same bad behavior in my own child," Jackie said, doing her share to lighten the mood. "I'm out of here."

TWENTY-ONE

———— ⚬⚬⚬ ————

IT WAS FINALLY WEDNESDAY MORNING, and Ella and I were walking near the house when Jackie emerged from another basic four-door rental. She looked our way and gave a delighted laugh.

"You look so pretty!" she gushed.

She wasn't talking to me. Rightfully, Ella was the recipient of her compliment. The pooch was stylishly turned out in a red-plaid Polytech coat with a thick mock sheepskin lining. We had done some serious doggie shopping yesterday. She also was sporting a new green leash and collar. A series of tags, including ID, rabies, license and microchip, jingled on her neck.

It was a cold, sunny morning, and Ella and I had been watching the vultures hitchhiking on the thermal currents that sent them soaring through the skies. They hunted for the dead while we sauntered along the water's edge. Suddenly, more than a dozen of them dropped out of the sky and landed on the bare limbs of a maple tree 20 feet from our house. One by one, they opened their wings and, facing the sun, allowed it to warm their bodies after the cold night. But then again, they didn't have a new red coat.

"Has she checked out the river yet?"

I had to laugh. "She was like an old lady in Miami Beach, dipping her tootsies in the water and squealing with distress. She ran back to the safety of terra firma and glared at the water. John's reaction? 'Not a retriever bone in that body.' Thank God, he hates hunting, so he wasn't disappointed.

"Well, Jackie, as enjoyable as the buzzard revue has been, it's time to go to the land of pit bull hell," I said. "Let me put Ella in with the pups. It was too cold to let them out. You want a to-go coffee?"

"Sure, I need all the fortification I can get before Hurlock."

We went through the kitchen door and were assailed with the smells of butter, yeast, almond and more butter. I was traveling in my kitchen again. This time, I went to France and made almond croissants. I put a few in a paper bag and grabbed a bunch of napkins. The croissants were already leaking butter.

"God, you are the best partner I could ever have," Jackie said. "Too bad our time together will be so short, since I'm going to die of a heart attack soon."

"You're right, but what can I say?" I said, tapping the fingers of my free hand nervously on the counter. "You know waiting makes me crazy. It drives me into the kitchen where I was born to bake. Grab a coffee and let's hit it."

Jackie and I headed to our 10 o'clock appointment with Carol Hayden. On the drive, we sorted out our plan. Once we arrived, Jackie opened her iPad and showed me where the memory disks were located on the receiver so I could pull them out and replace them. She would keep the realtor busy inside the house.

Carol opened the front door upon our arrival wearing a see-through blouse that immediately called to mind Lenny Bruce's line, "...and you don't want to." I kept my eyes locked on hers, never letting them dip below her shoulders.

Jackie asked to see the master bedroom first, since it was the farthest from the kitchen and the back door. I headed out without a backward glance or word. I went down the steps, bent over and felt for the receivers. I pulled them towards me, exchanged the old disks with new ones, and returned the receivers to their spot under the stairs. Two minutes later, I joined Jackie and Carol heading towards the living room. Jackie was quietly peering and poking around.

"I'm going to think about it for a couple of days," she said to Carol.

Her face flashed disappointment as she felt her fish wriggling off the hook, but she took a resolute approach. She told Jackie she understood that it was a big decision. Once in the car, Jackie told me she'd call her tomorrow and tell her she was going to move in with her parents.

I slipped one of the disks into my computer and began watching to see if we captured any images on the cameras. We had. The time stamp was dated yesterday afternoon at 3:12.

I watched the first few minutes and my stomach knotted so badly it felt like it had contracted to the size of a pebble. I could feel the blood draining from my face. My jaw locked and I knew it was bulging into what John called my Dick Tracy face. Jackie placed her hand on mine, which was shaking with anger and adrenalin.

"That bad, huh?" she asked, knowing that I wouldn't be so upset if it weren't. "Turn it off for now. Wait until we get to your house and we'll watch it together."

Jackie pressed down harder on the gas pedal and we sped back to Trappe. I went straight to the bar and grabbed my bottle of Pappy Van Winkle bourbon. I poured a few fingers of Bourbon and downed it in a couple of gulps.

"Jesus," was all Jackie said, and drank a matching shot out of self-defense, I suspected.

"Let me take Ella outside first," I said, surprised my voice was so calm. Even alcohol doesn't take effect that quickly. I was blocking. "Would you feed the puppies?"

Soon we were back in the kitchen, where I fed Ella. I let all the dogs stay with us. They were a comfort, even with Ella's scorched body. I attached the disk to my computer. Our television would have been way too large for such a horror show. We put the computer on the coffee table and sat next to each other on the couch. I hit the start button.

Antonio was instantly recognizable because of the deep scar that ran up the side of his face. He was holding back a tan-and-white, heavily scarred pit bull by its heavy harness. Jorge, his tattoos so dense he almost looked like he was in black face, dragged a small, starved, young pit bull into the fighting pit in the backyard, not too far from the house. The older dog, bristling and stiffening, locked its eyes on the terrified dog.

Jorge appeared to yell, "Ready?" Antonio nodded and walked away from his dog, which curled up and tried to flatten itself and disappear into the ground; in dog-fighting parlance it's known as "pancaking." Jorge let the pit go and it attacked the trembling "bait" or "cold" dog, which didn't have a fighting bone in its body. After it let out one plaintive howl, the muscled pit bull ripped it apart. It took less than 15 seconds. Jorge walked off-camera with the survivor while Antonio dragged the shredded remains of the dead dog out of sight towards the woods in back. The inactivity stopped the camera.

"That's as far as I got," I said. It was Jackie's turn. She grabbed my arm. This time I put my hand on top of hers, comforting her. I took a deep breath, waiting for the inevitable. The camera started up again. I looked at the automatic timer and saw it was just seven minutes later.

Jorge had the same tan-and-white pit bull, which now had a muzzle coated in drool and blood. He was roughly petting the dog on the head and giving him hearty body slaps, which from the dog's wagging tail seemed to be interpreted as affection.

Duncan Stanton now appeared with Antonio, the other Rivera twin, and a dark brown pit bull. The two dogs eyeballed each other, ominously silent. The men held them by their collars, keeping them separated by about 10 feet. They let the dogs lunge at each other, but pulled them apart before they could touch, ratcheting up their aggression each time.

Finally, frustrated and angry, they were allowed to fight, with Antonio and Jorge standing ready to separate them. I knew this process was known as "rolls" or "bumps." Despite the cute name for these encounters, the dogs were expected to try to kill each other. The brothers separated them again and again before they could finalize that act.

Then the Riveras looked at each other and nodded, a gleam of anticipation flickering across their otherwise dead eyes. They released the dogs. They flew at each other and collided. They rolled around, struggling for domination, teeth digging deep, jaws snapping. Suddenly, the brown dog began squirting blood from his neck. His carotid artery had been punctured, but the dog ignored the wound, continuing to fight for position, though he grew visibly weaker with every blood-spurting heartbeat.

Jefferson Brown appeared on camera and stopped the fight, having the Riveras pull the victorious dog off its victim. The twins looked pissed that the entertainment ended so suddenly.

"Oh God," Jackie gasped.

I didn't say anything. I was too busy beating myself up for not doing something sooner, somehow saving those dogs.

I watched Brown turn towards the dark brown pit. He barely resembled his old mug shot. He was wearing a perfectly tailored long, black leather jacket with the collar turned up against the cold. Brown had traded in his shaved head for a stylish "fade," and removed the grill and the gold chains. Now he had a neck; his shoulders no longer sprung from his ears. He looked very slick until the camera captured his eyes. They remained fierce and hard and a touch crazy.

Brown approached the dying dog, which was now shaking with tremors, going into shock. But when he saw Brown, he actually whined and used his last bit of energy to wag his tail. He tried to get up to go to his obvious owner. Brown looked down at his dog. I thought for a second he was going to help it.

Instead he pulled out a .45 Glock from his coat pocket and blew his dog's brains out. Then he turned and walked out of the range of the camera. Stanton grabbed the dog by the legs and dragged him towards the woods. The camera clicked off. The end. Thank God.

Jackie and I were pretty hardened to the results of animal abuse or we would never be able to do our jobs. I was luckier than she, if "luck" was the proper word. I usually dealt with animals when they no longer felt any pain. I was a scientist. I had trained myself over the years not to concentrate on the animal's life, but only on its death. I knew from having necropsied numerous pit bulls that this type of violence is often inflicted on them. But watching it, as opposed to knowing it, served as a stark reminder of how brutal these people were and how horribly these dogs were victimized.

"I need a cop," I muttered, dazed. "A cop with a gun and a dog."

TWENTY-TWO

───∞∞∞───

"SENIOR TROOPER THIBERT," HE SAID, answering his cell phone.

Damn it, I thought, hearing John's working voice. Obviously, he was busy. I could be equally professional, so I didn't beg him to come home.

"Hey, call me back," I said simply, watching a small tremor move my hand like it was palsied. I carefully clutched my glass and drained it of the last remaining inch of bourbon.

"You okay?" he asked.

"Sure, I was just wondering when you're coming home," I said keeping my voice even and sane. "I was thinking about making reservations for dinner."

"Sounds good," he replied. "We're having procedural meetings this afternoon, so it should be an early day. I'll call when I'm on the way home."

"Thanks. Love you," I said and disconnected.

I looked at Jackie. She mirrored my depression.

"You're the investigator. How do you want to handle this?" I asked her, sitting on the couch. I pushed the bottle away and leaned back. I was finished drinking. It was time to figure out our next step.

"I want to get a warrant to raid that place. Yesterday. Morning. Before all this happened. Short of that…." Jackie's voice trailed off.

"John will be home in a few hours. I want to show him the video, if you're okay with that. We're going to need some police power as we go forward."

"You're right."

"This is the perfect job for him," I added. "Only bad guys."

"Didn't he shoot someone through both kneecaps last year?" Jackie interrupted. "I've been meaning to ask you that forever. Am I remembering that correctly?"

"Yes," I said.

"You know I love John, but he can be a bit of a prick," Jackie said.

"A bit of a prick?" I said amazed at her power of understatement. I corrected her, "John can be a dick. And, yes, he did shoot someone through his knees. John was cruising a neighborhood at night and saw a man climbing through the window of a home. He arrived in time to see the perp standing beside the daughter's bed. The guy's gun and flashlight were resting on the night table and his hand was over the little girl's mouth. He had pulled down the bed covers, her pajama pants and was trying to open his fly."

"Jesus," Jackie said, her eyes wide, her hands fidgeting. "How the hell did I miss this story?"

"You were on vacation and then had to go to California or somewhere to testify on some puppy mill case that you worked with someone else. I guess by the time you returned the story had died down."

"Okay, go on," she ordered, more interested in hearing the story now rather than why she hadn't heard it before.

"Well, John crouched in the window, pulled his gun and aimed it downward and away from the girl. The perp was standing sideways to him, his hand still over the child's mouth. John didn't want to give him a chance to grab his gun off the night stand lest there be a shoot out in the girl's bedroom. So he yelled 'Police,' and shot him. The bullet went through both knees. According to John, he dropped like an anchor."

"Was that the perp who tried to bring John up on charges because he hadn't warned him before he shot?" Jackie recalled correctly. I nodded yes. "Okay, well now I have the whole story. I can't believe it took me this long to get it."

"Yep. John was suspended during the investigation. Once it was completed, the case against him was dropped and he was reinstated. The perp went to jail after he was released from the hospital. But John's supervisor, First Sergeant Stewart Parker, took a lot of heat, and was pretty pissed at John, as usual."

I was ready to leave memory lane and changed the subject. "I'm going to give the pups a once-over just to make sure they're as healthy as they look."

I checked their vital signs, looked in their ears and at their eyes. I pretty much figured their big tummies told the rest of story. I went through the same routine with Ella. Same result.

Unlike the well-fed dogs, my empty stomach rumbled and I realized Jackie and I hadn't eaten since croissants and coffee. But first, Ella needed to go out.

We went out through the sunroom's French doors. Fall was turning into winter. The leaves underfoot were crunchy reminders of warmer months. The wind coming off the water, roiling its surface as it traveled was a prelude to winter's imminent arrival. I looked at the clouds piling up in the distance, rolling and twisting towards us, possibly carrying a snowstorm to the shore.

We lasted only five minutes. I could feel my cheeks flushing and nose tingling with the cold, and knew Ella needed to get into the warmth of the house. We all ended up in front of the fridge. I reached for a container of yogurt and sliced up some fruit and sprinkled granola on top.

"I can't believe I'm hungry. I thought I'd never eat again after watching that video," Jackie said.

Her phone buzzed. She looked at it and said, "Hi, hon." She listened intently, the color in her face bleached by obvious bad news. She said curtly, "Is he okay? Are you sure? You wouldn't lie to me? Okay, I'm on my way. I'll meet you at the hospital."

"That was Thomas," she said, her voice cracking, her body flying through the house grabbing her things. "Michael was hit by a car while he was riding his bike. The woman who hit him called 911. It happened just down the street, so a couple of his friends raced to the house and got Thomas who had just come home. An ambulance is taking them to the emergency room. The EMTs stopped the bleeding and Michael's conscious, thank God. Thomas is sure the gash in his head will need stitches."

"I'll drive you," I said immediately.

"No, I'm fine. Well, not fine, but okay to drive. It'll give me something to do. Thomas swears he's all right. Well, except for needing stitches."

"Are you sure? I don't mind. In fact, I hate your being alone."

"I'll call you as soon as I get to the hospital. Really. I'd rather drive myself. It will give me something to concentrate on besides Michael."

"Okay, but promise me, if you need me you'll let me know."

"Of course."

I walked Jackie to her car and hugged her. "Drive safely." And she was gone. Life changes just that quickly.

It's one of the reasons I loved yoga. You live fully in the moment with no memories of the past or worries about the future. I grabbed my mat and as I unrolled it, I thought about one of my best friends. She used to say, "It's never the things you worry about that bite you on the ass." Then she bumped her head and drowned in a swimming pool accident. The ultimate irony was she had just become a five-year breast cancer survivor. I allowed myself to be sad: for the dogs, for Michael and for my dear friends.

Then I put my dour thoughts behind me, snatched an hour to practice yoga, and then went to the bathroom. I looked in the mirror and splashed water on my tired eyes. Sadness had softened some of the harshness that I often saw in my reflection. I brushed my hair and worked it into a French braid. A little eyeliner, a little lipstick. It actually made me feel a little better.

"Hey, where are you?" John called from downstairs. I hadn't heard him arrive.

"I'm on my way down," I yelled back, and headed towards him. We met up in the kitchen. I updated him on Michael's accident.

After he had all the details, John started to go upstairs when the phone rang. He stopped and came back to where I was standing.

It was Jackie. "How's Michael?"

"They want to keep him overnight for observation," she said, a quaver in her voice. I knew she was fighting tears. "He has a deep gash and a concussion, but the doctor assured us he'll be fine. Oh, Allison, it's so scary." And then she let go and cried.

I soothed her as best I could. "You stay home and take care of Michael," I said. "Everything will be fine on this end. Are you sure you don't want us to come to the hospital?"

"No. We're just going to stay with Michael. We'll be fine."

"Call me if you change your mind," I insisted. "Let me know how he's doing. My love to the three of you."

"Love you, too," she said.

"Do you think we should go to the hospital?" John asked once I had hung up.

"God, I love you," I said, somewhat of a non sequitur. "But there's nothing we can do tonight."

"Well, at least Michael seems to be okay, right?"

"Yes, but it's all downhill from here," I warned John.

TWENTY-THREE

—◈◈◈—

"MOTHERFUCKER!" THAT WAS THE SOUND of John exploding. He had my computer on his lap, leaning back on the couch, feet resting on the coffee table as he watched the horrors of Hurlock, as I would always think of it. He bolted upright. I figured his feet hit the floor at the precise moment the bullet killed the dark brown pit bull.

John's outburst startled the dogs and the cats, but I was expecting it. I could pretty much tell what part of the disk he was watching by looking at his face. I had no desire to see it again. I would never forget a moment of it. But John went through it again from the top. This time he took notes; his face emotionless.

Then he walked over to the bar and poured us drinks. He sat down next to me and handed me one. We both took a gulp.

"I want to kill that prick," John said.

"I know you do, honey. And the really scary part is so do I."

"Let me make sure I understand the timeline," he said, calming down. I could see the cop in him taking charge. "You traced Benji, the black American Pit Bull Terrier, that I found on the highway, back to this prick. Jackie got a warrant and you put up spy cams. Don't tell me again how you did it, because I swear I feel a heart attack coming on. You waited a couple of days and returned to Hurlock and pulled the cameras and receivers?"

"No, not exactly," I said softly, not wanting to cause his heart to stop beating. "I just pulled the discs. I didn't want to take a chance on being spotted, so I left the cameras in the tree. And the receivers under the back steps with new disks. They're probably still recording. Very long battery life."

"Okay, I can live with that." John relaxed a bit. "As long as you and Jackie aren't planning on going back, are you?"

I shook my head, and said, "I'm pretty sure we have enough evidence to raid Brown's place, but there should be more on the new disks if we need it. Jackie and I were going to talk to you about organizing a raid before she had to go to the hospital."

John sat quietly for a moment and thought.

"Babe, we can bust this hump right now, but the most we could get him on is animal abuse." He hesitated. "But we could also collect more evidence, bring down his entire operation and go after dozens of other dog fighters, too."

"You want to wait so you could raid a bigger fight?" I shrieked and looked at him like he had lost his mind. How could he ask this of me?

"Think about it for a second," John cautioned and put his palms up in a calming gesture. "We could get all of them. For dog fighting, drugs and guns, which seem to always go together. I know it entails doing what you hate the most: waiting."

He made sense, but so did rescuing Brown's dogs today. In fact, it made more sense than it did a week ago or even yesterday. But John seemed to have no doubt as to the path he wanted to travel. I didn't want to follow him down that road.

"As much as I hate to leave Brown with those dogs, I know you're right," I finally said. "But we can't wait too long, okay?"

"Not with these rap sheets," John agreed, opening the file on my computer and reading it. He handed it back to me when he finished.

"The police have had eyes on Brown since he was a kid and he hasn't been picked up for 20 years. That's pretty amazing," he said, scrolling through Brown's record now using his iPad. "There's a list of almost busts. Whenever there was a raid, he was miraculously never there. Or any of his crew. It has to be more than luck. The Baltimore County Police Department would get so close and then their cases would fall apart."

"So he moves here? Why? Maybe because this is the land that loves dog fighting." I answered my own question. "He can conquer new territories and still be close enough to Baltimore, Washington and Philadelphia to keep his old customers. And he can maintain a low profile. The most noticeable thing about Jefferson Brown is his high fence."

John looked puzzled. "But the only thing that brought him to our attention is the dead pit bull. Why would someone shoot it? And then why would they leave it where it could be found? Because of all the stink the Baltimore bicyclists made, the dog landed in the local papers."

"At least it brought some attention to the plight of pit bulls," I said, trying to be positive. "But Brown could have escaped notice for years, maybe even forever." I was standing up, pacing. "This doesn't make sense. We're missing something."

"A whole lot of something," John agreed, and looked at his watch. "I'll call Lieutenant Andrews right now and see if we can meet with him tomorrow. You available?"

"Yes. Any time he wants. But what about Parker? Isn't he going to be furious?"

"He's out sick. It's the best thing that's happened at the station in years – at least until he retires or dies. That would be even better."

Parker was John's nemesis and, unfortunately, his immediate superior. John often called him the missing link in the chain of command. Lieutenant Bill Andrews was John's go-to guy. And he went to him right now.

John picked up his phone and was talking to Andrews in a few seconds, asking if he could meet with us tomorrow. He must have asked why because John simply said "Jefferson Brown."

"Yes, I'll tell her." He put down his phone.

"Tell me what?"

"He said it will be nice to see you. It's been too long. But I'm afraid it's going to be a bit longer. He has to go out of town for a couple of days."

"Shit," I said and landed on the couch across from John. "But am I right in assuming Brown is already on Andrews's radar?"

"Yeah, as soon as I told him about the dead pit bull and you tracing it back to Jefferson Brown, Andrews pulled his file. And, like us, he's wondering what he's doing in Hurlock."

Unable to sit still, I jumped up and walked over to the light panel where I flipped on the outside floods. The sun had set more than an hour ago and I looked out just in time to see the last of the day's light being sucked over the horizon. I felt a hunger pang, still surprised that I had any appetite.

"You want to go out for dinner?" I asked.

"Absolutely," he said enthusiastically and added, "How 'bout a little down time first?"

I knew exactly what he wanted and followed him up the stairs. He closed the door behind us, a sure sign "down time" was just a euphemism. Duke wasn't allowed to watch us have sex because John worried that if we were too active or noisy, Duke might think his beloved master was being attacked. As the potential victim, I thought the closed-door policy was an excellent precaution.

"I love it when you make love to forget," John said, once we finished, his voice still husky with sex.

"That's not it," I said softly, feeling layers of release. "I'm not forgetting anything. I'm just concentrating on how good you make me feel – especially when I'm at such a low ebb."

A half-hour later, we were out the door and on our way to get some Italian food at Scossa in Easton. We were quickly seated at a table in the understated dining room with its impressive long mahogany bar and matching stools and the white-linen topped tables. The server arrived before we settled into our chairs. As soon as we ordered a bottle of

Barolo, I asked him for some of their crusty bread and olive oil. He sent it over with a busboy while he went for the wine.

I dove in. Our server reappeared with a bottle and showed off its label to both of us before he opened it. I appreciated his effort; I hate being treated like an oenophile idiot. I took an unladylike gulp of wine as soon as the server filled my glass.

"A belch would be the perfect touch," John said, staring at me with an amused look.

"You know, I'm hungry, thirsty, and we haven't even touched upon cranky yet. So don't push it, Buster." He patted my hand as I used it to soak more bread in the oil.

Ten minutes later, the server reappeared. We ordered and once we were alone, returned to our unfinished conversation.

"You have a plan," I surmised, running my other hand over his and giving him a crooked smile that almost always made him grin back. He did.

"Actually I have two. Or one plan with Part A and Part B. I have a creepy, horrible snitch that I want to send into pit bull hell. Hopefully, he will be able to find the next Big Fight. If he does, I will send in my favorite undercover cop, Cletus Garrison, providing Andrews agrees. As soon as he's in place and lets us know the fight is underway, we will bust the shit out of the bad guys."

"My God, you are the man with the plan, aren't you? I'm impressed."

"Babe, I'm good at a lot of things."

———&&&———

TWENTY-FOUR

I WAS PUTTERING AROUND THE house, staving off the depression looming on the horizon. I wasn't comfortable leaving Brown's dogs in his possession, and now we had to wait for Andrews's return. I was feeling increasingly anxious.

The phone rang. It was Helen. I tried to remember if she ever called with good news. The answer was no. It wasn't the nature of our relationship. We spoke during emergencies and disasters.

"Animal Control just dropped off a dead pit bull," she said, her voice flat as if trying to mask her distress. "It was killed in a fight."

"And you're calling me because...?"

"I want you to necropsy it and give the results to John," Helen explained, obviously prepared for my question. "For once, I'd like to see the assholes responsible for its death brought to justice."

"I'll be there within the hour," I said, glad to have something to do besides bemoan the fate of Brown's dogs.

I left Ella home and jogged over to the lab to pick up the Mobile Unit. I drove it to the back of the shelter where Helen met me. I was relieved to find that the dog weighed around 40 pounds, and lifted it from the shelter's refrigerator to my portable one. She handed me copies of the Animal Control reports but I didn't look at them right away. I knew Helen wanted me gone, so I signed for the dog and left. Involving me was definitely not normal protocol. But we were all feeling a little bit desperate.

Once I returned to my lab and placed the pit bull in the refrigerator, I took the paperwork to my desk and began going through it. Someone had actually called in the dog fight. Animal Control followed up and found the dead dog in the back yard of an abandoned building. Instead of it being the usual dead end, this time the tipster supplied several license numbers of cars parked in the vicinity. I couldn't remember that ever happening before. I called Jackie to tell her the good news, thinking she could probably use some right around now.

"Damn," she said. "If you want to wait a couple of days to do the necropsy, I can help you. Thomas can stay home with Michael for a few hours – he's not in court this week."

"Don't give it a thought," I ordered and felt bad I called her. "Michael needs his mom. I only called you to give you the news that someone had actually done something about a dog fight in Cambridge. I'll probably get to the necropsy later today or tomorrow. In the meantime, I think I'll check on some of those license plates."

"Allison, are you crazy?" Jackie said sternly, "Don't! Wait for me. You know it's too dangerous to go after these pricks by yourself. Shit, John doesn't like it when it's the two of us. This is not a good idea. Okay?"

"Sure, I'll wait for you," I said effortlessly.

"That was way too easy. Allison, please don't put yourself in harm's way. I'm begging you."

"Alright, alright, I'll wait for you," I said. But we both knew I was lying.

Next I phoned John. My call went to voice mail. So I texted him the license plate numbers and asked him to find out who they belonged to. I decided he didn't need any additional information such as the dead pit bull parked in my refrigerator. John sent me a list of addresses. Then he called.

"What's going on?" he asked, his voice curious. "What's all this about?"

I told him about Helen's call and the pit bull I had picked up from the shelter. Then I added, "I thought I'd take a look around. This is the first lead we've had into pit bull fighting in Cambridge."

"I'm sorry. I must not be getting this. Why isn't Animal Control following up?" his voice becoming more insistent and annoyed. "Or the police?"

"Oh, they are," I said innocently.

"And, of course, Jackie's at home?" he snapped and couldn't resist adding, "Where she should be!"

"She won't be back for a day or two. Just like Andrews," I shot back, and felt my frustration increasing to the point that I stood up and grabbed my coffee cup. I took it to the sink and slammed it down so hard it shattered. God, I felt like such a jerk. I cleaned up the pieces and forced myself to sit down and relax. John wasn't going to make it easy for me. He wasn't finished.

"So your answer is to put yourself in jeopardy? When did you become invincible?" he asked rhetorically and followed it up with, "Stop pouting and wait for help."

"Okay," I said right before I disconnected.

In response to the warnings I just received, I turned on Google Maps and entered the four addresses. I listed them in order of proximity. Then I threw on my parka, which covered my holster and gun.

Once in Cambridge, I swapped out my car at the Enterprise counter and headed for the closest address. It was an apartment complex where no dog training or fighting would occur, so I headed to the next one.

This address took me out of town a couple of miles towards Church Creek. I arrived at a ramshackle farmhouse with peeling paint, cars on cinderblocks and scrawny chickens pecking their way around. I ignored the NO TRESPASSING signs posted on every other tree, walked up to the front door and knocked. No answer. I called out. No response. I beat on the back door and didn't rouse anyone. I peered through the filthy kitchen window and saw two kenneled pit bulls. I could make out some fresh wounds and old scars on them.

I found a dog fighter. I started to walk back to the car, planning to call John and then Animal Control. I was feeling pretty good. But just as I turned the corner, I heard a shotgun being racked. I stopped dead in my tracks. I turned slowly towards the noise.

I was staring into the barrel. The shotgun was held by some withered, weathered piece of trash who was now standing in front of his open doorway. He was wearing oil-coated jeans and an equally dirty jean jacket over a ragged T-shirt. He was rapier thin, maybe because he was grinding his teeth so hard his jaws couldn't open. Since decades had passed since he was a teenager, I strongly suspected an addiction to meth caused his raging acne.

He looked at my hands and motioned the shotgun up and down in the international language of "Put 'em up!" I did.

"What the fuck you doing here?" he croaked and wheezed, another victim of too many cigarettes and COPD.

"I was hoping you could help me," I said, all innocence and interest. "I didn't mean to startle you. I did knock on the door and call out. I'm asking everyone around here if they've seen my dog.

She got loose this morning and I've been driving around. I live a few miles from here. Someone said they saw her heading this way. She's a small, tan pit bull with…"

"I don't give a shit," he interrupted taking a couple of steps in my direction. "What the fuck are you really doing here?"

I was asking myself the same question. I felt like the Revenuer who surprised the moonshiner. I needed to extricate myself quickly.

"I get it. You don't want to be bothered. I'll just get going," I said, and turned slowly towards my car, allowing my arms to drop down as I began walking away.

"Not so fast," he ordered. I looked at him over my shoulder in time to see him snap his fingers. A good-sized Rottweiler appeared from inside the house and stood by his side. Its eyes were fixed on me and he seemed to bristle with unspent energy.

I turned sideways so the man couldn't see me draw my gun. I held it against my right leg.

"No need for your dog," I said. "I'm leaving."

"No you're not. Why'd you really come here? I saw you peeking in the kitchen window. Too bad. Now you know too much.

"Git her!" he ordered his dog, right before he turned and walked towards his neighbor's backyard. The dog didn't notice. His eyes were locked on me.

He came at me at a full run. I dropped down on my left hand and braced myself as I bent my right leg at the knee and drew it into my chest. I calculated the ever-closing space between the dog and myself. When he was close enough that I could see the drool dripping from his opened mouth, I repositioned my right foot a bit and kicked the dog in the throat with all my might. It fell back with a grunt and shook his head.

It didn't take long for him to regain his desire to destroy me. He came at me again and this time I kicked and landed only a glancing blow. He threw it off, lowered his head and sank his teeth into my hip. My layers of clothing offered no protection. The searing pain knocked me back and to the ground. I cried out. The dog struggled to get a deeper grip. I tried kicking him with my other leg and beating his head with my gun butt. He didn't notice. The dog wouldn't release his hold and tried to dig in deeper.

That was when I shot him in the head. Only in death did he release me.

TWENTY-FIVE

THE DEAD DOG LANDED ON top of me, pinning me to the ground. I began to panic under its weight. I didn't want to touch the lifeless body. I was having trouble accepting the reality of its death. So I concentrated on my breathing. My basic instincts returned and I began to feel fear. I worried the dog's owner had heard the shot and could be on his way back.

I rolled out from under the dog, and shivered as it slid over my body. I grabbed my phone and used it to take photos of it and the surroundings. I ignored my torn clothing and flesh and the burning pain that radiated across my hip and down the outside of my leg. It forced me to limp when I wanted to run to the safety of my car so I could call John. I backed out of the driveway and parked a few houses over.

"I really messed up," I said simply when John answered. "I need help. I shot and killed a dog."

"Jesus Christ. Are you okay? Where are you?" his voice loud with concern and amazement.

I told him yes and gave him the address and asked him to send local police and Animal Control. I listened while he called Dorchester dispatch.

"They're five minutes out. I'll be there in under 15. Talk to me," he said struggling, I imagined, not to give into the anger he must be feeling.

I told John about my reception at the Church Creek house. He didn't say anything until I told him I was attacked, bitten and forced to shoot the dog.

"Just stay put until the police arrive unless you need to go to the Emergency Room," he said. "Allison, do you?"

"No. It hurts like hell but I don't think the puncture wounds are too deep. Maybe I overreacted and didn't need to shoot him." I started sniffling. "Oh God, John, I killed a dog."

"Allison, is there any sign of the guy? You're not still at his house, are you?"

"No, I parked down the street where I can still see the dog. I'm hoping the cops arrive before the prick returns. He's got fighters caged in his kitchen."

"Okay, it'll be fine," he said, his voice going from flat to soothing. "Animal Control is coming with them. The Sheriff's department will take the dogs to his facility."

The squad cars soon arrived in stealth mode, not sure what they would find. I stepped out of my car once they landed in the driveway and officers piled out of their cars. I recognized several of them. An officer, whom I didn't know, separated himself from the pack, walked over to where I was standing and began questioning me. I had just finished telling him I didn't need medical treatment when John parked his car and got out.

His eyes never left mine as he walked towards me. John was an easy read: his forehead was creased, his eyes brooding, his lips set and his body vibrating. I wasn't sure which way this was going to go. All I knew was I felt bad enough already.

The officer broke off once John arrived and introduced himself. John apologized for interrupting and told him to continue. Then he listened to me explain the "incident" again. He was glaring by the time I reached the shooting the dog part. It was horrible. I just wanted to get away.

I watched the crated dogs being removed and overheard one of the officers give John the name of the absentee owner. An APB was put out for him and several squad cars began cruising the neighborhood, while other officers began going door to door. I was allowed to leave the scene of my crime.

"Let's go sit in your car," John suggested, his voice neutral. I looked at him carefully. I could tell he was upset and concerned, but I couldn't judge how furious he was. We were slowly making our way to my car when I saw Michelle Manning's car pull in behind my own. She and Dwight jumped out and hurried towards us.

"We were at the shelter when the call came in from Animal Control that you had just killed a dog," Michelle yelled in her loudest and most accusatory way. "I called the Sheriff to find out what happened. He told me his Animal Control agent had brought a dead pit bull to the shelter to be necropsied and Helen gave you the dog. She had no right. This time she's going to be fired. You have cost her her job.

"I want the dead dog back!" she continued screaming and pushed her way into my space once again. "In case you haven't noticed or cared, we have our own vet to perform these procedures. Especially now that you're compromised."

"You really shot and killed a Rottweiler? You, the great protector," a smirking Dwight interjected, and started to chortle until he saw John's face.

"I will have Animal Control return the dog to your facility," I said, unable to hide my dejection. I blinked rapidly and was able to suppress the tears that were ready to slide down my cheeks. I needed to get the hell out of there. I put my hand in the door handle and tugged it but it didn't budge. That was because Michelle was pressing her heft against it making escape impossible. I turned towards her ignoring the pain in my hip and used all my self-control to stop myself from shoving her to the ground. I stood there, my insides shaking, and jammed my hands in my pockets so no one could see them trembling. The worst part was I knew I deserved her disapproval. She had a lot more vitriol to send my way and I stood silently and took it – for a while.

"That's all you have to say? You just killed a dog that probably could have been saved if you hadn't felt the need to grandstand. There are other people around here who care about animals. If anyone else did this, you'd be all over them," Michelle continued. "I will be contacting the HSPAC to request you be relieved of your duties. And I plan to take legal action against you as unfit to keep our three pit bulls."

John put his hand on my arm knowing what was coming, but I twisted away and walked straight into Michelle. I had agreed with everything she said until she threatened to take Ella and the puppies. She backed up a step. I moved forward. I put my mouth against her ear so no one else would hear my words.

"You don't care about any animals let alone pit bulls," I hissed. "You try to take Ella and the puppies, and I will ruin you. You have almost bankrupted the shelter. Gossip is that your own house is about to be foreclosed, no matter how much work you throw at your idiot husband. I can force an audit of the shelter's books, so don't fuck with me. And get off my car!"

I was so upset I grabbed the car's door handle again and pulled it with such ferocity it flew open and almost knocked me off my feet. I ignored the pain that shot through my hip and slid behind the wheel of my car before slamming the door and locking it. John got into the passenger side. Michelle gave up and stormed away.

"Can we talk later?" I asked, trying to avoid looking at John. "I have to return the car and pick up my own. I just want to go home."

"I have to go back to work, anyway," John said. I snuck a glance and saw him press his lips together. I had been fooling myself – he was too angry for words. "Let me see the bite first."

He unfolded his pocketknife and told me to put my leg across his lap. I did. He carefully cut away the material exposing my hip. It was bruised and the teeth marks were deep, but the flesh hadn't been torn, just punctured. It should heal quickly as long as I didn't let it abscess.

"I'll clean it up when I get home," I promised.

"Do you want me to come home early?"

"No."

"Okay," he said with a shrug.

"Hey, John," I said softly, "thanks."

"Yeah," was his only response.

"Oh no!" I wailed and pointed towards the TV news vans that were arriving. Michelle was racing to meet the first reporter who exited a vehicle. She pointed in my direction.

"Time for you to get out of here," John said. He jumped out of the car without a goodbye. I pulled away before the door had even closed.

I made it halfway home before I had to pull over. I turned off the engine. Tears were pouring out of my eyes and dripping off my chin within seconds. I wrapped my arms around the steering wheel, dropped my head and sobbed.

I couldn't stop seeing the dog's eyes glaze over in death and knew it really was all my fault. I was too willful and stubborn to listen to John's and Jackie's warnings. For the first time in my adult life, I felt like a failure. I cried even harder. Eventually, I pulled myself together and finished driving home.

John arrived a few hours later, took one look at my swollen eyes and said softly, "I hope you figured out you can't do this anymore."

I nodded yes and was speechless for once. I laid low the next day and nursed my physical and emotional wounds. I was grateful to Jackie for not lecturing me, either. She did, however, mention that Michelle had reported the incident to the HSPAC, and one of its lawyers had already contacted her. She pleaded ignorance of the situation, but did tell the attorney about Michelle Manning's insensitivity to animals and antipathy towards me. By the time she finished, Jackie said, the lawyer seemed quite sympathetic to my plight.

No matter what happened with my job, I had learned a valuable lesson. I now knew hubris was, indeed, a deadly sin.

TWENTY-SIX

⌘

BY THE TIME LIEUTENANT ANDREWS was back at work, my stoic resolve had returned; good humor would take longer. I had had my fifteen minutes of infamy, thanks to the Mannings' attempt to crucify me in the media. In one day, I was portrayed as a rabid, out of control veterinarian who ended up killing a dog because I went rogue instead of following legal procedures. I had to admit there was some truth in this portrait.

The attorney Jackie had spoken with contacted me. She interviewed me over the phone for a couple of hours. At the end of the call, she was kind enough to tell me she wasn't going to recommend that I be suspended or fired. But she did warn me that a letter of reprimand would be placed in my permanent file. All I felt was relief – I could get back to work.

I was now able to look forward to the meeting John had arranged with Lieutenant Andrews. I pulled up in front of the red brick, sprawling barracks in Easton that was home to the Maryland State Police. There were two small plots of grass on both sides of the walkway leading to the glass front doors and a bunch of flowerless azalea shrubs pressed against the building like suspects hugging a wall. I walked into the station house a few minutes before our appointed time and, as always, thought what a depressing place to work. No wonder John never wanted to be there.

He looked up when I walked in, as if feeling my presence before he saw it. His desk was wedged against the corner of the back wall in the large bustling center of law enforcement. John had worked long and hard for this space so he could be as far away as possible from the constantly ringing phones, snarling perps and ongoing conversations of his fellow officers. I walked past the monochromatic area filled with grey metal desks, chairs, computers and filing cabinets. Today, even the sky was a matching dull, leaden color.

John's smile cut through the gloom. That's why I wore my Chanel-red colored wool parka. Every eyeball in the place followed my progress to his desk. I usually tried to blend in, but today my wardrobe choice had been deliberate: I wanted to brighten John's day and my mood. It seemed to work on several others, too.

I sat down in the intentionally uncomfortable chair next to his desk. It ensured no one willingly hung around for long. For suspects, who were forced to sit there, it helped reinforce the fact that their butts were on the line. Subtle, but efficient.

Andrews was ready for us. We walked into his office, not much more inviting than the outer area. He, at least, had two chairs in front of his desk and a few folded up and leaning against a wall.

"Get a goddamn haircut," Andrews growled at John, his voice gravelly from years of cigarettes and whiskey. This, I knew, was his usual greeting to John, who simply ran his fingers through his locks and shook his head like a young stallion. I assumed that was his typical response. Time had perfected their routine.

The Lieutenant immediately turned an affectionate smile my way, which tilted the ends of his thick white mustache upwards. His snow-white hair was buzz cut so close to his scalp that it took on a pinkish tinge. Just a tad under 6 feet tall, with a straight spine and squared shoulders, Andrews was consumptively thin but that was not to be confused with weakness. His body burned thousands of calories a day with the ferocity of a hummingbird. His ropey muscles had the strength of ironwood. His hands were huge and looked like mallets when he rolled his fingers into fists, yet no one could remember him using them. He wasn't a fighter; he was too smart.

"Well, aren't you a spot of sunshine on a mournful day?" he said, somewhat courtly and Southern. We had worked on several cases together over the years and it had always been a good experience. Andrews maintained an interest in John and still occasionally pestered him about becoming a homicide detective.

John walked over to the farthest chair and lowered himself into it. He stretched his long legs, sliding his feet under the desk. "Check this out," he said when we were all seated. He had transferred the disk onto a flash drive, which he handed to Andrews. The Lieutenant plugged it into his computer.

John kept his eyes on Andrews's face as he watched the screen, just as I had done to John when I first showed him the clandestine video. Like John, Andrews clenched his jaws, and his neck muscles also twisted and bulged by the time he came to the end. His ruddy color had deepened several shades. Then John slid the rap sheets on Stanton, the Rivera twins and Diaz across his desk. He had already introduced Andrews to Jefferson Brown.

"You've been doing a lot of work that you don't get paid for," Andrews commented, tugging the ends of his mustache, first the right side then the left. He drummed his fingers on his desk. I couldn't tell if it was impatience or an unconscious habit.

"I'd like to be more involved in this case," John said simply. Andrews looked at him as if gauging his seriousness. "I know as a K-9 officer I'm not supposed to be, but I thought maybe…."

"You mean you're finally sorry you turned down all the opportunities I've offered you to advance your career?" Andrews interrupted, looking annoyed as he stared at John. "About time you got serious. You're too smart not to challenge yourself. Never mind that for now. We can revisit this conversation."

"Yes, sir," John replied quickly, and held Andrews's gaze. "This case, more than any other, has made me realize I want to be more involved. I'm a good investigator."

"Hallelujah!" Andrews said. "Why the hell do you think I've been pushing you? Because you'll make a goddamn good detective. Jesus, John. You fight me all the way."

"I know," John with a bit of a hangdog look, but shook it off with a grin. "So what can you do for me now?"

Andrews started to look pissed off, but couldn't hold back the smile that broke out across his face. He let loose a short bark of a laugh and said, "I will swear you in as a Detective Sergeant for this case. Don't screw it up."

John refused to look at me. He knew I'd be smirking. I had said my piece a few times over our years together, questioning why he didn't want to be an investigator. I knew how good John would be at the job and never understood his lack of drive.

"What do you need from me?" Andrews added, slapping the paperwork hard on his desk. His glance included me in the question.

"Would you call Cletus Garrison's boss and see if he can free him up? He's the best UC I've ever worked with," John added.

"Sure, that'll be Captain Alan Steinman out of Baltimore County P. D. I'll give him a call. Garrison's a good choice," Andrews added. "What are you planning on doing? And when do you want Garrison?"

"Pretty soon. But first I want to put my snitch on the case. I want to find out when and where the next fight is being held. My plan is for Garrison to go with him. Of course, we'll bust it, but I'm not going to tell my stitch. We can cut him loose after we pick him up. Okay?"

Andrews nodded in the affirmative.

"I'm going to need some money to pay him." John said, his foot tapping energetically under Andrews's desk.

"How much?"

"Five hundred for him to buy his way in and five to pay him."

Andrews pulled out a pad of vouchers and I could see him fill out the top one for $1,000. "Hope this is money well spent." He handed the voucher to John, picked up the rap sheets and began thumbing through them again.

"Thanks, boss," John said, appreciation in his voice.

"Now get back to work."

I loved it when I didn't have to say a word and things got done. Andrews walked around his desk and put his hand on my shoulder and gave a firm squeeze.

"And you are not going to go off on your own like some avenging angel again, are you?" he said.

"No, sir."

"Good. I hate being on the 6 o'clock news."

"Me, too," I said, right before goodbye.

John and I returned to his desk. He picked up his cell phone, thumbed through his contact list and called his snitch. He put him on speaker so I could hear.

"Hey, what's up?" John said with an unusual lilt in his voice. "Where are you?"

"Why?" Lincoln said suspiciously, clearly waiting for John's response. There was none.

"I'm in Easton," Lincoln finally said.

"Perfect! Meet me outside of Walmart in an hour. I'll drive past you and wait at the back of the building. You follow. There'll be a woman with me. Neither of us is in uniform."

"I'm with my auntie," Lincoln whined. "She's awful sick and can't be left alone."

"Hey Lincoln, I don't give a shit if she's having a heart attack and you're giving her CPR. Get your ass in gear and don't keep me waiting. Just think how lucky you are you're not in prison in case she takes a turn for the worse. You'll be able to make it to her funeral."

John disconnected and turned to me. "That stupid prick has no auntie. Doesn't he know by now I do my homework? You mind driving?"

"Not at all," I answered, "but I need to switch my plates with another pair. You know I never wear them to a crime scene or a criminal."

"Sure," John said. "I'll grab a couple of confiscated plates. And cash the voucher."

After returning, he handed me the plates and a screwdriver. Then John went to his car to retrieve his undercover outfit – jeans, of course, and a well-worn Eddie Bauer jacket, and went back to the station house to change. Meanwhile, I switched the plates and let

Duke out of the squad car for a quick walk. He nearly swooned when I grabbed his ball from the back seat. I threw it. He was on top of it in one high bounce.

After a half-dozen receptions, John reappeared in civvies. He opened the back door of my car and whistled. Duke jumped into the backseat carrying the ball with practiced nonchalance. John jumped into the passenger side and we headed towards Walmart. I looked at the clock and realized we had time for a quick lunch, brunch, whatever the menu offered. We opted for breakfast and chose pancakes at the ubiquitous IHOP.

Once there, I couldn't stop talking about John's potential promotion. I mentioned what a great homicide detective he'd be – he had the smarts and the instincts. John, the master of understatement, managed to reduce the benefits of such a promotion to discarding his uniform, which figuratively chafed him whenever he put it on. I shut up.

We made it to the corporate welfare state of Walmart at the appointed time. There wasn't a mom-and-pop store in the entire paved-over, cinderblock strip mall. So much for the charm of small- town America.

On the drive over, John told me about Duane Lincoln. Two years ago, he let Lincoln walk on a small-time drug bust, which was easy for John to do since he hated arresting low-level addicts. The problem for Lincoln was that the arrest would place him within the three-strikes-and-out zone. So he made Lincoln an offer that was quickly accepted: John would use him as a snitch until he felt he had paid his debt to society, or until someone else busted him.

"That's him," John said as we drove up on this banty rooster. "Yuck" was my uncensored response when we drove past a nervous-looking guy whose eyeballs jerked back and forth in their sockets. I wasn't sure if he was looking for us or someone from his past that he had pissed off. Lincoln saw John when we drove past him and slow-walked around the corner. I came to a stop. Lincoln slipped his hand around the door handle, ready to pull it open. Duke, as if on cue, snarled.

"No fuckin' way," Lincoln mumbled. "I'm not getting in there. Just shoot me now."

"God," I stage-whispered to John, "the decisions you have to make."

TWENTY-SEVEN

—⊗⊗⊗—

JOHN HID HIS SMILE AND relegated Duke to the way back of my car, freeing up the back seat for Lincoln. He scrambled into the middle and sank down, but I could still see him in the rearview mirror.

Lincoln had bought into the bald-headed, diamond-studded look made popular by sports figures, rap stars and ex-cons. No mistaking which group spawned him. My eyes dropped to his chest and took in his T-shirt with the word SNITCH circled and X'd out, and wanted to punch him right in center of the "nit." So much for my appreciation of irony.

Lincoln was a tiny, over-pumped, jailhouse kind of guy with a rubbery face that seemed to be missing the necessary tendons to hold muscle to bone. He literally had a detached look. His doughy smile and shuttered eyes did little to cover his truly malevolent nature that John held so dear. A better person wouldn't be such an effective snitch. All I knew is he creeped me out.

John took hold of the rearview mirror and angled it so he could see Lincoln. I didn't care, since I was pulling out of the almost empty parking lot, and took a right on Industrial Park Road, which rarely had any traffic.

"Look at me," he ordered Lincoln. I could still glimpse the snitch in the tilted mirror and watched John strain to make eye contact with him. But Lincoln's shifty eyes made it impossible. John finally gave up and continued, "What do you know about dog fighting around here?"

"Nothing. Not a thing," Lincoln said, his jumpy eyes landing on John's right shoulder. He uncrossed his arms and began cracking his knuckles, one annoying popping sound after another. I thought he looked so nervous he might have been hosting the dog fights himself. I'm sure John didn't believe a word passing through his mushy lips.

"You need to find the next big fight, probably around Hurlock," John said. "That is, if you want to get paid. I'm not interested in two guys getting their rocks off in the backyard with their dogs and a couple of 20-ouncers. I want the one with lots of dogs, lots of people and big money."

"I'm not sure what you're talking about," Lincoln whined in his weaselly way.

"Listen, Lincoln," John said softly. "I'm sure with all the people you know, you can find this information. You're resourceful. You're smart. I'm not asking you to do anything dangerous. In fact, this is a cushy job for you. You get to drink, do drugs and bet on dogs. And you do it on my money. Now, how bad is that?"

"How much you paying?" Lincoln asked, his fear fading fast. It was pretty obvious Lincoln's avarice would overwhelm his caution, the main reason he had spent so much time in jail and now was a snitch.

"You get $500 now to work with and $500 to keep when I get the info I want. Now take the flashing around money," he said, handing it to him. "And remember to make it last through the fights or you won't get your final payment."

John didn't say anything about Brown. We were both afraid Lincoln might sell our information to him. But if Lincoln brought us Brown's name, then he would be the one taking the risk. Besides that, no defense attorney could say we influenced the CI and set up Brown. The only thing John trusted about Lincoln was his ability to worm his way into the fight scene. He was the typical audience that got off watching dogs kill each other.

"Once you find out where the next big fight is being held, I want you to look around, bet on the dogs and drink. Lincoln, I want you to have a good time," John said, his voice holding enough menace that when he turned around to look at Lincoln, his snitch was forced to return his stare. "I just want you to tell me when and where it's being held. Don't fuck this up, Lincoln."

He looked at John and asked suspiciously. "What else you want? You ain't asking me to wear a wire? You think I'm crazy?"

"No, of course not," John said, shaking his head. "Hey man, this is the 21st Century. We've received a whole mess of surveillance equipment from the Feds."

He stuck his hand in his pocket and pulled out a tiny white box. He opened it and took out a black onyx-looking earring. It wasn't a real stone, of course, and it did have a major flaw – a pinhole camera in its center. As long as Lincoln wasn't in direct light and pushing his earlobe into someone's face, it wouldn't be noticed.

"Lincoln, take this, it's a camera," John explained as he dropped it into his extended hand. Lincoln looked it over. "Start wearing it now so people will get used to it."

"So nice to see federal dollars being spent in our small community," I interrupted, "and used for something other than the never-ending War on Drugs."

John shushed me with a look, but smirked a bit. Like many officers, he thought the War on Drugs was an intentional losing battle, wasting resources and time, especially his own. I agreed. We both believed it would never end as long as prison profiteers, drug cartels and private contractors, who I still called mercenaries, were making billions.

"Do you guys have any idea how dangerous this is?" Lincoln sniveled. "You ain't paying me enough to do shit like this."

John's grey eyes, which I could see in the rearview mirror, hardened to the color of gunmetal and he pressed his lips together as if to silence himself. I gripped the wheel tighter. John, ignoring Lincoln, reached into his pocket again, this time pulling out a pack of cigarettes. I noticed Lincoln's eyes finally stop shifting as he reached out for them.

"Not so fast," John said, palming the flip-top box like a catcher covering a baseball. "These are not for your pleasure. They are part of your job."

He half-turned in his seat, shifting towards me. I watched him from the corner of my eye open the box of cigarettes and take them out one at a time and put them in his lap. Then he turned the box over and a thin rectangular receiver fell into his hand. I glanced at it before he handed it to Lincoln, who barely looked. He was too fixated on the cigarettes.

"Hey, pay attention!" John ordered, holding up the 1-inch by 2- inch receiver. "This is an audio/video   recorder."

"That's amazing!" I was obviously a lot more impressed than Lincoln. "How does it work?"

"It has a mini hard drive and a battery, and can be plugged into a computer, phone, TV or whatever. The receiver fits into the bottom of the box. The cigarettes are a quarter-inch shorter than regular ones, so the pack looks completely normal."

"What happens when I run out of smokes?" Lincoln asked.

"Here," John said, digging into his pocket once again and coming up with another pack of cigarettes, which he threw into Lincoln's lap. "These are replacement cigarettes. Like the ones already in the box that are covering the receiver, these are a quarter-inch shorter than regular cigarettes. You turn the receiver on right before you get to the fight, put it back in the box and put the cigarettes on top of it. It's set up to record both audio and the visual your earring will provide. Only smoke these at the fight. Got it?"

"I ain't an idiot," Lincoln grumped.

John chose not to argue the point. Instead he asked Lincoln if he had a computer.

"Hey man, remember, it's the 21st Century," Lincoln snapped back. I almost laughed. I could tell John didn't find him the least bit amusing.

"Great. Then you can download anything you get and email it to me immediately. I'll write down my email address. Memorize it and throw it away. It would be a drag if someone found it and killed you, especially since you have my money and equipment. Okay?"

"Like I just said," Lincoln snarled. "I'm not an idiot."

I have never been happy to be at Walmart, but this time was different. I pulled into the back of its parking lot and hit the brakes hard enough to slam Lincoln into the back of John's seat. I guess he was an idiot – he wasn't wearing his seatbelt.

TWENTY-EIGHT

THE SNOW BEGAN FALLING AND dusted the windshield like powdered sugar as I drove John and Duke back to work. I loved winter, especially if I could watch it from the inside out, which I planned on doing once I made it home.

Soon we were pulling into the parking lot at the barracks. The minimalist grass in front of the building was coated in white and poked through like stubble on a man's jaw.

"John, I was thinking about calling the Everetts to see if they are ready to pick up Frick and Frack," I said, and immediately felt a pang of loss. It left me once I pictured the Everetts cuddling the puppies. "You have any thoughts?"

"No, you're the doctor."

"Okay. I'll give them a call while you're changing the license plates on my car," I said, pursing my mouth in a helpless way.

"Cut the crap," he grinned. "Remember, I know you and Jackie have put chains on the Mobile Unit during a blizzard. But I'll be happy to do it for you."

John wasn't nearly as happy as the Everetts once they heard my news. Mrs. Everett started listing the items they had already purchased in anticipation of the pups' arrival. I cut her off.

"I'll be leaving the Highway Patrol barracks in a few minutes," I said, "and the weather is getting bad. The snowflakes are morphing into cotton balls. Can you leave now and meet me at my house? The roads should be okay for another hour or so. Or we can wait until after the storm passes."

"Oh no, we'll start now and see you at your house. Bye," she said and hung up so quickly I think she was afraid I'd change my mind. I knew the puppies were going exactly where they belonged.

John, opening the back door to let Duke out, startled me. He walked over to my window, which I lowered so he could stick his head in. I was surprised by the drop in temperature in just a half- hour. He obviously felt it, too.

"Damn," he groused, his voice filled with annoyance. "I'll be on the road all day and, God forbid, night – one wreck after the other. I listened to the weather this morning and it was a 'quick moving front and maybe one inch of snow.' Now it's looking like 8 to 10 inches.

"No point in talking about the weather though," he continued, look-ing exasperated, "when I can be bitching about all the idiots out there speeding around in their all-wheel drives – until they crash. Light snow, my ass. I would have called in sick had I known."

"Yeah, right," I snorted. I couldn't remember the last time he had taken a sick day. I hated the fact that John was a cop because of the in-herent danger, but he was a good one. I had learned to worry about him silently. I did, however, give him a deep goodbye kiss.

"Hey, I'm not going off to war," he said. "I'll call you until you're sick of my voice. You better get going. The roads are getting slick and I hate it when I have to worry about you."

By the time I turned onto our road, the snowflakes were so dense they looked like a moving white wall heading towards me, forcing the wipers to work with metronomic ferocity. The Everetts were pulling into the driveway just ahead of me. I opened the garage door, went around them and motioned for them to follow. I pulled in as far as possible and they obviously got the message, because they parked on my bumper.

The wind was picking up and the sky continued to darken. There was nothing to do but hurry. I petted Ella quickly and said hello to the Everetts over my shoulder. We raced into the sunroom and I kissed Frick and Frack goodbye and let Ella give them a lick. Then I closed her in the sunroom.

I handed the puppies to the Everetts and we sprinted to their car and the crate they had placed in the back of their station wagon. I surprised myself and kissed both Everetts goodbye and was hugged back.

"Call me," I implored. "Let me know as soon as you get home, please. We'll go over things once you're settled in. Okay?"

I watched them back the car's nose out of the garage. Despite knowing they were going to a wonderful home, I felt my eyes misting up. I figured Ella would be missing them even more, so I lowered the garage door and went into the house through the kitchen.

I opened the sunroom door and gave Ella a big hug. She whined, looking for her puppies. Fortunately, she was easy to distract, if only momentarily. She tap-danced while I put her coat on. My phone rang.

"Are you home?" John asked. Actually, I was already outside with Ella, but he wouldn't care about that unless I was chauffeuring her around. Ella looked like she would have preferred that option, having tried to avoid putting her paws in the snow. She gave up and peed instead. Then she pooped.

"Yes," I said to John as Ella and I ran into the warm house. "The Everetts left with Frick and Frack a few minutes ago. I'm waiting to hear they made it home safely. How are you?"

"Following a snowplow. This is the good life. At least for now. I'll...." John's voice was drowned out by the squawk of the dispatcher. "Damn, got to go. Love you."

The line went dead. I had already taken off Ella's coat and was toweling her dry in the kitchen. I gave her a cookie and she took it back to the sunroom. Then she brought it back and dropped it at my feet. Ah, I thought, the heartbreak of motherhood. I put the kettle on the stove, filled a tea ball with Genmaiche and dropped it in the empty teapot.

I decided to call Jackie while I waited to hear from the Everetts. I hadn't spoken to her for a few hours. She answered on the first ring.

"It's me," I said. "How's Michael?"

He had been discharged that morning, she told me, and they were already home. Jackie wanted to stay with him for a day or two. No problem, I said, but I'd miss her. Then I caught her up on our meetings with Andrews and Lincoln.

"Well, things are moving along," Jackie said with a sigh. "You and John did good. I can do some research when Michael is sleeping or watching TV. That way, I can keep from fixating on him. God, Allison, this was so frightening."

I could hear the exhaustion in her voice, suggested she take a nap and promised to call her tomorrow. I sent Michael a kiss before I hung up.

The phone rang almost immediately. It was the Everetts; they had made it home.

Now I just had John to worry about. I pulled a quilt out of the linen closet, and Ella and I moved to the couch where we snuggled. The wind's unearthly yowl had turned into a nerve-wracking moan. It traveled through the trees and blew off some limbs. The snow, pelting the house's glass frontage, had intensified in the past three hours and was drifting into huge piles. John was out there, and I hadn't heard from him since our earlier call.

Finally, he rang in. I snatched up the phone like I was hatching it. John had trained me not to ask the dreaded question: "Are you alright?" His answer was always the same. "If I weren't, there'd be men knocking at the door, pretending to be sad, when they told you I was dead." I had stopped asking.

"Hey," I said mustering a nonchalance I was far from feeling.

"I just heard from Lincoln," John said. "It seems he loves his new toys. He just emailed a video he took at a bar and a note asking me to call him when I watch it."

"Oh God, don't tell me he went to a stripper bar!"

"Well, it is called Jugs," John said, and laughed when I said "Shit."

"It's just a sleazy neighborhood bar in Hurlock," he continued. "Someplace close enough for Lincoln to crawl to and from. It's a hangout for real shitheads. Anyway, he warned me it's very dark."

"Is that a psychological statement or a film critique?"

"Yes. Turn on your computer. I sent it to you. I'll conference call us when you're ready."

"Where are you?" I asked.

"Well, I was thinking of going to Jugs, but decided on grabbing some greasy food and coffee instead. Just got back to the car. We're hunkering down for a long, cold night. The good news is the roads are just about empty. The bad news: There are idiots stranded all over it. God only knows how many lives I'll save tonight."

"You may just put to bed the old saw 'Where's a cop when you need one?' You are impressive. Tell Duke to be careful. And don't be taking him to Jugs!"

TWENTY-NINE

———∞∞∞———

I CLICKED ON MY LAPTOP and found the file John had just sent. The
screen came to life like a black and white movie. It was your basic, dark
seedy bar. I guess no one in it wanted to see more than they had to.

"I'll get Lincoln on the line," John said. "Oh, and when he tells you
he just stumbled onto the fact that several dog guys hung out there,
don't laugh. I managed not to."

"Are you telling me that your delightful snitch is also a wannabe dog
fighting groupie? I'm astounded."

"Shush, phone's ringing."

Lincoln picked up. I noticed he had traded in his constant whine for
a good-natured slur.

"Lincoln, Dr. Reeves is on the phone."

"That's what I call a tall tail, if you catch my drift," Lincoln said with
a creepy giggle.

"Lincoln, shut up," John said. "Let's just watch what you sent."

The Lincoln show began with him standing in the doorway, probably
waiting for his eyes to adjust to the cave-like darkness. He gave a satisfied grunt and started moving down the bar. I could barely make out the
figure of a skinny African-American, dressed in black, who nearly disappeared into the background. Lincoln seemed to be heading towards him.

He walked past a table filled with badass types, all of whom followed
Lincoln with their eyes as he went by. I had a feeling from their pumped
size and demeanor, they were with the man in black.

146

"Hey, Ghost," Lincoln said, his voice filled with awe and subservience.

"Get the fuck away from me," the man he called Ghost warned, his eyes surprisingly visible in the gloom and doom of the bar. They were slits of anger, resentment and impatience. He turned his back.

"Hey man, don't be like that. Got me some money. See?" Lincoln said, fanning a few twenties through the air. Maybe it was so dark Lincoln couldn't see that Ghost had turned around.

"Fuck off," Ghost finally said over his shoulder, still not looking.

"I'm buying," Lincoln said, seeming impervious to Ghost's hostility. "Have one on me."

"Do I look like I need your drink?" he asked, deliberately holding up his left hand and shaking his wrist so Lincoln couldn't avoid looking at Ghost's garish, diamond-wrapped Rolex.

Lincoln was about to give up when a laughing, light-skinned, freckle-faced, middle-aged man walked over to him. His voice carried the patois of the deepest South. His belly fell over his belted pants, weighted down, I guessed, by the splendors of a life filled with po' boys, beignets and deep-fried anything.

"Yo, Creole Jackson, as I live and breathe," Lincoln said, giving us the newcomer's full name so John could instantly access his rap sheet.

I had already pulled up "Ghost," whose real name was Stephan Dupres. He had been a guest of the state for more than two-thirds of his life, starting in his early teens. He was now 46 and had been out of the system for the past two years. He always pleaded his innocence, but was found guilty on charges ranging from grand theft auto, B&E, and aggravated assault to attempted murder.

"Hey, Ghost. Lincoln, my man. Long time," said the man who was named Creole; it was not a nickname. According to his rap sheet, he was a very different type of criminal from Ghost. He had never done time. His belly may have been as country as cornpone, but his mind was as devious as a Wall Street trader dumping derivatives.

Creole, I noted, was not a nice guy. He scammed widows and veterans out of anything he could. If he had graduated from college and landed a well-paying job, he would have been called a "white collar" criminal. Instead, he was simply known as a con man. I thought of Creole and Ghost as country criminal meets urban psychopath.

"Hey Creole, help me out here," Lincoln said, and lowered his voice conspiratorially. "I'm looking to make a score. I just want Ghost here to give me a couple of tips. He's got some hellacious dogs, you know, always winning. Trying to get him to tell me his favorites."

"Don't know what you talking 'bout. But you better get the fuck away from me," Ghost said, his tone hard. One of his guys started to get up from his chair. Creole took it upon himself to wave him down. Ghost gave a slight "it's okay" nod and the guy sank back into his chair. Lincoln could have suffered whiplash with his "earring" taking in all the action.

"What's the deal, Lincoln?" Creole asked.

"Check it out." Lincoln flashed some cash at Creole. "I got money needs to be making money. Just want to place some bets."

"Whoa, who'd you jack?" asked Creole.

"You askin' the wrong question, Creole. Should be, who you find stupid enough to jack?" Ghost added, just being plain nasty. "Don't forget this ain't no mastermind criminal."

Lincoln kept his mouth shut. It was easy to tell he was scared by the way he let Ghost rain bullshit all over him. I didn't blame Lincoln; his fear was justified. Ghost, I had just discovered in the pages of his rap sheet had a penchant for one thing in life: his knife (or shiv if he was doing jail time.

"Let's just say I did a little business and came out on top," Lincoln said, and I could imagine his rubbery lower lip pushing outward into a pout that matched his tone. "You got some problem with me spending it here?"

"No sir," Creole said, and I could make out his face creasing with merriment. He was enjoying the show. "Long as you spend some on me."

Lincoln motioned to the bartender and ordered shots and beer backs. Ghost downed his drinks without a glance at Lincoln, but Creole picked up his glass, raised it towards Lincoln and then   drank.

"Look, I don't want no trouble. I'm going to take a leak and then I'm out of here."

"That's the first thing you said that I want to hear," Ghost said.

"Don't mind if I join you," Creole said to Lincoln. "I swear, the older I get, the faster the beer goes through me."

John and I watched them walk silently into the men's room. Creole turned to Lincoln once the door closed. "Ain't been no fights for a while and no talk of one," Creole whispered. "That's why Ghost's so pissed off."

"What you mean? They just stopped?" Lincoln asked. "Damn, just when I get me some scratch. What's going on?"

"Seems the guy running the fights came up against a problem," he answered carefully.

"You mean Jefferson Brown?" Lincoln asked, voicing genuine surprise. "Who'd fuck with him?"

"Hey man, don't be saying his name, even in here," Creole warned and paused.

"Yeah, say his name," I whispered, putting my hand over my phone so Lincoln couldn't hear me.

"Okay, okay," Lincoln said, "but what do you mean problems?"

Creole hesitated and then continued, "His guy Duncan Stanton has gone missing."

"No way. Who'd mess with either of them?"

"That's not all," Creole whispered so low I could barely hear him. "Brown's best dog was killed before Stanton disappeared."

"Which dog?"

"The big, black male with the white stripe. He was Brown's biggest winner ever."

He had to be talking about Benji.

Lincoln waited, but Creole had said his piece. So Lincoln finally said, "Hey man, thanks for the heads up. I'm out of here. I'd rather take a leak outside."

THE SUN WAS UP AND John was still out. I had slept enough to replenish my energy, despite my overall anxiety. I went downstairs and thought about putting on sun block.

The sunlight was bouncing off the river, pinging across the snow, and lit up the inside of the house like someone had turned on high-powered, Hollywood-style klieg lights. It felt as if the atmosphere was pulsating with white light, obliterating any negative ions that might have been hanging around. Good juju.

Suddenly, Ella started barking and I listened carefully. I heard an engine. I looked out the window and saw Vernon turn the tractor with the snowplow strapped across its front onto our driveway. I was about to go out and say hello when the phone rang.

"Hi, Honey," I answered, knowing it was John, and asked hopefully, "Does the fact that Vernon is plowing our road mean you'll soon be following?"

"How does 20 minutes sound?"

"Nineteen too long," I said and meant it, checked the clock and allowed the anxiety I had lived with all night to begin to dissipate.

I put Ella's coat on her and slipped into my parka, scarf, mittens and boots. We marched out the front door and headed towards Vernon, who jumped off the tractor to greet us. He and Ella romped around for a couple of minutes before I saw her start to shiver.

"Thanks for freeing us," I said, watching my breath hang on the air in front of me. Ella walked off to relieve herself, came back and pressed herself to my side. "I need to get her in the house. Her knees are knocking. At least I think they are – if I could see them under the foot of snow. Jeez! This was a bit of a forecasting disaster. You want to come in for a cup of coffee?"

"I'd love to, but I told a few friends around here I'd be by to plow them out. I just want to get it done so I can go home myself."

"Don't blame you."

Vernon accepted my offer for dinner tomorrow night on behalf of Gina and him, and drove off into the crystalline day. Fifteen minutes later, I was standing in the kitchen doorway eating a bowl of oatmeal, watching John drag himself out of the car and open the door for Duke. He bounded out. I gave them both a kiss when they reached me.

"God, you look tired," I said, as he took off his sunglasses upon entering the laundry room, squinted and put them back on. "You want breakfast? Bed? I'm assuming coffee isn't a priority."

"You're right. I want a shower, you and bed. And then I want to sleep until the sun sets."

"And you shall. I'll be right up. I'll finish my breakfast while you shower."

"Would you feed Duke?" I nodded. "And eat fast so you can wash my back?" he grinned.

"Done. See you in minutes."

John left his boots on the rubber mat and stripped off his filthy, wet uniform and threw it in the laundry room basket on his way upstairs. I soon followed.

I slipped out of bed after dozing off myself and began my day. I had a long chat with Jackie, who was at home, too – with Michael. We got through all the personal stuff and then turned the conversation to Jugs, the missing Duncan Stanton and the dead Benji. It was a short discussion since neither of us could make any sense of what was going on.

I went into my office, turned on my computer and entered the notes on the cats I had recently necropsied. I added my comments to the open file so I could begin closing out the Chestertown case.

That task completed, I went into the kitchen. I turned on my iPod, put in my earbuds and blasted early Rolling Stones. I had enough time to make a tomato sauce for pasta, sautéing a humongous amount of garlic until it caramelized and added tomatoes and fresh basil. I covered it and left it to simmer, stirring every half-hour or so.

I took Duke and Ella for a late afternoon walk, and returned home to find John awake and mobile. He was standing in the kitchen with a cup of coffee in his hand and his face in the fridge.

"I'm starving," he announced. "Early dinner?"

"Sure. Pull out some salad stuff and start chopping. You want to try an Amarone tonight?" I asked. When he nodded, I headed towards the bar. I grabbed a bottle, opened it to breathe and put it on the dining table.

"I fed the cats and they still don't appreciate me," John griped.

"Really? Oh, maybe it's because they're cats. That's why you never had any. You need constant attention and devotion. That's why you have me around."

"And I bless you for that."

Soon dinner was on the table and we sat side by side, watching the disappearing view of the river. The fire was blazing, the candles were glowing and the sun was setting, casting an orange blush over the room. We managed to make it through the salad and garlic bread before talking business. That was long for us, especially since we had yet to discuss Lincoln's video.

"Wow," I said. "And another wow for good measure. So someone's picking a fight with Bad Bad Jefferson Brown? Killed his best dog and maybe his best friend."

"Yeah, the wow factor sure increases," John said. "I wonder if this is the beginning of a range war."

"Or a country music song," I couldn't resist interjecting.

John ignored me and said, "Wouldn't it be great if they all just killed each other off?"

"Oh, I love it when you're optimistic. It's so infrequent. Makes you wonder who'll be next. I just hope it's not a dog. At least Lincoln didn't waste any time."

"Yeah, that's my snitch," John said. "I don't know anyone who can rat out someone faster."

"You have so much to be proud of," I joked.

"Hey, I thought you'd be happier," he said. "We now have a link to the dog fights, at least."

"Yeah, but it's the waiting," I said. "It's getting harder."

"Hopefully it won't be much longer," John said and patted my hand in a comforting gesture.

"Yeah, and we also have to pray that Lincoln doesn't drink himself to death or get killed for running his mouth. That's a whole lot of praying."

"Brown won't wait forever," John said. "No dog fights mean no betting, no drugs being bought and sold like hot dogs at Dodger Stadium, no guns and hookers changing hands. That cuts deep into his bottom line. And I'm sure he wouldn't want to take the chance of someone else moving in on his territories."

"I'm somewhat mollified." I smiled. "Very good. I'm coming in from the ledge, backing away from the cliff…"

"Got it," John interrupted.

"Fine. Anyway, I was thinking you could access ViCAP and look for any more of Brown's cohorts," I said, referring to the Violent Criminal Apprehension Program that was overseen by the FBI and comprised the largest investigative repository of major violent crime cases in the U.S. Its purpose was to collect and analyze information about homicides, sexual assaults, missing persons, and other violent crimes.

John's response was to get up from the table since we had finished eating and walk me into his Spartan office, filled with a few file cabinets, metal desk, desk chair and an extra one that rivaled the chair he had in the barracks for imparting pain. He turned on his computer while I pulled it next to him and watched. He opened the ViCAP website and entered his info. Soon he was feeding his search parameters into the system, and numerous rap sheets appeared on screen one after the other. He breezed through them with amazing speed, discarding most of them. I realized for the umpteenth time how good he was at his job.

After a few minutes, he hit the print button and the machine spit out three names with similar aptitudes and rap sheets to the Rivera boys.

"Check them out," he said to me while he continued looking at his screen. "See what you think. There are more, but these guys are my top candidates."

I could have been reading Brown's rap sheet – again and again and again. These guys were into the same activities, except – unlike Brown – they had all served hard time. Maybe one of them had freedom-envy. I went over the rap sheets again to see if anyone had recently been released from prison. Nope, they'd all been out for some time.

In alphabetical order, these Baltimore boys were Arnold Diaz, who we already knew about, Kawayne Johnson and Paul Salvatore. Hispanic, African-American and Italian descent. Seemed like being a dick encompassed all ethnic and racial categories.

"I'm not sure their own mothers would mourn their passing," I said, pushing myself away from the desk so I could stand up and allow the feeling to return to my rear end and added, "Maybe we'll find out – if we're lucky."

THIRTY-ONE

I WAS IN A DEEP, happy sleep when my phone woke me up. I looked at the clock. It was a little after 5 a.m. and still midnight dark outside. Nothing good happens at that time of day. I was glad John was next to me. He didn't have to be my first worry.

I looked at the caller ID and didn't recognize the name, but Baltimore County Police Department kind of said it all. By now, John had turned on the bedside lamp and was looking at me.

"It's a Sergeant Robert Brennan," I said, feeling my shoulders rise in a slight shrug, reading his name off the caller ID. John shook his head no as in he didn't know him. I answered, "Allison Reeves speaking."

"Dr. Reeves," Brennan said and introduced himself in a deep, crisp, wide-awake voice. He added, "I'm sorry to bother you at this hour, but I'm with the Homicide Division and we've discovered the bodies of a man and a pit bull that had been buried alive up to their necks. They were facing the incoming tide that drowned them both. We've made a temporary ID. I recognized the body. I'm sure it's Duncan Stanton. He's well known to us."

I wasn't sure if my gasp was audible. If it were, Brennan ignored it. He continued, "When I just called in to report the death of Stanton to my Commander, Lieutenant Steinman, he told me about the conversation he had with Lieutenant Andrews the other day about Cletus Garrison working a case on your side of the bridge. Steinman told me you necropsied a dog believed to be owned by Jefferson Brown. Is that correct?"

"Yes, I did," I said somewhat surprised at the question, having no idea where he was headed. "And we now know for sure the dog did belong to Brown."

John's eyes widened with surprise at the mention of his name. I picked up my pen and wrote on the notepad I kept by my side of the bed, "Duncan Stanton murdered in Fort Howard Park," and handed the paper to John. We were both fully awake now.

"Are you saying someone buried Stanton and a pit bull and left them to drown, as in 'Blackbeard' drowned?" I asked incredulously, thinking about the horrible last scene in an old pirate movie.

"Exactly," he said and added, "I was hoping you'd necropsy this dog, too."

"I'm on my way," I said, already out of the bed and stepping into the bathroom. "Send me the coordinates so I can find you."

"They're on the way."

"Fort Howard Park? How the hell were the bodies found?" I asked.

"Someone called it in. No name. Untraceable phone."

"So someone wanted them found. I guess there's not much point to creating such a horrific death scene if it goes unnoticed?" I commented. "How far away is the dog from Stanton?"

"About five feet. We're about to excavate Stanton. We can do it without disturbing your crime scene," he said, and I could hear the warning in his words. His team must have been standing nearby.

"I'm going to call my partner, Jackie Vincente. She's the HSPAC's lead investigator for this area. She'll probably get there ahead of me, since she lives in Annapolis. She can start taking photographs, if that's okay."

"Sure," Brennan said immediately. "I know her name, and I've worked with her husband on a few cases."

"I'll be coming from Trappe, so I should be there in 90 minutes or less. At least I'll miss rush hour – by a couple of hours," I noted before I said goodbye.

I quickly brushed my teeth and called Jackie while I threw on my clothes.

"What's up?" she asked her voice groggy with sleep."

"Any chance you can meet me in Fort Howard Park? Duncan Stanton's been located. A homicide detective just called with the news that the bodies of Stanton and an unidentified pit bull were found there buried alive."

I talked over Jackie's sharp inhalation and loud enough for John to hear. I repeated Brennan's conversation. I heard Jackie talking to Thomas, explaining the situation.

"I'll meet you there," she said, her voice filled with energy once she returned to the phone.

"Are you sure you're okay leaving Michael?"

"Yes, he's much better and our housekeeper will be with him."

"Hang on a sec," I interrupted when my phone pinged. I checked and saw it was a text from Brennan. "I just received the location; I'm forwarding it to you. I told him you'd be there before me and you'd start immediately, so go to it. I'll bring the shovels and additional muscle. I'll be there as soon as I can.

"Hey Jackie," I added. "I'm glad you're back."

I braided my hair without looking so I could give John my full attention. He was sitting up, staring at me with a quizzical look.

"So how did Brennan get to you?" he asked.

I explained the Andrews-Steinman connection and that Garrison is in Brennan's department, so Steinman already knew that John had found the dog and I had necropsied it.

John stood up and pulled on his jeans and headed for the bathroom. "I'll see you downstairs in a minute."

"No, go back to bed."

"Don't argue."

Ella followed me down the stairs and sat next to her coat that was hanging on the guest closet's doorknob. I didn't have the heart to tell her she wasn't coming with me.

I heard John's feet slapping on the steps and figured he could explain it to her. But he headed into the kitchen and then the garage. I heard the garage door open and my car's engine turn over. Bless him. He was heating it up for my drive to the lab and the Mobile Unit.

I bypassed Ella's coat and pulled out my warmest HSPAC jacket. I put it over my Polartec vest. Then I laced up my waterproof, wool-lined boots. Three days had passed since the snowstorm and it had warmed up a bit, but I knew it would be damp and cold near the water. I dove back into the closet for my hat and gloves when I felt John's hands on my shoulders. I turned into his arms. He gave me a hug and a kiss, pushed me away gently and wrapped my scarf around my neck. Then he took the ends of it and pulled me into him for a goodbye hug.

THIRTY-TWO

— ⊷ —

ONCE IN THE MOBILE UNIT, I drove to Route 50 and turned left. It was just 18 minutes after Brennan's call. I fed his info into my GPS system and put on Lambert, Hendricks and Ross's "Cloudburst" that dated back to the 1950s. They were the jazz wordsmiths of their time. I actually thought of them as the precursors of rap. They fit words into jazz solos that found their own rhythm in verse.

As I crossed the Bay Bridge, the sun began to rise and revealed a wall of steely grey clouds moving in from the west. Damn. I prayed the crime scene would be tented and, if not, hoped the rain would hold off long enough for Jackie and me to free the dog from the sand and collect any evidence the killer might have left behind. I started to call Brennan, but decided to give him the benefit of the doubt for professionalism.

Then I pushed all thoughts of the dead dog and the horrible way its life had ended out of my mind. I was compartmentalizing again. I chose to concentrate on what I knew about Fort Howard Park and its history.

The Patapsco Neck Peninsula, located in the southeastern part of Baltimore County, was rich in American lore. John, a true history buff, told me that when he took me on an ad hoc tour of the area a few years ago. As we crossed the Francis Scott Key Bridge, he pointed out the red and blue-striped buoy bobbing 100 yards off the western shore. It marked the place where the British Navy held Key captive on one of its ships. From there, he watched the overnight bombardment of Fort McHenry during the War of 1812. He wrote the poem that became "The Star-Spangled Banner" the next morning when he saw the American flag still flying.

The rain was holding off, but I knew it wouldn't for much longer. I was relieved when I finally saw the spine of the long, serpentine Key Bridge stretching far across the Patapsco River. Once I landed on the peninsula, I found North Point Road and followed it until dead-ending at the VA Hospital, a sprawling brick edifice that was slated for demolition. It reminded me of Shutter Island and its inherent spookiness.

North Point was the site of the largest invasion of the United States. Seven thousand British troops massed there in the hopes of capturing Baltimore, which lay to the north of the Chesapeake Bay. The troops were turned back and moved on to Louisiana, only to lose the Battle of New Orleans.

By the end of the 19th Century, but before the beginning of the Spanish-American War, the military became fearful of another attack on the Port of Baltimore. Fort Howard was built to repel the Spanish, who never showed up. A few years later, North Point was renamed Fort Howard Park. The fort and its coastal gun batteries remain to this today.

GPS told me to turn left, away from the small community of people and houses that were in the opposite direction. This path took me farther into the park.

I called Jackie. "Tell me the crime scene is tented."

"It is," she said. "Where are you?"

"I just turned at the VA hospital. You tell me."

"I should see you in around 10-15 minutes. You have to go real slow through the woods, especially with the Mobile Unit. It seems like the killer somehow made a pathway once the narrow road ended. It will take you all the way to the beach where we are."

"Where's your car?" I asked.

"I left it at Sparrows Point Restaurant on North Point Road, and had a cab pick me up there. You can drop me off and I'll follow you to the lab, if you need me."

"How's Michael doing?" I said, the van bucking and twisting. It forced me to slow down, which made me writhe inside.

"Probably great," Jackie said ruefully. "I have a feeling he's loving a day free of my smothering love and care."

"Well, I love knowing you're waiting for me at the literal end of the road. I think I can see some lights in the distance. That must be you guys."

I arrived at a full-blown crime scene with a dozen law enforcement vehicles parked in front of a tent set up on the sandy beach close to the water's edge. I knew the bodies were under it, protected from the elements and onlookers. The media was already there and being contained. I stopped in front of one of the officers and handed over my ID.

"Sergeant Brennan told me to let you through. Agent Vincente is already here," he said, pointing towards the tent.

I drove as far as I could, which was nearly to the tented area, and parked next to the coroner's wagon. I entered the tent just in time to watch four men heave Duncan Stanton into a body bag. I stared down at him. His face was immobilized in death – his mouth formed an unheard scream, a rictus of terror. His eye was open and bulging, bloodshot and speckled with sand and sea foam. The other one was missing, probably plucked out by a crab. Chunks of skin and hair had been torn away from his face and head. I almost felt some sympathy for him, but not quite. The most I could marshal was wishing the facial mutilation came after death. I was concerned with the true victim – the innocent dog.

Once Stanton was zipped into the bag, I switched my gaze to Jackie. She was ignoring the dead man, looking down at the top of the dog's head. She turned towards me as the tent flap closed and I moved forward. One look and I knew she was trying to hide her distress. I walked over to her and gave her a big hug. I was always surprised how little she was. She was such a large presence.

"A new low?" I asked, already aware of how Stanton had been whipped by the elements. I looked down at the dog. It was a brindle American Pit Bull Terrier with old scarring around his muzzle. His tongue was hanging out of his mouth, stuck to the sand. Tufts of fur and skin were chewed out of his face. I estimated he had been dead for at least 48 hours, but could have been buried alive three days earlier.

"This is a new form of torture for us," Jackie concurred. "If there is a God, and things like this make me question that fact, I pray we never see anything like this again."

"Amen," I said. I heard someone enter the tent behind me and turned to see who it was.

"Dr. Reeves," the man said, holding out his hand which I shook while he introduced himself, "I'm Robert Brennan. We're done here and, as promised, we didn't disturb your crime scene."

"I appreciate that. And thanks for the tent. Any idea how long your vic has been dead?"

"It's hard to tell. The coroner thinks less than three days, but he needs to run a bunch of tests. The line between dying and dead is pretty cloudy at this point.

"I had Stanton's file pulled. He was hospitalized as a teenager. He almost drowned. Because of that he was deathly afraid of water. Someone put a lot of thought into killing him. This was very personal. Never seen anything like it." He added, shaking his head in disbelief, "What a horrible way to die."

"Especially for the dog," Jackie interjected.

Brennan's words surprised me because they belied his eyes, which were cynical, intelligent and looked like nothing could shock him. His face was pitted with acne scars so severe I wondered if he ever had a date in high school. He was big-boned, large-nosed and wearing big black-framed glasses that rode the bridge of his nose, causing him to push them up in a gesture that I was sure was habit by now. His black pants were tucked into knee-high, black rubber boots, and I saw his plain white shirt buttoned up to the neck under a red striped tie. His look was conservative married, and I checked and found a wedding band on his left ring finger.

"We still have some work to do around here, but we'll be out of your way," he said considerately. "Maybe if we finish up around the same time, we could meet and grab a cup of coffee. I know I could use at least a pot at this point. I'd like to get your first impressions, give you mine and introduce you to my detectives who will be working this case."

"Sounds good," I said, surprised at his willingness to cooperate. A lot of detectives were real dicks. "Any chance you can leave the lights up in the tent? It would save us the time of setting up our own."

"No problem. In fact, I'd rather have my people working the exterior. We found some footprints and tire tracks. This storm isn't going to hold back too much longer," he added, opening the tent flap and looking towards the sky.

"Jackie is parked at Sparrows Point Restaurant on North Point Road. I'm going to give her a ride to her car when we're done. You want to meet there?"

"Sure, they do a decent breakfast," he said.

"After extricating the dog, I'm not sure how hungry I'll be. Coffee may be all I can handle," I said as my eyes made a return trip to the dog's head. I shouldn't have, but I allowed myself to imagine the dog's terror of being trapped in the sand with the waves lapping towards him. For a second, I worried my icy inner core was melting. Then I shook off these unwanted feelings and unwrapped my scarf and took off my wool gloves and stuffed them in my pockets. It was time to get to work.

THIRTY-THREE

RAINDROPS BEGAN GENTLY PINGING ON the roof of the tent and I was once again grateful it had been left in place. Jackie and I couldn't have put it up in time. I was also glad Brennen was collecting any evidence found outside the tent, secure in the knowledge that he was going to share. His was the perfect response to my willingness to perform the necropsy. I thought of it as working hand-and-paw with the law. Sometimes I just couldn't help myself.

"You finished photographing the dog?" I asked Jackie, back to the sad reality of now.

She nodded yes.

"I'll go grab a couple of shovels so we can extricate it," I said, pulling up the hood of my jacket and slipped out of the tent.

I returned quickly with a large plastic bag, two standard size shovels, two small ones and a brush with soft bristles. Jackie had put her Nikon back in the case and took a large shovel from me. We discussed our excavation strategy and decided to start on the left side of the dog and dig a four-foot wide hole the length of the dog's body. That way, we could lay the dog on its side once we freed it from its sandy grave. I would be able to do a cursory examination before we moved it into the Mobile Unit.

"Let's leave, what do you figure, six inches of sand next to the dog? You think that'll be enough to keep it upright until we can lower it to the ground?" I asked. This was a new problem and procedure for us, thankfully.

Jackie sighed and picked up a shovel. "We'll just go slowly and keep checking to see if the dog starts to shift. I don't know what else we can do," she grumbled and added, "Well, at least this made me realize how much I love my job. As ugly as the death of this dog is, and it is hideous, I'm glad to be here."

"I know what you mean," I said, flashing a smile at her. "I missed you. No one I'd rather work a skin-crawling crime scene with than you."

"Jackie?" I started to say, but instead grabbed the other shovel and placed the edge into the sand. I held the handle between my palms and jumped on the top of the blade, digging deep and coming up with a shovelful of wet, heavy sand.

"What?" she asked and leaned on her shovel, staring at me, her eyes searching my face.

"I'm afraid this might be one of Brown's dogs. I hope it isn't one we could have saved if we had just done something sooner, anything."

"Allison, let it go," she ordered. "Maybe this will lead us to the killer and the dog's death will mean something. That's the best I can do," she said with a rather pathetic look.

"Not bad," I said, giving her a small smile, which was the most I could manage.

We dug a large hole until our muscles were screaming from exertion. We took a short break. And drank a lot of water.

Then it was time to pick up the small shovels and begin the careful process of removing the sand from the top down that was pressing against the dog. We placed the sand closest to the dog in large buckets and carried them in the Mobile Unit. We would send them to the lab to be sifted for any potential evidence. When we had nearly freed the dog from its sand trap, I handed Jackie a pair of sterile gloves to put on, so she could hold it upright. I removed the last thin layer of sand with the wide, soft brush. It was a tedious process that made me feel like an archaeologist exposing a fossil. After a while, I could see the striations of a brindle pattern appearing on the dog's coat.

"Ready?" I asked and slipped on a pair of sterile gloves.

"Yep," Jackie said, holding up the rear end. I placed my right hand over the dog's back and my left hand went under its ribcage. We wiggled the dog out of its tomb and, at the same time, lowered it to the ground. I turned on my flashlight and used it to illuminate every inch of the dog. It was a male that had multiple bite mark scarring its body.

"Jackie, I may have good news, if you figure everything is relative. I'm thinking this dog may have died of hypothermia rather than drowning. Look here," I said, pointing to bare patches of exposed flesh. Then I turned the beam of the flashlight on the remaining wall of sand. Bits of fur clung to it.

"It could be a sign that this dog was shivering so severely that the friction pulled out those bits of fur. Of course, it could be that the dog was struggling to free itself, but I think it would have left larger tufts in the sand. If it were hypothermia, the dog would have been so cold that he would have become unconscious and died without knowing it. Drowning would have been torturous; think waterboarding."

"I don't want to," Jackie said. "Jesus, the things that make us happy. We are psychologically screwed."

I climbed out of the pit gingerly. My hip was aching and I reached into my pocket for the bottle of Advil I had been carrying around since I was bitten. I took several to tamp down the pain. Then I picked up the large plastic bag while Jackie went in for closeup shots with her Nikon. I waited until she finished before dropping down into the hole. She took the bag from me and put it on the ground next to the dog and opened the end. I carefully lifted his head so she could slide the bag under and around it. Working together, I lifted and she slid until we had the entire dog captured in the bag. Jackie tied off the end and reached into her pocket. She pulled out a tag and attached it to the bag. Then she took a pen and wrote the necessary info on it.

"You ready?" she said.

"Front or back?" I countered.

"Don't care."

I walked to the dog's head, since she was at the opposite end already. In unison, we bent our knees, placed our hands under the dog and straightened up, lifting it to waist height first and then up to our shoulders so we could place him outside the hole on the ground.

"Let me sit for a second," Jackie said and lowered herself to the ground. I plopped down next to her.

"You okay?" I asked concerned, knowing the past few days had been really hard on her.

"Yeah. For once, it's only physical."

She massaged her biceps and flexed her hands several times. Soon we were ready to get back to work and carefully picked up the dog and walked him outside and into the Mobile Unit. Jackie and I put him down on the examining table so I could open the refrigerator. Then we slipped the dog into it.

We returned to the burial site with smaller bags and collected the pieces of fur that the dog had dislodged. I found several spots where the dog had urinated on the sand and some feces, and shoveled samples of each into its own bag. Jackie tagged and ID'ed them.

"Well, we're done here," I said, feeling a deep sadness approaching once the work part was over. "That was pretty ghastly. Let's go find Brennan and see if he has any answers. I have so many questions."

We stepped out of the Mobile Unit as the rain intensified and mingled with an onslaught of snowflakes. One of the officers jogged towards us. He had a message from Brennan. The sergeant was waiting for us at the restaurant. His men would take down the tent. I told him we'd left the hole in the ground and he said they would fill it in. Jackie and I thanked him and returned to the Mobile Unit.

We drove to Sparrows Point Restaurant and found Brennan sitting at a table with two other people, a man and a woman. A waitress was just arriving with a tray of coffee cups.

"I took a chance and ordered coffee for you," Brennan said. "If you don't want it, I'll drink it. I'm several cups behind already. This is Detective Maria Delacroix and Detective Chuck Whitfield. Meet Dr. Allison Reeves and Agent Jackie Vincente."

We shook hands all around and settled on first names. Jackie and I sat down and gratefully grabbed a cup of coffee.

"In case anyone had a doubt about that being Duncan Stanton, we matched his fingerprints," Brennan said. "The only good thing about what happened is that I won't ever have to deal with him again. Every time I thought we had him and Jefferson Brown in our sights, they just faded into nothingness."

"You think there might be a leak?" I asked what I thought was an obvious question.

"Yeah, maybe one of our K-9s snitched to one of their pit bulls," Whitfield said in a snotty tone.

Delacroix's thin lips twisted in a poorly suppressed grin, making them all but disappear. She shot her partner a reverential look of appreciation, which somehow managed to escape from under her pudgy eyelids, nearly lost in the surrounding folds of flesh in her face. She reminded me of a Shar-Pei, especially with her chins hanging over her turtleneck sweater.

Whitfield, on the other hand, was a pretty boy, but not a nice one. He had perfected his jaded look, probably thinking that's what looked good on a detective. His hair was fashionably short and headed in several directions like a young TV show host. He had long black lashes wrapped around cerulean-colored irises, pouty, almost feminine lips, and metrosexual clothes.

"How do you explain Brown and Stanton escaping detection for so many years?" I questioned evenly, knowing my eyes had gone frosty.

The detective duo had nothing to say. Maybe they were just marking their territory and pissing on Jackie and me in the process.

"Did you come up with a time of death?" Brennan asked us.

"I think your assessment is close," I answered. "I'd say three days in the grave and two days dead. I'm figuring the decomposition was slowed by the lack of oxygen and the cool temperatures."

Brennan nodded and I continued, "I'll send the dog's DNA to the databank and see if it gets any hits. Maybe we can tie it to someone other than Stanton or Brown."

"You think the dog was the target?" Whitfield asked his voice now incredulous and downright nasty. His pretty lips twitched with amusement. He was beginning to really piss me off. Brennan shut him down with a dismissive flick of his hand.

The waitress, a thin slip of a girl with lots of tattoos, arrived at our table and handed us menus. I looked at Jackie and we shared a silent understanding.

"We're going to get going," she said, and put her menu on the table. I stood up quickly, nodded to everyone and said to Brennan,

"We'll let you know what we find out," I added. "I'd appreciate it if you keep us informed on your end."

"Of course," he said politely, and did a half-rise from his chair and dropped back. "Thanks for coming. I appreciate it," he added pointedly, sending a message to his subordinates.

As we left the table, Jackie and I heard Whitfield, his voice packed with sarcasm, say, "Are you kidding? They're Doggie Dicks."

I noticed Jackie's body start to turn back to them and I gently pushed her between her shoulder blades, ensuring her forward mobility. When we got outside, I braced myself. She didn't disappoint. "Fuck them!" exploded from her lips.

"That was good," I said, patting her on the arm. "You made it out the door. But really, 'Doggie Dick'? I'm thinking I want that inscribed on all my official clothing. So much catchier than Forensic Veterinarian."

"Yeah, right," Jackie said, a reluctant smile nudging at the corners of her lips. "I so wanted to run my fingers through that jerk's perfectly organized disorganized hair and bitch slap that Shar-Pei."

"Right there with you," I said, laughing at Jackie's description of Delacroix. "I thought the same thing, but felt I was doing a disservice to the breed. They, at least, are cute. She was like some gnome that they'd put in a scary garden in a creepy movie."

"The worst part is I'm hungry," Jackie said. "I really wanted breakfast."

"Can you make it over the bridge?" I wanted to know. "We can stop at Cracker Barrel, if that works for you."

"Yum," was Jackie's one-word response and she was happy again.

THIRTY-FOUR

———— ❧ ————

THE DOWNPOUR SLOWED OUR RETURN to Trappe from the restaurant. As soon as I neared the house, I called Jackie, whose headlights were visible in my rearview mirror.

"Hey, I want to stop quickly to pick up Ella on the way to the lab," I said.

"Okay, I'll meet you there. It'll be nice to see the girl."

"You want anything from the kitchen while I'm home?"

"No, I'm full. I'll put up some coffee when I get to the lab. It's already been a long day."

"I know. Be right behind you," I said, and disconnected. I headed to the house and saw Jackie peel off towards the lab.

Ella began barking as soon as I pulled into the driveway. I unlocked the front door and let myself in, petted the delighted Ella and put on her coat. We went outside into the stinging sleet, carried on the gusting winds. Ella put her head down, lowered her eyelids and trotted to the edge of the woods and quickly relieved herself. I called her to the Mobile Unit, where I had opened the passenger door and patted the seat. She immediately jumped up and looked out at the blustery weather. Then she gave a comfortable snort, circled and landed.

Jackie must have been watching for us because she opened the lab door and walked outside before I could put the van in park. She opened Ella's door, kissed her on the nose and looked her over.

"A miracle," she said simply. "You still feeding her 20 times a day?"

"Actually, I've cut her back to 12. And no infections. She doesn't seem to miss her K-I-D-S anymore."

Jackie smiled, scratched what was left of Ella's ears and slid past her to join me in the back of the van. Together, we removed the brindle pit bull from the refrigerator and took it out the back. Jackie had left the door ajar, so we could easily enter the lab. Ella scampered after us. We placed the dead dog on the examining table, which Jackie had readied for the necropsy.

I changed into scrubs, and looked the dog over with a magnifying glass. I found tiny patches of scraped flesh where the fur was missing. I pointed them out to Jackie, who switched lenses so she could zoom in on those areas. Then I radiographed the dog but didn't find any broken bones or undetected gun shot wounds.

"I get why someone could want to do this to Duncan Stanton, but why this dog?" I almost whined. "Ah, crap, how many times have I said that – the part about the dog, not the shithead? But I don't get it. And I don't want to. I just want to prove to myself the dog was unconscious before the tide came in. At least he would be spared the terror of a pro-tracted death."

I was relieved to discover the visual effects of hypothermia. There was a noticeable buildup of fluid in the dog's face and paws. And when I shaved the fur off, I uncovered a purple tone to the skin and violet patches on the dog's leg joints. I lifted the dog's rear leg slightly and revealed its scrotum had a bluish cast. These are the body parts least protected by fur.

Following procedure, I exposed the dog's internal organs one by one and took samples from each and placed them in formalin. As usual, Jackie labeled each container.

I removed the bladder and managed to draw a few drops of urine from it. I would send it to the lab tomorrow to test for a high concentration of catecholamines (dopamine, norepinephrine and epinephrine, formerly named adrenalin), a chemical produced in the adrenal glands, which produces fight/flight response. Total urinary catecholamine content is increased in hypothermia deaths and, if it were found, would confirm this was the cause of death.

I found more results attributable to hypothermia. There were macroscopic signs of gastric erosions and acute renal and hepatic degeneration. I worked my way through the rest of the dog's organs. No other abnormalities. Next, I detached the heart and lungs and put them on the table before I separated theformer.

"Well, Jackie, I know you'll be shocked, but I can prove this dog was used for fighting – just in case the bite marks weren't enough of a clue," I said sardonically, after I incised the four chambers of the heart and studied each one. "The linings of both the left and right ventricles show the effects of anabolic steroids and endurance training."

Then, I drew a longitudinal incision down the side of one lung and used my fingers to pry the lobes open. I found no congestion in it or any pink frothy fluid in the bronchi or trachea. I explained to Jackie that froth is a symptom of drowning.

"So the dog didn't drown," Jackie said, and stopped typing my findings into the computer, which I was restating in medical terminology. She put her hand on my shoulder and patted it.

"If I didn't have to stay sterile, I'd turn around and hug you," I said.

I examined the brain, which showed no abnormalities, and removed a sample. That was that. The dog had, indeed, died of hypothermia before the tide came in – a horrible death to be sure, but one that could have been much worse. Often in my line of work, that was the best I could hope for.

"It's a wrap," I said, and began folding the white paper around the dog's organs before I disposed of them. Jackie packed the containers of samples in FedEx boxes. My scrubs went in the laundry basket.

I looked at Ella who was at the door, just knowing she was going somewhere soon. I was only too happy to take her there. But my phone rang instead. It was Barbara Montrose. I immediately sat down at my desk and grabbed my notebook.

"Allison," she said warmly. We'd been talking cases and strategies for years and had formed an effortless and friendly alliance. She was my working West Coast Jackie. "I bring you lots of news," Barbara explained. "But first, tell me how she's doing. Thanks, I think, for sending the photo. Jeez, what a nightmare. I'm so glad she's with you."

"Me, too. She's gained enough weight to fill out her ribs and she can cope with being a few feet from my side – well, one foot – without suffering separation anxiety. She does go out with Duke. She adores him; he tolerates her."

"Send me a healthy photo, okay?"

"You mean after she has plastic surgery?" I joked. Barbara chortled.

Jackie bundled up, ready to leave. I mouthed "goodbye." She waved to me, petted Ella and disappeared into the night.

"We just completed a necropsy on a pit," I explained. "I'm going to send you a DNA sample tomorrow. I'll also send my report. I can't go through it now."

"You sound exhausted," Barbara said.

"It's been a long day," I sighed. "Anyway, back to Ella. I'm too tired to complain."

"I haven't had any success in finding her dam, but I do know who sired her," Barbara said with enjoyment. "The dog you identified as Benji is Ella's sire."

"No shit!" I was so amazed I think I shouted my response, and fell back into my chair.

"Benji? Really, Allison?" she questioned and continued without waiting for my comment. "Anyway, the math works. Benji was stolen three years ago and Ella is somewhere between 18 months and two years, right? I wouldn't have known that without the hair samples you sent me from both of them. Neither one was in our system."

"Hey, first of all, I didn't name him," I said in self-defense. "Second, he wasn't in your system because he was a fighter and then a family pet until that son of a bitch Brown turned him into a fighter again. He's the one I watched shoot one of his other dogs. I feel my professional detachment waning."

"Now that I had Benji's DNA," Barbara continued, pretty much ignoring my tirade, "I found he sired another female, an American Pit Bull Terrier named Weather. She was traced back to dogs belonging to Tyndall Garcia-Lopez of Philadelphia. Unfortunately, I received Weather's DNA after she was found dead in a Dumpster in Baltimore. So I think it's safe to say these guys are interbreeding their dogs. I had a couple more hits on Benji's progeny. One dog, Maco, was confiscated in a fight in Florida, but his DNA was also traced back to dogs bred by Arnold Diaz several generations ago. And there was another dog, a female, who was found hanging from a tree in Fort Howard Park. We had no information on her lineage until now."

"Well, Jefferson Brown seems to have a penchant for killing his dogs," I said, and told her about the video we pulled from his house. "And it goes on," I said, my voice sober with the realization of how many pit bulls died violent deaths, no matter how hard we tried to prevent it. "Garcia-Lopez is a known associate of Brown's. And their good buddy, Duncan Stanton, turned up dead with the pit bull I just necropsied."

I stood up and started cleaning up my workspace, knowing our conversation was winding down. I began to scoop up the instruments to put them in the sterilizer for their water bath. Once that was completed, I would wrap them into packs and autoclave them. I do it tomorrow, I decided. Now I just wanted to head home.

"Allison, this is a whole lot of crazy stuff. You be careful," Barbara warned. "But I don't need to tell you, do I?"

"No, I have John and Jackie for that," I said with a rueful laugh.

I locked up the lab and left. It had been a tough 15-hour day, and I was glad it was ending.

I could see the house lights through the trees as we drove from the lab, so I knew John was home.

He had a fire blazing in the living room when I dragged myself through the front door with Ella. The fire was the first bit of cheer I had experienced since I left the comforts of our bed that morning.

"Honey, I'm home," I shouted. Duke's bark welcomed me from upstairs. John yelled he'd be down in a second.

"Ella is almost home," I continued, taking off my boots, jacket and shook out my hair. "She's outside taking a whiz. No, now she's inside."

Ella, wet and wiggling, ran past me when I opened the door for her and shot up the stairs to say hello to Duke and John.

"Oh no, it's a wet dog attack," John roared, and I smiled as I heard the thud of man and dogs collide. The next sound was the click-clack of dogs' nails on the hardwood floors overhead, and I made a note to clip them after dinner. I heard John's footsteps coming down the stairs and walked into his outstretched arms when he reached the bottom. In unison, we turned towards the living room and sat on one of the couches and put our feet on the table.

"How are you?" John said, looking me over. Obviously, he found his answer, because he rose and walked to the bar. He poured me a glass of bourbon. He took rye.

I waited until I swallowed two mouthfuls, letting each one individually slide down my throat, enjoying its mellow warmth all the way down to my aching feet.

"I have the most amazing news," I said, which surprised John, since I wasn't given to hyperbole. "I spoke with Barbara Montrose today. You know I sent her Ella and Benji's DNA. She was able to track Benji to several other dogs that he sired. I'll email you the info later. But that's not the amazing news.

"I know who's my baby's daddy," I paused, milking the Maury Povich moment for all it was worth. "It's Benji!"

"Holy shit!" was all John said until he added, "I hope the rest of your day was as productive."

"That would be a strange way to describe it," I said and told him about the horrors we found at Fort Howard Park and the results of the hours Jackie and I spent in the lab.

Once I finished, John said apropos of nothing, "Let's get out here. Can you bear going out to eat? I'll even carry you."

"God, you had me at dinner."

THIRTY-FIVE

─────⊶⊷─────

WE LANDED AT BISTRO GARDEN in Cambridge, not too far from our house, one of the better restaurants on the Eastern Shore. The upscale French eatery was buzzing, serving up excellent food.

The snow had stopped, but the temperature had dropped with Arctic intensity, so I ordered my Grey Goose martini straight up. I had had enough ice for one day. John stuck with rye. I sipped slowly but steadily until an alcoholic flush warmed my bloodstream. I didn't need another.

My stomach relaxed enough for me to turn my attention to John's plate of escargot. He ate the snails and I dipped my bread into the garlicky butter left behind. We moved through the menu quickly, both of us glad to be sitting, eating and making normal couple conversation.

That feeling ended on the ride home. John's phone rang and I could tell from the way his lip curled, it was Lincoln. At least we had finished our meal, so we didn't have any appetite to lose. John put him on speaker.

"Hey man, I just found out there's a fight tonight," Lincoln said, his voice filled with enthusiasm.

"What?" John exploded. "When?"

"I'm just waiting on Creole to pick me up to go somewhere in Hurlock."

"You asshole!" John roared. "You were supposed to let me know way ahead of time."

"Hey man," Lincoln whined. "I just found out. I thought you'd be glad to get the news. I've been wearing my earring since you gave it to me. Man, I don't need this shit."

"Yeah, you do, Lincoln. So shut up. Here's how this is going to go down. I want to know where you go tonight. I doubt if there'll be an exact address, but get the roads and cross streets as you go. You film every detail. Every person. Every dog. Kind of like I was THERE!" he shouted. "Then get your ass home after the fight, upload the video into your computer and send it to me. I will call you when I get it so we can all watch together. And you can do a running commentary. Shit, you can be the fucking John Madden of dog fighting."

I thought I heard Lincoln whimper, at least I hoped so.

"And," John added, "you better never let this happen again. I'll snatch you off the streets so fast you won't know how you got back to jail. I want to know when the next fight is days before. Not minutes. Fighters have to be readied; people have to travel. I know the word goes out several days ahead of the fights. You better lock in on those in the know."

John angrily pressed the End button. I managed to wait until he calmed down a bit before I spoke.

"Asshole," I spat, and couldn't stop myself from asking though I knew the answer, "We could have had Jefferson Brown, his crew and his dogs tonight?"

"Yeah, if Lincoln wasn't such a fuck up. But it shouldn't be much longer. At least the fights are up and running again. We knew waiting was a risk. But we're getting close."

We arrived home and immediately took out our dogs. John and I held hands and tried to pretend we were doing anything but waiting. We came back in the house. I looked at the clock. It was too late to call the Everetts to tell them the good news – that Ella was a descendent of Benji's so he was alive in the genes of their pups. I would call them in the morning. I tried to lock onto that happy thought, but it dissipated in the miasma of my anxiety.

John and I waited for three excruciating hours. We tried watching television, reading and playing cards. Time dragged no matter what we did. We were sprawling on one of the couches, staring into the fire, when John's phone finally vibrated. We both sat straight up. John listened and then turned on his computer.

Once he finished downloading the file Lincoln sent onto a flash drive and placed it in the television, he called Lincoln and told him to start the video. John began at the same time. It was time for "The Lincoln Show," which he would narrate.

The opening shot showed the warehouse where the fight was being held. People loitered around the outside of the nondescript cinderblock building where the double doors were swung open. Two humongous guys stood on each side of it, both wearing matching black windbreakers and holding TEC-9s. They frisked every arrival and confiscated all the phones, dropping them into a box near the doorway. No one was allowed to photograph the fights. Too many YouTube videos had previously led to way too much trouble.

"Where were you?" John asked.

"A couple miles past East Main on Route 307, in Hurlock. I don't know nothing else. I wasn't doing the driving, just the drinking."

"Just go on," John said, his distaste for Lincoln flashed across his face and pulled his lips into a snarl.

"That's Creole," Lincoln said, forgetting we had met him at Jugs. Lincoln turned his head a bit to capture his friend handing over his cellphone to the guards at the door.

Lincoln headed through the doorway and entered the warehouse. His overview showed the milling crowds, a few dogs and, behind them, the warehouse windows, which were blacked out like London during the Blitz. Lincoln was proving to be the Martin Scorsese of dog fighting.

He keyed in on the skinny black guy from Jugs, whose life of death and drugs lined his malevolent face.

"That shithead is Ghost," Lincoln nearly whispered, again forgetting we were already familiar with him from his first video. "And that beige-and-white female is one of his top fighting dogs. I saw that bitch fight a while back. She lasted for three hours and made me a bundle."

"Shut the fuck up, Lincoln," John said. "Identify people and dogs. No other comments."

"See the guy standing to the right of Ghost?" Lincoln asked.

"The white guy?" John said, looking at a 30-something man with colorful neck tattoos and major diamond studs in both ears. He had a crowd around him.

"Yeah, that's Paul Salvatore," Lincoln said. "He was a Philly boy, but moved to Baltimore a year ago. Got into the game big time. He had a couple of dogs fighting tonight."

"How'd they do?" I asked, trying to sound nonchalant. I wanted to know how much of the business Salvatore had taken over, but was careful not to sound too interested.

"Man, that dude is moving up fast," he answered, his voice filled with admiration. "He's got lots of money and buys lots of dogs. His black-and-white male ate up Ghost's cousin's dog in less than two minutes. There's talk Salvatore's trying to set up a fight with one of his pits against Diaz's tan male, The Rock. I can't wait...." Lincoln stopped in mid-sentence. It seemed even he was learning when to stop talking.

"Speak of the devil." Lincoln allowed himself a laugh. "That's the white boy's dog, named Doc, which you're looking at now. And what's left of Diaz's dog. Man, someone just threw that dead dog out of the ring and I almost fell over him. Diaz was pissed. He left the fight before it was over. No one saw him for the rest of the night.

"There, you can see the dog in this shot," Lincoln continued. "I told them I could sue them if I tripped over it and got hurt. Everyone thought that was pretty funny." Lincoln's jarring *cinema vérité* showed a different pair of Brown's black-jacketed enforcers holding the dog by its legs and throwing it against the wall. "I was getting dizzy moving my head around to get all these shots."

"Enough," John warned, standing up and walking behind the couch. He rested his hands on my shoulders and began kneading the muscles that were twisting in rebellion at watching the video.

Next, two dogs entered the fighting area. They were brought to the scales and weighed before being washed by their handlers. In the past, dogs had been covered in poison in the hopes that it would kill their opponents when they bit down. Hence the hosing.

"That's Ghost's dog, right?" I asked. "So who's the other one?"

"The brindle is Salvatore's. Oh man, this was the fight of the...."

He didn't need to be told to shut up this time either.

I knew what was coming and forced myself to watch. The dogs were placed in opposite corners of the pit behind the "scratch line," diagonal lines drawn in front of each corner. They were held behind them, eyes fixed on each other, until the referee ordered the handlers to release them. The dogs collided in the center of the pit and the fight was on until one dog "turned," as in literally turned away and stopped attacking.

At that point, the dogs would be separated, returned to their handlers and dragged behind the scratch lines again. The dog that turned is given the chance to attack his opponent while the other one is held in his corner. If it attacks, the other dog is released and the fight continues. This goes on and on until one or both dogs turn and refuse to fight, or a dog gives up, dies or jumps out of the pit. Fights can be as short as minutes or as long as hours. The longest fight on record was more than five hours and took place in Colorado.

This fight went on forever. But to me, a minute is forever when watching such cruelty. The dogs were hanging on each other, teeth buried in flesh. The crowd leaned in, cheering for the winner or laughing at the flailing loser. The fight ended with Ghost's dog lying down, unable to continue. He was dragged out of the pit and Lincoln captured the dog lying down, dazed, torn up and bloodied.

I was glad when Lincoln turned his attention and the camera away from the carnage and began shooting the crowd. He walked up to a betting area manned by two more large guys in black jackets, one of them taking cash, the other handing out chits.

He continued filming this cast of hundreds, also taking in the women who were cooking ribs and chicken in a makeshift kitchen, and their young children playing nearby. Teenagers were running the food to the crowd and taking the money to a barrel-shaped woman who was piling it up in a large metal box. Bottles of beer and pints of booze were being sold at extravagant markups at another table, while drugs changed hands with more subtlety. Lincoln captured it all.

There was a weird, frightening normalcy surrounding the savagery of the fighting dogs and cheering, jeering people. Except that wherever money was collected, there were guys wearing black windbreakers that had bulging pockets that, John pointed out, would probably be more TEC-9s.

I was starting to breathe easy, figuring the horror show was ending. I was wrong. Lincoln turned his camera towards Ghost's defeated dog, which was still down.

"Who's the guy in the hoodie with the tan-and-white pit bull?" John asked.

"That's Ghost's nephew."

He was a skinny teenager who looked like a younger but-not-nicer version of Ghost. Suddenly Ghost came into view. The dog struggled to sit up and looked at him. Ghost lifted his dog's head, tilted it back and slit its throat with his knife and smiled as his dog fell on its side and died. Then he bent over and wiped the blade on the dog's fur.

"People was talking," Lincoln said. "Ghost was fucked up out of his mind. He had raised that dog since it was a pup. Man, that was cold, even for the fight game. I never seen nothing like that before. Man, he don't fuck around. He learned it all from Diaz. Check this out," he said proudly.

Lincoln had turned his camera from the dead to the living, providing a panorama of the crowd. He worked his way across the fighting pit to the audience, finally landing on Jefferson Brown, flanked by the

Rivera twins. They had the only seats in the house – and, of course, the best view of the bloodshed. Although he looked directly at Lincoln, Brown didn't acknowledge him.

"That was the last fight," Lincoln said. "People started leaving and I didn't want to be noticed hanging around. Creole said a few words to Ghost, but I didn't want to get near him. Not after I watched him with that knife. Ya know, I think I might be moving on. This life is getting too dangerous."

"Lincoln, I don't care where you go," John said coldly. "I just care about when. You finish this job and we'll talk about getting you some get-out-of-town cash." He added, his voice low and threatening: "You seem to be a part of the fight scene in Hurlock, so don't you ever pull this shit again. I don't believe for a second you didn't know this fight was happening. When the next one rolls around, you better be damn sure we have the info on it well in advance. You get that, shithead? 'Cause you ain't getting another pass from me if you don't."

"Hey, I did everything you wanted," he said, his voice returning to his unpleasant whine. "You don't need to be such a hard ass. I'm putting my life on the line for you."

"No, Lincoln, I'm putting your life on the line."

THIRTY-SIX

IT WAS SO BEYOND OUR bedtime that John and I staggered up the stairs and fell on the bed. He stretched out on top of it, tucking his hands behind his head, and stared up at the ceiling. I sat cross-legged and stunned. I wiped the tears out of my eyes.

"Let's put a plan in place so I can get some sleep tonight," I grumbled, miserable and exhausted. I straightened my legs and pulled myself over them by wrapping my hands around my feet. I flattened my rib cage onto my thighs, chest to shins, and rested my forehead on my ankles, stretching out my aching back. John put his broad hand on the middle of it and massaged his way up to my shoulders.

"I'm going to call Jackie before I send her Lincoln's video to prepare her for it," I decided.

"What?" he asked. "I can't hear you. You're talking to your feet."

"Oh." I used my arms to lift me up to a 90-degree angle and repeated the information I had just confided to my ankles. Then I stood up, stripped and grabbed a long-sleeve T and a pair of flannel drawstring bottoms and pulled them on. The bedroom temperature was dropping into our sleep zone – think hibernating. John removed his jeans and shirt, a man of few clothes, and slid into bed where the warmth of his body met me under the covers.

"I'll call Garrison and see when we can meet up," he said, rolling on his side so he faced me. I stroked the hair that fell across his left eye and saw a few new grey flecks. "You have anything planned for Sunday?"

"No," I said, making room for Ella who had discovered the delights of human beds. She was allowed cuddle time before being relegated to her cushy bed on the opposite side of the bedroom door from Duke. That was John's training – keep your dogs separated in case of intruders. Who knew if Ella would ever have a protective bone in her battered body? We didn't care. We trained her like she was a "normal" dog, and loved her like she wasn't.

"I was also hoping you could ViCAP the new name Barbara supplied. I'll start putting a doggie DNA chart together." I had to stop talking. My eyes were filling with tears. I couldn't stop seeing the fighting dog. "Oh Jesus, John, that was awful."

Without a word he pulled me toward him and held me until I was able to fall asleep.

The next day was a testament to climate change. The snow had been baked away by a sun that pushed the thermometer north of 70 degrees. Weird. John and I had a lazy breakfast and a long walk with the dogs before we began our pre-assigned tasks.

I went into my small office that had a simple mahogany desk and a comfy, ergonomically correct chair, a huge potted palm to the side of a narrow floor-to-ceiling window with a chair next to it. I didn't need much space since I had the lab down the road. I put my feet up and called Jackie.

"Tell me we're going to work, please," she begged. "My one day in Fort Howard made me realize how much I miss the daily grind. I was born to be a detective. How did I become a housewife?"

"You married and had a child," I reminded her. "But you can take off your housecoat and turn on your computer. Poof. You're an investigator again. Lincoln called us last night to inform us the Friday night fights were back on."

"As in last night?" Jackie's voice rose. "You're telling me he knew there was a fight and he went and gave us no time to put a raid together?"

"Exactly. The asshole called John while he was waiting for Creole to pick him up and take him to Hurlock. I think the only reason John didn't spend the entire night planning his death is that the video was really good. But not in a good way," I warned.

"Just send it," Jackie said sounding more resigned than excited now. "I'll call you back after I watch it and can talk without sobbing."

I waited until the end of our conversation to drop the other bomb. I pushed back in my chair and allowed my feet to hit the floor so I was sitting upright. That was when I told her Benji was Ella's sire.

"Wow!" she said, and I could imagine her large brown eyes growing even bigger. "She must take after her mother."

"Don't be mean," I said, but smiled because I had had the same thought. "Jackie, all I keep thinking is how did she end up at the shelter and not hanging from a tree?

"I'm looking forward to asking Jefferson Brown about that, which brings me to the other reason for this call. John is contacting Cletus, 'Don't ever call him Cletus,' Garrison, his favorite undercover cop, to come for brunch tomorrow. He's supposed to hang out with Lincoln and, hopefully, go to the next fight with him. Anyway, can you, Housewife of Annapolis, make it?"

"Are you kidding? I'm on my way now."

"In that case drive slow, real slow."

Conversation over, I stood up just as John appeared in the doorway. It was nice to be together. I cynically figured we'd remain a couple forever since we spent so much time apart. I knew that was part of my unwillingness to have a child. I wasn't finding marriage so outlandish anymore, but I questioned spending all that "family time" having a baby would demand. Then I noted I had been giving this a lot of thought lately. I put it aside and wrapped my arms around John's neck.

"Hmmm," I sighed as I put my lips up to his ear and exhaled, "I love you."

Twenty-five minutes later were still entwined, but now we were on the floor.

"Oh, by the way, Jackie can make it tomorrow," I said, when my breath and brain returned to functioning.

"Garrison, too," he said, pulling on his pants and then extending a hand to pull me up. I took it. "I'm starving."

"Me, too," I said. "I'll turn on the oven and heat up the leftover Eggplant Parmesan. Salad?"

"Sure. I'll start it. Why don't we eat outside?"

"Sounds good. Strange, but good."

I went outside into the balmy day and cleaned off the teak patio table, grabbed a few chair cushions from the shed and put them out. John tossed the salad while the eggplant warmed. I went back inside for a couple of beers and John carried out our plates. The dogs ran in joyous circles and the cats begged for food, even Daisy. I helped her on the seat next to me that was in the sunshine.

After we ate, John and I cleared the table and brought out our iPads. If the trees hadn't been stripped of their leaves and the grass hadn't turned a greyish-brown, I would have sworn it was springtime.

"Give me the new name again that Montrose gave you yesterday and I'll pull his jacket," John said.

"Tyndall Garcia-Lopez from Philadelphia."

He pulled up several screens at a time and scrolled through each one. Every so often he would jot down notes on a pad. His foot was tapping to some internal biorhythm, and his brow furrowed in increasing concentration.

"Boom, got it!" he said. "Here goes: as we know Jefferson Brown was essentially the first born and baddest of the bunch. He crawled his way to the top of the drug, guns and dog heap. The big three of quick cash. He was busted at his house on a gunrunning charge more than twenty years ago. Arnie Diaz was with him at the time and let go. Brown made bail and later beat the rap. Of course.

"Enter Tyndall Garcia-Lopez, but not permanently," John continued, leaning back in his chair. "He was picked up at the same time and also released. He would go back and forth to Philadelphia. His known associates are the Hurlock contingent and Diaz. Diaz, in turn, has been busted with Garcia-Lopez and Salvatore in Philadelphia, but that was years ago. This is where it gets interesting: Garcia-Lopez's sister is Belinda Marquez, who lives with Jorge Rivera in Cambridge."

"Oh God, no," I added and felt my skin crawl. "These horrible people are interbreeding? Please let them all be sterile."

"Honey," John said, looking amused, "when you dream you sure dream big."

THIRTY-SEVEN

—⊸⊶⊷⊷⊶⊸—

It was high noon on Sunday. Jackie and Garrison were sitting on stools at the kitchen counter. Jackie looked all new and shiny. Her hair gleamed and her eyes sparkled. She had even polished her nails. I guess she really was a bored housewife. She was wearing a white linen button-down shirt, black jeans and snuggly boots. Jackie was back and I was glad.

Garrison was smiling at Ella. She had sidled up to him for a pet. He obliged. His smile revealed his perfect bell-shaped teeth. I had a thing about teeth, maybe because braces hadn't redirected my own crooked tooth during my teen years.

He was nothing like I expected. Garrison brought us a lovely bunch of deep purple irises, a good Cabernet, and charmed me with an easy smile and warm handshake and a man-hug for John, who didn't recoil. He was tall, rangy but muscular, and bi-racial. His copper-colored skin had a burnished tone of a Rolls Royce's wooden dashboard. His shaved head reflected the sun that had stuck around for the weekend. I could tell from the way Jackie sneaked a peek that she, too, was surprised. Garrison was just plain handsome. Even in his dirty undercover persona, I suspected he'd be pretty good-looking.

"Jesus, Garrison," John said, giving him a hard stare. "So that's what's under your disgusting stocking cap, straggly beard and filthy clothes. Look at you, all citified and wearing Weejuns. I only know that because Allison, my preppy girlfriend, has a pair. How'd you know about them?"

"Reading fashion magazines that people throw in the trash can where I live," Garrison joked, I think. John had called him an enigma wrapped in a dirty newspaper. I was beginning to understand.

"Hell, I had to shave. It's how I keep the lice under control," he said, adding with a laugh and rubbed his chin, "Just kidding."

John and I were on the other side of the counter putting the finishing touches on breakfast. He opened the oven door to take out the herb frittata we had made together. I hip-checked him, moving him over so I could rescue the egg twist loaf from over-browning.

I had woken up early and couldn't get back to sleep, so I started baking at sunrise. Caffeine had fueled my kitchen creativity for hours. Now everyone was drinking coffee except for me. My hands were shaking too much to hold the cup.

"Hey, Garrison, would you take the coffee to the table? Jackie, take this please," I said, passing the platter of eggs over the counter to her. She, in turn, took it and headed towards the dining room. John left the kitchen with a heaping plateful of bacon and followed Jackie. Garrison followed the meat with his gaze first and then his body. I handed off a pitcher of fresh orange juice to John, who had returned to the kitchen and was standing in the doorway waiting. I grabbed the braided bread and walked it to the table.

"Did you make that?" Jackie asked. I nodded. "I'm so glad we're eating first. This way, I don't have to drink my brunch."

We smiled, knowing exactly what she meant. We were all seasoned to the harsher aspects of life, but none of us wanted to bring it to the breakfast table. There would be time later. I sliced several pieces of bread and sent the cutting board around the table. The omelet and bacon were already circling. I sat down and said, "No business until we finish. Agreed?"

Everyone mumbled their assent through full mouths. No one wanted to do much talking about anything. John went so far as to turn on a football game in the living room. Though he muted the sound, he could still see it from his seat.

We finished the meal and took our mugs into the living room. I followed with a warmed coffee cake that I didn't have to make. Thank God for good bakeries. I put it down on the long glass coffee table, and returned to the kitchen to retrieve a fresh pot of coffee. I refilled everyone's mug and then landed on the couch beside John and facing Jackie.

Garrison waited until I sat down to throw out the first question. It was all business now.

"Where're you at on this?" he asked John, crossing his legs, and massaged his knee with long tapering fingers whose tips disappeared into the fabric of his charcoal grey twill slacks. He noticed my gaze and said, "Gunshot."

"Bullshit," John laughed.

"Jesus, I forgot how annoying you can be," Garrison said with a slow smile that showed off those perfect teeth. "Anyhow, bullet just seems so much more romantic than arthritis. And fitting with this group. But never mind. Just tell me what's going on."

"I did the paperwork for the warrants yesterday," John answered, taking his eyes off the television to give Garrison his full attention, despite the fact that the Steelers were about to punt. "I should be able to pick them up tomorrow. No big hurry, since they always seem to hold the fights on a Friday night, but we'll be ready if anything changes."

"So what's my job? As if I couldn't figure it out," he added, his expression turning sour.

"Well, if you're thinking you'll be hanging out with our talented cinematographer, you'd be right," I said, which caused him to chuckle.

"Yeah, but I call him 'our douchebag snitch,'" John said, crossing his leg so his ankle rested on top of his knee. "After an hour with him, you'll probably be ready to get back to your trash can. Especially since you are about to become his long lost best friend. I don't envy you. You start by hanging out with him at Jugs, the neighborhood dive. Ingratiate yourself. You know the drill. You need to become a familiar face so you can get into the next fight."

"Pretty much what I thought it would be. You want to hook me up with Lincoln tonight? I can funk myself up pretty good by then. Call Lincoln and tell him I'll be in touch this afternoon."

"You got it," John said, looking a bit relieved. Suddenly it dawned on me that he was as concerned as I was about leaving the dogs at Brown's. "And remember, I want all the information, anything we uncover, kept on this side of the bridge. I noted numerous raids out of Baltimore County that didn't pan out. All the info was good, but no one was home when the troops arrived. That's pretty strange. Makes me think leak.

"Can you ask around?" he continued talking to Garrison. "Maybe somebody you know knows something. I spoke to Andrews and he agrees with this cloak-and-dagger shit. Hell, we're not even going to tell our guys about the raid until it's underway."

Jackie leaned forward and put down her coffee mug, but she kept her plate on her lap, starting on her second piece of cake. I had noticed she had put on a few pounds, which I thought looked good and healthy. She surreptitiously opened the button of her jeans. I couldn't help myself. I smiled. She caught me in the act and, with even more stealth, gave me the finger – for a change.

"It's a long shot," added Jackie, "but some of my rescue and shelter contacts may have heard something. Many of them are put on notice when a raid is going down. John, how about you get me a list of the raids that failed and I'll cross-check the names involved in each one?"

"Good idea," John said. "Allison?"

"Jackie and I will bring the Mobile Unit so we can start triage, which I'm pretty sure will be necessary," I said, and stood up. I was a pacer when given the room. I walked to the wall of glass at the end of the living room and went back and forth to the table while I discussed our plan. "We'll also have local shelter staffs, vets and Animal Control on site. That way, they'll have vehicles to transport the dogs after I examine them."

"You're going to cut out the Cambridge shelter completely?" John asked. I could see he was enjoying the thought of not giving Michelle Manning any chance of looking like a savior. He slouched back into the couch and stretched his legs under the table.

I felt a smile crease its way up my face and crinkle the corners of my eyes. I said in the softest voice, "Screw Manning and her photo ops."

Jackie beamed her approval. John waved his hand at Garrison, dismissing the topic with, "It's a long story."

"Anyway, I'm charting dogs and owners with Barbara Montrose, who heads up Canine CODIS, which is the doggie DNA data bank," I explained to Garrison. "I'll send out what I have tomorrow. Barbara emailed me that she might have some DNA info in the next 24 hours on the dog that was killed with Stanton.

"The interchangeable dog owners are Jefferson Brown, maybe Antonio and Jorge Rivera from Cambridge, definitely Charm City buddies Arnie Diaz and Paul Salvatore, and Philadelphia's Tyndall Garcia-Lopez. Oh, and our very own Eastern Shore shithead, Ghost."

"I know Brown and his Baltimore boys from their drug trading/gun running days," Garrison said, interlacing his fingers into fist, looking as if he wished he was squeezing their necks. "I'm glad someone killed Stanton, even if it wasn't me."

"Or me," John said. "But you can have the pick of the litter of the rest of them. Wait, I take that back. I want Jefferson Brown."

Garrison snorted. "No way! I've been after him for years. You take the Rivera twins. That way you get a twofer. And they are on your home turf. You know that's fair."

"Not having it," John said, creepily sounding like Dana Carvey's Church Lady.

"Well, I'd like to put in a bid for Ghost," Jackie said, and raised her hand enthusiastically.

"Stop it," I ordered. "No divvying up the bad guys. First we have to catch them. Then you can kill them. I'm joking. But seriously, please let's get them at the beginning of the night before any dogs have to fight. I feel bad enough about the ones we left behind at Brown's."

"I'll get tech to put a transmitter in my collar," said Garrison. "I'm sure I'll be searched when I get there but I'll turn it off in case they 'wand' me. I'll turn it back on as soon as I pass inspection so I can contact command central when the fight begins. Then it's up to you to kick it into gear."

John added thoughtfully, "If for some reason our main targets aren't in attendance, we pull the plug and come back another night. Agreed?"

We all nodded our heads reluctantly. I refused to even consider that possibility.

"Just remember," Jackie warned. "I'll never give up the Ghost."

THIRTY-EIGHT

——⁕——

I WAS SPRAWLED ACROSS THE couch with my computer on my lap, staring out the living room's glass wall. Spring had ended after a brief, weird 24 hours. I was mesmerized by the snowflakes lazily drifting sideways instead of downward. Perhaps the weekend's unnaturally warm temperatures had slowed them down. They seemed to lack the energy to reach the ground.

I was fighting off the Monday morning blues, while somewhat grudgingly reading the *New York Times* online and stroking Daisy, who was nestled against my hip. Since I moved down here, I had to wean myself from newsprint. Some Sundays, John and I would go to the Hyatt Resort in Cambridge to have brunch and pick up a "real" *Times*. But this was Monday.

I was waiting for Barbara's call. She had emailed me last night that she was expecting the DNA results on the hypothermia pit bull to be on her desk when she arrived on Monday. Taking into account the three-hour time difference between our coasts, the earliest I expected to hear from her was 11. I still had an hour to kill.

The sun was pushing its way out of the clouds, and the river was beginning to sparkle. Ella was standing at the door with what I thought was perfect timing. I put on our respective coats and we went for a brisk, in every sense of the word, walk. She was effortlessly trotting alongside me and broke into a run when she saw a squirrel. I let her go several yards before I called to her. She instantly returned to my side. My girl was healthy.

We raced back to the house; I let her win. Once inside, I hung up our coats. For some reason I found myself fixating on the small white patch on her chest. It jogged something in my brain.

I couldn't get to my computer fast enough. I opened Lincoln's latest video and began watching. It wasn't as hard to view this time since I was looking for something specific. I finally found it. I actually gasped. Not at the part where Ghost slit his dog's throat. I was too busy staring at the tan-and-white dog sitting in a crate behind Ghost. I already knew the skinny teenager in the hoodie standing next to it was his nephew.

I zoomed in on the dog. It was a female, but I was much more interested in the huge patch of white across her chest that reminded me of a map of the United States. I felt all shivery. I had seen a similar marking before, but I had no idea where.

I framed the shot and printed it out. I then shifted my focus to the guy in the hoodie and turned him into a photograph. I sent the dog picture to Jackie with the caption: "Do you know this dog?"

I was staring intently at the pit bull when my phone rang. It startled me. I had forgotten all about Barbara's call.

"Once again the name of Arnold Diaz comes across my computer screen," she said instead of hello. "I traced your hypothermia brindle pit bull's DNA back to a female who was confiscated from him five years ago. And Big Deal, a brindle male who was taken from Stephan Dupres a.k.a. Ghost at the same time. I checked the records and neither Diaz or Dupres were brought up on charges.

"That's no crazier than what's been going on here and in Baltimore County. Who would want to kill a dog Diaz and Ghost had bred? And kill Stanton? Damn it. I don't get it."

"Just keep the DNA coming," Barbara said. "I'm now invested in your mystery."

"Thanks," I said. "There is one more thing. Can you email me the names of the agencies that sent you the DNA samples of dogs that weren't attached to people? In other words, discarded or dead dogs that had no known owners."

"You'll have it this afternoon at the latest."

"You're the best," I said simply. I wasn't sure if she heard me before she disconnected.

I returned to staring at the dog's chest, willing my brain to make the connection. I started speeding through mental images. I revisited the raids I had been on and the live animals I had examined at them. Nothing. Then I thought about pit bulls I had examined over the years. I moved my mind to shelters and rescues where I often volunteered my services. That was when I finally put dog to .place.

"Oh, my God," I shouted out loud and smacked my thigh so hard near where the Rottweiler bit me, it made me yelp. I had seen that dog or one just like it at the Cambridge shelter. It was several years ago when Michelle Manning first took over as president of the board of directors. I speed dialed Helen's personal phone.

"Hey, Allison," she said. You just can't sneak up on anybody anymore.

"Helen, I need to talk to you," I said, hearing my own sense of urgency. She picked up on it.

"Sounds serious. What's going on?"

"Can you come to my house?" I said. "Have you had lunch yet? I'll feed you."

"In that case, I'll be there in about half-an-hour," she said.

I called Jackie next and told her about the dogs Barbara had mentioned, my own discovery, and the call I had placed to Helen. I explained how I purposely didn't mention the map dog. I wanted to see if Helen recognized it without my input.

"What can I do?"

"Would you look through your files, and anyone else's you can access, and see if you can find photos of the dogs Barbara mentioned? There's a chance we might recognize them. By the way, she's going to send us the names of the agencies that forwarded the information to her this afternoon."

"I'm on it," Jackie said.

Next I called John. I told him about recognizing the dog from the Cambridge shelter and Helen's imminent arrival. He asked which one.

"Remember when Ghost slit his dog's throat? Like you could forget," I said, nearly gagging over the question. "His nephew was standing right behind him next to a crate with a tan-and-white dog. That's the one I'm referring to."

I was up and pacing. I stopped in front of the fireplace and stirred the logs. I dropped another one on the fire. It immediately crackled as the flames encircled it. I looked out the living room windows to see snowflakes falling with a new-found determination.

"Helen should be here in a few minutes. I'm feeding her our dinner, so call me before you come home. Maybe you could pick up something?"

"Sure."

By now, I was in the kitchen, staring into the refrigerator. There was a bowl of minestrone that Gina had dropped off last night when she and Vernon came for dinner. We often swapped food. I took it out and transferred it to a pot and put it on the stove. I pulled a salad together, whipped up a sesame oil dressing, and set it to the side. Yesterday's braided bread reappeared on the table. I put a cheese plate together and lunch was complete.

As Helen's navy SUV pulled into the driveway, I turned the heat on under the soup and stood in the open doorway with Ella. We hugged our hellos. Helen, the unflappable, actually squealed when she saw the girl. She dropped to her knees and cuddled Ella, who was doing her happy dance.

Helen stood up and stomped her feet on the doormat and shook off any loose snow. She began to take her boots off before she came in the house and I told her not to bother. The dogs never did.

"What's going on?" she asked, peering at me with a look I swear she borrowed from Miss Marple.

"A lot, I hope," I said.

THIRTY-NINE

—∞∞∞—

I SWORE HELEN TO SECRECY over a bowl of soup. She crossed her heart, located somewhere behind her ample breasts, and stared at me with a seriousness I found reassuring. We were sitting opposite each other at the dining room table. I could see dread mingled with curiosity flash across her deep-set brown eyes.

I had planned to wait until we finished eating to talk business, but I felt like I was just prolonging her anxiety. So I told her only what she needed to know: A CI had attended a dog fight and I had a video of the event. I wanted her to look at it and see if she recognized any of the dogs. She looked puzzled and continued slathering a piece of bread with butter.

"Finish lunch and I'll put on the video," I said.

"How 'bout I eat while I watch?"

"If you can," I said, and shrugged. "Follow me."

I walked her into the living room and put her salad plate on the coffee table next to the bowl she brought with her. I had already lost my appetite, because I knew what was coming. I positioned Helen so she was sitting on the sofa nearest the kitchen that faced the 60-inch flat screen TV.

I took the flash drive that John had previously downloaded from Lincoln's video, and slipped it into the TV's USB port. I turned on the set, imported the video and hit the Play button. It came on ugly and large. I watched it on the big screen and it sucked the oxygen out of me.

Helen sat silently, her hand over her mouth. Suddenly she emitted a low moan. We were watching the two security thugs lift the dead dog and throw it against the wall.

"Stop! Go back!" she ordered, looking stricken. I hit reverse and pause so we could see the dog being held upside down by its legs.

"Oh, my God, Allison," Helen gasped. I could see her fingers dig deep into her thighs and her shoulders sag. "I swear that's Petey Jr. He has the black ring around his eye, but look at his tail. It has a black tip and a double black circle at its base. I'd never seen those markings before or since. He was confiscated in a raid. I worked with him for a few weeks, and he was really coming around. He loved everyone. I was so happy when I heard he was sent to a pit bull rescue."

"What do you mean he was sent? Where were you?"

"I had taken off for a month when my husband had a heart attack." Helen stopped talking and I knew she was struggling not to cry.

Her eyes were wet with tears that made them glisten. She blinked rapidly to contain them. But she was a tough broad and pulled herself together.

"You looked surprised." I had my guard down; usually I wasn't such an easy read. She studied my face and astutely added, "So Petey Jr. isn't the dog you had in mind, huh?"

"You're right," I admitted. "When was he at the shelter?"

"Nearly three years ago or so. Right around the time you stopped coming."

I stood up and walked over to my laptop, which was on the other end of the coffee table. I returned to the couch, opened the computer and started making notes about Petey Jr. I picked up the remote, looked at Helen, who gave me a go-ahead nod, and the video proceeded, until she yelled, "Stop!"

We were looking at the tan-and-white female with the map of the U.S. emblazoned across her chest.

"You remembered her, didn't you?" she said, staring at me and trying to judge my reaction. "That's why you wanted me to watch this."

"America! That's what you named her," I recalled suddenly and stood up to pace. I was enraged. I didn't even want to look at Helen. I could imagine her pain. She had cared for these dogs, and thought they had been saved.

"Allison, what the hell is going on? How could these dogs end up fighting? We were always so careful with our pit bulls. I know the Sheriff and Animal Control are, too."

"Helen, I have no idea, but we will find out. This is what Jackie and I do." I gave Helen's hand a squeeze. Her fingers were so tensed up they looked like a talons. They didn't relax under my caring pressure.

She picked out one more dog, a brindle male she had named Jackson. We had to watch him fight and win, but at a terrible cost. He, too, had been at the shelter after I had stopped volunteering, and before the board put a moratorium on pit bulls.

"Well, Allison, that was truly awful. You won't find me rude if I don't thank you for lunch," she added, looking disheartened. "I'm going back to the shelter and check the files on the three dogs. I'll call you as soon as I can."

She stood and wrapped her navy cardigan around her chest and kept her arms crossed in the defensive posture she so often employed. We walked to the front door and she only uncrossed her arms when she had to put them into her coat sleeves. We gave each other a supportive hug, before she gave Ella a goodbye kiss.

"At least we know where you are," she murmured into her ear so softly I almost missed it.

"I'm going to edit a photograph of each dog from the video so Jackie can send them to her sources and find out if anybody recognizes them." I told her. "I wonder if any other shelters are involved in this thievery."

"Let's find out. Soon!" Helen said, disappearing into her car and driving off.

As soon as she left, I called Jackie. I told her about America, Petey Jr. and Jackson. They had all been residents of the Cambridge shelter. She, too, was stunned.

"Why don't I pull individual shots of each dog?" Jackie asked. "I'll send them to the area shelters and rescues, and see if anyone recognizes them."

"Wow, we are the same person," I said. "I was just about to start doing that, but go ahead. This is so your bailiwick."

Once the call ended, I took a long, deep breath and unrolled my yoga mat in front of the fire. It was catnip for Tom. He immediately started kneading it until I shooed him off. Ella lay down next to it and soon Daisy joined her. They were forming a girls' alliance. Or, more precisely, we were.

After an hour, I felt stretched, energized and relaxed. I went upstairs and grabbed my book off the night table, Phillip Kerr's *March Violets*, a murder mystery set in Nazi Germany, and then went downstairs. After I tended the fire, I turned on the lights and lay down on the couch. Ella climbed up next to me. I stared at her burn marks and found myself wondering for the umpteenth time about the deep sickness inside people that found its relief, if not joy, in hurting and maiming animals. I doubted if I'd ever find the answer to the "why," which depressed me even more. How can you prevent something you don't understand?

The phone rang. It was John.

"Hi, hon, I'm leaving in ten," he said cheerfully. It was the end of his workday. He was always happy about that. "I'll pick up dinner. What do you want?"

"Pizza and Coke," I ordered.

"What do you want on your half?"

"No halves tonight. I want pepperoni and lots of it. And Coke."

"That's not a good sign," he sighed.

"I know," I said, my voice choking on the words. "I'm having a pepperoni depression and that ain't good."

FORTY

THE SUN WENT DOWN, THE barometer dropped and my spirits sank even lower. I was lying on the couch wrapped in a quilt with Ella pressed against my feet and Daisy draped across my midriff. Tom, his independent self, was sleeping on the ottoman. I hadn't bothered to turn on the lights. The room's only illumination came from the dying flames of the depleted logs.

Helen had called a couple of hours earlier. She was so upset she could barely get the words out. She had looked for the records of America, Jackson and Petey Jr., and there were none. They had all been deleted. She had no idea how that was possible. Then she repeated the gut-wrenching question that I had been asking myself: How many other dogs had disappeared? And from how many other shelters? That's what had laid me flat on my back.

Ella heard John's car before I did, jumped up and waited in the kitchen at the door to the garage. At least I think she did; she disappeared into the darkness. I heard the rumblings of the garage door opening and made the supreme effort to sit up.

The kitchen light went on and I blinked with its brightness. John stood there for a second and bent down to greet Ella. Duke trotted into the living room to check me out.

"Allison?" John called, squinting into the darkness until he made out Duke standing next to me. "Oh, there you are," and quickly walked towards us. "Should I use my flashlight or may I turn on a light?"

Without waiting for an answer, he flipped the lamp switch. He tried to hide his surprise when he saw me. "Honey, are you okay?"

"Not really. I mean, I'm okay, but...." Words failed me. John nudged me over so he could sit down beside me.

"I'm glad you're home," I said, and ran my fingers through his hair and stroked the side of his face. I kissed him. He almost always made me feel better. I looked at his uniform, taking in the insignias on his sleeves, the empty holster at his hip and thought how far I had come from my black cashmere sweater and cultured pearls upbringing.

We just sat quietly for a while until he stood up to rescue the fire. I couldn't stand it.

"Everything sucks," I bemoaned. "Dogs we rescued are being returned to the fighting pit. The bad guys are winning, and they always will. And I killed that poor dog. I don't know how to forgive myself."

"At least they found the prick who sicced him on you. You'll help put him in prison. Now isn't that a happy thought?" John said hopefully.

I shrugged and told him I needed a bath more than conversation.

John stood up and tenderly pushed me down when I started to rise. "You stay there," he ordered, walked over to the fire and brought it back to life. "Now I'm going upstairs and draw you a bath, complete with that bath oil you love and I, by transference, have learned to desire."

I looked at John, the hard angles of his sculpted face, his penetrating hawklike eyes and noted the downward turn of his usually impervious mouth. He looked concerned and tired and moved slowly towards the staircase.

"I'll feed Duke and the others while you're upstairs," I said, standing up.

"No, you won't. I can turn on the tub, run down the stairs, feed the guys and get back to turn off the tap before it overflows. I am a multitasker. Why don't you pick out something pretty to put on, or your usual flannel pajamas? How 'bout dinner in bed?"

"That sounds good," I said, feeling loved and a little better. "New plan. I'll start the fire in the bedroom. That way, I can take over bathtub detail so you can pour us both a drink. I'll have mine in the bath, so make it a martini on the rocks, please."

I could see a bit of happy returning to John's eyes. We climbed the stairs together, and he insisted on making the fire. I took a left into the bathroom and turned on the bathtub taps. Then I trotted into the bedroom and opened my closet door. I started to reach for a pair of flannel jammies, but decided to dress up a bit. I picked my heavy cotton white nightgown covered with tiny embroidered pink flowers. It reached my ankles, but showed a bit of cleavage.

I was deep in the tub when John arrived with my martini. He put it into my outstretched hand and said, "I fed the dogs and those other four-legged things."

"Cats, dear. They're cats. And we all thank you," I said, taking a long drink and letting it roll around in my mouth before swallowing. "Oh, that's good."

"The oven's preheated, so all I have to do is put in the pizza. I bought an antipasto, also. Let me know when you are five minutes away from tucking yourself under the covers," John said, leaning against the doorframe with his arms casually crossed. He ran his fingers through his hair. "I think my hair is frizzing up from the humidity."

"Jesus," I said. "At least we've dealt with your split-end problem."

My tub time had ended, and I stood up and walked into the bath sheet John held open for me. He wrapped it around me and rubbed me all over. I put my arms around his neck and kissed him. He kissed back. And then pulled away.

"I'll see you in bed after I deliver the pizza. Oh God, I sound like I'm straight out of a porno."

My laugh echoed in the bathroom. John looked relieved and left. I finally looked in the mirror. My lips were pressed together and my jaw bunched like Dick Tracy's, yet again. My laugh lines were nonexistent; I was aging before my very eyes. So I stopped looking. Instead, I put on my pretty nightgown and brushed my hair and my teeth.

John entered holding a large tray with a pepperoni-topped pizza. I had already put up our bed trays. We were not novices when it came to reclining dining.

I pushed the plate away. "God, I must have been near suicidal if I thought eating unidentifiable dead animal parts would make me feel better."

"I'll be right back," John said. He returned in a couple of minutes with a bottle of Coke tucked under his arm, two glasses filled with ice and another dinner plate, which he exchanged for the one on my bed tray.

"I bought a non-pepperoni pizza just in case," he said, looking pleased with himself. I certainly was. I looked at the olive oil swirling on top of the melted cheese and tomato sauce. I sniffed it with giddy pleasure – and ate wholeheartedly.

John flipped on the television and "Monday Night Football" took the place of dinner conversation. The Redskins were playing. In deference to Native American Indians everywhere, I now referred to them as the Washington Rednecks. If the owner didn't want to change the team's name, I would. While John watched the game, I took the dishes downstairs, let the dogs out and cleaned up the kitchen. I was back in time to watch Washington score a touchdown before halftime to tie the game. John muted the television.

"What happened today?" he finally asked. He was looking at me intently.

"Helen recognized two more dogs on the video," I said, hearing my words but not feeling them. "They had been at the shelter after I stopped volunteering there. The dead dog Lincoln almost tripped over? Well, that was Petey Jr., named and cared for by Helen. She has no idea how he ended up fighting again. She also identified America, the dog with the map on her chest. I didn't say anything. Just let the video play. Then she saw a dog she had named Jackson. She's totally freaked. So am I. How many others are out there?"

I threw back the covers so I could get up and start pacing. "It began with Benji going from a pet to the pit. Then watching the training sessions at Brown's and leaving those dogs behind. So what do I do? I go and kill a dog."

"Allison, you've got to stop. Why are you continuing to make yourself feel bad?" John interrupted. "I've never seen you beat yourself up like this. It's crazy."

"I never killed a dog before," I mumbled, feeling awful.

"Babe, come back to bed."

I crawled under the covers.

"Have you ever thought of taking some time off when this case is finished?"

"Why?" I said suspiciously, moving the pillows so I could sit and lean against them.

"Well, we could get married and go on a honeymoon," he said tentatively, an unusual tone for him.

"Oh, my God," I said.

"I'm worried about you," he said, resettling himself so we were now at eye level. "Maybe a break would be good for you. Maybe marriage would be, too. We could stay like this, sure, but maybe there's more. I just want you to think about it."

"Maybe you're right," I said slowly. "Maybe I could use a break. And… maybe more. But you want a baby and I don't."

"Well, I want you more," John said.

For the first time in my life I thought marriage might be a good thing. As a young girl, I never dreamed of having a 'white wedding,' the beautiful gown, the appreciative guests and the momentary sparkle that ended in a life of boredom, depression and probably divorce. I surprised myself thinking about getting married in a positive light, but then again I never thought I could live with anyone else with such comfort and enjoyment. The common denominator was, of course, John. I loved him and found this next step in our relationship somewhat appealing.

"Well, that's better than your usual 'I don't want to talk about it.' I'll take it as an 'it's possible.'"

So formalizing my relationship with John didn't seem so threatening. But children? I always thought I didn't want any. I really loved Michael, who always called me Aunt Ally. He was the only one I'd let shorten my name. He adored being with John and me when Jackie and Thomas went on vacation. But my own? I just wasn't sure. I would have a lot to think about in the light of day. For now, it was enough that blue Monday was drawing to a close.

⎯⎯ ✺ ⎯⎯

FORTY-ONE

THE SKY WAS A CLOUDLESS blue and the unfiltered sun threw a gold glow over Annapolis. I drove past the shimmering State Capitol – so old that Benjamin Franklin oversaw the construction of its lightning rod – on my way to Pickney Street where Jackie lived, just a few blocks from Spa Creek.

I pulled into her driveway, parked behind her silver Prius and stared at her house for a moment. I loved the simplicity of the American Foursquare set in Annapolis's historic district, a land filled with frilly gingerbread Queen Annes and multi-colored, decorative Victorians. I always thought Jackie's boxy brick house, with its barn-red shingles and broad front porch, reflected the sense of order she had established in her life.

Jackie and Michael were standing in the doorway, watching Ella and me walk up the brick path. By the time we reached the porch steps, Michael had launched himself into my outstretched arms. I caught him and he wrapped his legs around my waist.

"Aunt Ally," Michael said with a huge grin hugging his somewhat bucked teeth. Adorable, I quelled inwardly, and carried him up the stairs. He was tall like his dad, with the same hooded eyelids and wide mouth, but he had his mom's solemn, dark brown eyes and bouncing curls.

We had been buddies since we were introduced when he was two. He was over the moon for John and Duke. Both John and I adored him. But as soon as Michael's feet touched earth, he dumped me for Ella, who instantly licked his face.

"How you feeling, hardhead?" I asked Michael, after he and Ella enjoyed a few bonding moments. He leaped up to show me his wound.

"Cool braid," I said, looking at it intensely to see how long the gash actually was. I guessed about two inches. Instead of using sutures, the surgeon had closed the cut on Michael's head by braiding the hair together on both sides of it. "Man, you're lucky braids are in. Yours look great."

Jackie was listening, standing a few feet away. I was amazed she could still look like a teenager. Wearing jeans, Keds and a V-neck sweater, she had captured her own curls into a short, bobbing ponytail. She eyed me with suspicion.

"I'm glad you're here. You sounded awful on the phone and you don't look so good," she said, pushing me away so she could scrutinize me.

"I know," I said. "Every so often, I am reminded I am human."

"Come on in," she invited. "I have my three in the backyard. Ella and Michael can join them so we can talk without interruption. At least for 10 minutes."

Jackie was referring to her dog pack of rescues: mixed breeds, mixed sizes and mixed ages, all victims. Ella fit in perfectly. Jackie bundled up Michael and we all walked into the yard. Once peace reigned, we left Michael in charge.

Jackie poured me a cup of coffee as I looked at the plate of sour cherry scones still emitting whiffs of steam on the countertop. They were her specialty. On the spot, I vowed never to have a partner that didn't bake.

We took the movable feast to the red-topped Formica table with a tubular chrome frame and sat down on the matching cantilever chairs with red vinyl seats. Jackie and Thomas loved the '50s furniture that lived in this 125-year-old house. It warmed the clean, simple lines of the kitchen filled with built-in oak cabinets painted white, set against the dark-stained oak floors.

I glanced at a manila folder Jackie placed on the table.

"What have you got?" I said. "Wait. Let me have a scone first."

"Good. I'd rather talk about you, anyway. What's going on?"

I told her about my meltdown and John's surprising response.

"Why don't you get married?" she asked with an exasperated look. "Maybe it's the next step in your relationship. Remember, nothing stays the same. It seems quite doable to me. You guys are great together."

I paused, having given his proposal nonstop thought on my drive over. "I never wanted to get married, but I never thought I'd find someone I loved as much as John. The concept doesn't make my skin crawl anymore."

Jackie laughed and, knowing John wanted a child, said, "What about having a child?"

"Can I just have Michael?" I smiled. Then I grew serious. "He really wants one. He said it's okay if I don't, but I'm sure he'll end up resenting me. I'm just not sure I can be a full-time mom."

We had walked into the living room so we could take a gander out the windows facing the backyard and Michael. He was rolling on the ground with the dog pack. It was impossible to tell that both Michael and Ella had recently been hospitalized. Ah, the healing power of love, I thought, not sure if I was mocking the concept or myself.

"I think you'd be a great mother, but obviously...." Jackie's voice trailed off as we returned to the kitchen. "You haven't ruled it out completely, have you?"

"No, I guess that's why I feel so conflicted. But I can't think about it now," I said with finality. "Not with this case unsolved. What have you got for me?"

I put down my coffee cup and picked up another scone and downed it in a heartbeat. I guess depression burned up a lot of energy – I refused to admit I was simply Jonesing for a sugar high. I took my eyes off the scones and gave Jackie my attention.

"I put out calls to the list of law enforcement agencies Barbara sent us," she said. "I started yesterday and continued through this morning, asking each one to send us photographs they might have of dead or confiscated pit bulls from the past five years," Jackie stopped, popped a piece of scone into her mouth. She chewed and added, "By the way, if anyone was an asshole, I gave John their number."

"Kind of like batting cleanup for him," I noted.

"Exactly!" Jackie said, and returned to her debriefing. "Then I contacted just about every shelter, rescue and Animal Control agency from

Maryland to Pennsylvania and Virginia to Washington, DC. I sent them the photographs I pulled off Lincoln's video, and asked them to check each dog against their intake records to see if they recognized any of them. On a whim, I also included the two dogs we saw fight in Jefferson Brown's yard."

My eyes roved to the manila folder again. Jackie followed them. "What?" I said, knowing she was sitting on some info.

She started to reach for the folder, but Michael and the unruly dogs came bursting into the kitchen, demanding all our attention.

"Ella started whining," he complained. Then he softened. "I think she missed you, Aunt Ally."

I looked at Ella. She was exhausted. I explained to Michael that she was just tired. I left out overwhelmed. That was too long a concept to get across right now. Ella had curled up at my feet and put her head across one of them. I bent over to pet her. She was sound asleep. Michael looked at her, dropped to the ground and kissed her on the head. His dogs had already landed on the living room couch.

Michael leaped up, his nose running and his cheeks flushed with the outdoors, and grabbed a tissue from the box on the microwave. Without asking, but careful not to disturb Ella, he climbed up on my lap.

"Impressive," I joked. "Good to know your momma doesn't have to wipe your nose any more. Soon you'll be driving."

He giggled like a seven-year-old. Jackie, who had left the table upon Michael's entry, returned with a cup of cocoa and put it in front of him. It was loaded with marshmallows. Michael picked up the cup and blew on it before taking a sip. He lifted his head to show off his marshmallow mustache.

"I'm going to be shaving soon, too." He laughed. His attention shifted to the folder and his dark eyes brightened and he started to reach for it.

"Michael!" Jackie said sharply and his hand stopped in mid-air.

"Work stuff, huh?"

"Yep. Why don't you go play video games?"

"Sure. Aunt Ally, will you come watch?"

"Of course. But first, your mom and I need to finish working. Okay?"

He nodded gamely and left.

215

"Okay, spill it," I demanded, pointing to the manila folder.

"A couple of hours before you arrived I received these photographs from Nina Walker," Jackie said, referring to the director of the Talbot County Humane Society located in Easton. Jackie opened the folder and pulled out the two pictures Nina had supplied in response to Jackie's request for information. One was of the dark brown dog; the other showed the tan-and-white pit bull. They were the dogs we saw fighting at Jefferson Brown's house. According to their Talbot Humane records, they had been there within the year.

I just stared at Jackie and then back at the photographs, recognizing the dogs but not understanding. It took me a moment to find my voice so I could ask, "How the hell did Brown acquire these 'rescued' dogs? Jackie, what's going on?"

I stopped talking and went back to reading. I noted both dogs had been sent from Talbot Humane to a Restore Pit Bull Rescue in Hurlock. I looked up at Jackie again, even more puzzled.

"I never heard of it. Have you?"

"No. So I contacted everyone again. This time I asked if any of their dogs went to Restore Pit Bull Rescue?" Jackie slapped down three more photographs on the table. "These just arrived from Jamie Levine's assistant at BARCS (Baltimore Animal Rescue and Care Shelter)."

I picked them up and was staring at a brown and white pit bull, a black one, and a tan one with a white muzzle. I looked at their accompanying records. They were young fighting females that had been rescued during the past three years and sent to BARCS at different times. Within a couple of days of each one's arrival, it had been transferred to Restore Pit Bull Rescue.

"Do we know how the dogs ended up at Talbot and BARCS?" I asked.

"They were picked up in raids in Easton and Baltimore, and sent to the appropriate shelter. A couple of K-9 officers dropped them off. Both work out of Baltimore County. I called them and neither had heard of Restore Rescue."

"At least we have some paperwork now. But how come we've never heard of it?" I asked.

"Because it doesn't exist!"

FORTY-TWO

I WAS SPEECHLESS. JACKIE AND I just sat staring at each other. Neither of us had any idea what this meant. Two shelters – Cambridge and Talbot — had released pit bulls that had somehow become fighting dogs again. BARCS had dogs that had simply disappeared. And none of us had no idea how it happened.

"But fighting dogs are always intact," I finally muttered. "And our shelters never release pit bulls unless they are spayed or neutered."

"My thoughts exactly," Jackie said. She pulled the tie off her hair and ran her fingers through it so it immediately returned to the bouncing Slinky look. Then she took the tie and threaded it over her index finger, wrapped it around her thumb and shot it into the sink.

"Feel better?"

"No. But it'd be nice if it were that easy. Anyway," she continued, her voice still edged with anger, "Talbot County and BARCS checked their records. In each case, it was noted Restore Rescue would take care of the spaying or neutering of each dog and signed the appropriate papers."

"Yeah, appropriate my ass," I snorted. "What the hell is going on?"

Suddenly I was standing and walked over to the sink, putting my hands on the edge of it and stared out the window straight into the neighbor's empty kitchen. Leafy trees blocked the view in the summer months. Winter bared more than just branches, I thought, as I could see stacks of dirty dishes on the neighbor's counter. My fingers drummed on the sink impatiently.

"I really cross-examined Helen right before you arrived," Jackie said, once she had sipped her coffee. "If she says anything to you, tell her I'm sorry. I just couldn't figure out how those three dogs could have been adopted without her knowing. I asked her if she'd ever heard of Restore Rescue. She drew a blank. Helen called me back to say she went through her files after speaking with me. She couldn't find any dogs that went to Restore."

"So we don't know for sure if her three went there, since the files are missing. This just keeps getting crazier."

I returned to the table and sat down so hard that the seat of the cantilevered chair bounced up and down. Jackie didn't say anything. She just picked up our cups and tossed the lukewarm coffee in the sink. She poured us a fresh cup, sat down and pantomimed plunging a knife into her heart. Neither of us smiled.

Ella lifted her head off my foot and looked towards the dining room. Soon Michael came charging through on his way to visit us. His dog pack was at his heels until Jackie barked at them to sit. Michael dropped to his knees and slid across the kitchen floor until he made contact with his new friend, who was standing to greet him. It was a good time to see a happy pit bull.

"Aunt Ally, do you know who did this to her?" he asked when Ella rolled on her back and revealed her scarred belly.

"Not yet," I said. "But your mom and I are going to find out. That's one of the things we've been so busy with. You aren't feeling ignored, are you?"

Michael took that as an invitation to crawl into my lap again. Ella pressed against our legs. I think she actually sighed. Jackie looked at the three of us and picked up her cell phone and turned it into a camera.

"Want to do something?" Michael asked.

"Yeah, but not now. Your mom and I need to finish our work and I need to get home. But, I was thinking, maybe you could visit John, Ella and me and stay overnight real soon."

"You mean tonight?" Michael said, twisting around so he could show me how enthusiastic he was about his potential trip across the bridge.

"No, we all have too much work right now and I'm no fun. But I'm thinking maybe in a couple of weeks. I want to make sure John isn't working so you two can hang out. I know he'd like that."

Obviously, this was acceptable because I received a hug before Michael slid off my lap and was gone with all the dogs in pursuit.

"Where are you at?" Jackie asked me.

"I've been putting together a DNA chart," I said, and opened the file on my iPad so she could review it. "It's not much yet, but I'm hoping we will collect a lot of DNA when we raid the Friday night fight. With Barbara's help we should be able to trace the dogs back to where they came from and find out who brought them. Then we can rescue them and send them to a farm in the country – for real."

Jackie pretended to pull the knife out of her heart. That made me smile.

I put my elbows on the table and cupped my chin in my hands. Jackie and I looked at each other for a second. We didn't seem capable of doing much else right now.

"You realize," I finally said, "we've had all of these names – Brown, Stanton, Rivera, Diaz, Ghost – from the git. And we still haven't figured out who killed Benji and why? Who killed Stanton and the unnamed hypothermia dog? How did Ella end up at the shelter? And when is the next goddamn fight? Now we have another unanswered question. What the hell is Restore Pit Bull Rescue?"

My voice had risen with each question, and I took out my frustration on the kitchen table, smacking it so hard I made the silverware jump. I was interrupted by the ringing of my phone. I could hear Jackie mutter "Thank God" under her breathe.

It was John. Before I could say hello, he said: "Babe, I'm going to rock your world."

FORTY-THREE

I QUICKLY CUT JOHN OFF and explained that would be difficult and vastly improper, since I was sitting with Jackie at her kitchen table. He chuckled and asked to be put on speaker.

"Hey, Jackie," he said. "Listen in because I'm going to rock your world, too."

"You can try," Jackie challenged with a smile that was wasted on John, but matched my own.

"What's going on?" I asked. "Tell me it's good news. We need some."

"It is," he said.

The cloud that had been blocking the sun for the past few minutes passed and the kitchen brightened as if a light switch had been thrown on. Let it be a good omen, I prayed. I stood up to begin pacing. John's words stopped me in my tracks.

"I just heard from Lincoln. There's going to be a fight Friday night."

"Oh, thank God!" I said and gulped. "I can't believe I just said that, but you know what I mean."

John said he had the same reaction and explained he had called Garrison to double check that it was true, since he had been hanging out with Lincoln nonstop. He already confirmed.

"I thought we could meet again at our house, so there's no risk of Garrison being seen with us in public, and coordinate our efforts," John said. "Jackie, how's tomorrow morning for you?"

"Yesterday would have been better, but I can wait," she said.

I was already going through a checklist in my mind of whom I could trust to involve in our part of the raid. I planned to ask Jackie to come up with her own list so we could compare them.

"Garrison said he could come over any time tomorrow. Jackie," John inquired. "What works for you?"

"Name it and I'm there," she said, her eyes suddenly sparkling with anticipation. We loved our job in these moments. We had spent the last few days stuck in the weeds; hopefully, we'd soon be barreling down the highway to Hurlock.

"Great," John said. "I already suggested breakfast to Garrison so we could get an early start. He said not to cook; he'll bring food from Baltimore. I tried to argue, but he said 'smoked salmon' and I caved."

Jackie thanked him for being so easy and then brought him up to speed. She told him about our phantom Restore Pit Bull Rescue, explaining how both the rescue and the dogs that had been placed there had vanished.

"Want me to call my FBI guy?" John said. "I haven't asked him for a favor in a couple of hours. At least he likes to have me in his debt. Jackie, is that okay with you?"

"God, yes!" she said so loudly, Michael called out wanting to know if she was okay. She quickly reassured him.

"I'll call him as soon as I hang up," he said. "Then I'll head home. What time are you going to be home?"

"Let's see," I said looking at my watch. "If I wait 20 minutes, I'll hit the beginning of rush hour, so I guess I better kick it into gear. I'm out of here in five. Home in under an hour."

"Want to pick up Thai food?"

"Emphatic yes," I responded.

That settled, we said our goodbyes. I stood up and started to help Jackie clear the table, but she shooed me away. I told her I was going to say goodbye to Michael and collect Ella, and went upstairs to his room. I knocked on his bedroom door.

"Aunt Ally?" Michael asked.

"It's me."

"Come in."

He had made a tent by throwing a blanket over the space between the twin beds. Two dog tails were sticking out from under the sheet that comprised the entrance. I couldn't see Michael. But Ella poked her head out. I was delighted she had left my side and was enjoying her own play date.

I hesitated for a second, thought about the traffic that would soon be backing up on the Bay Bridge, shrugged, and dove under the sheet. Instantly, I was flat on my back with Michael and the dogs crawling on top of me. Michael smiled and gave me a quick kiss on the cheek. I gave him a hug and extricated myself so I could sit up.

"Honey, we have to get going," I said reading his disappointed face. "We'll see you soon. I promise. Remember, you're going to stay with us for a night or two. However long I can wrestle you away from your parents. Maybe you could stay until you leave for college."

I was rewarded with a giggle before we all crawled out of the tent. Jackie was waiting at the foot of the stairs. I loved the way her face softened when she saw her son.

"You better hit it," she warned.

"I'm out of here," I said, petting each dog and then giving Michael a hug. I snapped on Ella's leash and buzzed Jackie as I raced past her on my way to the car.

"See you tomorrow," I yelled out my open car window.

"Drive sa…." She didn't bother finishing her sentence, probably because she was talking to my rear bumper.

FORTY-FOUR

———✦✦✦———

THE DOGS, OUR FOUR-LEGGED DOORBELLS, went off before Garrison even turned into our long driveway. I was reading in the sunroom, listening to some soothing classical music, when I heard their warning barks. I hurried across the length of our house. I told Duke and Ella to sit. They did and I opened the door in time to see Garrison slide out of a 1970 Chevelle SS, the eye-popping ride he had liberated from the impound lot to enhance his new image. His clothing told the rest of his invented story.

I wasn't sure I would have recognized Garrison if I weren't expecting him. He had transformed himself from preppy to street. He had traded in his Weejuns for de rigueur Timberland boots, black baggy jeans that rode low on his hips and cuffed in folds on top of his footwear and a blindingly white T-shirt. A hoodie and sunglasses hid his identity. Garrison's diamond earrings rivaled TV's famous judge, Judy Sheinelin, who packed several carats on each earlobe.

"What, no chains?" I asked by way of greeting.

"They're in the glove box," he said, returning my smile. "I don't put them on until I have to. I hate it when I bend over and they slap me in the face. Afraid they'll chip a tooth."

"That would be horrible," I grimaced.

"Yeah, my mother would kill me if anything happened to these teeth after all that orthodontist money she invested," Garrison said, giving off a huge smile. "Thanks, mom."

He carried two large shopping bags – one in each hand – from Lenny's Deli, one of Baltimore's finest. I moved on to licking my lips.

"What have you done?" I marveled, expectancy making me salivate. Just the word "deli" had a salacious effect on me. We made it through the doorway where Ella and Duke were waiting with John. Garrison put the bags into my outstretched hands so he could greet all life forms and I proceeded into the kitchen. Soon we were crowded around the shopping bags.

The dogs were instantly banished and John began pulling down platters and bowls. Jackie arrived in time to set the table while Garrison opened the multiple packages. I laid out the thinly sliced smoked salmon, whole whitefish, smoked herring, assortment of cheeses, olives, cucumber salad and pickles. I sliced mounds of bagels and red onions while John squeezed a huge pitcher of orange juice. Jackie worked on the coffee.

Once seated at the dining table, no one spoke for the first 15 minutes of mouth-stuffing ecstasy. But the excitement of the impending raid took over and we peppered Garrison with questions. He gave up on the bagel he was building with cream cheese, salmon and onion, put it down and looked up at us.

"I called Lincoln as soon as I left you guys," Garrison said, beginning at the beginning, "and arranged to meet him at Jugs at 8 o'clock that night. I've been there ever since, nursing drinks and dropping enough names and info to be taken seriously. It's like being encased in perpetual nighttime with creepy monsters. Can't wait to get back to my trash can."

"You know where the fight is?" John asked. He waved a forkful of whitefish near his mouth. He finished his sentence and then the fish. His eyelids closed in momentary appreciation.

"I've heard mumbles of Hurlock, but don't have an address yet," he said.

John stood up and started pacing. I kept silent and watched his energy propel him around the room. He swung by the table and grabbed his half-eaten bagel. Then he walked out of the room and returned with a full mouth and his laptop.

"My friend, who still remains nameless, and I have been looking at Brown's holdings," John said, opening his computer and turning it on. He was shifting it on the dining room table, blocking out the sun's reflection, when his phone vibrated next to it. John picked it up, listened, thanked the voice on the phone, and smiled. He returned his attention to his computer while telling us that was his Feeb friend. He had just sent him the info he had asked for.

I was looking over John's shoulder and noted lots of FBI emblems on the pages he was flipping through. John caught my gaze and said, "My friend was happy to help. Now I owe him a favor, which he'll call in pretty quick. Things just work out sometimes."

I put together another bagel and fixings, cut it in half and put a piece on John's plate. "Like this," he said, picking up his food. "I was just thinking I want more food and, boom, it appears."

He turned back to the computer. "Brown owns 50 acres with a smallish warehouse on the property at 395 East Meadowbrook Lane in Hurlock. But it's not off Main Street like Lincoln mentioned when he went to Friday night's fight. That piece of property – which has a large warehouse – is right off East Main Street. I'm betting that's where the fights are being held. We'll track Garrison's car in case I picked the wrong property. We'll just reroute everyone, but I don't think we'll have to.

"Both properties are buried under the weight of several dummy corporations and tons of paperwork, according to my friend," John added. "I want to think our Jefferson Brown keeps lots of lawyers, accountants and business managers on retainer. Because if he did all this shit by himself, he's freaky good. Like archenemy villain good."

I dusted a few crumbs from my pants and went into the kitchen.

Our dogs were on them instantly. If you didn't mind a thin veneer of saliva on your floors, they were the perfect cleaning implements. I boiled water for the next pot of coffee, ground the beans and poured them together into the French press. I could hear John talking about having the necessary warrants in place.

I brought the brewing pot of coffee to the table, set it down and made one more trip to the kitchen. This time, I returned with a chocolate Babka cake that weakened my knees with each step. The scent of butter, chocolate and sweet yeasty dough swirled upward, filling my nostrils with memories of my father taking me to his favorite New York deli for lunch. Before he forgot he had a daughter.

John had moved on to the different agencies that would be involved in the raid when I put the Babka on the table. I stood next to him and surgically sliced through the streusel topping and soft dough. John rose to his feet and removed the dirty dishes with Garrison's help. We returned to the table and the coffee and cake. Again, the food's allure lasted only so long. John picked up the thread of his conversation.

"Andrews and I aren't telling anyone what's going on," he continued, as if never interrupted. "We're just giving instructions to each unit commander about when and where to meet us. Other agencies will keep to the same schedule, but take different routes so they aren't noticed moving through town."

"Good," I said, before I looked at Garrison and asked, "Did you hear about the pit bull rescue that isn't?"

"Yeah," he said, "John filled me in. This whole case is odd. I don't get how none of these guys have been picked up for anything in recent years. On the whole, they are not that smart to go undetected. And we're not that dumb. Who's watching out for them? And why?"

"Exactly," John said quietly. "That's why we're keeping the raid a secret until we bang on the door. Jackie, you want to work with me on which Animal Control and K-9 agencies you want to bring in?"

"Sure, that would be great," she said, licking her fingers before she wiped her mouth.

"Allison, any thoughts?" John queried.

"Of course," I said with a smile. Everybody laughed, or more accurately, sniggered. "Jackie, will you drive the Mobile Unit? I'd like Penny Truhane to help us. She has a private veterinary practice in Easton," I informed Garrison. "I was thinking she could travel with me. She's a great surgeon and I know I can trust her. But I don't have to. I'm sure she'll help once I tell her we're going after a hoarder in Hurlock. Who could refuse such an opportunity?"

I continued, "I'll also contact Wicomico Humane and reserve some kennel space, if we need it. And I want BARCS and Talbot County Humane to take some dogs. They'll send their own people, too. As I said before, I don't want anyone from the Cambridge shelter involved. Now that we know the three disappearing dogs on Lincoln's video was an inside job. I'll call Helen and explain and apologize after it's over.

"John, who are you inviting to the party?" I asked.

"Andrews wants SWAT on point, which I'm all for. We've lined up ATF, DEA and have additional State Police on standby. I wanted to talk to you before I contact Jim Phillips," he said, referring to Dorchester County's Sheriff, who also oversaw Animal Control and its three agents.

"Let's hold off if we have enough bodies. At least until the raid is underway. I'm pretty sure the leak isn't coming from his department, but I can't be positive. He'll be pissed, but I'm sure he'll understand once it's explained – by John," I said, and plastered a cutesy smile on my face. It did no good.

"Not happening!" John responded with a shake of his head.

"Fine, I'll talk to him. For our part, Jackie, Penny and I will go in as soon as the place is secured. You know my motto: You guys get the animals; we get the dogs."

FORTY-FIVE

———∞∞∞———

THE DARKNESS ROLLED OUT OF the east and pushed the sun off the edge of the Earth. The energy shifted as daylight disappeared into night. My stomach lurched in reaction.

The raid was less than 90 minutes away.

I was sitting on my yoga mat in the sunroom, practicing breathing exercising called Asanas to center myself while I waited for Jackie and Penny Truhane. I had called Penny a couple of days ago and asked for her help with a hoarder in Cambridge. I would tell her the truth when we were heading towards Hurlock.

Once I felt calm and invigorated, I rolled up the mat and left it in the corner. I ran upstairs and threw on my evening work clothes: black jeans, black boots, several layers of shirts, topping them off with my bulletproof vest and a black zip-up hoodie. I would carry my HSPAC jacket until I needed it so I didn't pass out from heat stroke.

I returned to the sunroom with Ella underfoot and Tom and Daisy sprawled on the loveseat. I concentrated on the calmness I was experiencing so I could re-create it when I needed it tonight. This wasn't my first raid-eo.

I was sitting on the couch when Ella jumped up, thought about barking and followed through. She had found her solo voice. I figured she was announcing Jackie or Penny's arrival, so we loped to the front door. I opened it as Jackie's headlights lit up the driveway. She parked and was just getting out of her car when we saw Penny's vehicle winding its way down our road. She pulled in behind Jackie and popped out from behind the driver's seat and met us in the doorway.

"Oh my God, who's this beautiful girl?" she said, giving Ella a pet. Then she straightened up and walked over to Jackie and me. Penny had chopped her long, bright red hair into moussed spikes.

Her nostrils and eyebrows were nesting places for rings and silver doodads, and her brilliant green eyes were ringed with coal. She was an oddity for the Eastern Shore and most points south and north and west, but her clients and patients loved her.

"Allison, it's good to see you," Penny said, her hand outstretched. I gave her the warm, two-handed shake. I was feeling pretty guilty about lying to her. Then I introduced her to Jackie.

"What's going on?" she asked both of us.

"We'll talk in the car, okay? Here, take this," I said, and grabbed a bulletproof vest out of the trunk of the rental and tossed it to her.

"Really," she said bleakly, her straight nose wrinkled, proving it could still move under the weight of all the metal dangling from it. "Not your average hoarder, hmmm?"

"Yeah, you could say that," Jackie said circumspectly and looked at her feet.

"Let's get going," I said, cutting off any further conversation. "Penny, we'll drive Jackie to the Mobile Unit so I can show you around. We'll leave from there."

The three of us drove to the lab in my rented station wagon.

"Wow!" Penny said when we entered the Mobile Unit. "I've never seen anything like this."

I quickly showed her where everything was located though the draws and cabinets was labeled. A few minutes later Jackie took the wheel of the Mobile Unit, and Penny and I returned to the car. We headed towards Hurlock and I offered an explanation for our true destination.

"I'm sorry I couldn't tell you earlier," I apologized.

229

"It's okay, no problem. Wait a minute, though. I'm digesting," Penny said, haphazardly pulling on the ends of her hair. Then she gripped her knees. "Bottom line, you've discovered pit bulls that were supposedly rescued from shelters back in the fight game? No wonder you're keeping this one under wraps."

"I knew you'd understand."

"I'm glad you included me," Penny said, her voice soft and thoughtful. "I've never been on a raid before. I've worked on the aftermath of them and always figured if I ever came across the people who fought those dogs, I'd kill them. I can't, can I?"

"You've met John?" I answered her question with one of my own.

"Sure," she said.

"Do me a favor, huh? Don't ask him." We both laughed.

We drove slowly, with Jackie following us through the back roads from Trappe to Hurlock, staying out of sight as much as possible. John, Jackie, Garrison and I had all pored over Google maps yesterday, plotting out pathways for everyone involved in the raid. No one could know we were coming.

The moon, nearly full, was bright enough so I could cut my headlights. I could see the outline of other cars crawling along like an army of sightless ants, traveling the back roads of Hurlock soon to converge on the warehouse.

We were nearing John's hiding place that we had chosen together when the image of the Mobile Unit vanished. I knew Jackie had turned onto a farm road, another parking spot we had discovered. She would be waiting for my phone call to join us. We were no more than an eighth of a mile from the warehouse. The dashboard clock read 6:51.

John and I had spoken a couple of times as the forces were gathering. Earlier, he had passed on the info he received from Garrison: The fight was at the warehouse off Main Street. Then 20 minutes ago, John called to tell me Garrison's Chevelle SS had just driven past him and he could make out Lincoln in the passenger seat. Now my phone rang again.

"We're closing down the roads, supposedly to check for seatbelts, so no one will get through until we give the word," John explained, an undercurrent of excitement and tension in his voice. I called Jackie to tell her to get moving. My phone beeped as I was about to hang up. It was John again.

"Slow down," John warned me.

"What? To a complete stop?" Which is what would happen if I went any slower.

"Yeah, exactly," he said. "I'm going to pull out in front of you."

"You're tracking me on GPS?"

"Of course," he said. "Stop now."

I used the handbrake to come to a complete halt so my brake lights didn't come on. John appeared from his parking place and led me down some unnamed road toward the warehouse. We crawled the last hundred yards or so and turned down its driveway. I could now see the outline of the Mobile Unit in my rearview mirror.

Directly ahead, I saw dozens of law enforcement vehicles creeping along until they formed a phalanx around the entire warehouse. We followed John, who pulled in next to Lieutenant Andrews, standing beside his car. He was waiting for John at their prearranged meeting place near the front doors. Jackie and I parked behind the first line of offense – the SWAT team – but close enough to arrive with the initial wave. I watched John began walking the perimeter with Andrews.

"This isn't the usual pit bull raid, is it?" Penny asked with a puzzled expression on her face, looking around slowly, taking it all in. Car doors opened stealthily and its inhabitants dropped onto their haunches using their vehicles as both protective barriers and gun rests. "How many agencies are here tonight?"

I rattled off the list of law enforcement groups, Animal Control, shelters and rescues that were in attendance. I stopped talking when I noticed John and Andrews had returned with a bunch of division heads.

They stood around talking and pointing, as if divvying up the areas of responsibilities. Suddenly, Andrews put his fist up in the air – the pre-arranged signal that Garrison had notified him the fight was in progress and Jefferson Brown was in attendance. The group broke ranks with the enthusiasm of football players leaving the huddle.

The SWAT team, encased in body armor and helmets, trotted to the entrance, falling in behind their man wielding the battering ram.

"Are you okay?" Jackie whispered so Penny couldn't hear, searching my eyes for my non-verbal response as well.

"I'm fine," I said, but recognized the testiness in my voice.

"Got it, but what I really want to know is if you feel any anxiety. You *were* just attacked."

"I said I'm fine," I answered, hearing a sharpness I had never before directed at Jackie. I guess I wasn't okay, but this wasn't the time to talk about my innermost feelings. There usually never was a right time. "Sorry. I just want to get going."

It was as if SWAT heard my request. They clustered around the door and turned towards Andrews who was directly behind the team. All eyes were locked on him. He looked over the field and made sure he held everyone's attention. Then he raised his hand and lifted one finger, then another. When the third finger went up, the SWAT team yelled "Police!" and smashed through the door. The yells of "Police! Get down on the ground!" were met by shrieks and curses from inside the warehouse.

I looked for John, figuring he would be among the first to enter, and there he was – right behind the SWAT team. I moved forward and grabbed Jackie and Penny. We disappeared amongst the horde of second responders and pushed our way into the warehouse with them. I was glad we hadn't waited for the "Clear" that would come from SWAT; we were already needed.

FORTY-SIX

———— ≈≈≈ ————

LAW ENFORCEMENT AGENTS ENTERED FROM all sides, smashing out windows and pouring over the sills with drawn guns. Personal preferences in weaponry abounded. Handguns ranged from Sig Sauers, 9mm Glocks, Berettas, Heckler & Koch and the legendary Colt 45. Others wielded semi-automatic Uzis, AK-47s, AR-15s, or anything else confiscated from gang members who are usually better armed than most police forces.

The SWAT team used their bodies to clog the doorway they had crashed through seconds earlier. Several of them pressed old-fashioned, crowd-stopping shotguns to their shoulders as if daring the crowd to try to escape. No one was that foolish.

The confused horde, which had started moving aimlessly, suddenly stopped when scores of cops began permeating its outer edges, yelling, "On the ground. Hands behind your back!"

Those who didn't move fast enough were shoved to the ground. Once everyone dropped face down on the floor, officers circled the crowd forming a periphery and turned their guns inward. Other cops began walking through the rows of people, pulling their arms behind their backs and tightening flex cuffs around their wrists before continuing to the next prone body.

As cops walked towards some adults – probably parents, I imagined – they grabbed sobbing children and pulled them to the ground beside them. I viewed these kids as animal-abusers-in- training. Yet when I looked at their terrified little faces, I felt sorry for them.

But I passed them at a dead run. In truth, I was much more interested in the two dogs that had been left in the pit to fight to the death than the kids that had been brought to watch them. I tuned out the chaos and commotion and, with Jackie and Penny, raced towards the dogs. I never took my eyes off them, especially as we approached the pit. Neither noticed us enter their space. They were too busy rolling around, struggling for an even deadlier grip. Each American Pit Bull Terrier was around 45 pounds of muscle, growls and teeth. A ratty piece of blood-stained carpeting covered the typical 12-foot by 12-foot pen. The portable plywood walls, about three feet high, were splattered with blood and saliva. Jackie and I leaped over them and landed in the pen.

"Penny, we've got this," I said over my shoulder, and motioned for her to stand back. I gave a quick look around and didn't see any Animal Control people. We had beaten them into the warehouse.

Jackie moved towards the brindle male, whose teeth were sunk into the white pit bull's head. Far from giving up, the white pit shook the other dog's shoulder, grinding his teeth into the top of his leg.

Jackie and I pulled break sticks from our pockets – a de rigueur tool in the world of pit bull fighting. They are hammer-sized pieces of hardwood with a handle and a flat wedge-shaped end that make quick work of disentangling fighting dogs.

I shouted: "One! Two! Three!" Jackie and I simultaneously grabbed the back of the dogs' necks and slid the break sticks behind their molars and turned them, unclenching their jaws. We gripped tightly so neither dog could move its head, thus preventing any further damage, and then pulled them apart.

I held the white pit bull's neck and immediately slipped the snap-on leash around it, as Jackie did the same with the brindle. Then we pretty much laid on top of them, pressing them into the ground until the aggression oozed out of them. Only then did we loop the leashes around their muzzles.

I went through the motions without thinking. That was because I was concentrating on a new feeling coursing through my being: fear. I was always anxious before a raid, but this one had my stomach churning. Granted, it was one of the largest I had been on, and, Lord knows, I had waited long enough to rescue Brown's dogs, but that wasn't why my stomach churned. I felt the pain of my bite wound flame up when I had bent over the dog to separate it. For a second, I remembered the Rottweiler's teeth digging into my hip, relived killing it and feeling the suffocating weight of the dog when it died on top of me. But I wasn't fearful about physical harm. I was worried about screwing up again. I was still trying to redeem myself – to myself.

"Now, Penny!" I ordered, looking at the injured dog underneath me. "Take Jackie's dog!"

She leaped into action. Penny handed me a compress for my dog's head before I could ask. Then she placed another on the brindle's leg and shoulder wounds and applied pressure. Jackie backed away and began looking around for more help.

I checked out the white pit bull, who was oblivious to the deep puncture wounds in his skull. He was calm and begging for attention. I unwrapped the leash so he could nuzzle my hand. I continued to apply pressure to his head wound to staunch the flow of blood, and forced him to remain on his side.

"How's your dog?" I asked, when I saw Penny shining a flashlight into the gaping tear right below the shoulder.

"I think the triceps tendon has been detached from the proximal olecranon humerus, but I won't know without an MRI. How about I sedate him now and put him in a Velpeau sling so he can't do any more damage to himself? That way, I can keep him at my hospital overnight, and tomorrow I'll do an MRI and operate if he needs surgery."

"You'll find bandaging materials in the Mobile Unit in the cabinet over the microscope," I told Penny, knowing she would need it to wrap the dog's flexed leg against its rib cage so he couldn't move his shoulder or put his leg down.

"One problem solved. Thanks," she said.

"This bad boy will probably require drains and an Elizabethan collar," I noted. "Hey, Penny, can you handle both dogs at your clinic or am I asking too much? We'll reimburse any expenses."

She clucked her disapproval at the thought. "What, are you trying to ruin my tax write-off?" she smiled, her silver lip rings flashing under the overhead light. "I'll sedate Legs and then I'll work on Blockhead. I'll call one of my vet techs to come in so we can send them to my hospital whenever you're ready."

Jackie jogged up to us with Talbot County Animal Control agents Regina Simpson and Daniel Millbrook in tow. They arrived in time to hear the tail end of our conversation.

"Penny, that's great," Jackie said, her cheeks pink from racing around the warehouse. "I'll see if I can find someone from K-9 to travel with the dogs, unless Regina or Daniel wants to take them."

Jackie noticed Penny's curious look so she added, "These dogs are evidence, so they need to travel with someone from Animal Control or a K-9 unit. Someone who can attest to the chain of evidence in court, if necessary. Buzz me when they're ready for transport, okay?"

Penny nodded, twirling the stud that pierced her face right below her cheekbone. I took the moment to open my jacket and pulled off my knit hat, starting to sweat from the exertion of separating the fighters.

Jackie tucked her hair behind her ears and off her face. I spoke to Regina and Daniel.

"We need these two dogs moved to the Mobile Unit after Agent Vincente photographs them in the fighting pit," I said. "I'll go grab a couple of stretchers."

"Hey, Doc," Regina said as soon as I returned and handed over the stretchers. "Did you separate the dogs?" An unhappy ridge formed on her broad brow. She was a big, curvy woman who filled out her uniform. I smiled disarmingly in the face of her displeasure. As a veterinarian, I was supposed to hang back until Animal Control or K-9 secured the dogs. Sometimes I just couldn't wait. That was a reoccurring problem, it seemed.

Regina took the white pit, now officially dubbed by Penny as Blockhead, by his back half and Daniel lifted his front while I kept pressure on the head wound. I counted to "Three!" In unison, we put the white dog on the stretcher and strapped him down. They ran him into the Mobile Unit where Penny stayed with him, and waited for them to bring her the brindle called Legs.

Once Jackie had finished collecting evidence, including blood samples from the fighting pit and discarded break sticks and harnesses (which probably held fingerprints of their owners), she called the directors of Wicomico and Talbot Humane Society and BARCS who were waiting outside with vets, vet techs and volunteers. They arrived en masse, and I sent a vet and two techs to help Penny.

Jackie reported her findings from her quick tour of the warehouse to us all. "Two Animal Control agents just corralled two loose dogs – that's what took so long. There are 10 crated dogs in here. From what we saw outside, there are multiple pit bulls stashed in cars and pickups, probably waiting to be sold."

"A regular flea market," I managed to everyone's amusement.

That was the last laugh any of us would have for a while.

FORTY-SEVEN

———— ✺ ————

PEOPLE STARTED SCREAMING BEFORE I saw the first pit bull charging through the crowd. Then I saw another and another. They, of course, saw or smelled each other, and soon there were the sounds of growls and the thud of dogs' bodies crashing into one another. They were attacking each other from one end of the warehouse to the other, and people were screaming in terror.

"Goddamn it! Regina, Daniel, get the two over there!" I yelled, pointing to the two pits rolling around in the center of the warehouse. Jackie and I were already running towards the corner where two other pits were locked in battle. We separated the dogs in a few seconds and handed them off to two Animal Control agents who were quick to follow us.

Next, Jackie and I sprinted over to three dogs fighting in a rotating pile. Two of them ganged up on the third and start mauling it. Another K-9 officer joined us in our sprint to the roiling dogs. To my horror, I saw several cops lifting their handguns, preparing to blow the dogs away.

"Don't shoot!" I screamed. "Stop! We have this! Don't shoot!" They didn't hear me. Instead they aimed their guns at the dogs. People were scrambling to get away and, thankfully, some of them crossed into the line of fire, causing the police to hesitate. Jackie and I ran faster, if that was possible, closing in on the shooters. I screamed again, just a few feet from the closest trooper, "Don't shoot!" She finally heard me and looked startled. But she held her fire.

Jackie and I and the K-9 officer created a wall around the fighting dogs, making it impossible to shoot them without hitting us.

"You two take the top dogs. I'll get the one on the ground," I shouted. "Now!"

Jackie and the K-9 guy grabbed the fighters by the back of their necks, put a break stick in each mouth and pried them off their luckless victim. I looked at the black pit on the bottom lying on her side. As soon as the two females had been removed, she shook herself and jumped up. She ignored her wounds and was bristling with vengeance. But I was ready. I snatched her up by the back of her neck with my right hand and managed to slip the leash around her head with my left one. I pulled the leash downward and used my weight to lean against her hindquarters, trying to force her to the ground. She was bucking and twisting, trying to throw me off, but I managed to wrestle her down.

"It's okay, girl," I said softly, talking calmly though my anxiety level was nearing an internal scream. I was fighting to maintain my position without getting bitten. I was also afraid that if the dog got away from me, she would be shot. As soon as Jackie and the K-9 guy removed their dogs from her view, the fight went out of her.

"What a good girl," I murmured and petted her. I took her to a quiet corner so I could check her wounds. Miraculously, they were minimal. She had suffered numerous bite marks, but the two dogs didn't seem to have the time to do any deep muscle damage. A series of antibiotics and some decent care would be all she needed.

The unexpected fracas had put a hold on the raid. Everyone had frozen in place while the dogs were loose. Now police continued rounding up people and moving them out. The dogs had been placed in any available crate. I still had to evaluate all of them and decide where to send each one.

I was on the way to the Mobile Unit with the black pit bull to get him cleaned up and walked past dozens of handcuffed people sitting on the ground who were waiting to be lined up and put on buses that would take them to jail. This was SOP. I was startled when I noticed Ghost sitting sideways and handcuffed next to an empty crate. He grinned at me, which was much more frightening than his usual furious glower. Then he ran his fingers over the latch on an empty crate, opening and closing it. He wanted me to know, I supposed, that he had let out one of the attacking pit bulls. Others had obviously followed his lead. I didn't know if he had hoped to get away in the pandemonium he created or if this were just his parting "fuck you."

Regina intercepted me and we discussed the black pit bull. "Can you take her to the Mobile Unit? We'll figure out where to send her later. Okay?"

"Sure," she said and took the leash from me and petted the dog.

"Thanks, Regina. Great job as always," I said, smiling my appreciation. I took the opportunity to tuck in my shirt, which had been pulled out during my tussle with the dog. "How are the other dogs?"

"A few bites, but nothing awful. They got pulled apart pretty quick. We are damned good," she said with a self-satisfied smile.

I nodded at her, but I was already thinking about what needed to be done next. Jackie sidled up to me.

"Don't ask," I ordered.

"When did we get married?" she asked.

"I'm fine. I didn't even think about the dog attacking me when we went after those pits," I assured Jackie. I didn't want to talk about it.

I finally had a chance to look around the warehouse. A thick cloud of cigarette smoke was trapped against the ceiling. CSI units were packing up dropped guns, knives and bags of drugs. There was so much spilled crack, heroin and cocaine on the ground that all I could think of was the Nutcracker Suite's Waltz of the Snowflakes.

Crime Scene tape was wrapped around the fighting pit and every remaining pit bull crate holding a dog. It was showtime for Jackie and me. We checked out each dog for injuries. A few were a little worse for wear from their brief but forceful encounters, and I tagged them to go to the Mobile Unit. Others were tagged to be placed in Animal Control trucks.

I wanted all of them moved to BARCS, since it was the farthest away and none of these dogs had life-threatening injuries.

Only then did Jackie and I begin methodically collecting evidence. She photographed everything before we numbered, bagged and tagged each item as we walked around the crates. We picked up any discarded break sticks that had been dropped pretty sure we would pull fingerprints and human and canine DNA off them. Canine DNA samples would be forwarded to Barbara to be checked against the existing database or added to it. Anything human would be given to Lieutenant Andrews

"Let's hit the ref's stand next, though it looks like someone already did," I half-joked, since the stand was lying on its side, papers scattered around. "Please, please let there be the names of the fighters and their owners," I begged, and helped Jackie right the stand. We picked up the papers and I quickly shuffled through my half. "Shit. I have a list of dogs' names, weights, ages and brief descriptions and, damn it, no owners' names just some kind of code. These assholes aren't as stupid as I wish they were. You have the same results?"

"Yep."

"Can we get to work yet?" Lieutenant Andrews interrupted, appearing at our side. "Crime scene guys are waiting in the wings to start fingerprinting. We've collected everything that's not connected to the remaining dogs. We'll break down the fighting pit and store it as evidence, if it's alright with you?"

"Of course," I said, while glancing around. "The dogs will be out of here in 15 minutes. Okay?"

"Sure," he answered and started to walk away.

I stopped his departure with a question. "Hey, Lieutenant, have you seen John around?"

He turned and hesitated. Not a good sign. "He went after Jefferson Brown," he said, his tone measured. I swallowed my response, which was a caterwauling, *Oh, God, no!* in favor of a weak, "How did that happen?"

"He told the K-9 officer watching Duke that he had followed Brown and the Rivera twins through a trap door in the warehouse. It led to a tunnel that opened in the woods."

"He went after them by himself?" I managed to get the words out without my voice rising. I did, however, feel my heart sink to my ankles. I was so busy with the dogs I hadn't notice Brown's absence. "Didn't he take any backup?"

"Yes and no," Andrews said, and I could see his brow crease and his eyes narrow as he chose how to phrase his   reply.

"Lieutenant," I interrupted his silence. "You can tell me. I promise I won't faint."

"That's not it, Allison," he said and I wasn't happy with the uncertainty in his voice. "John called for Duke to be released. He said the Rivera twins couldn't keep up with Brown and had veered off the path and were heading south. He had us send officers with dogs to track them. Once Duke arrived at his side, he called back to say he was following Brown."

Andrews stopped and held up his hand while he talked into his earpiece. "Got it. You bring them out. We'll have two squad cars waiting on the edge of the woods. Any sign of Thibert?"

He listened briefly and ended the one-sided conversation without uttering another word. I saw him push a worried look out of his eyes and avert them slightly from my intense stare.

"The Rivera twins have been captured," he said immediately. "John's still out there. Last anyone heard from him, he gave the 'K-9 Loose!' warning and said he'd call for assistance if he needed it."

"You're not going in?" I asked, though I already knew the answer. Once a K-9 was working, no one would interfere.

"No. I'm going to wait until he calls for assistance – like he said."

I could tell neither of us was happy with that answer.

"Okay," I said, with what I hoped was a plucky smile. We still had a bunch of dogs to process and hopefully many more to save tonight. But I was thinking of John.

FORTY-EIGHT

I TURNED MY ATTENTION BACK to Jackie and the papers we were holding. I shuffled through my half and found I had the fight schedule in my hand. The next dog on the roster was Dustup.

The heavyweight hadn't been one of the escapees and was still in his proper crate. He was the size of a mini-fridge standing on long legs, unusually large for a fighting pit. His head lolled benignly on his substantial neck. He was beige with a splatter of brown across his chest, the size of a pillowcase. As with all the other dogs, a chain with links as thick as piano legs hung from his neck.

Dustup jumped up and wagged his tail when Jackie opened his door. She slipped a leash over his head and took off the chain. I was about to check him out when I heard several gunshots from outside. My head snapped.

"Go on," Jackie ordered, "I'm fine. Be careful."

I ran. First thing I saw was a crowd of police gathered in a circle. I couldn't see what was at the center of their attention and elbowed my way forward. I saw a body lying face down. It wasn't John.

The crowd parted for EMS to come through. They turned the body over. It was Ghost. One of them checked for a pulse and shook her head no. Just like that, Ghost was dead. I looked for Andrews to ask him what happened, but he wasn't around. I talked to a couple of officers standing in the circle, but no one offered an answer. All I learned was that, for some inexplicable reason, Ghost had decided to escape, refused all orders to stop and was shot and killed.

I looked to see if John had reappeared. I couldn't find him, but my eyes locked onto Garrison's instead. He was handcuffed and standing in line, waiting to get on a police bus. I knew the plan was to cut him loose before he was processed. It was good there were so many being busted. He could just disappear. Lincoln was a little less fortunate. He was going to spend the night in jail and be released in the morning.

Andrews appeared and walked over to Garrison, pulled him out of the line roughly and talked to him briefly. Then he shoved Garrison on the bus. Andrews grabbed another body off the line, pulled him aside, talked for a minute and then pushed him into the bus. He did this a few times so Garrison wouldn't stand out, I figured.

Andrews saw me watching him and walked over. He pulled his wool cap over his nearly naked head, zipped up his windbreaker and plunged his gloved hands into his pockets. He looked cold and weary, but managed a thin smile.

"What's going on?" I asked, as I turned towards the warehouse. "Can you walk with me? I have to get back to Jackie. I know she'd like the details on what happened. Me, too."

"Garrison took credit for sending Ghost to his death, but he didn't have time to say how, damn it."

Our conversation ended when we stopped in front of the parking area near the warehouse. My attention turned to the Crime Scene tape placed around the numerous vans and pickups parked close to the entrance that were housing more dogs.

"We have a few more dogs left inside and then we'll get to these," I assured Andrews and paused. I knew the answer, but couldn't help asking, "Any word from John?"

"I would have told you," he said.

"I know," I answered, hearing resignation in mine. "See you later."

It was now unsettlingly quiet as I took one more look around for John before I entered the warehouse. The long lines of handcuffed prisoners had disappeared onto the buses, most of which were on their way to State Police headquarters. I had seen the Department of Social Services arrive and take sobbing children from their parents and place them in protective custody. I shook it off and returned to my work with Jackie.

She had been busy filling evidence bags that rested on top of Dustup's crate. She looked at me and said, "John?"

"He and Duke are still chasing down Brown. It was Ghost who was shot dead. Garrison had something to do with it, according to Andrews, but he hasn't been able to explain it to him yet," I said. I didn't want to discuss John, and Jackie knew it.

I began checking out Dustup. "We should all be so healthy," was my final diagnosis. I took a swab of his saliva for the DNA data bank and said, "Move him out," to Daniel, who was now hovering. Jackie called BARCS to come and collect the warehouse dogs to take them home.

At last, we were able to process the dogs behind the taped curtain. Of the 33 that had been left behind in their owners' vehicles, all were reasonably healthy, probably because they were hoping to sell them. All of the dogs were sent to shelters. This time, for real, their fighting days were over.

Suddenly a group of officers began running towards the woods. I joined them. The moon was so bright I had no trouble distinguishing John walking towards us, shoving a barely mobile, stumbling Jefferson Brown. I wondered why John was walking so slowly and not dragging him. Until I saw Duke limping alongside him.

"Get this piece of shit away from me," John ordered, and pushed Brown so hard towards the arriving cops he fell to the ground. Duke bristled and gave a full-throated growl, which caused John to sharply say, "Nein!" Then he bent down and picked up his dog.

I took one look at John's angry, worried face and simply said, "Bring Duke to the Mobile Unit. What happened to him?"

"That prick shot him," he said, his voice flat, his eyes furious.

I jumped up the stairs ahead of John and went to one of the surgical tables. Penny, who was cleaning up, looked at us and began disinfecting it so John could put Duke down. I saw the bullet hole – it had entered his chest, traveled behind his leg and exited in front of his ribs. It had caused the least amount of damage possible.

Penny shaved a small patch of fur from Duke's front leg a few inches above his paw and sterilized it, so I could give him an IV of short-acting anesthesia that I had drawn into a syringe. John held Duke and was saying something in German, which I hoped was "don't bite the nice doctors." Once Duke was sedated, I inserted a soft plastic tube into the dog's windpipe and connected it to an anesthesia machine that delivered an anesthetic mixed with oxygen and other gases.

I attached a pulse oximeter to his tongue, a small sensor device that registers the oxygen saturation level in his blood. Perfect. John watched me irrigate the bullet hole with a syringe filled with antibiotics to wash away any visible and microscopic debris, a process known as lavage. Then I put drains in both ends of the wound, secured them and gave Duke a shot of antibiotics. I turned off the anesthesia machine. Now there was nothing to do but wait for him to begin to regain consciousness and his swallowing reflexes. Only then would we take out the tube in his throat. Penny would monitor Duke until he was fully conscious.

"John, come talk to me a minute," I said. "Duke is going to be unconscious for a while. You can stay with him, of course, but I have to get to the other dogs. You okay with that, Penny?"

"Sure," she said, and scanned Duke's numbers on the pulse oximeter.

John followed me around to the back where no one could see us, and I wrapped my arms around him. He hugged me back. We stood like that for a minute.

"What happened?" I asked.

"I saw Brown and the twins slip through a trap door right behind their seats," he said, sounding tired and depressed.

"I know." I cut him off so he wouldn't waste his words or time. "Andrews told me you called for Duke and he met you in the woods."

"Yeah, he picked up Brown's scent and was on him in a flash, knocking him to the ground. Brown rolled over with his gun drawn and was trying to get a shot off when Duke grabbed his wrist. I heard a gun shot and a sharp snap that was almost muffled by Brown's scream. Duke had broken his wrist, which was fortunate. It changed the trajectory of the bullet and probably saved his life. I didn't even know he got hit," John stopped, staring at the Mobile Unit, "He's going to be okay, isn't he?"

"He'll be fine," I gave a slight smile wanting to reassure him. "And you're right, Duke pretty much saved his own life. I gave him a very light dose of anesthesia, so he'll be coming around soon."

John continued, still reliving the incident. "Brown couldn't use his gun, so he started kicking him. That's when Duke grabbed his foot and bit his way up his leg, locking onto his kneecap. I continued questioning him. But all he did was curse me. I guess he finally realized he wasn't going anywhere. I was asking him who shot his black pit bull with the white stripe and buried Duncan Stanton alive and the dog. He finally muttered Arnold Diaz. Was he here tonight?"

"I didn't see him, but I wasn't looking for him, either. Did you ask Brown about Restore Rescue?"

"Yeah," John said, sounding even more pissed off. "He asked me what that was. That's when I ended the interview."

I pulled off John's baseball cap and lightly kissed him. I could relax a bit. John couldn't.

"I'm going to check on Duke," he announced. "I'll call Andrews and ask him to start looking for Diaz."

We returned to Duke and it was John's turn to relax. His boy was starting to come around. I removed the tube from his throat. John could see Duke was going to be okay and he now had a new mission: find Diaz.

FORTY-NINE

———⧉———

ONCE THE DOGS HAD BEEN moved out, we formed a procession traveling from the warehouse to Jefferson Brown's house to confiscate his fighters. SWAT took the lead, John and several patrol cars followed, then my car and the Mobile Unit. Duke was still in it, being cared for by Penny and a vet tech. Behind it were more squad cars, traveling veterinarians and their techs, and bringing up the rear were the remaining Talbot and Wicomico Counties' Animal Control trucks. Jackie called to tell me she'd alerted Sussex County Animal Control. No one knew what to expect.

The line of law enforcement vehicles drove onto Brown's property without slowing down and encircled the house and large fenced-in yard. Car doors blew open and officers exited their parked cars and again used them as shields not knowing what they were facing in the darkened house. They pulled their guns and leveled them at doors and windows. SWAT made their way to the front door with shields, a battering ram and more drawn guns.

John was right on their heels when they smashed in the door. I waited in the doorway and watched SWAT go from room to room before giving the "Clear." No people. No dogs. John, Jackie, Penny and I ran through the house and into the backyard.

My body actually jerked when I realized there were no dogs there either. I had to remember to exhale.

"Where the hell are they?" John asked, moving his flashlight back and forth across the tree-lined property. "I was sure they'd be here."

This was the one scenario I had never anticipated. I was stunned. We went to Brown's house and located his home office. Jackie pulled out all the desk drawers and began rummaging. John went to work on Brown's computer and I dumped every trash can and read each scrap of paper.

I was rewarded first. I found a sales receipt for a couple of hundred pounds of raw organic meats. I read it carefully and ascertained it was a standing weekly order. I checked the address where it was delivered on my phone's GPS and discovered it was only two miles away, deeper into the woods. I handed the receipt to John. He, too, checked it out.

"It's a good address," John agreed. "I Googled the location. It's the parcel of land I looked at the other day that Brown owns. Give me a minute to call it in for a warrant."

Jackie and I spent the time looking around the house. The interior introduced us to a different Jefferson Brown. He either had a great sense of design or hired someone who did. Each room had lots of comfortable, stylish leather furniture and beautiful, simple wood pieces. It was masculine without being a man cave. There were lots of windows and tall plants, dark wood floors and expensive rugs. There was nothing thuggish about the house. This was the kid that donated to libraries and instituted profit sharing; not the man that killed and maimed.

I was drawn to a baby grand piano in the massive living room. It had the requisite number of framed photographs. No dogs, just people. Looked like grandparents, parents, sons or daughters, nieces or nephews. There were several pictures of Brown with a beautiful woman. Girlfriend? Sister? I turned away, realizing I didn't care.

I checked out his bedroom and the walk-in closet, and discovered Brown also had a fine taste for designer suits and automatic weapons. I looked through all the drawers, but didn't find any paperwork.

John called for us and once again, we packed ourselves into our vehicles, formed a line and proceeded down the road from Brown's house to, hopefully, what would be his kennel. We arrived at a huge piece of property that appeared to be solid woods. We drove slowly and followed the lead car, which turned down a dirt path, just wide enough for one vehicle. It ran alongside the edge of the property until it sharply turned left, farther into the woods.

A quarter-mile later, the vehicles pulled into a clearing where a one-story, cinderblock warehouse had been erected. My anxiety level soared. How many dogs were trapped inside the building? What condition were they in? I found some solace in watching law enforcement encircle the third structure of the night, and was even happier when SWAT jump out of their vehicles and rammed their way into the warehouse. They smashed through the front doors and we could hear them bellowing "Clear" from inside. We were standing way off to the side. I knew we were supposed to stay put until we were waved in, but in the gloom I could make out a few dogs.

I couldn't wait and began running towards them. Penny and Jackie were at my heels. Our arrival tripped the outdoor sensor lights, and the muted illumination revealed a show of horrors.

We were looking at the disposable pit bulls chained to stakes in the ground. I counted 11 lying unprotected on nothing but dirt and frozen slush. They had no blankets, no water and no food. All of them were too weak to sit or stand, their chains anchoring them to the earth. A half-dozen metal barrels, lying on their sides, were interspersed among them.

"Jackie, call any available vets and Animal Control."

People began running up to us within seconds. Jackie raced to the Mobile Unit and reappeared carrying stacks of foil blankets that she handed out so the freezing dogs could be covered. I had already started checking them out. I was surprised that the heavy chains tied around their scrawny necks were long enough for some of the dogs to huddle together. If the pit bulls in Brown's yard were touching each other and not fighting, they would probably be used as bait dogs.

I called them victims. Our arrival had spared some of them this hideous death, but we were too late to save many. With one quick look, I knew in my sinking heart most of them were dead or dying.

"We need more blankets!" I shouted. "I want every dog covered until we can move them out."

Jackie left my side and raced back to the Mobile Unit. She returned with another pile of foil blankets and handed them off. Then she and I launched into triage mode while the others covered the dogs. I looked over the field in order to pick out a dog we might be able to save. My eyes skimmed over the ones I knew were dead, which I counted at three. I asked Penny to check them out and make sure they had expired. She had just walked away when an emaciated dog began gagging and went into convulsions.

We sprinted over to it. Jackie took the chain off its neck while I wrapped a blanket tightly around the dog, protecting it from itself, until the seizure passed. I talked to the dog and stroked it. It was unconscious and dying. Its breathing was shallow, its gums were grey and it was shivering uncontrollably.

Jackie handed me my vet bag. I listened to its faint heartbeat and congested, rattling lungs. I pulled out a case that held a dozen full syringes. I always prepared them before a raid. Jackie held her flashlight steady and applied pressure to raise the nearly collapsed vein in the dog's foreleg. I quickly slid the needle into it, pressed down the plunger and euthanized it. I silently said goodbye to the dog, feeling the usual mixture of sadness and relief.

I caught Regina's eye and waved her over while I talked my notes into my tape recorder and walked over to the next dog. I left Jackie behind to ID the dog as #1 and photographed it. I knew she would place it in a bag and tag it. Later, we'd return to this spot to collect any remaining evidence. I overheard Jackie ask Regina to put the dog's body in our refrigerator.

All of a sudden, the area was flooded in intense light. John had turned night into day, having his officers erect portable lights around the clearing.

I gazed at a now-easily visible dog some several yards away that was trying to sit, but shaking so hard I feared it would topple over. I ran to it. Jackie was soon next to me, photographing it while I removed its chain and wrapped a foil blanket around the scrawny, beige, female pit bull. I took her temperature – low but not deadly. I checked her with the stethoscope and was relieved that her heartbeat was steady, her lungs wheezy but functioning. She was savable.

By now, several vets were standing around waiting for orders, and I began giving them. I asked for a show of hands of who could take dogs to their hospitals. Everyone raised a hand. Then I pointed to the dogs that needed immediate care and assigned a vet to each. If the dog needed emergency surgery, Penny, who had just returned to my side, would find space for it in the Mobile Unit.

"How many dead?" I asked her.

"Four," she said, and then added, "I covered them."

"Penny, you feel comfortable in charge of the Mobile Unit?"

"Sure. You'll be around if I need you, right?" Her eyes were a tad wider than usual.

"Jackie and I will be right here," I said, and handed her the little dog I was holding. "This is #2 when you're filling out the paperwork. Jackie already photographed her."

"Penny, if a dog is healthy enough, send it to Sussex or Wicomico Humane," I continued, bending down to examine the next dog. "If it needs surgery, please oversee the vets who will be introducing themselves to you."

Two vets, each one holding a dog I had already tagged for possible surgery, turned to follow Penny to the Mobile Unit. Jackie and I hurried to the nearest barrel. In Brown's world, these were doghouses. Freezing metal in the winter, boiling in the summer: a home designed in hell.

I looked around and waved over two more vets from Caroline County, who were standing in a group with Animal Control agents and vet techs. I knew all of them by sight, if not name.

They arrived at the barrel en masse. I flashed my light into it. A teeny white pit with brilliant green eyes struggled to her feet, but didn't have the energy to get to us. I heard the click of Jackie's camera before I crawled into the barrel and removed her heavy chain. The little female shook her head, took a couple of steps towards my outstretched hand and licked it. I coaxed her closer and removed her, talking calmly all the time. Jackie photographed her again as she collapsed in my arms, overwhelmed by the strain of standing. Jackie tagged the dog.

One of the vets came forward, wearing scrubs under her heavy jacket and a stethoscope draped around her neck. "I'll examine her, if you want. I don't think this little girl is going to a shelter tonight. If you want, I can take her to my hospital."

"Dr. Truhane is set up in the Mobile Unit. She'll find space for you to work. And thanks."

It was a tough night. Of the 11 dogs left out in the elements, only four survived. Four had already died, and I had to euthanize three more. The barrel dogs did a bit better. One was healthy enough to go to a shelter; three needed intense medical care, and I had to euthanize two.

Once all the dogs were cleared from the area, I finally had time to wonder where John was. I texted him. He told me he was waiting for me inside the warehouse – with more dogs.

FIFTY

JACKIE AND I TRUDGED OVER to the warehouse and found John standing in the doorway waiting for us. I read his face. He seemed pretty relaxed. I breathed easier. There were several SWAT guys milling around in the front of the building, looking rather disinterested. Another good sign.

"No one home? I asked.

"Nope. SWAT chased after two young guys who were trying to escape out the back door, which was an unfortunate choice for them. I was checking out the backyard and they almost ran into me. Not sure who was the most surprised, but I was definitely the fastest. I drew my gun and pointed it in their direction and they put up their hands. We had a little chat but, unfortunately, they knew nothing. They were hired by Duncan Stanton and never talked to anyone else. But Stanton had told them to ignore the outside dogs."

"Like in let them die?"

"Guess so."

"Well, maybe he did deserve the way he died." I was furious.

"I know, but hang on a sec," John said, and reached to open the front door and went through it ahead of me. He turned towards me and said, "I just want to see your face when you walk inside."

I stood in the doorway and blinked several times. John laughed; I had provided him with the exact reaction he was anticipating. I felt like I had slipped through the looking glass and entered a parallel universe to the horrific one outside. Here the dogs were fat, sassy, bright-eyed and warm.

I did a quick count that added up to 18 dogs living in large, deluxe, well-spaced kennels with beds and bowls filled with food and water.

I took in the landscape. The place was immaculate with terracotta vinyl flooring and white-painted walls. There were high, horizontal windows that let in sunshine and kept out curious eyes. The kennels were lined up against the wall to the right of the entryway. On the opposite side was a dog-sized swimming pool. And, in the center of this huge space, was every piece of dog training equipment ever invented.

"This is crazy," I said out loud, wondering why Brown would put so much money into a fighting dog. What was the lifespan of a fighter? Especially if it pissed him off.

I finally felt warm enough to take off my gloves and scarf. I figured by tomorrow I might remove my jacket. Staring at the dogs, I reached a new level of amazement: most of the dozen female pit bulls were pregnant. The others would have to pee on a stick for confirmation. At least a quarter of the dogs were black with a white stripe. Suddenly it started to make sense. I was beginning to understand the true importance of Benji. I would bet John's parents' farm that he was the progenitor of Brown's fighting line of American Pit Bull Terriers.

"Penny, how's Duke?" I asked, noticing her standing next to me.

"He's conscious and looking good. Vitals are great. So I left him with one of the vets and vet techs to see if I can help here."

"As you can see, these are the lucky dogs. They're in great shape. You can go home, if you want. Someone can drive you to my house and your car. I'm going to check out these guys and swab them. I'll send all the DNA samples to Barbara in the morning," I said.

"I'll stay. I've never seen anything like this," she said wide-eyed, but her mousse-spiked hair was starting to bend with fatigue.

"Me, neither," I admitted, still stunned by our find.

Penny watched as Jackie and I hit our stride. I took blood samples from the females to confirm how many were pregnant. Jackie collected the evidence strewn around the area. We finished in record time, due to the good health of these dogs. I took the last one, a male, out of the kennel.

"Jackie, look at this guy," I said sharply. I didn't say anything else. I wanted her reaction.

"Oh God, it's the tan-and-white dog that fought with the dark brown pit that Brown shot, isn't it? He's the only one with fresh scars. I wonder if Brown was looking for a replacement for Benji?"

"Well, this old boy is throwing in the towel. He's out of the fight game forever," I said emphatically, putting the dog back in his kennel. I petted his head.

"Jackie, I'd like to keep these dogs together until we can figure out what to do with them. Do you want to call Sheriff Phillips?" I asked.

"God, no! I don't want to explain how we kept him away from the raid. You tell him."

"Wuss," I said. She didn't relent. "Fine, I'll call."

I woke up the Sheriff, and explained the situation, at least in part. I promised him more info later in the day. He was a lot nicer than I would have been when I told him about the raid, and said he would call his Animal Control agents and would arrive with them ASAP. And yes, he did have kennel space for the dogs until they could go to rescues. He even ended the call with a pleasant goodbye.

"Holy shit!" Jackie shouted, recapturing my attention.

She had opened a door and was staring into a closet. The shelves were packed with bottles of steroids, antibiotics, tranquilizers and syringes. The top shelf was stacked with break sticks. Another closet held boxes of latex gloves, antiseptic and cleansing fluids and paper towels. Leashes and harnesses were hanging on pegs attached to the inside of the door next to a couple of cattle prods. On the floor were several pairs of rubber boots. It was OCD-organized.

We opened another door and found an office with a couple of cots, a table and several chairs. Apparently, our raid also interrupted a card game. There was a door off to one side of the room that opened to a bathroom. Next to it was another door, but this one was locked and bolted. I called John, explained the situation, and asked him to send me someone with a bolt cutter. He arrived and removed the lock.

I called Jackie over and we all walked into a small, windowless room. John flipped on the overhead light. Several objects stood out: a safe, a surgical table and a raised wooden platform holding half-dozen tanks. There was a six-foot long counter on which the microscope and centrifuge rested. Underneath was a stack of cabinets with wooden drawers. A comfortable stool completed the room's furnishings.

John eyed the tanks with a curious expression. "What's that?"

"They're semen holding tanks."

"Do you think the pregnant dogs out front were artificially inseminated?" Jackie asked.

"I'm sure they were," I answered, glancing around the space again. "That's what all this equipment is used for. I have the same microscope in my lab. It's perfect for evaluating the viability of sperm."

I turned to John and asked, "Do you have anybody here that can open the safe?"

"Hang on a sec," he said, taking out his cell phone and looking at the face of the safe. He took a photo of it with the manufacturer's name and serial number and texted it to Andrews. "He probably knows someone at DEA who can do it."

John was right. Soon, an officer with DEA emblazoned across every piece of clothing arrived. He said he had already been in touch with the manufacturer, who gave him the necessary information to unlock the safe. In less than five minutes, he swung open its door and left us to explore the contents. We clustered around John, who pulled out two ledgers and handed one to each of us. Then he pulled out a computer.

"Hallelujah!" I said, thumbing through the pages.

"What have you got?" John asked.

"I have a list of more than 600 collection dates for a dog with initials BB, which go back almost three years," I said. "If you figure the averages, a dog produces about 50 million sperm per ejaculation, enough to fill 10-20 straws, which are the size of coffee stirrers. Usually 3-6 are needed per insemination."

"That's a lot of puppies," Jackie said and asked, "What happens to the straws?"

"Nine or ten of them are placed into containers called goblets," I recalled while I flipped through my stack of papers. "If I'm remembering correctly, I think these type tanks would hold 5 or 6 canisters, which hold the goblets. Then they are attached to canes and are placed into the tank, which is filled with liquid nitrogen. Brown must be maintaining them himself. What have you got, Jackie?"

"I hit the mother lode – literally," she said. "I'm holding a list of hundreds of females that Brown either considered breeding or bred. I have here the owners' and dogs' names, dates and information obtained from vaginal smears detailing the four stages of the breeding cycle. All the notes are in the same handwriting."

Jackie began opening the wooden drawers and pulling papers from it. I asked her what she was doing.

"I'm looking for a sample of Brown's handwriting. I suspect these are his notes, but it would be nice to be sure."

John and I began rummaging through the other drawers, peering at papers until Jackie announced she found a handwritten note signed by Brown. She put it on the countertop next to the lists of female dogs. We all agreed it was the same handwriting.

I picked up the list of females and looked through it. Each dog's file ended with the result of a pregnancy test. A quick glance told me Brown's success rate was astronomical. I relayed this fact.

"So Jefferson Brown took pit bull breeding to a whole other level," John said, running his hand over the stubble that had sprouted across his jawline. "Do you think that made Benji expendable?"

"As in Brown might have killed him?" I said. "Why?"

"Who knows?" he said, his voice expressing the exasperation we were all feeling.

FIFTY-ONE

LIEUTENANT ANDREWS'S ARRIVAL ENDED OUR conversation. As the resident vet, I explained to him the significance of the items in the small room. Then we all walked to the training area. From past experience, I figured the Crime Scene Unit would break it down and transport everything to the lab in the barracks where it would all be tested for prints, DNA, anything that would give up any information.

"Any sign of Arnie Diaz?" I asked Andrews. He shook his head no.

"So we now have another mystery to solve?" Jackie griped, sounding as cranky as I was feeling.

"Damn it, we do," I said. "Everyone is accounted for except Diaz."

"I managed to get a message to Lincoln, and he said he hasn't seen Diaz since the night of the fight he taped for us," John said, looking more annoyed as the conversation continued. "Let's just get finished here and I'll see what I can find out tomorrow. Right now, I want to check on Duke. Then I'll be back."

So Jackie, Penny and I began boxing all the contents in the closets and marking them. We would turn them over to Andrews to keep with the other evidence of Brown's misdeeds. With the arrival of Sheriff Phillips and his Animal Control agents, we quickly moved the dogs from the kennels to their trucks. I took a few minutes to explain the situation to Sheriff Phillips and the need for secrecy. He understood and he gave me a "Good job," before he went on his way with the healthy dogs. He was lucky. It was after two o'clock and we were all exhausted, but we still had more items to pack up.

"What is all this?" Penny asked, looking around the training area for the first time. "I think I can figure out some of the machines on my own, but I'm hoping I'm wrong."

I followed her gaze. She was staring at a piece of equipment that had a metal base and two padded stirrups projecting upward from it. There were straps over the stirrups.

"It's called a 'rape box.' The females, too, are trained to fight, so they can't just turn the male loose to breed with her, so they strap her down. These dogs really never know a 'normal' moment, including now being artificially inseminated."

"The only thing I recognize is the treadmill," Penny said, her face pinched with distaste. "What's the machine next to it?"

"It's called a catmill," I said, following her finger, which was pointing at a pole with a long beam centered and attached across the top of it. "A dog is chained to the end of the beam and a small animal, usually a cat or tiny dog, is tied to the other end. The dog races after the bait, turning the pole. That's what caused that deep groove in the ground – the pitter-patter of big paws racing after some terrified creature. When the dog finishes exercising, it gets to kill it."

"This is really horrible," Penny said.

"Yes, it is," I agreed. "But here's a thought that might make you feel better – the best thing about a Friday night bust is no one gets out until Monday morning."

"It doesn't," Jackie said.

"I was talking to Penny," I said, and found myself smiling. The thought that I could placate Jackie with such a simple statement was a joke. I knew exactly how she was feeling. I looked over the paperwork again and couldn't find Diaz's name on any pages. "Well, he wasn't breeding dogs with Brown, according to these records."

"So we pretty much came up empty," John said, walking into the room.

"Every answer just leads to more questions," I said. "At least you can tell me how's Duke."

"He was happy to see me. The vet who was with him said he's doing well."

"Good news," Jackie chimed in, looking relieved. Then she asked, "Hey John, can we have the files, computer and anything that was in the desk first? I'd like to keep all of it for a couple of days."

"As long as we can have the computer when you're done," John responded.

"Sure," I said, answering for Jackie. "Why don't we just take the file drawers and stack them in the rental car? There's plenty of room."

We all agreed and proceeded to load it up. We were saying our thanks and goodbyes when an unmarked sedan pulled in next to us. Driving was Garrison. The undercover wunderkind had taken off his chains and pulled up his pants a bit, but otherwise was wearing his street uniform.

"How'd you do it?" John asked. We knew he was asking about Ghost.

"He was one crazy mother," Garrison said, though that information came as no surprise to any of us. "His greatest fear, of course, was going back to prison. So when the raid was going down, I kept talking to him, telling him I'd be looking at a life sentence just like him if I went back. I managed to stand next to him when we were handcuffed. I kept saying I had to get away. Pointed out how close we were to the woods and, with so many people being taken away, the cops would be too busy to catch us.

"He was so tweaked, it was easy to make him believe we could slip away. I just told him what he wanted to hear, that it was safe to go. Ghost ran and I hung back. He was ordered to stop and chose not to. I'll always think of it as suicide by cops. Somehow he had to know that was going to happen."

I felt a twinge of conscience, only because I couldn't have cared less about Ghost's death. I would never forget him slitting his dog's throat and the hideous smile that lit up his face.

FIFTY-TWO

THE TEMPERATURE WAS HOLDING STEADY at frigid and the wind had risen to a howl. I salvaged some warmth thinking about all the dogs we had rescued and were safe from the elements. And the night wasn't over yet.

John was speaking nonstop into his earphone, acquiring more warrants and divvying them out to local K-9 and Animal Control teams. He had his guys call in every license plate attached to a car that had been parked at the warehouse.

"You get anywhere on Diaz?" I asked when he stopped talking. "Not yet," he answered, the lines across his forehead deepening with concentration.

"I'm going to look at Duke before we take off," I said. "Then I just want to go home, okay?"

"I still have some warrants to check on, but I can do that from the car," John answered.

"Do you want to stop at our house?" I asked the others. "You can rest, shower, eat, talk, in any order you prefer."

"I'm exhausted," Jackie said. "I'll take you up on your offer."

"I'll stay for breakfast. It is being offered, right?" Garrison said, definitely a foodie. "Then I'll hit the road. My job seems to preclude sleep on a daily basis."

"Penny?" I said, turning to her. She looked wiped out.

"I'm going to get my car and check on the two dogs in my hospital. I want to send my vet techs home. I can crash there; I have a roll-out bed for just such occasions."

The rest of us decided to meet up at the house. We'd unload the Mobile Unit at the lab tomorrow. As soon as I turned on the engine and blasted the heater, I called Gina. I knew she and Vernon were early risers. She answered her phone immediately and I was sure I heard Ella bark in the background.

"Are you at our house?" I asked, not that surprised.

"Yeah, how did it go?"

"The bad news is that Duke was shot. He's okay, but needs to rest for a few days. On the other hand, we saved many more dogs than we lost and put a lot of assholes in jail, which I guess makes it a good raid," I said, wishing I could sound more enthusiastic. "Everything okay at the house?"

"I kept Ella at our place so she wouldn't be alone. I was just returning her. Tom is indignant and Daisy is sleeping. The usual. I was going to text you and see what time you'd be home."

"We're leaving Hurlock now," I said, looking in the rearview mirror to watch the minimalist streaks of light breaking through the darkness caused by the rising sun.

"Good. Vernon's cutting up fruit salad and I was planning on making waffles and bacon. How many will there be?" she asked.

"John, Jackie and Garrison, whom you haven't met yet. You'll stay for breakfast?"

"You know you'll end up talking business or else you'll want to. We'll get together some other time."

I passed along the word that breakfast would be waiting for us. A hungry John flipped on his lights and siren and goosed the gas pedal. We were home in drag racing time.

Penny insisted on leaving and we said our goodbyes as we all walked her to her car. I thanked her for her invaluable help and gave her a big hug.

John set up a large crate for Duke in the sunroom and I grabbed a couple of thick quilts to put on its floor. Then John and I returned to the Mobile Unit and retrieved Duke, put him on a stretcher and carried him into the house. Once we had settled him, I rechecked his vitals which were good, but I was concerned about all the exertion he had undergone. So I gave him some more subcutaneous fluids to insure he wouldn't become dehydrated.

When I returned to the dining room, I found Gina and Vernon finishing up in the kitchen. Gina, the mother I'd always wanted, told us to wash our hands before we ate and then ordered us to sit down upon our return. We did. Our caregivers slipped out once they served up the food, despite my protests.

I instantly started shoveling waffles – the ultimate vehicle for carrying maple syrup – into my mouth. I gulped down a glass of milk and hid a burp, or so I thought, until I saw John smirking at me.

He lifted a forkful of food towards his mouth and stopped, seeing Garrison staring at him.

"So Andrews told me Brown's kneecap needed more stitches than a baseball," Garrison laughed and added, "Police dog brutality? Really?"

"He shouldn't have shot Duke and then he certainly shouldn't have kicked him," John said without hesitation.

"So Brown escaped through a tunnel?" Garrison wanted to know, losing interest in Brown's condition. "I saw the Rivera boys being thrown into squad cars. What a wonderful sight."

"Almost as nice as Duke bringing down Brown. You would have loved that one. That jerk was running and sweating through the woods, making it easy for Duke to pick up his scent. I told him to get him, in German, of course."

I started to smile but stopped when I noticed John's mood suddenly change. He looked tired and dejected, especially when he began speaking again. "Damn it, after all that, Brown basically gave me nothing. He denied knowing who killed Benji, Duncan Stanton, and knew nothing about the dog that was buried beside his number one guy. And so on. Finally he blamed everything on Arnold Diaz.

"Christ, I didn't even realize the prick had shot Duke. I heard the gunshot, of course, but Duke never let out a sound," he said, and looked so guilty I wanted to get up and hug him. That thought passed quickly.

"So where is Diaz?" Garrison asked, looking as puzzled as I felt.

"Who the hell knows?" John said angrily and added, "Maybe he's hiding out at Restore Rescue."

FIFTY-THREE

A SILENCE HAD FALLEN OVER the table. None of us looked happy. So I asked, "What do we know about Diaz?"

"Well," Jackie said, "he was fighting the three rescued pit bulls from Cambridge on Lincoln's video. Duncan Stanton and the pit bull were killed and buried near his house in Fort Howard Park, so maybe he and Brown really did get a murderous divorce. Perhaps Diaz killed Benji, and then took out Stanton."

"Why?" I asked, thinking out loud, "He and Brown were partners, even childhood friends. So why would Brown mention him if it wasn't true? To send us in the wrong direction?"

John stopped eating and picked up his phone. "McDonald, it's Thibert," he said, so I knew he was talking to one of the desk sergeants at the barracks. "Would you check again to see if you booked an Arnold Diaz tonight from the Hurlock raid? Yeah, I'll hold." We all waited with John. "Are you sure? You still processing people? Shit!" John barely managed a "thanks" before disconnecting. He punched in another number.

"Hey Lieutenant, it's Thibert," he said, up and pacing around the kitchen. "Has anyone heard anything about Arnold Diaz?"

He listened and his eyes widened and then tightened in anger. His face flushed with fury.

"How the hell could that happen?" he almost shouted at his boss.

He stopped and listened. Without another word he ended the call.

We looked at John expectantly. I could tell he was getting himself under control before he spoke. It took a while.

"Somehow the warrants got away from us and Andrews thinks some asshole took it upon himself to send the one for Arnold Diaz directly to Baltimore County P.D."

"Oh, no!" I moaned. "After all our sneaking around …."

"How the hell could that happen?" Garrison jumped in, angry and scowling.

He took one look at John's face and said, "Never mind."

"When I was checking out Brown's properties, I also looked into Diaz," John reported. "I found out he owned a non-working farm with a large barn about a mile away from his house in Fort Howard Park. As usual, the title was buried under a bunch of corporations. I had warrants issued, but I told the clerk to put Diaz's on hold. Somehow it wasn't. Baltimore County P.D. served it. Big surprise: Diaz's house was empty. And the barn where I suspected he kept and trained his dogs? It burned down tonight.

"There were no dogs in it, but there were a bunch of kennels and cabinets, which had been emptied, left in the rubble. God damn it!" he exploded. "Where the hell is Diaz? And his goddamn dogs?"

Garrison smoothed and folded his linen napkin next to his plate, a study in calmness and good manners. "I think the more important question might be: 'Why wasn't he at the fight?' He couldn't have been warned to stay away, since no one knew."

I was all talked out, which was good since again I had no response. So I stood up and picked up my plate. Everyone else followed my lead. The sun was bright and the river was glassy, but no one seemed to notice but me.

We all watched John grab his buzzing phone off the dining table. He listened for several minutes, barely saying a word before he disconnected.

"That was Andrews," he said, sitting next to me and putting his hand on my knee. I wrapped mine over his. "He traced the goddamn warrant for Diaz to Baltimore County P.D. and then to Fort Howard Park K-9. It was never served. So now I'm going on the assumption that someone in the department saw the warrant, kept it and warned Diaz not to be waiting for us at his home."

"I give up," Jackie said having trouble keeping her eyes open. She had taken off her shoes and was massaging her instep. She swung her foot down, pushed her chair back, picked up her boots and announced. "I'm exhausted. I'm going to grab a few hours sleep and then head home."

"Hang on a sec," John said, finally taking his face out of his iPad. "I actually have some good news. Andrews just emailed me the stats on the raid. There were five different law enforcement agencies on the scene," he said in his most official voice, as if reading a government report. "So far, the number of people arrested is 257, a lot of them owners and trainers, but mostly 'sporting enthusiasts.' Home followups are being done now, so we should have more dogs, more charges and a lot more people. It will probably take some time, since many of these assholes are from out of state – we confiscated driver's licenses from as far away as the Carolinas, Florida, New York and New Jersey. DC and Baltimore were heavily represented. The money's been counted and the unconfirmed amount is $415,000. Oh, and Jefferson Brown is being held on $2 million bail.

"Child Protective Services pulled 11 kids out of this mess," John continued. "Four-year-olds were watching dogs tear each other apart. One seven-year-old was actually running food his mother was cooking and selling. Like eating french fries is normal while watching a dog being eviscerated."

John picked up his mug and put it down without taking a sip. I had the feeling he didn't want to be awake much longer.

"What was the largest purse of the night?" Jackie asked, pale with exhaustion. Smudges formed under her eyes. She looked so tired, I knew I didn't want to look in a mirror.

"A cool $150,000. In the esteemed words of Joe Biden, this was a Big Fucking Deal."

"And so," I said, "why would Arnold Diaz miss it? He didn't even have a trainer there with any of his dogs?"

"Who knows?" John shrugged his shoulders, putting an end to that conversation. "I need a few hours of sleep before I head into work. I want to go over all the arrest records. And Andrews texted me about an hour ago to stop by his office this afternoon."

"Why?" I wanted to know. John's shoulders shrugged again. I interpreted that to mean he knew nothing.

"I'm going to check on Duke," I said. "It's time to give him some more pain meds. I was thinking about asking you to bring him upstairs, but he's better off not being moved. I'll set the alarm and get up in three hours to recheck him."

"No!" John said, and smiled. "If you don't take this personally, I'll sleep with my dog tonight."

"Fine," I said and grinned. "I'll miss you, but I understand."

With that, we all stood up and congregated at the front door. John and Garrison exchanged a couple of back slaps. Garrison gave Jackie and me brief hugs goodbye and walked out into the sunlight of the new day. Jackie crawled in the direction of the guestroom, or her room, as I thought of it.

John opened the closet door and pulled out our jackets. "Come on," he coaxed.

"I want to go to bed. It's seven o'clock. You go."

"We'll take Ella for a quick walk, you'll get cold and then I'll take you upstairs and warm you up." He pushed my jacket towards me. I took it knowing John was a man of his word.

FIFTY-FOUR

THE ALARM DRAGGED ME OUT of a deep sleep. I had passed the REM stage, but not by much. That's because it was 11 a.m., and I had slept for only three hours. Obviously more than John had, since he left a note on his pillow telling me that Duke had a good night and he was gone. Ella and Tom were lying next to each other at the foot of the bed, a sight that shocked me into wakefulness. Daisy was pressed against the side of my pillow.

Duke was sitting up in his kennel when I entered the sunroom and wagged his tail to let me know he was feeling better. I let him out, put on his leash and took him for a short, slow walk with Ella. We returned and I fed the two dogs and switched Duke to pain pills.

I took my cup of coffee to my desk where I sat at my computer and started my workday. I emailed Barbara to expect the DNA samples from the raid and pled my case: My samples were the most important in the world and therefore needed her immediate attention. While I did that, I called Penny.

"How's Duke?" she wanted to know, before I could ask her about Blockhead and Legs. After I finished telling her he was better, she said, "The dogs are doing really well. If they had a home, I'd say they could leave tomorrow, but...."

"I know," I sympathized. "I have a friend who is a director at BADRAP, one of the rescues that did such a great job with some of Michael Vick's dogs. Maybe it has some room. I'll call her and let you know."

"If they can be socialized I'd adopt them. I can't believe how sweet they are."

"Oh, Penny, that's great. Let me see what I can do. I'll get back to you."

Then I called Gina and asked her if she could stay with Duke while I worked in the lab. I didn't want to leave our warrior dog alone. She assured me she and Vernon would watch over him as long as they were needed. I poked my head out of the front door and sighed with happiness. The sun was warm on my face. I ducked back into the house, threw on some clothes, and jogged with Ella to the lab.

My phone vibrated. I looked at the text John just sent in reply to mine, wanting to know why Andrews had called him in. According to him, Andrews had rescinded his detective privileges, handed him a slew of materials to study for his upcoming detective exam, and then questioned John to make sure he hadn't changed his mind overnight. He hadn't, John promised Andrews.

Jackie arrived soon after and, once I told her, was almost as delighted as I was with John's career choice. We spent the rest of Saturday performing necropsies on the dogs we had brought in last night. We continued on Sunday and finally finished the last two dogs around noon on Monday.

Jackie took off to keep her prearranged meeting with John at Baltimore County P.D. in Towson. It had been postponed until today since everyone there had been busy investigating a cop killing and the suspect hadn't been arrested until this morning. Everything had been put on hold.

Garrison had already talked to his boss, Captain Steinman, who in turn spoke with Sergeant Brennan and Lieutenant Andrews and John. To a man, each was concerned with the apparent leak within the Fort Howard Park Police Department. It had been arranged that Jackie would hand deliver Brown's computer to Brennan. In exchange, she and John would be granted access to the computer files, raids and arrest records of known dog fighters in Baltimore County.

I cleaned up and came out of my lab an hour later. Ella and I sprinted home. My phone rang on the way. It was Barbara.

"I've just faxed you some of the DNA profiles I collected from your samples, but I wanted to tell you this myself: I found Ella's dam. It's Dervish, who belonged to Antonio Rivera. I double-checked the findings by separating Ella's genetic markers. As you already know, I found the sire to be Benji. You sent me Dervish's DNA. She was picked up in Friday night's raid."

I came to an abrupt halt and Ella skidded to a stop next to me. I exhaled sharply. "Antonio Rivera!" I said, genuinely surprised. "Well, Barbara, I think I know how Ella ended up at the shelter. And yes," I said before she could offer her usual warning, "I'll be careful."

I left Ella at the house and jumped in my car. I drove to Cambridge, stopped at the local Best Buy and bought two burner phones and returned to my car. I had a plan.

"Oh shit!" I said out loud, took my foot off the gas pedal and started to brake. I realized I was once again putting myself in jeopardy. But the thought didn't last long. I reasoned that those arrested Friday night were currently being arraigned and wouldn't be free yet. So I drove to the Chesapeake Estates subdivision where the Rivera twins resided. The only vehicle parked at Antonio's condo was the red Mustang, just as I hoped. Had I seen any other cars, I would have kept on driving. Instead I parked, hesitated for a second and then jumped out of the car. I walked to the condo's front door and rang the bell.

Sandre Washington opened the door. At her side was a blue nose pit bull puppy, probably the one I had seen her carrying from Jefferson Brown's house. We stood staring at each other for a couple of seconds. She was model-thin and well-dressed in skin-tight black leather pants and a thick, dark-grey cabled cardigan sweater that she wrapped around her body. Her skin tone was a rich café au lait color – French Roast with a heavy hit of milk. Her eyes were as dark as espresso beans, and anything but innocent. She had a world-weary look. Her hair fitted like a skullcap, accentuating her ancestral broad cheekbones and generous wide mouth. Even without makeup, she was beautiful, despite her broken nose and bloodshot eyes.

"What do you want?" she finally said, her voice soft, but suspicious. "Who are you?"

"I wanted to thank you for saving her life," I said, and handed her a photograph of Ella, all healthy and happy. I gave Sandre an easy smile. I really meant it.

"I don't know what you're talking about," she said, just going through the motions of denial. Her eyes were shifting up and down the street behind me. "You've got to get out of here."

"No, I have to talk to you," I said, and held my ground. "I took this dog, Ella, from the shelter, and helped heal her wounds. I know you saved her life and her puppies."

"I can't talk to you," she said, her nervousness seemed to grow and she backed into her house. I stuck my business card and one of the phones in her hand before she could close the door. I took it as a good sign that she didn't throw it at my head. "I programmed my phone number into it. I bought a burner for myself. Please call me." Then I loudly apologized for ringing the wrong doorbell and returned to my car. I stopped in front of several other houses looking lost, I hoped.

I had been home for more than an hour when the burner phone rang. "What do you want?" Sandre asked, her voice even softer.

"I want to know about Ella," I said.

"How did you find me?" she asked.

"I saw your Mustang parked in front of Jefferson Brown's house. You were carrying a pit puppy to your car. I traced your license plate and found your address."

"Oh, my God!" she gasped, her panic almost vibrating across the phone. "You know Brown? Do you have any idea what he'll do to me if he finds out I've spoken with you?"

"Yes."

"Then you know he'll kill me. What they did to Ella would be nothing to how they'd torture me." Her voice cracked with fear.

"No one will find out through me," I said quickly. "I just want to know about Brown and Arnold Diaz. You know them, don't you?"

"They were partners," Sandre said succinctly.

"How so?" I prompted, knowing I had to go slow or I would lose her.

"They've known each other since they were kids in Fort Howard Park. They do business together. Or rather did."

"Dog business? I don't care about anything else," I said, explaining I worked for the HSPAC, not any law enforcement agency.

"Yes," she said, "they owned pit bulls together. But, in the last few years, Brown became interested in breeding his fighters and pretty much stopped fighting them. He's been adding to his stock and I think Diaz felt left out. I'm not sure."

"Who bred Ella?"

"Brown," Sandre said. "He bought a black pit bull from some crack-head a few years ago. He had old fighting scars so Brown immediately began training him to fight and when he found out he was a natural, he started fighting him. The dog kept winning. So he bred him to all his females. He looked at Big Ben to give new blood to his dogs. He was that incredible. His fights lasted no longer than a few minutes."

"You're talking about the black pit bull with the white stripe under his chin?" I asked, now sure that Benji, renamed Big Ben, was the "BB" listed on Brown's breeding records.

"Yes," she said, sounding startled.

"So he bred Big Ben to Antonio's Dervish?" I said, taking her back to neutral ground. Something about Ella's plight had forced her to act.

"Yes," Sandre said, and added suspiciously, "How did you know about Dervish?"

"It doesn't really matter, does it? Let's just say I've been doing my homework, okay?"

"Yeah, you're right. Let's just get this over. Dervish had five pup-pies. Four were great. Antonio sold them. Your Ella was the runt. He kept her and tortured her for fun, as you can tell. Brown was furious when he found out Antonio had let her have puppies. He didn't want her breeding. She was the runt and had none of the qualities he wanted in his fighters. He told Antonio to get rid of them all. That night when

Antonio went out, I dropped them off at the Cambridge shelter. When he got home I told him I drowned them. Jesus. He believed me. How sick is that? Anyway, if he ever finds out she's alive, he'll kill me."

"Trust me," I said with sincerity. "Your secret's safe."

"Hey, what happened to the puppies?" Sandre said. She sounded concerned. "I figured with Ella as the mother, they'd be safe at the shelter. No one would expect them to be fighters."

"What do you mean?" I said, surprised by her comment, not understanding it.

She hesitated. I let her proceed at her own pace. I took five interminable, long, deep breaths before she continued.

"Some pits bulls were taken from the Cambridge shelter," Sandre finally explained. "I found out about it one night when Antonio and Diaz were out of their minds high. I was in the bedroom, but I could hear them talking. Diaz was bragging about just getting three young dogs from the Cambridge shelter. They had been confiscated in raids on pit bull fights and were supposed to go to rescues. Diaz was saying he was going to get them fighting again."

"How did he get the dogs?" I asked, praying Diaz had been loaded and indiscreet enough tell Antonio.

I was glad I had taken all those deep breaths because now I was holding mine, waiting for her response. And waiting. An eternity. Finally she spoke.

"You know the bitch who runs the shelter?" she asked.

"You mean Helen?" I replied, surprised and dreading her answer.

"Is she the one who looks like a sausage – you know, like she's been stuffed into her clothes?"

"No, that's Michelle Manning. She's the director of the shelter's board," I said, knowing who she meant immediately and feeling a rush of relief.

"Black-haired bitch?"

"Yes. Are you telling me she gave Diaz the dogs?" I asked, my voice rising in disbelief.

"No," Sandre said, and paused again. Her answer was worth the wait. "Her husband sold them to him."

FIFTY-FIVE

Dwight?" I asked incredulously, shocked into momentary silence. Then I thought maybe I heard wrong, so I said, "You're telling me it was Dwight Manning?"

Sandre hesitated long enough for me to realize I needed to keep my reactions to a minimum. I waited for her response.

"Yes," she said after another long pause.

"Do you know why?" I said, managing a conversational tone. I stopped pacing the length of the house and plopped down on the couch and was quiet. Unfortunately, Sandre was, too. She was exhausting in her stops and starts. I understood how hard this was for her, but jeez.

She finally continued, "Brown was getting pit bulls from shelters around here. I think he was using a K-9 guy to spot dogs for him that had been confiscated in raids and sent to shelters. They all grew up together. His name is something like Harriman or Harrington."

"Is that when he started Restore Pit Bull Rescue?" I interrupted.

"Yes," Sandre said, sounding startled. "You know about it?"

"So where does Dwight fit into all this?" I asked, ignoring her question and quickly changing directions. There was so much I wanted to know.

"I think the K-9 cop is that Dwight guy's cousin," Sandre went on, seeming to gain some confidence as she ratted out Brown. "I think he must have heard about the dogs from his cousin and wanted in on the action. So he took three dogs from the shelter and sold them to Diaz. Antonio warned him to keep his mouth shut when he told him about buying the stolen dogs. No one wanted Brown to find out. He'd go crazy."

"Did Antonio mention if Diaz fought those dogs in Hurlock?"

"Yes," she said, really sounding surprised now. But she couldn't resist adding, "He told me when he got home that night. It was the ultimate fuck you to Brown. Diaz put the dogs on the ticket a few weeks ago. I heard one of them got killed."

I had watched it happen. Now I wanted Diaz as much as I had wanted Brown.

"Do you know why Diaz wasn't at the last Friday night fight?"

"No," she said. "Everybody's wondering. Look, I have to go. I've been talking to you way too long."

"Just one more question," I begged. "Please."

"What?" she said curtly. She was pretty much done.

"Tell me about Restore Pit Bull Rescue?" I asked.

I could hear the gears in her head turning while she decided how much to tell me. I wanted to put my hand down her throat, fish around for her words and yank them out, like a magician with scarves. Once again, I was reminded why I work with the dead. The living was too exhausting.

"This is the last question," she warned, and went on to answer it. "Brown, not Diaz, put the K-9 guy, Harrington or whatever his name is, on his payroll. His job was to tell Brown what dogs had been picked up at raids and where they were being held. Brown would decide which ones he wanted 'rescued' and have them brought to him. He was using them for breeding only, not fighting. I think he would train some of the pups he bred if he liked them and was offered enough money."

"Where did he keep them?" I asked. It was the most important question I had put to Sandre.

"I don't know and I don't want to," Sandre said, starting to sound annoyed.

My time with her was ending, but I refused to stop. "Who would pick up the dogs from the shelters?"

"Any of the creeps that worked for Brown," she responded. "They would slap on a Restore Rescue uniform, hand in phony documents and walk out with the best-looking fighters."

The phone went dead. She didn't even say goodbye. Sandre just hung up on me. I didn't care. All I wanted to do was call John and Jackie, but my phone rang first.

It was John. We both began talking; we each had news.

"Hey, why don't you conference Jackie into this conversation before I continue?" I suggested, "She'll want to hear this, too."

"She left an hour ago," John said, to my surprise. I hadn't heard a word from her all day. "She's probably home. I stayed and looked over their K-9s for a while. They have some new dogs they were training. I'm on my way back to the barracks now."

"Hang on, I'll call her," I said. I punched in Jackie's number. When she answered, I told her John was also on the line and I was calling with good news.

"I have good news of my own," Jackie said, cutting me off in her excitement.

"You go first," I said with unaccustomed graciousness. God, I was feeling good.

"Okay," she said, jumping in with enthusiasm. "As soon as I got home, I sent photographs of the dogs we confiscated last night to all the shelters and rescues in the area. I received a call from Jaime Levine at BARCS an hour ago. She recognized two of the pregnant pit bulls we liberated from Jefferson Brown's kennels. They had been at BARCS a few years ago, but not for long. They were sent to Restore Rescue."

"And that's not even the big news. Now wait for it," Jackie paused. "Ready?"

John and I both yelled at her to continue. She almost giggled, enjoying the moment.

"Jaime's been to Restore Rescue!" she ended triumphantly.

"What?" I shrieked. "When? Why?"

"Five years ago," Jackie continued. "She began sending dogs there after a K-9 officer contacted her and told her about a new pit bull rescue in Hurlock. Jaime started asking questions and the officer offered to meet her there and introduce her to the staff. She arrived at the facility and the first thing she noticed was a large sign over the front entrance: Restore Pit Bull Rescue. She looked on the wall inside and it had all the necessary permits posted to run a rescue organization.

"Over the years, Jaime said, she talked to other shelter directors who had established relationships with Restore Rescue, too," Jackie continued. "The "rescue" would call them when they had space and send a the Restore van to pick up the dog or dogs."

I was somewhere between thunderstruck and dumbfounded. This was so brazen, such a lie. And it had worked.

"How could she be duped so easily?" I asked, settling on astounded.

"She wasn't," Jackie said. "She checked out the place online and it had a website. The mission statement said it was founded to help fighting pit bulls find forever homes. It had pages and pages of testimonials and photographs. Obviously the website was taken down once the rescue's credentials were established, since we couldn't find it."

"Did she remember the name of the officer? Where he was from? Anything?" John wanted to know.

"Jaime said he was wearing a Federalsburg police uniform and his name was Warren Tull. She had called his station house and spoke to the desk sergeant who verified he worked there.

"I did some quick research and found a photograph of Tull," Jackie added. "I faxed it to Jaime. He wasn't the man who showed her around Restore. She's completely freaked out. Just to make sure we were talking about the same facility I sent her a picture of it. She recognized it."

"Well, now we have an actual witness who saw the operation," I said, feeling the hair stand up on my arms. It was starting to come together. Maybe we'd even find the pretend policeman. "Did she say if there were any dogs there?"

"Yeah, she told me she saw around a dozen. They all had fighting scars. But she didn't recognize any," she said before I could ask. "At that point, there were no exercise machines. Just big, beautiful kennels and outdoor runs."

"Any sign of Jefferson Brown?" I asked.

"Of course not," Jackie responded.

"Why am I not surprised?" I said. "By the way, didn't you already talk to BARCS after we found the three dogs fighting on Lincoln's video?"

"Yeah, but Jaime had been on maternity leave. This was her first week back. She hadn't heard about the disappearing/reappearing dogs until we just spoke. She said Restore Rescue picked up two more dogs six months ago."

None of us said a word for a minute. It was a lot for us to take in.

"What's your news?" Jackie nudged me. John chimed in.

I took them back to Barbara's morning call, telling me that she had matched Ella's DNA to Antonio Rivera's bitch, Dervish, who was confiscated in the Hurlock raid. She had been bred to Benji.

"Jackie," I asked, "remember the woman who left Brown's house carrying a pit bull puppy and drove off in the red Mustang?"

"Yeah," she said, sounding mystified.

"Well, that's Sandre Washington," I continued. "John, you ran her license plate for me when we first found Brown's house. I traced her address to Antonio Rivera. They live together. She was so gentle handling her puppy, it surprised me. So when Barbara tied Ella to Rivera, I just made the leap to Washington. I couldn't think of anyone else in that crowd that would have tried to save Ella by taking her to the shelter. So I contacted her and she was willing to talk to me on the phone. She explained Antonio kept the runt around to torture her.

"I think we found our leak," I continued. "Washington told me Brown worked with a K-9 cop who he grew up with in Fort Howard Park. He would look over the pit bulls that had been confiscated statewide and alert Brown as to what dogs went where. Then Brown would decide which ones he wanted and have one of his lackeys dress up in a Restore Rescue uniform and pick up the chosen."

"You didn't get a name, did you?" John asked.

"She wasn't sure, but said it might have been something like Harrington. Is that any help?" I asked. "Oh, and she thinks he's Dwight Manning's cousin."

"Holy shit!" John boomed. I heard his sirens come on and could hear his tires screech. "I'm on my way back to Towson to give that piece of information to Whitfield and Delacroix and get to work. Jackie, you want to meet me there?"

"What's going on?" I demanded, feeling out of the loop.

"Jackie and I met there as planned, and Brennan gave us access to the time sheets of his K-9 officers and everyone else involved in each dog fighting raid," John said. "We put together a list of cops that were on duty when the raids were successful and another for when they didn't pan out. Then we cross-referenced the lists. We pulled a few names that could have been passing on the information. One of them was a George Hennigan. He's with Baltimore Police Fort Howard Park's K-9 division. Harrington, Hennigan, I think we found our man, whatever the hell his name is."

I summed up my conversation with Washington about Brown's foray into breeding dogs rather than fighting them, and leaving Arnold Diaz to go it alone. And, yes, Brown used Restore Rescue to steal dogs from various shelters and hide them there to breed. I also explained that Antonio had bred Ella against Brown's instructions.

"So Antonio is Ella's torturer?" John interjected.

"It would seem that way," I said slowly, knowing where this conversation was headed.

"Well, I know exactly where he is now so I can get my hands on him," John said, his voice frightening with anticipation.

"John," I warned, "it's not worth it."

"Yeah, it is," he countered.

"Please leave it alone, at least for now. Can we talk about it later?" I pleaded.

"Sure. Sorry," he said. "Don't worry."

"Okay. Let's move on, please, because that's only part of my news," I said and added, "Washington said that Dervish was bred to Big Ben."

"Benji's fighting name?" John said, quick on the uptake. "He was the BB on the breeding list?"

"Yes, exactly," I said, once again enjoying myself. "But I'm not done yet. In fact, I'm getting to my favorite part. Washington also overheard a conversation with her boyfriend and Arnold Diaz. It seems that Diaz was the one buying dogs from the Cambridge shelter, not Brown. As Jackie would say, now wait for it. But I won't make you. I will simply tell you Dwight Manning was the one selling them!"

John found his voice first and said, "Dwight Manning, as in Michelle Manning? Did you just say that? This day just keeps getting better."

Jackie joined in, "Oh, God, I love it! Do you think she knew and that's why she stopped allowing pit bulls?"

"No, I think the reason she doesn't want pit bulls at the shelter is they might screw up her adoption rates. I doubt if she knows what he did. At least I hope not. I want to be the one to tell her. Right before you put the handcuffs on him, John."

"That's my little pumpkin," John purred.

"Hey, that prick sold the three dogs to Arnold Diaz," I shot back. "That's how they ended up fighting in Hurlock, and Petey Jr. is dead and the others are missing, so screw the Mannings and the poor dogs they rode in on."

"By the way, why would Washington tell you all this?" he questioned.

"Oh, I forgot to mention her broken nose and black eyes. She's ready to move on. I think she's hoping Antonio will be put away for a long, long time. Me, too."

"Well, he had an outstanding warrant for a DUI so that will keep him in jail a little longer. Brown made bail an hour ago, but we can also file new charges on him – stealing dogs from shelters. God, what a shit-head. I'll put out an APB on him."

"Good. But I'd feel a lot better if he were in jail right now."

"You get anything else from her?" he asked in a flat voice.

When I said no, he continued questioning me, "Allison, how the hell did you know she had a broken nose and black eyes?"

Oh shit, I thought. Once again I was busted.

"I showed her a picture of Ella and gave her a burner phone with my number programmed into it and asked her to call. She did."

"You went to her house?" John yelled. "Are you crazy?"

"Allison," Jackie said with a moan. "You went by yourself? Again? You are crazy!"

"Don't waste your breath, Jackie," John shouted his outrage.

"Hey, I figured the bad guys were in jail and this might be the only chance I had to talk to her. Jesus, get off my back."

John was done talking to me. Instead he said, "Jackie, Brennan gave his tech geek Brown's computer and he's been working on trying to open it since you signed off on it. You want to meet me in Towson?"

"Thanks for the offer, but I don't want to go anywhere. I'm sure you've got it covered. What a good day this is turning out to be – except for my partner's stupidity."

"Okay, I get it," I muttered.

"I wish I could believe that," John said. "Jackie, I'll let you know what we find out." He hung up without saying goodbye to me.

I called BADRAP and found my friend in her office. She was willing to take Blockhead and Legs, and work on rehabilitating the dogs in the hope Penny could adopt them. I called her with the good news. Then I spoke with Barbara and gave her Benji's fighting name: Big Ben. At least I didn't disappoint everyone.

FIFTY-SIX

―――&&&――――

I LOOKED AT ELLA, WHO had turned out to be the surprising key to the puzzle, and gave her a treat. I remembered I hadn't let her out for hours and decided to take her for a long walk. The sun was warming the earth through the leafless trees, but the breeze was gentle.

We took a long walk along the river trail. My phone rang and I answered to hear a hysterical Sandre Washington.

"Oh my God, he knows," she shrieked. "I'm at the 7-Eleven in Easton. You have to come get me. Someone saw your car. You said you'd help me."

"Who?"

"Brown," she screamed at me as if talking to a deaf moron.

"I'm on my way," I said, startled by her desperation. "Just stay out of sight. I'm driving a dark grey Lexus." I hung up.

We raced back to the house which took almost 10 worrisome minutes. Ella beat me through the door to the garage. I thought about putting her back in the kitchen, but decided it would be faster to take her with me. I was getting frantic with worry.

I passed Gina and Vernon's house and was about 200 feet from reaching Route 50 when I saw a black Hummer sitting on the edge of the road. It came to life and barreled towards me, pulling directly in front of my car and forced me to hit my brakes. Before I could catch my breath, the driver's door opened and Jefferson Brown emerged.

I was staring into his expressionless black eyes. My gaze dropped to the gun in his left hand. It was pointed at my head. Despite a pronounced limp – more like he was dragging his leg – he was quickly beside my car and tapped my window with the muzzle of his .45 automatic.

I looked around trying to find an escape route. The gun in my face made that impossible. I tried to push down the fear that was rising inside me. I knew it would make me useless. I had to keep it together for my sake and Ella's. I had put us both in jeopardy. I only hoped I survived to hear John's inevitable lecture. But I had no idea how I was going to do that.

"Get out," he ordered. His right wrist was in a cast and the part of his hand and fingers that were visible were bruised and swollen. I looked him over, forcing myself to take in all aspects of Jefferson Brown. It was how I viewed a crime scene – one detail at a time. Following my usual protocol calmed me down a bit.

I noted he was dressed in money, from his long black down coat with its mink-lined hood to his black insulated Gore-Tex ski pants tucked into L.L. Bean waterproof boots.

He was a tall man who had replaced the gangsta slump with a straight spine and squared shoulders. His unzipped coat revealed a thin, self-indulgent layer of fat over a well-developed six-pack that must have kept him in the gym for hours a day. The scowl he showed in his mugshots had been perfected and now dug in deep across his broad forehead and mouth. He was large and menacing.

I tried to shield my right hand from his view by shifting in my seat a little so he couldn't see me slip my hand over the gear stick. My plan was to put the car in reverse and gun the engine to get away from him. I didn't have a chance.

His arm snaked out and he smashed my window with his gun, shattering it. "Now get out, or I'll shoot you right here. Your dead body will be the first thing your fucking boyfriend finds when he comes home."

Suddenly Brown's eyes shifted and my stomach lurched – he was staring at Ella. He leveled his gun at her and said "Pow!" Then he laughed, exposing teeth that were as perfect as Garrison's, now that the grill was gone. It was as if he had transitioned from rapper P. Diddy to entrepreneur Sean Combs. My mind was bouncing around uncontrollably like my stomach.

"You've been pretty busy," he said softly, scaring me into focus, but I'd die before I let him know that. I knew that's exactly what he was planning for me.

"Sandre explained how you found her because of her car and somehow tied that fucking runt to her and me," Brown said, his fury pouring out of him like sweat on a hot day. "But there is some justice in it. I found you because you used your own car. Did you really think I don't have eyes everywhere? You're as stupid as Sandre. And now she's dead. You soon will be."

"She's dead?" I asked in disbelief. "She can't be. I just spoke to her."

"Right after I made her call you, she had a terrible accident. I shot her. Rather, Arnold Diaz shot her. They'll find his blood under her nails. She's in the back of my car, all wrapped up like a present – just for you. You'll see her when we arrive at our destination. I plan to have you bury her right next to you."

I couldn't help myself. I groaned out loud, I didn't want to believe I had caused her death. Washington had warned me about Brown, and I convinced her I could keep her safe. I couldn't even keep myself safe. I wanted to cry, but I knew better than to show any weakness. That's what Brown wanted.

"Now get out, or I'll shoot the runt," Brown threatened. "And give me your phone."

He snatched it out of my hand, dropped it on the ground and stomped on it. Ella was on the floor of the car, cringing in fear as soon as she heard his voice. I opened the car door and was about to swing my legs out when he grabbed me by the hair and dragged me out. Ella growled and, despite her terror, jumped out after me and tried to bite him. He kicked her, and I watched Ella fly through the air and land with a thud that nearly knocked her out.

Brown watched me carefully. I refused to react. So he swung his hand across my face so fast and hard that my head snapped back. "You're going to be Diaz's last victim, you and that fucking dog."

He grabbed my wrists, oblivious to his broken one, and tightened his grasp as he pulled my arms behind my back. He picked up Ella's leash from the car, placed his gun between his knees and tied my hands together. Brown put the gun back in his left hand and went over to Ella, who was trying to stand, and lifted her by the collar. Her gurgling noises were horrific. He opened his passenger door and threw her onto the floor. Brown grabbed my hair again and hauled me into the passenger side of his car. I fell forward, so he shoved me in the belly, forcing me back in the seat. My arms felt like they were going to snap as he put the seatbelt on me. I worked my elbows up and out, relieving the unbearable pressure. I put my legs lightly over the shaking Ella, trying to comfort her.

We drove over the Chesapeake Bay and the Severn River, heading north towards Baltimore. I saw the signs for the Francis Scott Key Bridge and soon it lifted us over the Patapsco River and past Sparrows Point. Brown followed North Point Road until it dead-ended at the shuttered Fort Howard VA Hospital, and took a left. We were heading to the Park where Stanton and the dog had been buried. I knew he planned to add Ella and me to his growing death list.

"How'd you get to me?" he finally asked. I said nothing, until he pounded his fist on top of my thigh. Then I sang out. It felt like Brown had shattered my femur.

I started with John finding Benji, tracking the dog through his microchip to the crackhead to the Rivera twins to Hurlock and him. Brown's brain seemed to get stuck in the first part of my recitation.

"Who the fuck microchips a pit bull?" Brown said, banging the steering wheel with his good hand. All I could think of was thank God for stupidity, and people who wanted their pets back, except I was going to die as a result.

"How'd you find out about the fights?" he asked.

I continued spilling my guts. I told Brown about the warrants, the cameras, and how it was all because Ghost gave him up when he was busted a few months ago. Brown went apoplectic when he heard this. He argued that it couldn't be true. I insisted it was. Ghost was dead, which made him a perfect scapegoat. And Brown's world was so duplicitous that he would eventually believe Ghost had sold him out. Lincoln would live to snitch another day.

By the time I finished telling my story, I realized we were on the trail I had followed in the Mobile Unit on my way to the bodies of Stanton and the pit bull. A heavy metal gate had been put in place by the police, and it stopped us from continuing down it to the beach. Brown hit his brakes so hard he almost swerved into a tree, yelled "Shit," that turned into a stream of invectives, and threw the car into reverse spinning his tires like a drag racer.

His sheer fury engulfed the inside of the Hummer, and I felt it crushing any hope I had of escape. Brown backed up and jerked the vehicle to the left and bowled over a mess of shrubs. We continued plowing through the trees, snapping them like twigs and widened the path all the way to a strip of sandy beach and the Patapsco River. He stopped and turned off the engine and sat.

I knew he was waiting for the sun to disappear. He lit a cigarette, cracked the window and a chill filled the car. Great, I thought, we'd follow the hypothermia dog and freeze to death before we drowned. I felt panic set in as we sat doing nothing. I couldn't stop myself from picturing Duncan Stanton's terrified, ravaged face and knew Brown had the same death planned for me and Ella. I thought about grabbing her and making a run for it, but I was sure my escape would end with a bullet in my back. As soon as I thought that might be the easiest way out of this situation, I forced myself to follow my breath and calmed down a bit.

Brown slid his seat back and lowered the backrest, pushing his hood off his head and rested his gun across his lap, aiming it at me. He closed his eyes. I said nothing. Time passed. So did the sun.

"Fort Howard Park, huh?" I asked passively. I looked at Brown out of the corner of my eye. Now I knew why he was in cold weather gear. "So you killed Stanton and the dog and let everyone think it was Diaz. Why?"

Brown ignored my question. Instead he said, "I'm going to stay to watch you watch the runt die. Then I'm going to hang around to see your final gulp or heave. Or maybe shudder. It's almost time to find out what it will be."

FIFTY-SEVEN

I FIGURED I'D DIE FROM exhaustion before I could dig three graves, albeit one small one. It was cold, windy, and wet on the water and only growing worse. Brown stood close to us, watching my expression as he walked us about two feet from the waterline. He was carrying what I could only assume was Sandre Washington, wrapped in a tarp and tied up with rope.

"High tide is at 3 a.m. and it's going to be nine inches tonight," Brown explained, appearing gleeful, not a reassuring emotion to see in the eyes of a sadist. He dropped his bundle with a thud. It made me shudder. "That's not a lot of water if you were going wading, but not so good if you're buried up to your chin when the tide comes in."

Ella was sitting on my foot. Brown pointed his gun at her again. He knew how to make me work. I took the shovel from his hand. I dug. He sat. Ella whined. I dug and dug. I finally finished my first vertical grave. He had me stop digging when just my head was visible. My back was aching, my feet were numb, my arms shook with fatigue and my hands were blistered and bleeding. I had to climb out by myself, pressing my feet against the sides of the hole for leverage and inched my way up and out. I fell forward and couldn't move, my lungs heaving.

"You're not done,' Brown snapped, rose and started toward me. The last glimmer of sunlight sank into the darkness of his menacing eyes.

"I just have to catch my breath," I wheezed.

He was quiet. I petted Ella who had crawled to my side. The silence was lasting too long, so I thought I'd use it. "Just tell me one thing. Please.

I know what you were doing. You were breeding magnificent fighters. You hung your legacy on Big Ben, right? You didn't kill him, did you?"

"Shut the fuck up."

"Come on, Brown. Think of it as my last request. Tell me who killed him."

"Tough girl, huh?" he said grudgingly. "Get up and dig and maybe I'll talk."

I gingerly rose, noting my muscles had lost their elasticity and now demanded my full attention to get them functioning. I put one foot in front of the other and deliberately walked over to the shovel and picked it up. I couldn't believe I was about to say this, but I did, "Can I dig a horizontal grave since Sandre is already dead?"

Brown almost laughed. Beyond creepy. "Good point. But do the fucking runt next. I'll think how I want Sandre positioned."

Brown liked playing games.

"You want to know about Big Ben, huh?" he asked. I nodded. "After you tell me what made you look into Restore Rescue."

I started digging and my body rebelled. I put more back into it and lifted a shovelful of sand. I grunted. All the time I was going through my options as to what to tell Brown. I decided to follow Antonio's counsel and not mention the Manning/Diaz thievery. I stuck with Ghost and played him to the bitter end, which was looming all too quickly.

"Ghost took a video of the fight for the police," I told him, substituting his name for Lincoln's and providing Brown with misinformation. I didn't want to be responsible for any more deaths. "My partner and I ended up watching it. She thought one of the dogs looked familiar from a raid, but she couldn't remember when or where it took place. It turned out she was wrong, but in the meantime she pulled photos off the video and sent pictures of each dog to area shelters and rescues. People recognized several dogs and checked their files. All were sent to Restore Pit Bull Rescue. That would have been great, except, as you know, it didn't exist."

He smiled.

"Now will you tell me how Benji died?" I said hopefully.

"His name was Big Ben. He was a Grand Champion. Don't disrespect him," Brown corrected me, his voice growing irate as he let me know his dog had won at least five major fights to claim that title. He lit another cigarette. He took a deep, ragged inhalation and let the smoke trail out his nose.

"As soon as I saw the photograph of Big Ben I had to have him," Brown said, and I was shocked to see him give a genuine smile at the memory. "I could tell he was a Colby pit bull by the slope of his shoulders and the size of his neck. Maybe you know John Colby started breeding these American Pit Bull Terriers more than a century and they are the gold standard. Big Ben was about 15 pounds larger than the typical Colby dog, which may be why no realized one realized his pedigree. But despite his size, I'd never seen a dog that so agile and quick. He had such confidence and heart. He was the perfect American Pit Bull Terrier. That's why everyone wanted one of his pups."

"You didn't kill him, did you?" I said putting some sympathy into the question. "He meant more to you than money, didn't he?"

"I had never seen a dog like him," Brown admitted. "That's why I retired him after 18 winning months and used him only for breeding. I had been at it seriously for a few years before and had produced scores of winning dogs. But Big Ben was the best. His pups are selling for $25,000 to $35,000," Brown stated, looking as proud as any father whose child was a straight A student.

"Why'd you name him Big Ben," I couldn't resist asking.

Brown studied me before he decided to answer. "He was wearing a collar with 'Benji' stenciled on it. Whoever named him that deserved to have him stolen."

I didn't think I could hate Brown more – I was wrong. I could have wept for Benji, the Everetts and myself, but that would have made Brown happy. I wouldn't give him that.

"I've been cleaning up, betting on them when they fought," he continued. "Diaz and I had been partners in the fight business, but I didn't want him involved with breeding. That was all mine. Then he started talking shit about how his top dog, Hammerhead, could take Big Ben. He knew he was retired, but he started running his mouth that I was too scared to accept his challenge. Man, the guy was crazy."

"Was Hammerhead a brindle?" I asked, making the connection to the hypothermia dog.

"I guess you're not so stupid – except you're about to die," he said with a nasty laugh.

"You had been friends since childhood, right?" I said, ignoring his twisted humor. "What am I missing?"

Brown looked surprised at the question, and then thoughtful. His first response was to stroke his gun. I didn't want to know what that was about. I just wanted to keep him talking so I could try to figure out a way to escape.

"I didn't realize how fucked up Diaz had become," Brown resumed. "Antonio warned me, but I didn't believe him. I didn't want to think that Diaz wanted to destroy me. He spent too much time in the joint. He turned into a stupid thug and I was done with him.

"So he went to Stanton. He promised him half of his dog fighting business if he would kill Big Ben. Those fools thought they could just disappear my best dog. That was supposed to be the first step in taking me down."

I stopped digging for a moment, resting and thinking how well that plan worked. Brown was caught up in his thoughts and didn't seem to care. He gave a harsh laugh, shook his head in what I interpreted to be disbelief and continued, "I had cameras all around the place that no one else knew about. When the kennel boys called to tell me Ben was missing, I pulled the disks and there was Stanton, just walking Ben outside and putting him in his car. Next thing I hear is a bunch of guys found the dog dead in some garbage dump."

I finally found out what had happened to Benji. Now I hoped I would survive to tell the tale.

"I hired a couple of guys no one knew and had them follow Stanton," Brown continued. "They reported to me and after a few days I saw a pattern emerge. Stanton drove Diaz's top dog from his house to his kennels twice a day to work out.

"One fine morning, I cut him off on the road, kind of like I did you. I jumped out like I needed help and the motherfucker gets out of his car. I Tasered the shit out of him. Dragged him into my car. Went and got the dog. And we all went for a day at the beach – just a few one yards from this one, but you already know that."

His eyes swept the beach and landed on me. He noticed how little progress I had made digging Ella's grave. He waved his gun in my direction and then the shovel. He didn't need to tell me what he was thinking. I went back to work.

"Stanton talked his head off while I made him dig the graves." Brown was suddenly quiet, as if reveling in the pleasure of that moment. He started talking after a couple of minutes and sneered, "Like words were going to save him. Told me he shot Ben in the woods. But the impact of the bullet knocked him back and he slid down the hill. He might have gone unnoticed, but he landed in that makeshift garbage dump. Before Stanton could retrieve him, the bicyclists arrived. And that's where you and your boyfriend come in. You know he's next? And his fucking dog."

I shivered despite myself. The wind off the water seeped deep into my bones. I struggled to relax and keep the blood flowing through my extremities.

"Now it's all gone," Brown said, looking crazy with anger and disappointment. "At least he'll be my alibi. I put Diaz's fingerprints all over the shovel you're holding."

"Did you kill him?"

"Let me put it this way – he'll never be found," Brown sparkled with joy for a second.

"Did you take his dogs?"

"They'll never be found," he said looking even more pleased. "But they will be seen fighting all over the country."

"Okay. Just tell me who picked up the dogs from the shelters in the Restore truck?"

"Anyone I wanted!" he roared, and grabbed me by the hair again.

He had nothing to say except, "Shut the fuck up and dig!"

FIFTY-EIGHT

THE CONVERSATION WAS OVER. ELLA growled at Brown and he pulled his booted foot back and went to kick her.

"Ella!" I screamed. "Go! Go! Run!"

She looked at me, startled. I yelled again for her to "Go!" and pushed her with my foot. She got the message and ran down the path the Hummer had bulldozed through the woods.

"Oh no, I'm not going to miss the pleasure of watching you see her die," Brown shouted. He dragged me to the rolled up tarp, took his knife out of his back pocket and cut off the rope wrapped around it. Then he punched me between my shoulder blades, knocking me to my knees. Next he kicked me in the back of the head. I fell forward and felt jagged pieces of shell cut into my face. In a moment of pure vengeance, Brown stepped on my head and pressed it hard into the sand.

It hurt so badly, I hoped I would pass out, but I didn't. I figured he wasn't going to kill me yet – he would just torture me. Death would arrive with the incoming tide. I shook that thought off. It terrified me and I knew I had to keep my head, so to speak. My cheeks burned: one side cut with shards of shells and embedded with small stones, the other, I was sure, bearing the waffled imprint of Brown's heavy boot. He finally took his foot off my face.

Brown wasn't done hurting me. He straddled me and savagely yanked my arms behind my back and pulled my wrists together, quickly slipping the knotted rope over my hands. I used all my strength to strain against it, creating a fraction of space between my wrists. Brown ordered me to put my legs together and bend my knees. I instantly knew he was going to hogtie me. As soon as he wrapped the rope around my ankles, I flexed my muscles and again pulled against the tautness of the rope.

He had unwittingly placed me into one of my favorite yoga poses – Dhanurasana, also known as Bow Pose. In this posture, I would hold onto the top of my feet with my hands, pulling my shoulder blades together, bending my spine backwards and lifting my chest and thighs off the ground.

Finished trussing me up, Brown limped after Ella, who I hoped had put some distance between him and her. I prayed his injury – thank you, Duke – would slow him down enough so Ella could escape. I knew this was the only chance I would have to get away and help her.

I began working against the ropes with frantic determination. I pressed my wrists and ankles together and deepened the bend in my legs and back. I created a bit of slack in the rope and worked my hands and wrists unmercifully. Finally, I was able to slither them free. I rolled over, sat up and pulled the rope off my ankles. Then I ran over to the shovel, grabbed it and took off after Brown and Ella. Adrenalin had taken over.

In the distance, I heard Brown yell "Got you!" followed by Ella's mangled howl. I was sure he was dragging her back to me.

I hid behind a tightly-packed grouping of scrub pines. I could hear Brown cursing and Ella gurgling. He would have to walk past me to return to the beach. He had a gun and my dog. I had a shovel and surprise.

I knew I had one chance. I couldn't let my chattering teeth give me away. I focused on my breath, following it in and out of my body, until it calmed down.

I heard them closing in on me. I turned the shovel upside down and gripped it in both hands like a bat. Soon, I saw the outline of Brown framed by the rising moon. His face was turned towards Ella, who he was lifting by her collar with his broken hand. Her feet had found a toehold in the fabric of his coat. Her gurgling noises subsided to a wheeze.

I forced myself to wait. I tightened my hands on the shovel, ignoring the pain shooting through my torn and bleeding palms.

They were almost next to me when Ella suddenly whined, picking up my scent and tried turning in my direction. My heart nearly stopped. But fortunately, Brown looked straight ahead, following the beam of the flashlight in his hand. He passed within feet of my hiding place. I could see a malevolent grin frozen on his face.

I silently slipped out from behind the trees, lifted the shovel as if it were a baseball bat and hugged it against my right shoulder. I looked at his hoodless head walking away from me. I took a couple of silent steps forward and closed the gap between us. I pulled the shovel back, lifted my left elbow, shifted my weight forward onto my left leg, ignoring the pain shooting through my hip, and swung with all my might.

The shovel didn't bounce off his skull like I expected – it sank into it. The sound wasn't explosive; it was more like a crack, followed by a wet sucking noise. Brown crumpled to the ground. His fall ripped the shovel from my hands, the edge of the blade wedged in his skull.

I vomited. Ella was cringing. She was trying to walk to me, crying out with every step. I scrambled to her and stopped her from moving. It was too cold for us to stay there, so I scooped her up, trying not to touch her ribs. I could see at least two of them were fractured. She yelped, anyway. I opened my coat and tucked her inside it and cradled her to me. Only then did I bend over Brown, put my fingers to his neck and found no pulse.

Jefferson Brown was dead and I had killed him. All I felt was relief, nothing else. But I was devastated that I had nearly gotten Ella killed. I was certainly responsible for causing her injuries. If it weren't for my actions, she never would have been in   jeopardy. I couldn't even think about Sandre Washington now. She would be alive if it weren't for me.

I finally began to feel my own injuries. My hip was screaming, my wrists were aching, my hands were bleeding and my face was on fire. I was hurt. But right now it didn't matter. I had to save us.

FIFTY-NINE

———∞∞∞———

I MOVED ELLA AND ME to the Hummer. As soon as I hoisted us up into the front seat, my whole body started shaking. Thank God, the keys were in the ignition, as I had remembered. I cranked the engine and turned the heat to full blast. Then I began searching for Brown's phone, growing more and more frantic when I couldn't find it. Dread overwhelmed me. The phone had to be in his coat pocket. I started gagging once I realized that not only would I have to see Brown's dead body again, I would have to touch it.

I left Ella and stumbled my way back to the scene of my crime. I avoided looking at Brown's clubbed head and his seeping brains and instead concentrated on his clothing. I felt bile burn its way up the back of my throat. I swallowed, turned my head away from Brown and just managed not to vomit on him. I wiped my mouth with the back of my sleeve and thrust my hand into one pocket after the other. I found the phone on my third try. I clamped my jaws together, blinked back the tears and forced myself not to cry. Only then did I call John as I made my way back to Ella.

"John," I said in a strangled voice, "Oh God, I just killed Jefferson Brown."

"What? What are you talking about? Where are you? Are you okay?" he asked, questioning me non-stop. He took a deep breath and settled on one: "Where are you?"

I told him I was on the beach in Fort Howard Park near where Stanton and the dog had been buried.

"Honey, I'm on my way. Talk to me while I drive. Tell me what happened."

"He tried to kill Ella and me," I managed to get out. I was entering the second stage of hysteria – I bypassed tears and went straight to hiccupping. "He made me dig my own grave. He hurt Ella."

"Allison, do you need an ambulance? Are you okay?" he repeated, his voice rising in insistence and fear, nearly drowning out my rhythmic hiccups. "Answer me, please."

"No. Sorry," I said, snuffling and wiping my dripping nose again on the back of my sleeve. "I'm okay. We're in Brown's Hummer with the engine running so we can warm up. Oh John, I'm so sorry. I'll never go after anyone again by myself. I promise." I started crying.

"Allison, stop! It's okay. I just wish I were there with you. I'm calling Brennan. He's closer to you than I am. He'll get there faster. You haven't called the police have you?"

"Just you," I answered.

John put me on hold for a couple of minutes and returned to the line to tell me Brennan was on his way. I could hear John's sirens in the background and knew he was speeding toward me. Then John told me he would stay on the phone until Brennan arrived. If I ever needed proof that John loved me, I had it. He was willing to talk on the phone for an unlimited amount of time.

I explained what had transpired from the house to the beach. And then I told John about Diaz convincing Stanton to kill Benji, which was why Brown killed both of them, and Diaz's best fighting dog. By the time I finished, John mentioned he was crossing the Keystone Bridge.

During our conversation, I had been busy examining Ella. I ran my fingers over her ribs and then felt around her neck. She moaned. She'd be sore for days, if not weeks, but she would heal. She was still shaking uncontrollably, though the car was pumping out heat. My poor pooch was in shock. I wrapped her in my jacket. I poured a little water in her mouth from a bottle I found in the car, and took a huge gulp myself.

I could hear sirens closing in, and soon I saw the lights flickering through the trees, heading towards me. I flashed the Hummer's lights. Cars began pulling in around us. Brennan barely waited for his driver to stop before he jumped out and ran towards us. I opened the Hummer's door.

"Stay there," Brennan ordered. "John told me what happened."

An ambulance screamed to a halt beside us and two paramedics leaped out of it and ran over to me. A young woman in her mid-to-late 20s was the first one in my face. I already had looked over my wounds in the mirror while I was waiting, and nothing was too terrible. I would have scabs and possibly scars, but didn't require any stitches and all my shots were up to date.

I recognized I was reacting to this nightmare the same way I did as a child when I felt overwhelmed. I withdrew. As politely as possible, I waved away the attention of the paramedics, mumbling I was fine.

Brennan seemed to understand what I was going through and turned his attention to Whitfield and Delacroix, who had arrived right after their boss and were standing a few yards behind him. He asked me where Brown's body was, and I pointed at the narrow beach. He and the detectives headed in that direction. A CSI van pulled up behind the detectives' car and its occupants were soon heading towards the water, too.

I just sat, staring out the window into the darkness, waiting for John. He came into view running past the parked cars, his legs and arms pumping. I rolled down the window and yelled, "John!" He changed direction slightly and was soon jumping into the passenger seat. He put his arms around the two of us. I dropped my head against his shoulder, resting my face against his neck, and relaxed a bit. He gave me a few moments before he put his hands on my face and moved it so I was staring him in the eyes. He searched mine intently.

"Are you okay?" he asked for what seemed the umpteenth time.

"Maybe I'll feel differently tomorrow, but right now I'm glad he's dead and I don't mind that I'm the one who killed him. He killed Sandre

Washington," I said and started crying. Then I added, "But Ella needs help now. He broke her ribs."

"You need some medical attention yourself," he said, trying to hide his distress from me. He looked at my bleeding palms and then the cuts on my face. "These need to be cleaned up."

"I just sent the paramedics away. Did you tell Brennan I needed an ambulance?" I asked and could hear the belligerence in my tone. "I'm sorry. You know I hate to be the center of attention. I'm fine."

"Allison, I'm not going to argue with you," he said, looking and sounding resigned. "Stay here while I talk to Brennan. He probably wants to get your statement."

They returned together. John looked angry; Brennan appeared pensive. They walked to the driver's side and I opened the window again.

"We'll take your statement at the precinct. I'll have a medic there to check you out. John insists and I agree. I know you're worried about Ella. Do you want to call anyone to get her?"

"No," I said, forcing myself to be civil though I wanted to scream. Now I knew why John was annoyed, though Brennan was just following protocol.

"Dr. Reeves," he said, "I'd like you to walk me through what happened. Are you up to it?"

I nodded. "The one thing I would like is some pain medication – Tramadol – for Ella."

"We'll do that," he said. Brennan quickly talked into his phone. I closed the window, left the engine running, opened the door and resignedly handed Ella to John. I swung my legs out and started to lower myself from the Hummer when I lost my balance. John, still holding Ella, reached out his other hand and grabbed my elbow, which stopped my downhill slide. He didn't let go until I was standing steady. One of Brennan's men trotted to the car carrying two blankets. I handed one to John for Ella and wrapped myself in the other. Then, with John holding her and half-supporting me, we headed towards Brown's body.

It was already nine o'clock and the wind had died down, leaving a calm, starry night behind it. The crime scene was lit up. The photographer was putting away his camera. I began my narration as we walked, pointing out where I was dragged near the water, hit, forced to dig my own grave and hogtied after Ella's escape. I pointed to Sandre Washington's body and explained what had happened to her. Then I showed them where and how I had freed myself, hid from Brown and surprised him with the shovel.

I finally looked on the ground and was relieved to see Brown had been zipped into a body bag. I watched an officer wrap the shovel and walk it to the CSI van. My teeth started chattering, making any more speech impossible.

"That's it," John said. "I'm putting her in my car. Our dog needs some care, too. We'll meet you at your precinct."

I looked at John, whose slate-grey eyes had turned steely and cold. Brennan also noted his checked anger.

"I promise to get you all home as soon as possible," he said, trying to negate our distress. "I don't want anything about this investigation to come back and bite us. I can't give you special treatment, as much as I wish I could."

"I understand, Sergeant Brennan," I said, this time putting a hand on John's arm to cut him off. I just wanted to get home.

SIXTY

WE MADE IT TO BALTIMORE County P.D. in Towson in just over 20 minutes, cutting the normal drive time in half. I think we went airborne at certain points. We arrived at the mirrored building nicknamed the "flash-cube" because it looked like one. John and I followed Brennan into a large, slow elevator and then to his office on the 9th floor.

He opened the door and as soon as we walked in, I saw a bottle of Tramadol on his desk. Without a word, I picked it up, read the strength and dropped a pill down Ella's gullet. "I'm going to need some food for her, okay?"

Brennan picked up his phone and asked someone to go for sandwiches and a can of dog food. There was a knock on the door a couple of minutes later and I was surprised at such quick service.

I needn't have been. It was the same paramedic I turned away at Fort Howard Park. She smiled in my direction and said, "Trooper Thibert called and requested we come back.

"What you went through tonight was horrific," she said with an understanding smile. "But I would just like to clean out your wounds and bandage the ones I can."

She stood in the doorway with her medical bag in hand and waited for my response.

I tacitly gave her my permission by turning my face in her direction her so she could work on it. She walked over to me, opened her bag and took out a bottle of disinfectant, antibiotic ointment and bandages. Her motions were quick and efficient. She cleaned my wounds and closed a couple of the facial cuts with butterfly bandages, and wrapped my shredded palms and wrists in gauze. I didn't mention my hip. I'd look at it myself when we got home.

While she worked on me I looked around Brennan's office. It was impressively large, yet suffocatingly crowded with filing cabinets pressed up against every inch of wall space. Files were stacked on any available surface, including the floor. Brennan reorganized several columns of papers, thus freeing up the two chairs in front of his desk.

"I keep the files on my chair so no one stays too long," he said with a smile. He absently-mindedly pushed his glasses up to the bridge of his nose. They immediately started their descent. "I'll call in someone who can type your statement. That way, it won't have to be transcribed, which will get you out of here quicker. I'll print it, you sign it and you're gone."

There was a polite knock on the open door and a young man, geekishly spindly with a pencil mustache, maybe an ode to Baltimore artiste John Waters, waited for Brennan's nod before he walked into the office. He was balancing a cardboard box filled with coffees and sandwiches on one hand. The other held a can of dog food. Brennan waved him forward and the young cop put the items on his desk and backed out without a word. John opened the can and scooped some of it out and hand fed Ella. She took a few bites. Brennan handed out the coffees and passed around the box of sandwiches he had requested. I rooted around until I found a cheese-on-rye. I shared it with Ella who managed to eat a little more.

Brennan stood up and closed his door. He gave us a conspiratorial wink, which seemed out of character for the man with such deep frown lines, and returned to his desk where he opened the bottom drawer. He pulled out a bottle of Jim Beam Black Label. He held it up and turned John and I into nodding bobbleheads. I ate and drank and drank some more.

I perked up a bit. Brennan picked up the phone and said one word: "Now." The same young officer, who he introduced as Richard Flemings, returned holding a laptop. He moved some files off the couch, sat down and opened the computer. We began.

Brennan asked questions; I answered them. This went on for almost two hours. Fifteen minutes later, I was reading the typed transcript with John looking over my shoulder. I made a couple of innocuous changes and initialed them. We could finally go home. Or so I thought.

"Sergeant?" Flemings said, looking uncomfortable, probably more used to dealing with machines than men. Brennan turned his attention to him. Flemings ran his fingers across his wispy mustache.

"I've been going through Jefferson Brown's computer and found some encrypted files," Flemings said with growing enthusiasm. "I've been working on them since this afternoon, and finally was able to open them. I think you'll want to see what I've uncovered."

"Email the files to me and I'll print out a couple of copies for Trooper Thibert and Dr. Reeves," Brennan said, leaning back in his chair. Flemings and then the Sergeant hit a few keys on their computers. Brennan's printer started spitting out pages. He picked them up, made two stacks, stapled them and waved them towards John. He stood up, took them and passed me a copy. Brennan pushed up his glasses and peered at his computer screen.

There were several files listed under the heading of Restore Pit Bull Rescue. At this point, I was most interested in the Events section and skimmed the pages that listed dates, owners, fighters, winners, losers and each purse. It gave us additional ammunition to go after the Rivera twins, Paul Salvatore, Tyndall Garcia-Lopez, Kawayne Johnson and every other name on the list.

"Oh, my God, it's a Who's Who of dog fighting," I said, swooning with joy. "Just think. If Stanton hadn't killed Benji, and Dwight Manning hadn't stolen those dogs from the Cambridge shelter, Jefferson Brown would never have come to our attention.

"Brown never knew that Dwight Manning was the reason we started looking at all the shelter dogs and stumbled onto his Restore Rescue operation. It's kind of too bad, but I don't think I'd wish

Jefferson Brown on anyone, even Dwight Manning. But I am in a weakened condition."

John's phone vibrated and I watched him pull it from his pocket to see who was calling. He excused himself and softly said his name, and then just listened. A smile lit up his face for a second and disappeared like a shooting star – a beautiful, if temporary, sight. Without another word, he ended the call.

That was Lieutenant Andrews," John said, leaning forward in his chair and cupping his knees in his palms. He looked directly at me and added, "He's got a present for you."

"What?"

"Speaking of Dwight Manning," he said, "we've been invited to sit in on the Lieutenant's interrogation of the Mannings. I know you're exhausted, but I thought maybe you could find the energy...."

"Both of them?" I cut him off.

"They've been brought in?" John nodded.

"Is it okay to invite Jackie? I'm sure she'll want to be there."

"Sure. Want me to call her?" It was my turn to nod.

"Do you mind?" John asked Sergeant Brennan.

"Of course not," he said.

I brought Brennan up to speed about the Mannings while John called Jackie. He hung up and said, "I'll call her when we're leaving here. Amazing how energized you both became." He tapped the face of his watch.

I and returned to the files. There was one that listed names of dogs, births, deaths, and breeding records. It even listed shelters and dates when and where dogs were removed from them. More interesting were the reports Brown received from someone with the initials G.H., as in *George Hennigan*. I moved on to the payroll sheet and found the same set of initials on it, too. It appeared he was on a monthly retainer.

Brennan was reading along and must have made the same connection because he said, "Got him, the son of a bitch! Now our investigation begins." He smacked his hand on his desk like an exclamation point. He picked up his phone, punched in a number and said, "I need a warrant for the arrest of George Hennigan. Immediately."

"Whitfield and Delacroix were interviewing him when I left." John said, crossing his ankle over his knee and tapping his fingertips on his boot while he talked. "Where's Hennigan now?"

"We had to let him go," Brennan answered, shaking his head. "No hard evidence. He had an attorney before he sat down to be questioned. But we've kept him under surveillance."

"Jesus," I said, taking it all in and rubbing my temples. Fatigue began to weigh me down. I yawned. "Sorry. It's hard to stay perky."

"Why don't you two get going?" Brennan suggested. "I'm going to call Agent Vincente and see what she wants us to do with Brown's computer. Also, I'll tell her we're arresting Hennigan and you're heading to Easton. And, I'll mention your near death experience today, so she won't panic when she sees your face."

"Is it that bad?" I asked.

"Yes," they said in unison.

John shook hands with Brennan, who finally unloosened his tie and unbuttoned his shirt collar, as if signaling the end of his day.

"You've had a hell of a day, Dr. Reeves," he said, turning to me and shook my hand also.

"I can honestly say this been the hardest day of my life. I would say worst, except I survived it. I only wish Sandre Washington had."

SIXTY-ONE

THE PAIN IN MY HIP forced me to limp so severely that John told me to wait in the lobby while he retrieved the car. He placed Ella in my outstretched arms and disappeared into the night. When he returned, I declined his offer to carry me and was about to start shuffling towards it when I noticed detectives Whitfield and Delacroix. They were heading our way from the parking lot.

"Oh shit," I moaned, "not them."

"Be nice," John teased, "They're my new partners."

"Dr. Reeves," Whitfield said once he reached us. His ears were red-rimmed from the cold and the lids of his perfect blue eyes drooped with fatigue. The short Delacroix looked like a moving medicine ball. She was encircled in a down coat with a scarf wrapped around her face and a ski cap covering her head. Only her eyes showed. They looked benign, for once.

"I didn't get a chance to talk to you before," Whitfield said warmly, much to my surprise. He even wore a sheepish expression. "I'm glad we ran into you. Detective Delacroix and I owe you and Agent Vincente an apology. You guys really did a great job. Would you tell her for us?"

"Sure," I said astounded, but managed to thank Whitfield in turn, trying to keep any amazement out of my voice.

"You must be ready to drop," Delacroix said solicitously, her eyes peering at me with concern. "It must have been horrible for you. I'm glad you and your dog are okay."

At least I think that's what she said. Her voice was muffled in her muffler. I wondered if that was why they called them that.

I looked at Ella, who was back in John's arms. She was sleeping the sleep of the dead, if the dead snored. I sagged against John and he pulled me towards him so I could use him as a leaning post.

"I need to get my girls home," he said, and gently rested his chin on top of my head.

"Of course," Whitfield said, and extended his hand to shake John's. "But I've got to tell you something before you take off. When we were checking into Hennigan's background, we came across the name Dwight Manning, who you mentioned to us this afternoon. He and Hennigan are first cousins."

"So I've heard," John muttered, looking tired.

"Brennan just called and told us you were going to question Manning now," Whitfield added with a slight smile. "You can tell him Hennigan ratted him out, 'cause you can be sure as hell we're going to tell Hennigan that Manning snitched on him."

"Thanks for the heads up," John said and gave a full smile. "Let's compare arrests tomorrow."

We said our goodnights and John opened the door for me, helped me into the car and, once I gingerly sat, put Ella on my lap. My hip wound was burning and my hands and wrists ached, but I was smiling with anticipation about confronting the Mannings.

I woke up with John calling my name and gently shaking my shoulder. We were parked outside the barracks and Jackie was opening my door. As soon as I stood up, the muscles in my legs and arms started to spasm. Jackie was there to catch me in a huge embrace.

"Oh, God," she said when she felt the tremors vibrating up my body. When they passed, Jackie stepped back, holding me by the shoulders to keep me steady and stared at my face. I guess I didn't look too good, because she pulled me to her in a big hug and I think I heard a few sniffles. "Oh, Allison, you're killing us."

"I'm sorry, Jackie," I sniveled back. "God, I'm so sorry. I know I've said this before, but I really mean it this time. I almost got Ella killed, too. And Sandre Washington is dead because of me. Brown killed her. Never again. I swear."

"You swear? Well, I swear if you do anything so stupid again, I'll kill you myself," she threatened. "Let's get you inside and seated."

Without a word, John passed Ella to Jackie and then scooped me up, carrying me down the narrow corridor that led to the Interrogation Rooms and stopped at the first door on the right. After he put me down, he knocked and entered. Andrews waved us in.

Michelle and Dwight Manning were seated next to each other and opposite Andrews. The room's bright fluorescent lights revealed dirt-streaked beige walls, scuffed brown linoleum and a beat-up rectangular table surrounded by a half-dozen chairs.

Both Mannings looked like they had been dragged out of bed, because they had been. Dwight's face was crimson with anger and probably soaring blood pressure, his lips curled in a disdainful sneer. He leaned back in his chair and looked dismissively at the four of us. He acted as though his imminent arrest was an impossibility. Michelle, on the other hand, looked terrified and was sobbing.

"Shut up," Dwight snarled at her. It made her cry harder.

"Knock it off," Andrews snapped at him. "Open your mouth again and you can sit in a holding cell until I'm good and ready to talk to you. And that could be days."

Andrews waved us into the empty chairs on his side of the table. John chose to stand and lean against the wall, taking in the entire tableau. Jackie began asking questions about Restore Pit Bull Rescue. John wanted to know about his relationship with Arnold Diaz. How many dogs did Dwight sell to Arnold Diaz? Who else? All questions were answered with a sneer. Finally, his face darkening with frustration, John took out his phone and made a call.

"Has Hennigan talk yet?" he asked, and listened to the answer. Dwight's cocky sneer disappeared at the mention of his cousin/partner. John broke his silence with one more question, "Did he give him up? Good. Yeah, I'm looking at him right now. Send me the transcript of his confession. Thanks."

Michelle turned on Dwight. "What did you do?" she screamed at him. "You stupid son of a bitch!"

"Shut the fuck up," he shouted back, but he was crumbling before our very eyes. The bravado had been replaced with fear and sweat beaded up on his thick forehead and upper lip. I wondered which he found more terrifying – jail time or his wife's mounting fury.

I miraculously found my energy level rising, especially when Andrews asked Jackie and me to stay put while John was told to take Dwight into another Interrogation Room. John rose and marched Dwight away. Panic crossed Michelle's face and she was shaking so badly she gripped the table for support.

"You're going to be in a world of hurt if you don't start talking," Andrews warned her, his voice becoming more menacing. He ran his hand over his bristled hair and then tugged on the ends of his mustache, one side, then the other.

"I don't know anything," she wailed, her face sallow and blotched. I looked at her carefully and thought she was breaking out in hives. I didn't care. I was tired, cranky and in pain and just wanted her to talk.

Andrews was silent and turned his gaze on Jackie and me, inviting us to join in. I put my hand on Jackie's arm and leaned forward, letting her know I wanted to go first.

"How close is your husband with George Hennigan?" I asked keeping my voice level and innocuous.

"Who?" Michelle replied, a smirk starting to form on her face. I was surprised she was going with defiance instead of cooperation. I fully expected her to place all the blame on Dwight and to start out saying he and Hennigan were best friends. Oh well, the night was young – at least for her.

"Michelle, this isn't going to fly," I said. "Are you asking us to believe that you've never met Dwight's first cousin? Who lives a couple of hours away from you? Who grew up with your husband? It makes me think that you were involved in selling those pit bulls and are trying to protect both of them. Are you prepared to go to jail with Dwight?"

"Why are you doing this to me?" she asked her face crumbling before our eyes. "You've always hated me, but interrogating me like I'm a common criminal is beyond crazy, it's cruel."

Jackie leaned forward, laying her forearms across the table and stared into Michelle's watering eyes and said sharply, "Do you have any idea what your husband did?"

"What are you talking about? I know you two hate me, but going after him to get to me? Really?"

"Michelle, you are hateful, but that has nothing to do with this," Jackie said with surprising equanimity. "This is about your husband stealing three pit bulls from the Cambridge shelter, your shelter, and selling them to Arnold Diaz, who fought them. Dwight was also either working with or for his cousin, George Hennigan, who's already given him up. So cut the crap."

I joined in. "Do you remember the white pit bull with black markings named Petey Jr.? He was one of Helen's favorites. She thought he went to a rescue. We watched him get killed in a fight. That video will be used in court when they prosecute your husband.

"He stole that dog and sold it without Hennigan's knowledge," I continued, beginning to enjoy myself. "Can you imagine how he's going to react when he finds out Dwight screwed him over? In fact, the three dogs that your husband stole helped lead us to Jefferson Brown's pit bull fighting ring. Hennigan worked for him. We'll make sure he finds out that Dwight's the reason he'll be doing jail time."

Michelle gulped, emitting a gagging noise, and swallowed hard. She focused on me and looked thoughtful for a moment. Then she said, with an obvious change of attitude, "I didn't know anything. I never would have let that happen to a dog in my care."

It was Jackie's turn to put her hand on my arm. She didn't want me to say a mean word.

"Be that as it may, Michelle," Jackie said with a soft look and a gentle voice, "do you know George?"

"Yes, but I didn't know anything about them stealing and selling dogs. I swear." She began crying again.

"This is all your doing, isn't it?" she said, accusing me, her eyes narrowing with hatred as they bore into me.

"No, Michelle, this is about your husband. He did this to you, not me," I said and I let my voice harden. "But I am going to insist you vacate your position on the shelter's board. If you don't, I will take every legal action at my disposal to have you removed. But, most important, you are to reinstate Helen. She's the best thing that's ever happened to that shelter. With you gone and Helen truly in charge, the place can become a safe haven for animals once again."

Michelle started to say something, but Lieutenant Andrews cut her off. "You may go home. Don't leave town. Your husband's bail will be posted some time today, in case you want to get him out of jail. You can use the phone out front to call for a cab."

He stood up without giving her a glance, gave us a nod and headed for the door. Jackie and I followed on his heels, leaving a forlorn and battered Michelle sitting by herself.

John was standing in the hallway waiting for us.

"How'd it go?" Andrews asked. John's smile told it all.

"Dwight gave up Hennigan and Diaz, but swore he never had any contact with Jefferson Brown," he said. "But he is sure Hennigan had some cops helping him locate dogs. Also, I asked him when he last saw Diaz, and he said it had been a couple of weeks. He did say there were rumors going around that something had happened to him."

"Yeah, Jefferson Brown happened to Arnold Diaz," I said repeating to Jackie and Andrews what I had already told John and Brennan. "Brown told me Diaz and his dogs would never be found and he put Diaz's blood on the shovel and under Sandre Washington's fingernails so he would be blamed for all the deaths Brown intended to commit.

"Hey, John," I said, interrupting myself, "did Hennigan really give up Dwight? I have to know."

"Shit no," he grinned. "I bluffed. I didn't want to spend the rest of the night interrogating that asshole."

His Lieutenant beamed at him, stuck out his hand, which John shook, looking a bit surprised when Andrews said, "Well done." Jackie winked at me. She knew this moment had been a long time coming.

The three of us went outside, me under my own power this time, and we hugged our farewells. John, Ella and I were finally going home.

"Do you want to get checked out at the hospital?" John asked.

"God, no. I just want to go home and go to bed for at least a week. Call Vernon or Gina, please, since I'm wearing gauze mittens and can't. Find out how Duke is, okay?"

"Could you stop worrying about everyone and everything and just concentrate on yourself?" John grumbled.

"Yes, I can," I said and nodded my head. "In fact, when I thought I was going to die, I found myself thinking about my life, and I was filled with just one regret. Other than being responsible for Sandre Washington's death...."

"Allison, please. What?"

"Do you still want to marry me?" I asked. The terror that had been gripping me since the kidnapping and killing of Jefferson Brown was beginning to recede a bit and I could concentrate on John.

His response was to pull over, hit the brakes, slam the gear stick into park and flip on the inside lights. He turned towards me and stared.

"Are you proposing to me?" he asked, his smile matching my own.

"No, I'm responding to your proposal. It just took me a while."

John's laugh was short and happy and he started to hug me, but stopped.

"Damn it," he said. "I'm afraid to touch you. Is there any part of your body that doesn't hurt?"

"Yes, my lips."

He kissed me gently, pulled back and said, "I love you."

"I love you, too," I said, "more than I ever thought possible."

"What a day you've had," he said, pulling out onto the road. "Not only did you break up an interstate dog fighting ring, save your life – after putting it in jeopardy, of course, rid the world of the evil Jefferson Brown, force Michelle Manning into retirement and help arrest Dwight Manning, you got engaged to me. Pretty damn impressive."

"Ah, it was nothing," I said, putting my bandaged hand on John's thigh, "just another day in the life of a Doggie Dick."

About the Author

GAIL BUCHALTER IS AN AWARD-WINNING journalist who was a staff writer for *People* magazine, a contributing editor at *Parade* magazine for more than 20 years, and arguably one of the longest surviving freelancers at *Forbes* magazine. She wrote about film, television and recording artists, sports figures, entrepreneurs and her true love – animals. Gail was born and raised in Manhattan, lived in Nashville, Los Angeles and Southampton, NY, before moving to rural Maryland, where she opened a yoga studio in 2002. A board member of the local humane society, she was also instrumental in helping create a low-cost feral cat spay/neuter organization. She has adopted and fostered numerous cats and dogs, and today lives with three dogs and two cats on several acres in the woods.

31239186R00182

Made in the USA
Middletown, DE
23 April 2016